Jeremy

God bless

the RKBA!

Skip

Excerpt from *Church and State*

"Repent and seek the Lord's face! Confess your sins to God and he will forgive you!"

Joshua turned his back on the police and walked away. The Lieutenant with the bullhorn tried one last time to stop him.

"Stop! Get down on the pavement or we'll open fire!"

The newscaster then broke in with a commentary, but the camera remained on Joshua.

"He's just walking away now, Jamal. He's ignoring the police as if he's not even afraid of them. I think they're going to shoot him if he doesn't stop! I'm not sure, but I think the police are going to kill an unarmed man just because he's talking about God. He just keeps ..."

Suddenly, a shot rang out, then another, and another. Soon a whole chorus of shots exploded into the air and Joshua turned to meet the hail of bullets.

Why you can't miss *Church and State!*

Before buying a book, I look it over carefully, always reading the synopsis, the *about the author* section, the quotes and a few excerpts. I don't have time to read half a novel and then lose interest. I only buy a book I KNOW for sure will captivate me from first page to last. *Church and State* IS that book!

Here is what you should know about *Church and State.*

First, this is a political thriller written by a person who dislikes politics. Now, don't get me wrong, I love my country, I campaign, I vote, but, for me, politics leaves a nasty taste in my mouth. I dread election years. This book is about friendships.

Second, I dislike certain aspects of organized religion. Christianity is not about church, though I attend. Christianity is about that one-on-one friendship with the God of the universe. This story is not preachy, and Christians and non-Christian alike will enjoy it.

In summary, if you love reading about action, suspense and entangled relationships; if you love God, Family, and Country; if those are the priorities in your life, then you and I are on the same page and you will love this story. Happy reading.

— Skip Coryell —

SKIP CORYELL

White Feather Press

Making the world a better place - one reader at a time.

Church
and
State

Other Books by Skip Coryell

Bond of Unseen Blood
We Hold These Truths
Blood in the Streets
Laughter and Tears
RKBA: Defending the Right to Keep and Bear Arms

Available anywhere books are sold.

Signed copies are available only at www.whitefeatherpress.com

Cover design created by Ron Bell of AdVision Design Group (www.advisiondesigngroup.com)

First printing by White Feather Press, LLC, in 2007
Second printing by White Feather Press, LLC, in 2009

ISBN - 978-0-9766083-1-8

Printed in the United States of America

Dedicated to my wife, Sara. Thank you.

Also, many thanks to the following for their input and support in writing this novel:

Pastor Jeff Arnett
Dr. Dianne Portfleet
Dr. Hadley Kigar
Pastor Timm Oyer
Dave Maqueen

Prologue

Frank Blocher stood on the ledge of the observatory deck, high atop an office building in Washington DC. He looked out at the skyline, recoiling at the white, jutting spire of the Washington monument off in the distance; it seemed to be giving him the finger. Frank looked down at the pavement many floors below, wondering if he would jump this time. No one was watching. No one would even miss him, except perhaps when the child support checks stopped coming in at the end of every month. He looked up at the heavens, searching for God, but saw nothing. Sometimes he believed in God, sometimes he didn't. His pastor told him that it was all about faith, that he had to believe in things not seen. Today, he looked inside his heart, but all he could see was darkness.

He thought about his little girl, hoping above hope that she would remember him after he was gone. Then he thought again; maybe it would be better if she didn't. Only her smiling face had kept him alive this long. He had heard it said once that people who jump from skyscrapers die of a heart attack before hitting the ground. He wondered about that and hoped it was true.

Frank was an overweight, balding, middle-aged accountant who had never quite reached his prime. He wondered about that too. He wondered why some people just never seemed to amount to anything. Back in high school and college, he had looked down on people less fortunate than himself, because he knew that Frank Blocher was on the fast track of life. Frank Blocher was destined for great things, but the great things had never come to him. Indeed, only bad things had offered themselves.

The sunshine glinted off the chrome trim on the soda machine off to his right. It was a hot today, and a lot of people came up here to the observatory deck to use the telescopes and just to feel the cool wind on their faces, especially over lunch and breaks. He was alone now and on the verge of getting fired, but he didn't care, not anymore. Frank pulled his wallet out of his back pocket and flipped it open. The picture of his 1-year old little girl, Missy, stared up at him: blonde curls, perfect, white skin, smiling blue eyes; they rebuked him now for what he was thinking.

Frank put the wallet back in his pocket, brushed his fingers through what remained of his short blonde hair, and backed carefully away from the edge. He walked over to the Pepsi machine. The caffeine wasn't good for him; it made him jittery, and, over the years of divorce, remarriage and divorce again, the sugar and caffeine had taken its toll, decaying his teeth and helping him gain weight. Regular Mountain Dew was his favorite, but he seldom bought that one anymore; it just wasn't good for him. Besides, he was on a diet.

He reached his right hand deep down into his front pocket and fished out 4 quarters and a dime. The dime dropped on the cement and rolled around lazily at his feet before coming to a rest against his shiny, black shoe. Sweat dropped off his brow when he reached down to pick it up, and then he inserted the coins, one by one, into the slot. He scanned the selections and resisted the temptation to buy the sugary Mountain Dew: 170 calories per serving. But when he pressed the Diet Mountain Dew button, the words lit up "Make another selection". He sighed. The same thing had happened with his first wife. He pushed the Diet Pepsi button instead, but the incessant words howled back at him again, "Make another selection!"

And then, like a siren, like a modern-day muse calling out to his beleaguered sense of reason, his eyes rested on the other Mountain Dew button, the one with all the caffeine and calories. It suddenly seemed larger than the others, and he reasoned to himself. What difference does it make? I'm going to kill myself one of these days anyway.

Frank reached down, his hand poised over the button, hovering there, suspended between resolve and despair. Someone had once told him that people lived or died based on the decisions they made. He agreed with that and pushed the button.

Immediately, the circuit closed, sending electricity to the detonator on the nuclear bomb hidden within, and Frank was instantly vaporized, along with most of Washington DC. The terrorists had planned and executed their job well, and within a few hours, eight other bombs were detonated in major cities all across America.

"*I contemplate with sovereign reverence that act of the whole American people which declared that their legislature should "make no law respecting an establishment of religion, or prohibiting the free exercise thereof," thus building a wall of separation between Church and State.*"

— *Thomas Jefferson* —

1

"But you can't say that, Mr. President! Not on national television! The House and Senate would go crazy! They've already threatened to impeach you if you continue defying the law."

President Dan Vermeulen furrowed his brow, obviously stressed at what his top advisor was telling him. Vicki Valence had never been one to mince words. She sat across from him, staring intently at him with large, brown eyes, determined to make her point. Ever since the other side had regained their majority in both houses in the last election, the country had been turned upside down. It was just another outcome of the war. When feeling insecure and threatened, people would give up almost any measure of freedom to feel secure. He sighed to himself. There was nothing he could do about it, at least not right now. One wrong political move by him, and they'd have the White House as well.

"All I want to do is say God bless America at the end of my speech and pray a blessing onto our country. Presidents used to do that all the time – even the ones who didn't mean it! Our founding fathers would go nuts if they saw America today! Everything is all backwards!"

The President bowed his head, sagging at the shoulders, and ran his hands through his black, graying hair from front to back in exasperation.

Behind his desk in the oval office in Omaha, Nebraska, he felt like a beaten man. He wielded power, great power, and he had proven that in the war when he had turned the Moslem holy city of Medina into a heap of radioactive rubble. Then, he had quickly promised to do the same to Mecca, should the radical Islamic extremists explode one more nuclear bomb on American soil. In all, the terrorists had exploded nuclear bombs in nine American cities: east coast cities included Washington DC, New York, Philadelphia, and Boston. On the west coast, they bombed Los Angeles, San Francisco and San Diego. In the middle, Chicago and Detroit were vaporized. In a matter of two hours time, the terrorists had succeeded where the Soviets had failed; they had reduced America to a second-class world power. Over 20 million Americans had died in the first 30 days, with more to come later through disease, famine and the resulting anarchy, and America's financial stability had threatened to collapse entirely. To top it all off, Mexico had stood poised on the Texas border to invade, saying it was a relief effort and a temporary measure to restore stability to the region. They had quickly backed off after the bombing of Medina.

In his first term as President, Daniel Vermeulen had acted boldly and decisively and saved America. He had been the most popular President in American history, at the most precarious and crucial time in her history. But now, only six years later, so much had changed. He was a lame duck. No, more than that, he felt crippled and beaten and hopeless. Much of America's military might had survived, and he had the power to wage war, the power to send a nuclear strike that would annihilate the globe, but he was impotent to pray a simple public blessing on the country he loved. His advisor interrupted his self-pitying daydream.

"I'm sorry Mr. President. But the Supreme Court has ruled against you on this one. The Freedom From Religion act expressly forbids any public expression of religion for government officials, even for the President. You can't get around that."

The voice of Vicki Valence softened as she spoke.

"I'm sorry, Dan."

She had met the President years ago at a political rally, had been his friend and confidante for close to two decades, and she felt pain for him now. He had already been in his second term for two years, and had accomplished less than any second-term President before him. All his judicial appointees were being filibustered in the Senate, and none of his proposed legislation had made it out of committee. The country was falling apart and he was nearing despair. Vicki could feel it, and she could see it in his blue eyes. He looked over at her now, pleadingly, and she wanted to help make it right for him, but knew she couldn't, not this time.

She reached over and placed her smooth, soft hand onto his own and stroked it slowly.

"It's okay, Dan. You're the President. Your God will not forsake you. He brought you this far didn't he?"

The President nodded and forced a tiny smile onto his lips. It always made him nervous when she touched him like that. He laughed weakly.

"That's funny, Vicki. You don't even believe in God, and you're encouraging me to trust him?"

Vicki's thin lips returned his smile.

"Well, perhaps I believe more than you think. Besides, I'm just doing my job, Mr. President. Just doing my job."

Inside, she frowned, wondering if he had any notion how she really felt about him. She withdrew her hand reluctantly and turned and walked away to attend another meeting.

• • •

The President watched sadly as Vicki left the oval office. He found her very attractive, and, in different circumstances, he just might

4

... Dan let the thought go unfinished. Besides, it didn't matter, because the circumstances weren't different, and there was still the matter of Jeanette. Still, after all these years, he felt like he was cheating her memory when he even thought of another woman, though, in reality, he knew better.

After Vicki left the room, he was alone, alone with his fears, alone with his pain, and alone with everything else that made him human and just an ordinary man like everyone else. At least when his aides and dignitaries were with him, he felt propped up by their sycophantic encouragement and praise. But Vicki was no sycophant. He knew that, and that's why he had placed her so highly in his administration, why he valued her counsel, and why he spent so much time with her. Well, not the only reason. Sometimes he longed for a different set of circumstances, while, at others, the idea of another relationship terrified him and riddled him with guilt. He let that thought trail on off into time and space and turned to the business at hand. He had to write a speech.

President Vermeulen cast his deep, blue eyes down at the blank sheet of paper in front of him; the sheer audacity of it stared back up at him, mocking him, accusing him, daring him to write what he felt. But he didn't dare express what was on his heart. It was forbidden, under penalty of law, a law that he had signed. He swore at his own stupidity and weakness, and reached down with his left hand and crumpled the parchment beneath his fingers. It was thick, textured paper and it gave way grudgingly beneath the pressure, as if it was alive and refusing to die. He found himself thinking, 'Why do they always buy the best of everything here at the White House?' A simple spiral notebook would have sufficed, but no, everything surrounding him had to be the best money could buy. Dan felt guilty about that, had even tried to change it, but the White House Staff resisted all his efforts to cut costs.

Poverty and disease were up, children were hungry, and jobs were scarce, but here he sat in a brand new White House in Omaha, surrounded by hundreds of people who waited on him hand and foot. His late-wife, Jeanette, had never liked it either, believing they hadn't come to the Presidency for the fame and prestige; it wasn't the elegance and glamour that had lured them here. Both he and his wife had just felt that perhaps fate or maybe some other unknown thing was calling them into politics for some unseen reason, something buried, something shrouded in mystery and shadow. Then the first bomb had exploded and it had all become clear to Dan. God, not fate, had raised him up for that one decisive moment in time, to either stand and win, or hesitate and fail. And the odd part was that while he had grown up believing in the existence of God, he had never given him more than lip service. That was why he had signed the Freedom from Religion Act. Besides being politically expedient for him, he hadn't believed it would make much difference to the country. But he had been wrong, very wrong.

But now, sitting alone at his desk in the oval office, that one victorious and decisive moment seemed light years away. Dan let his forehead drop down onto the big wooden desk with an agonizing thud. Even Vicki, a professing agnostic, had warned him against signing the Freedom From Religion Act. "It's not right Dan. It just doesn't feel right. I don't know why. It feels instinctively wrong." And she had been correct. The erosion of freedom and the fallacy of the separation of church and state had become inevitable with the signing of that one bill into law. Dan felt as if he had failed his people, and, more importantly, failed his God.

Yes, those victorious first years of office were light years away, and his Jeanette was light years away as well. His wife and two children had been in the west wing of the original White House when the first bomb had exploded without warning. The fact that they hadn't suffered gave him no solace. Just a few hours before the attack, he had been called away for an emergency summit on the rise of tensions in the Mideast. It was supposed to be a whole weekend away from the distractions of friends and family, where they could hammer out a plan to negotiate a truce with the Palestinians and the Israelis.

Since the loss of his family, and all the tragedy that had followed, Dan had suddenly drawn himself much closer to God. Now, with his hands massaging the sides of his face in an effort to relieve the tension, he missed his wife and family more than anything, and only the great need of the country had kept him going. There had never been sufficient time to grieve his loss, what with the pending Mexican annexation, the threat of more bombs in more cities, the massive and unprecedented relief effort for the millions of Americans affected. Only the business of work had kept him alive, but now the work was becoming a draining routine. There were no immediate crises, no foreign enemies to conquer, only a congress and supreme court who would see him destroyed should he turn too far to the right or to the left.

With his face nestled in his palms, Dan was reminded of King David, one of his heroes of the faith: "Be merciful, O God, for men hotly pursue me; all day long they press their attack. My slanderers pursue me all day long; many are attacking me in their pride."

Dan knew his enemies. He knew who wanted him gone. Senator Devin Dexter was the leader, the head of the snake that would bite him sooner or later, but he felt impotent to stop him. Just two more years and he would be free from the curse of this office.

Dan knew for certain that his biggest failure had been his signing of the Freedom From Religion Act. At the time, before the death of his family, spirituality had not been important to him. He'd referred to himself as a deist, much like some of the founding fathers, but the death of his family and the ensuing pain and suffering had changed all that – had changed him as well. He still remembered the day after the first blast, the one in which his wife and children had died. He had been on his knees in his private office on Air Force One, crying, weeping before God at the mass of his loss, and at the hugeness of his charge. At that moment, he'd asked God to curse him and die. He didn't want to live without his wife and kids. But, instead, God had reached down and caressed his heart, had given him strength, new purpose, and a new will. In return, Dan had pledged his life, his fortune, and his sacred honor to the cause of Christ. At the time, he hadn't realized the ramifications of that decision. So much had happened, so much in so little time, that Dan's head and heart had reeled. But he'd made a deal with God: "Give me strength, courage, and wisdom to save America, and I'll serve you to the end of my days." And God had been true to his word, but with an errant stroke of his pen, Dan had repaid God almighty by signing the Freedom from Religion Act into law, thereby curtailing the rights of all public servants to speak publicly about their faith. It remained his most dismal failure and his greatest regret.

But now, more legislation was pending. One bill would strip churches of their tax-exempt status, while another would make them register with the federal government and meet a host of guidelines, rules, and regulations. Still another would remove the phrase 'In God We Trust' from all currency. It would mean the death of the open church, and the government would finally control the one thing they never could before: the God of our fathers.

Dan buried his face in his hands. He felt the wetness on his cheeks and tried to wipe it off, but the tears came faster than he could wipe them away. In desperation, he spoke out loud.

"When I am afraid, I will trust in you. In God, whose word I praise, in God I trust; I will not be afraid. What can mortal man do to me?"

The unknown voice thundered back at him with hurricane force.

"Whatever we can, Mr. President! We'll do whatever we can!"

2

Vicki Valence stood nervously off to one side of the podium, waiting for the President to begin his speech. She had read and edited three different drafts, carefully, and incrementally purging it of all religious overtones. In the end, it hadn't been all she'd wanted, but it would be enough to keep Dan in the White House for two more years. And that's all she really cared about. It was her job, and she owed it to her friend.

The President stood behind the podium now, looking down at the papers in front of him, as if confused, as if he wasn't sure what he was doing there. Vicki wanted to rush over and prod him into speech, but she didn't dare. He was the President, and he must appear to stand on his own two feet. He must look strong and presidential. The muscles around her spine tightened, and she squeezed her hands together until they hurt. Right now she wished she believed in a personal god, just so she could talk to him.

"My fellow Americans."

Vicki breathed a sigh of relief. Thank god. He was talking. It would be okay now.

"I come before you today to discuss the problems that America faces.

I come to discuss what must be rebuilt, what must be healed, and what must be made whole."

Vicki smiled proudly. Those were her words.

"Today, I come to you ..."

The President hesitated and his voice trailed off and became silent. He cocked his head off to one side and looked up at the ceiling as if listening to the silence of an unheard voice. Vicki followed his gaze upward but could see nothing. People started looking around the room at each other, wondering what was going to happen next. Vicki started shifting her weight from one foot to the other, waiting for him to talk, waiting, waiting, waiting.

The President looked back down at the paper and smiled softly, and when he spoke again, his voice had a different quality, one that Vicki had never heard before. And she thought she knew everything about Dan.

"America, these pages represent the contents of a great political speech. Perhaps the greatest ever written. But, unfortunately, they are not my words. Because, you see, I'm not a politician. In fact, I hate politics. Always have and always will."

The President picked up the small stack of paper and tossed it onto the floor, where the individual sheets separated and each went its own way.

"There! That's what I think of politics."

And then he smiled again.

"You know, that felt kind of good. I've been wanting to do that for years."

He placed his elbows on the podium and leaned forward, looking directly into the camera. All the blood was suddenly draining from Vicki's face.

"Did you know that George Washington never wanted to be the General of the Continental Army? He never even wanted to be the

President. He just did it because no one else was willing and able. He did it to serve his country. George Washington, like most of our founding fathers, was a man of great conviction. He saw something wrong, and he fixed it, no matter what the cost."

Dan looked over to Vicki and smiled. He knew what she was thinking, that she was afraid for him. And he appreciated her loyalty. The weakest part of him wanted to comply with her wishes, to take the easy, political way out, but, if he did, he couldn't live with himself. She would have to understand and support him in this.

"George Washington was afraid of the British Army. They were the most powerful military force on the face of the planet, and he only had a few thousand men, most of them untrained farmers, shopkeepers, blacksmiths, you name it. They came from all walks of life. They were just ordinary people, common folk who had virtually no chance of winning. But they fought anyway. They fought, they bled, and they died!"

The President stood up straight and pounded his fist onto the oak podium and roared out his next words with surprising passion.

"And they won!"

Vicki's heart stopped for a moment. Where was he going with this?

"They were the very first Americans, and they were afraid. But they didn't let fear make decisions for them. They fought for what they believed in, no matter what the consequences, no matter what the odds. They stood up – they took a stand! They fought! They Bled! They died! They won!"

The President's face was overcast now, like a cloud threatening to storm.

"And with their blood and the blood of their sons and daughters, they bought our freedom - freedom from a government who no longer protected the people they served, freedom for us to govern ourselves, freedom to elect those who serve, and to fire those who cease to serve.

They bought and paid for our freedom to worship, freedom to speak out, freedom to gather, and freedom to keep and bear arms in order to protect those freedoms."

The President's brow stood furled, like the flag he represented so enthusiastically. But he unfurled it now with pride and with words of force and power.

"I used to be so proud of America! I used to be proud to be your President! But not anymore. I stand before you in shame. I stand before you as a broken man, because I have failed you. The President is supposed to lead, and in the quest to hold on to my title and the power you have loaned me, I have compromised my beliefs and have ceased to lead and to serve."

Vicki stood off to one side, both disappointed and relieved. She knew what was coming next. She sighed and let her shoulders slump down. She had held him back as long as she could. That was her job – to keep him in power. She had done her best, but, in the end, she had failed.

"But I will compromise no longer. I will not remain silent while the country and the people I love fall apart in ruin, even if it means breaking the law. Laws of man come and go, but the laws of God remain forever, more immutable than the rock on which they were carved."

The President leaned forward again, moving closer to the microphone.

"The United States Congress has threatened to impeach me should I continue to mention God in public. They say I'm breaking the law; their precious Freedom From Religion Act! Well, not only do I detest politics, but I also detest religion. In the name of religion, Islamic extremists flew two airliners into the Twin Towers, killing 3,000 Americans. Do you remember the Twin Towers? I do! Do you remember what it felt like in the pit of your stomach when you watched that first tower fall? In the name of religion, Islamic extremists exploded nine nuclear bombs in cities all across America, killing twenty million Americans, including ..."

The President hesitated. A tear welled up in his eye.

"Including my wife, Jeanette, of 20 years, my seven-year-old daughter, Sandra, and ... my three-year-old son, Michael."

The President looked straight into the camera, but this time let his tears stream down his cheeks unhindered.

"I have more reason to hate religion than anyone. Religion is a terrible thing, and that's why our founding fathers were against the establishment of a national religion. But belief in God is not religion. It is deep; it is personal; it is strong and powerful and transcends any human law."

The camera zoomed in.

"I hate religion, but I love my God. I love my God and I love my country. And, I stand before you today, willing to die for both."

"So, in closing, America, now is the day when you must stand and be counted. You must decide what you believe. Here's what I say. I believe that God is alive and well. I believe he's watching us. I believe he loves us. I believe he wants us to be free. And I believe that God hates religion more than I do."

The President leaned back and straightened his tie.

"So now, if you're going to impeach me, then do it quickly. But if you believe as I do, then find a way to make a stand. Whatever you do, don't just sit there while America teeters on the brink of her sunset. Pull her back from the edge. America is worth saving, but only if its people stand and be counted. America isn't the government. America is We the people, we the farmers, we the factory workers, we the moms, we the dads, we the students, we the shopkeepers, we the people who live, and breathe, and bleed and die in this great country!"

The President looked from one camera to the next, as if making eye contact with every person in America.

"God once said, 'If my people, who are called by my name, shall humble themselves, and pray, and seek my face, and turn from their wicked ways, then I will hear their cry, and I will heal their land!'"

The President nodded.

"And that's what I believe America. I'm the President of the United States. I'm your President. You hired me, and that's where I'm leading you. Now, please, make a stand. Help me save America!"

The President smiled and strode away quickly and resolutely, leaving the sheets of parchment lying still and silent on the floor beside the podium.

3

Vice President David Thatcher hung up the phone and leaned his tall, slender frame back in his padded chair. That was the fifth call this morning complaining about the President's speech. And this last call from Senator Devin Dexter had been the worst. That man gave him the creeps, and he didn't trust him any further than he could throw him, but still ... Vice President Thatcher thought about it for a moment. It couldn't hurt to keep his options open. Things were going to be happening soon, and he wanted to be appropriately postured in the event that things went south for the President. Dan was his friend, but ... he needed to show some prudence, especially since he planned to announce his candidacy soon.

The Vice President reached up with his left hand and stroked his chin thoughtfully and then touched his fingers against his silver hair in his most prevalent nervous habit. Yes, perhaps a little distance was in order. He didn't want to be too close should the hammer fall. On the other hand, he didn't want to appear ungracious either. He didn't want to come off as abandoning his friend. He could play both sides, if he had to.

But he would have to be careful, very careful. Politically speaking, Senator Dexter was a powerful and dangerous man, and David couldn't afford to take him on, at least not now. Yes, he would leave his options open, play both sides, at least until he could determine what was right for him in this situation.

David Thatcher swiveled slightly to the left and looked down at the solid, oak desk resting beneath his right hand. Lately, he just didn't feel as good about himself as he usually did. The job was no longer a joy to him, but more of a burden than anything else. But, no matter how much he hated to play political games, he had to, at least for now. It was a necessary evil.

Suddenly, there was a dull thud behind him and he quickly glanced over his shoulder at the window to his back, just in time to see a small bird bounce off the thick, bulletproof glass. He got up from his chair and walked over to the window and peered down. The bird was flopping on the grass below. Dave watched for a few moments, and then the bird stopped moving. In front of his face, he saw a bit of blood on the glass and he shivered.

Dan Vermeulen was his friend, but ... yes, he would have to be careful.

• • •

Senator Devin Dexter was at the pinnacle of his career and his power. In fact, it had been said in hushed tones in board rooms across America, that Devin was the most powerful Senator in the history of the United States. He never argued that point; it served no purpose. Besides, he didn't want to be the most powerful Senator. He wanted to be the most powerful President!

The Senator looked out across the sea of press reporters. He thought it amusing that he could call a press conference at any time of the night or day and they would all scurry to him like lab rats, and then repeat whatever he told them. Devin stretched up to his six feet of height and ran his fingers casually through his full head of gray hair. Devin was 53 years old, and had been in politics now for over 20 years. He was proud that no one could out-politic Devin Dexter!

He held his hand up and the sea of reporters grew calm and silent at his bidding.

"Thank you all for coming today. I know you are all very busy."

He laughed inside. They were busy all right, busy waiting for him to tell them what to print.

"As you all know, the U.S. House of Representatives has been very disturbed at the latest speech of President Vermeulen. So disturbed, in fact, they have just voted to pass articles of impeachment against him."

He paused for effect, and then feigned an outward frown, all the while smiling exuberantly inside.

"And, as you also know, it grieves me deeply to see the President sully our nation's highest office with his many arrogant and reprehensible breeches of trust and poor judgment."

He pretended to glance down at his notes. In reality, he had no notes. Devin had been preparing this speech for months now, planning for it, conniving, maneuvering, all for this one moment in time when he would challenge the President of the United States of America.

"So, it is with great remorse and a heavy heart that I announce to you, that the United States Senate will fulfill its constitutional obligation and will begin impeachment proceedings against President Vermeulen at the earliest possible convenience."

He waited for them to soak it all in.

"President Vermeulen must be sent the sharpest message possible – no one in this great country is above the law! Not even the President! Mr. Vermeulen must be held accountable for his words and for his actions. The President has proven, time and again, by flagrantly breaking the law of the land, that he has lost the ability to lead."

Devin reached up his left hand and wiped an invisible tear from his eye.

"I, Senator Devin Dexter, am bound by my oath of office to hold President Vermeulen accountable. Indeed, I would be derelict in my duties if I were to turn a blind eye to his repeated criminal offenses."

Senator Dexter looked coldly into the nearest network camera and smiled inside, all the while, knowing that Daniel Vermeulen was watching and listening.

• • •

"Oh, forget it, Vicki! I don't want to listen to that old windbag! He's one of the biggest liars I've ever known. Besides, I don't care if they impeach me anymore. That's not important. What's important is that I do the right thing."

Vicki shook her head from side to side, wondering how to get through to him. She reached up and began nervously squeezing her right ear lobe. Then she caught herself and quickly pulled her hand down again.

"Mr. President, if you don't listen to me, then you're going to lose your presidency!"

Dan Vermeulen smiled and made eye contact with her. She immediately melted under the gaze of his thoughtful, blue eyes.

"Vicki, you are the most loyal person I've ever worked with, and I appreciate you so much. I don't think I could have made it through all this without you."

Vicki's visage softened along with her voice.

"Thank you Mr. President."

"But will you please stop calling me Mr. President? It's okay in public, but not here in the Oval Office. Vicki, you're not just my advisor, you're one of my best friends on this earth!"

Vicki started to blush, but quickly fought to regain control of her feelings.

"I'm sorry Mr. President. It's just a habit."

Dan looked at her and a smile formed on his lips. She always called him 'Mr. President' when he was displeasing her. He liked that about her. He never had been a leader to collect agreeable worshippers around him, and Vicki would always speak her mind. She wasn't afraid of him at all. He admired and respected her, even trusted her more than anyone else in his life.

He looked over at the television where Senator Dexter was announcing the impeachment proceedings, but quickly turned his gaze back to Vicki. She was an attractive woman, looking 10 years younger than her age, and, more importantly to Dan, she possessed impeccable strength of character. Dan was happy to have her.

"No matter what else happens, Vicki, I have to spend the rest of my life knowing that I did the right thing, that I did what God wanted me to do. Do you understand that?"

Vicki looked up and met his eyes with her own.

"I'm afraid for you, Dan. Senator Dexter isn't just a regular politician. There's something creepy about this guy. I can't explain it, just that whenever he's in the room I feel ... somehow, unsafe."

Dan furrowed his brow as if contemplating her answer, and then his face relaxed back into his normal smiling ways.

"Don't worry, Vicki. I'll protect you. I am the Commander-in-Chief, you know."

Vicki feigned impatience and got up to leave.

"It's not me I'm worried about. He doesn't want my job. He wants yours, and I don't think there's much he wouldn't do to get it."

She spoke abruptly while striding defiantly towards the door.

"I have some papers to go over, Mr. President! I'll be in my office if you need me."

The President of the free world watched as she stormed out of the office. It was just a small hissy fit, but this time it was different. Dan could tell that she really was scared. And Vicki Valence didn't scare easily.

Dan looked over at the TV screen. Senator Dexter had finished and now the newscaster was commenting.

"And there you have it, Mike. The Senate Majority Leader has called the President an arrogant criminal and has sworn to hold him accountable. The stage has been set for a political showdown of epic proportions, and now the whole world waits to see what will happen next."

Dan shut off the television set and threw the remote onto his desk. He plopped himself down into his chair, placed his elbows on the desk and his face in his open palms.

"Dear God. Please help me. Give me courage. I can't do this without you."

4

Retired General Thomas Taylor looked a lot like a bulldog. He was short, only 5 feet 6 inches tall, and his face seemed rather flat when compared to others. More importantly, his personality matched his looks. Once the man set his mind to a task, he never gave up until he could claim victory. He sat beside the phone, waiting for the call that he knew would come. He was still watching the 24-hour news channel as Senator Dexter turned his back on the microphone and left the podium. He had been watching the President's speech, Senator Dexter's rebuttal, and all the endless commentary and speculation for over 4 hours. He was convinced of it now; there was going to be a change of power, either through political or through hostile means.

The general's career had been distinguished: 30 years in the Army, serving in the cold war, the Gulf War, and throughout the War on Terror. Then, he had been called upon to work for the Director of Homeland Security as a special liaison to the military, and that's how he had met the President and Vicki Valence. The time he'd spent with him, however brief, had convinced him that Dan Vermeulen was a man of honor. Then, after the bombs had exploded across the country, the general had retired, hoping to live out the remainder of his days in peaceful seclusion. He had even taught military strategy and tactics for 2 years at the new academy in Omaha. Now, the most excitement he hoped for during any given day was the prospect of walking his little terrier, Rufus, who now lay snuggled between his slippers on the floor at his feet.

However, fate sometimes had different plans. The President had been correct in his speech about General Washington, the reluctant father of our country, how he had agreed to serve, but had never been anxious for the mantle of power and leadership to fall upon his shoulders. That was the difference between Senator Dexter and himself. Dexter craved power and leadership, while Taylor avoided it, though it had been thrust upon him again and again throughout his service. But, if his country and his President needed him, he would serve one last time.

The sixty-two-year-old general never thought he would see the day when it was against the law to speak of God in public – not in America – the land of the free. He had always thought they would eliminate the right to keep and bear arms long before the right to worship, but he had been wrong. He was a student of history, the founding fathers, and of the U.S. Constitution, and he had been surprised when President Vermeulen had signed the Freedom From Religion Act, and even more shocked when the Supreme Court had ruled it constitutional. So much had happened after that, and so quickly.

This whole episode in history reminded him of the Jews in World War II, how they had passively accepted the loss of freedom and constraints put upon them. That was the biggest problem with Christians and Jews: they were too peace loving, and they would suffer almost any trial in order to avoid conflict. The immortal words of Benjamin Franklin came to mind. "*They that can give up essential liberty to obtain a little temporary safety deserve neither liberty nor safety.*" It appeared that the Christians just didn't have the spine or the will to protect their own freedom. What was it Jesus had said, 'Turn the other cheek'? That was a one-way ticket to bondage! Act like sheep, and you'll be eaten by wolves; there was no other way to look at it. There were only two kinds of people in this world: sheep and wolves. And General Taylor was neither. He was a lion, a predator who gave no quarter and took no prisoners. He remembered turning the other cheek just one time, but never again. He had walked away with two black eyes instead of just one. Never again.

He wasn't even a religious man per se. Sure, he believed in God and the Bible, but he had never been a fanatic about it. Church had been a special occasion for him, and he attended only on holidays and before going into battle. God was a power he had always called upon to keep his men safe and help him win in combat, but never a close, personal friend, the way some people professed he could be.

The phone rang beside him, and his heart quickened inside his sixty-two-year-old chest. But he didn't move to pick it up. He knew who it was and what she wanted. He also knew that the moment he answered the phone, his newly found, quiet, peaceful life would be shattered forever. The phone rang again. General Taylor steadied himself. It rang a third time. Finally, he picked up the telephone and pressed it closely against his right ear.

"Good evening Vicki. How may I serve my country?"

• • •

Vicki hung up the phone and chills ran through her body. That man gave her goose bumps every time she talked to him. He was always so calm, so collected, always in charge, maybe even superhuman. But dark times were ahead, and the President would need the general, should it come to that.

She put her cell phone on the night stand and rested her head back onto the down pillow on her bed. She was wearing a pink satin camisole with white lace around the hem, but she felt anything but feminine. Vicki was 40 years old, but looked closer to 30. By most men's standards, she was a beautiful woman, but Dan had never shown her the slightest hint of a romantic interest. She reasoned that he was still grieving the loss of his wife and children, but sometimes she wondered. Maybe he just didn't see her that way. But how much time did he need to grieve? Vicki whipped herself inside for even thinking like that. But she couldn't help it.

Dan would be very upset if he knew what she was planning with General Taylor, but she had to risk it. It was for his own good. And she wanted him now, lying down beside her, even though she knew it was wrong. She had always wanted him, even before his wife and two children had died in the first explosion of the war, destroying Washington DC and half the United States Government. Of course she felt bad about that, but there was nothing she could do. She was in love with the President.

She smiled weakly and snuggled her face deep into the pillow. It was profoundly ironic that the President of the United States, with all the intelligence and resources at his disposal, was totally unaware of her feelings for him. But, after all, he was just a man, and men knew amazingly little about their own hearts or the hearts of the women around them. Unless she put it in a memo or in his morning briefing, he would never figure it out, at least not for another two years when he left office. Then she would find the courage to help him along.

Tears welled up, but she forced them back and closed her eyes. Just two more years, and she would find out his true feelings. But first, she had to keep him in office and alive. Vicki reached over and turned out the lamp, dreading another sleep sequence, another night of unbridled contemplation … one more night, one more lonely night. Then, tomorrow, she would get up and serve him, take care of him for another day. One day at a time. That's all she could do. She was in love with the President.

24

It was her job.

With a firm and steady resolve, Vicki rolled back over and picked up her cell phone again. She punched in the number and waited.

"Eleanor, how are you tonight. I hope I didn't wake you."

She spoke with the Vice President's wife for 20 minutes before hanging up satisfied. Eleanor had always kept her confidence, and she would do so again now. Besides, Eleanor, like herself, understood that men were only capable of so much, and then they needed a little help from the women behind the throne.

But still, there was a lingering doubt in her mind. She didn't like what she was doing. Nonetheless, it was necessary, so she brushed away the doubt and rolled back over inside the fluffy bedding, finding little or no comfort inside the furls of her down-filled comforter.

Yes, he was the President, but it was her job.

"Walking the wall of separation between Church and State is like balancing on the apex of the knife. On both sides are razor-sharp thorns. Fall to the left or to the right, and find yourself painfully entangled in the utmost controversy."

5

Sweat dripped down the old man's face, forming little rivers – rivers which followed the deep lines of his face before raining down into the freshly plowed soil. It was turning out to be incredibly hot for mid April in southwestern Michigan.

The old horse plodded slowly on ahead, pulling the plow, while the big, barrel-chested man guided and shifted and turned, all the while holding man, machine, and beast on course, working in concert, heading toward that one common goal of putting the seeds in the ground. Joshua looked ahead, fixing his bright, turquoise-colored eyes on a point at the end of the field.

For many decades, countless years, Joshua Moses Talbert had plowed this gentle hillside, laboring from dawn to dusk, reaping the fruits of the earth by the sweat of his brow. God had been good to him, giving him meaning and purpose, a hope ... and someone to love. That is ... until last fall.

His Sara had died slowly, leaving him lonely and void. At 66 years of age she had gone with a smile on her face and a song in her heart. For so many years she had anticipated her death, which to her was not death at all, but freedom and renewed life. She had been saddened to see such harsh times come upon the Earth: terrorism, nuclear war, famine, and disease. In a way, Joshua envied her, because her struggle was over.

The sun was down on the horizon now, so Joshua ceased his plowing and led the old horse back to the barn. After finishing his chores, he went back inside the big, white farmhouse and sat in the living room in the overstuffed chair. For many years, people had laughed at him for using a horse and plow, but he didn't care. He liked horses. He liked old things. They didn't laugh as much since the bombings. Horses made more sense now; they didn't need gas or spare parts, and, for the most part, the American dream was a little bit harder to come by these days. These were hard times.

Usually, Sara would have dinner ready for him, and they would sit together at the table, hold hands and pray. Joshua always ate in silence as she read aloud from her ragged, old King James Version of the Bible. Sara had read everyday to him for almost half a century.

At first it had bothered him, and he had told her so, and harshly.

"You knew I wasn't religious when you married me, woman, so don't be trying to change me now!"

But Sara was a spunky little lady, full of spirit and a mind of her own, and his protests had fallen on spirit-filled ears, while his complaints had only emboldened her and made her read all the more. The battle had raged on for 5 years, until finally, one evening after chores, she had sat down at the table without the Bible. Joshua had been taken aback, and spoken to her in a sarcastic tone.

"What's the matter? Aren't you going to preach to me tonight?"

Without a word, his Sara had broken down and wept uncontrollably as if her best friend had just died. Joshua had listened to her sobs for half the meal, but finally could take it no more. She had been a good wife to him, humble, hard-working, and loving. He had never seen her cry before. Feeling like a heel, Joshua Moses had gotten up from his chair and walked over to the mantle where she kept the big, black leather Bible. He'd picked it up and brought it over to her and placed it solemnly on the oak table beside her.

"Something from the Old Testament please."

Joshua had sat back down as Sara's sobs slowed and then faded. That was the last time he had ever complained to her about the Bible, and it was also the last time he'd ever seen her unhappy about their marriage.

He missed her voice now - her reading, her singing, her praying – and he longed for the smells of her cooking, the joy of her countenance, the strong, spiritual sunlight she brought with her whenever she walked into a room. He looked over at the empty piano and imagined her sitting there on the bench, playing and singing to him and to God.

But she was dead now – gone - forever.

Joshua looked around at the darkened room. There were shadows everywhere, black, sinister shadows that were crowding in against him like demons. He missed her profoundly, and he found himself ill-equipped to handle the pain of her absence.

On the lamp table beside him was Sara's beat-up old black Bible. He picked it up and pressed it close to the gnarled muscles of his 70-year-old chest, and then he raised it to his face and smelled the musty old pages, imagining her scent. Her fingers had touched this Bible more than any other object in the house. How he longed for her to read to him again. He had never paid much attention to her words, but the love in her voice had always solicited a soothing effect on his soul. But now, sitting alone in the dark with nothing to look forward to, he became restless, and for the first time in his life, terrified of the silence.

Suddenly, something prompted him to turn on the light, and he did. The same unseen something caused him to look at the worn leather binding of Sara's Bible and then to open it. His gaze fell immediately to these words.

"Thou, which hast shewed me great and sore troubles, shalt quicken me again, and shalt bring me up again from the depths of the earth. Thou shalt increase my greatness, and comfort me on every side."

Joshua read the words over and over again beneath his breath.

"Comfort me on every side. Comfort me on every side. Comfort me on every side."

Then, slowly, gently, and methodically, he did feel comforted. And, once again, the same gentle prompting caused him to come to his feet, and then to kneel with his elbows propped on the seat of the overstuffed chair. Finally, for the first time in his life, Joshua whispered a prayer of childlike faith.

"Dear God. You were Sara's best friend. She loved you in a way I can't describe or understand. I can't be with her anymore. But I can't make it alone either. Sara was my reason for living, but now she's gone. Please be my best friend the way you were to Sara. And please give me a reason to live again. Amen."

As if in answer to his prayer, a sudden wave of peace came over Joshua's body and soul. The heaviness in his heart lifted, and he went to bed and slept – no longer alone.

• • •

The next morning, true to his word, Joshua began his day with this simple prayer.

"Please be with me today Jesus. Comfort me, and I will follow you."

And then he cooked and ate a full breakfast, and read Sara's Bible which now belonged to him. He let the Bible fall open just as the night before. That's the way Sara had always done it. "Let the Lord decide," she had said.

"And Jesus said unto him, 'No man having put his hand to the plough, and looking back, is fit for the kingdom of God.'"

Joshua had been guiding a plow since he was a boy, and he understood this better than most. How can you turn a straight furrow if you don't look where you're going? The secret was to pick a spot out on the horizon and keep your eyes upon it. The plow always followed your eyes, always. And now, Joshua understood why Sara had always said, "Keep your eyes on Jesus."

And so Joshua did just that. He plowed all morning, and then took a break at noon to eat and read and pray. He had made a commitment to the Lord, and he would follow through with it. Besides, the closer he drew to Jesus, the closer he felt to Sara.

That afternoon was especially hot, and the sun beat down on old Joshua hard and without mercy. Once, in the middle of the afternoon, he stumbled, but then regained himself and sat down in the coolness of the newly plowed dirt to rest. After sitting for a few minutes, Joshua thought he heard a voice.

"May I have a drink of water please?"

Startled, Joshua looked up and saw a man standing beside his plow. The man had white hair, but his face was young and perfect. Joshua stood slowly and moved to get a closer look.

The man was very tall, and his eyes conveyed the paradox of both gentleness and power. Without saying a word, Joshua extended the plastic jug of water out to the man. The man took it.

Joshua wondered where he had come from. They were standing in the middle of a 10-acre field. Why hadn't he seen him coming? The questions faded away and slowly soaked down into the soil beneath him.

The man took a small sip and handed it back to Joshua. Then he smiled, and Joshua smiled too, not really knowing why. The man spoke again, but this time his voice changed and the gentleness was gone, causing Joshua's heart to race uncontrollably.

"My master has heard your prayer, and all of heaven rejoices."

Then suddenly, without transition, the man's voice boomed out like thunder, and Joshua's legs began to tremble and go weak. He fell down in the dirt.

"Behold the word of the Lord!"

"And you shall leave your plow and not look back. You shall go forth into the wilderness for 40 days and 40 nights. Then you shall enter the city gates with praise and thanksgiving. You shall go forth with the power of Elijah, and you shall proclaim these words: Behold, the kingdom of the Lord draws nigh. Believe on the Lord Jesus Christ. Repent and be saved."

The man took a step closer and Joshua tried to slide backwards but couldn't move. He was frozen in the dirt with fear and awe. The man reached out his hand and touched him on the forehead.

"You shall no longer be called Joshua Moses. Your name is now Faithful, since you have willingly pierced your ear with God's awl. Receive God's anointing. Go in spirit and go in power."

Joshua felt the white light of power flow into his forehead and work its way from molecule to molecule until it had saturated and transformed his entire body. He never felt his head hit the ground, and he lay there asleep in the sun, receiving that which the spirit bestowed upon him.

• • •

The very next day, in obedience to God, Joshua had left his home and he now stood on the brink of the desert, a man-made wasteland, void of human life, but brimming with radioactive dust and debris. There were still tall skyscrapers jutting up, forming a skyline, but the black and battered buildings seemed angry and misshapened, seeming to cry out to Joshua in fear and foreboding. 'Don't come near. Unclean! Unclean!'

Joshua took one more look behind him as if to say good bye to his past and all he'd known. Once he stepped into the radioactive rubble, there would be no turning back; indeed, no chance to turn back. He would either live or die, but the nagging question in his mind kept coming back at him again and again: 'why would God send him into a radioactive city' and then, after that, 'would he protect him?'

Resolutely, he buried the past, took a deep breath, closed his eyes on his old life and stepped into the remnants of Chicago; it was a catacomb, a burnt-out funeral pyre for a million people. Joshua walked through the deserted and wreckage-strewn streets, as a man driven by a heavenly purpose. He was the only living person for miles around, and he would not be bothered here. But he couldn't help but wonder. "What does God have for me in this place? Why am I here?"

He took one step further, and his life was changed forever. There was no turning back now.

6

The two small children were playing in the garden again, while their middle-aged mother sat on the grass on a blanket, waiting patiently for her husband to return from a business trip. The picnic lunch was ready, but he had been unavoidably delayed.

The boy appeared to be about 3 years old, and the girl about 7. They were playing their own special brand of tag, something called Chicken Tag. The little girl was clucking like a hen, strutting around the lawn, chasing her little brother who was trying desperately to get away.

The President watched from off in the distance, surrounded by Secret Servicemen, always on the lookout, always paranoid, always keeping watch over him. Sometimes he wondered if they were loyal to him because of who he was as a person or just because he was the President. He preferred the former, but doubted it was the case. After all, they were being paid to protect him.

The little girl caught the boy and they both fell down in a heap, rolling around on the green grass. The mother cautioned her to keep her dress pulled down, but the little girl didn't appear to be listening.

Dan chuckled to himself from off in the distance. They looked so much like his own kids. He stopped, and looked again. Wait a minute;

those were his kids, and that was his wife, Jeanette. How could this be happening? He jumped up and began running across the lawn of the White House toward them. The Secret Service sprang into action and quickly ran with him, shielding him from harm on all sides.

"Jeanette! I'm here!"

The woman heard the yell and looked over, but she had to shield her eyes from the sun.

"Sandra! Michael! It's me. Daddy!"

Dan ran as fast as he could, and the secret servicemen, loaded down with gear, labored to keep up with him. Finally, his wife appeared to recognize him and stood up to greet him.

"Sandy, Michael. Look, Daddy's here for the picnic."

The two little ones got up and began running to meet their father halfway. Dan smiled and slowed to a trot as he neared them. Tears streaked down his cheeks as he came close to his family. It had been so long since he'd seen them.

And then, just as he was about to scoop his little girl up into his arms, the ground shook beneath him, and the sky appeared to catch itself on fire. The fiery, white cloud boiled up from the ground like a giant mushroom, quickly taking shape, rising into the sky above them. The nearest secret serviceman dove onto him, knocking him to the ground and shielding him from the deadly radiation. The other three piled on top, giving him further protection.

Dan looked up through the pile of safety, watching helplessly as his wife and two children were incinerated before his eyes. He saw his son's lips form the scream, "Daddy! Save me!" But he couldn't get up. He was loaded down with too much protection.

The President watched as his daughter's pink and white dress burst into flames, turned to ash and fell to the ground. He looked on helplessly as his wife's flesh melted from her face and dripped down onto the grass like wax on a hot summer's day.

A few moments later, they were gone, only charred and blackened outlines on the green grass. The secret servicemen were gone too, and he got up slowly, choking on the powdery ash of their bodies. But they had kept him safe, all of them. He was alive, and they were dead - so many dead - so many had died. But he was alive. He wasn't even hurt, and the thought disgusted him.

He screamed up to the heavens, cursing God for the air he breathed and the blood that pumped through his veins.

"Why, God! Why!"

But the mushroom continued to turn black and malevolent, eating everything in its path.

"No God! Kill me too!"

Then he felt someone touching his shoulder and he rolled over in his bed.

"Mr. President! Wake up sir! Wake up, Mr. President!"

Dan looked over at the clock; it read 2:13AM. Then he noticed he was still screaming and closed his mouth.

"I, I, I'm sorry, George. I didn't know I was dreaming."

The black-suited man nodded his head and stood back up.

"Yes, Mr. President. I understand. Another bad one?"

The President sat up in bed and wiped his eyes before responding.

"Yeah, I guess so. My wife and kids again. I hate that one. It always seems so real though."

He looked up at the icy, stone face of his protector.

"Will you be okay by yourself now, sir?"

Dan sighed and turned away. He wanted to talk about it, but knew it would be inappropriate. He just nodded his head.

"Yes, George. You can go now. I'm okay. I'll see if I can get back to sleep."

"Very good, sir. Good night sir."

The man turned and walked out of the room, closing the door behind him. Dan liked most of his secret service detail, but this George fella really spooked him. He never cracked a smile, never showed any sign of emotion. He just did his job, and that was it.

Dan lay back down and rolled over onto his side, pulling the covers back on top of him. Tonight he had drawn his wife and kids – he hated watching them die. In last night's dream he had been forced to watch the city of Medina burn to the ground. One of the two dreams visited him almost every night now, and it was starting to take its toll on him both physically and emotionally.

He was the President of the United States, and all he wanted was to die and go to heaven to be with his family. That's all he wanted, just death. He prayed to God for it everyday, but God had other plans, it seemed. Dan Vermeulen wasn't yet done here on earth. God had something else in store for him. The thought of it made Dan shudder in terror, but he would keep the faith. He would keep on believing and obeying God.

He closed his eyes and whispered a prayer.

"Please, God. Send help. Send help, and let me sleep."

A few minutes later, his chest rose and fell to the rhythm of his peaceful breathing, and he slept mercifully for the remainder of the night.

Outside his room, Agent George Stollard stood with his ear to the door. He heard the breathing and backed away slowly.

7

Joshua Talbert sat beside the culvert; it was just a 12-inch diameter, ribbed steel tube coming out of the ditch, but there was water running out of it, and it appeared to be clean. He bent over and cupped both his hands, letting the water flow into them. His mouth moved down and sucked up the cool, fresh liquid until he was no longer thirsty.

When he looked up, he saw a man sitting about fifteen feet away from him. At first he wondered if this was the angel that had met him in his field, but he looked into the man's eyes and quickly dismissed the notion. This was evil. His *new* eyes discerned it.

"Hello, Joshua."

Joshua wiped his mouth with the sleeve of his flannel shirt, but soon grew tired of the man's annoying stare and answered him.

"Hello."

The stranger answered with a smile.

"You're not afraid of me, are you?"

The other man chuckled, but Joshua's face remained stern. Before replying, he took a mental note of his heart rate. It was steady and slow.

"No."

The stranger nodded and breathed out an impatient sigh.

"That is most unfortunate. This whole affair would be so much easier on everyone if you were terrified like the others I come across."

He looked down at the rocks in the ditch. The sun burned down, but he appeared not to feel the heat.

"I find fear to be one of the best motivators, don't you? I've used it so many times over the years."

Joshua reached down and let the water trickle across his fingers as he spoke.

"It's an effective motivator I suppose, sometimes, but I wouldn't call it the best. I wouldn't even call it good."

The man's smile slowly faded away, and the air around him began to chill. When he spoke, it was with a newfound sneer.

"Oh really! And just what do you think motivates people? I'd like to hear this."

Joshua smiled, and was surprised at his calm demeanor. A few weeks ago he would have been terrified of this man, assuming he really was a man and not some twisted apostate from hell.

"I think faith is a good motivator."

The other man scoffed out loud.

"Faith! Is that the best you can come up with? I could reduce your faith to a sniveling whimper given enough time. And I've got all the time in the world!"

Joshua's smile broadened.

"But you don't have all the time in the world. Your days are numbered, just like mine."

The man's face contorted into an evil smirk, and his gaze burned into Joshua with more malice and hatred than he'd ever thought possible.

"My days may or may not be numbered. That remains to be seen! At any rate, faith is only as strong as the man who wields it. And no man is as strong as me."

Joshua maintained his calm and quickly changed the topic.

"But what about hope? Hope is a good motivator."

"Hope! Hope is dead! At least for mankind it is. Look all around you."

He spread his arms out and the fabric of his gray robe hung down from his wrists, leaving dark holes where Joshua expected light.

"You dare sit in the rubble of this place of death and speak to me of hope? That's madness! I killed over a million people in this city alone, and they died, void of hope, bereft of all comfort and solace."

Joshua waited a moment before answering. Was this man a demon, or was he the devil himself? He didn't know. But it didn't matter. There was only one answer to give.

"No where on earth, past or present, has hope ever been silent. It has always been here, calling out to those who would choose it. Even in the darkest of times, there have been some who have clung to God in hope and earnest. There have always been people of faith – people of faith who placed their hope in God, even unto the end. You know that. You've seen it, and it frustrates you to the core of your vacuous soul."

The man's arrogant smirk grew even larger.

"Oh yes. I'm beginning to like you, Joshua. A man with attitude! I will enjoy owning your soul. I love a good challenge. But every man has his weakness, and I will find yours as well. What is your weakness, Joshua?"

Joshua looked straight into his laval eyes.

"Everything … and nothing."

The man laughed out loud, his voice echoing off the walls of the dead city around him.

"Why do humans always speak in riddles when they don't know what to say? Defense mechanism I suppose. But mark my words, Joshua, I will probe you out, and I will find your weakness. In a matter of months, you'll abandon your faith, and give up your hope. Then you will curse

God and die!"

Now it was Joshua's turn to smile. His voice remained steady and strong, and he knew the Spirit of God was helping him remain so.

"You couldn't break Job, and you can't break me. Do you want to know why?"

The man turned away as he answered, showing a sign of slight weakness.

"Job is just a story! That man never existed! I don't want to hear your lies!"

Joshua held firm.

"Do you want to know what I want, Lucifer?"

When the man looked back at him, a red fire had welled up in his eyes, and his voice took on a deeper tone, reverberating off the air and rubble around him.

"So, you know my name. Good. Then you also know I can give you the whole world, in return for special favors of course."

Lucifer's smile returned slowly.

"What do you want, old man? Tell me and it's yours. Just don't go through with this ridiculous plan of his. Oh, how I hate him so!"

Joshua nodded his understanding but remained steadfast.

"It's simple. I want Sara."

Lucifer squinted his eyes.

"Why? That's crazy! She's old and wrinkled. I can give you a new body, and then I can give you women of incredible beauty who will do anything you desire! I can give you all that. I can give you any woman you want!"

Joshua smiled and answered softly.

"Then give me Sara."

The devil's eyes grew even redder and appeared to boil and fester inside their sockets.

"But she's already dead! Her dried old bones can do nothing a man

40

could want! Choose something else instead!"

Joshua's voice boomed out like thunder.

"I want Sara!"

Lucifer stood on the rock, his fiery eyes bearing down on Joshua like laser sights.

"You can't have her. She's dead!"

Joshua smiled again.

"Only her body is dead. Her soul lives on. And I want her."

Suddenly, clouds began appearing in the sky, dark clouds, and the light was blotted out from the city.

"Why! Tell me why you want her!"

"It's really quite simple, though I doubt you'll understand it. I love Sara. And that's the greatest motivator of all. Fear works. Faith and hope are good. But love is the greatest and the strongest."

Joshua cocked his head to one side and smiled ever so slightly.

"I should think that someone of your stature and longevity would have figured that out by now."

The fire in Lucifer's eyes spread to the rest of his face as he burned with anger. He rose up to his full height and towered over Joshua, looking down on him with hatred and malice. And when Lucifer finally spoke, Joshua could almost feel the contempt physically splashing off his own skin and falling to the ground

"Go ahead little man, get cocky! But rest assured, before I'm through, I will kill you!"

Joshua's pulse began to quicken, but he called on God and was given strength in return.

"Only if you bore me to death. Now go away! Be off and don't bother me again! I grow weary of your lies!"

The dark clouds grew black and they boiled and churned around Lucifer's head, but Joshua's courage only grew stronger in the face of it.

"I said go away! Scat!"

Lightning flew out from Lucifer and concussions of thunder broke the air. But Joshua sensed that it was for show and waved him off with a flip of his hand.

"By the power of Jesus' blood, I command you to leave me!"

The thunder abruptly stopped. The lightning echoed off into the distance and faded away. The black cloud began to evaporate, turning gray, and then white, until there was nothing but sunshine on the water and the rocks. And Lucifer was gone.

Suddenly, the full portent of what he'd just experienced came over him like a flood, and Joshua collapsed onto the culvert and fell into a deep and restful sleep.

8

"Let's just say that my employer was very impressed with your resume."

Aric, a 26-year old former U.S. Army officer, seemed surprised. His resume was splattered with black marks, and he'd already been turned down by dozens of prospective employers.

"Are you telling me that my felony conviction was no problem for him?"

The man across the table was dressed in a tailor-made business suit and tie. His platinum-blonde hair was perfect, and his watch and gold chain on his wrists were the best that money could buy.

"No problem, Aric. We've all sewn our wild oats. You just had the misfortune of getting caught, and then you hired a lousy lawyer."

Aric ran his fingers through his short, black hair. He looked confused.

"What about my dishonorable discharge and the court martial?"

The other man looked back at him with his aquamarine eyes.

"Those were events that have no bearing on your job duties. In fact, they may even turn out to be useful life experiences."

Aric looked over distrustfully. He placed his forearms on the table and leaned down hard. He'd thought that his life was over, but apparently he was being given another chance – a new lease on life.

"What do I have to do? Kill somebody?"

Aric laughed, but the other man did not. Aric's laughter faded, and his smile went away.

"Are you with the mafia or something?"

The other man remained silent, so Aric pressed him further.

"Is this a legitimate job?"

The man nodded. He was big, and he filled up his entire side of the booth in the family-owned restaurant on the outskirts of Omaha.

"I assure you it's legitimate. On paper, you'll be listed as a business consultant. You'll own a house, come and go as you please, have opportunities for world travel. You'll even pay taxes and vote."

Aric's suspicion grew. This sounded too good to be true. In his experience, that meant that it probably was.

"But I can't vote. I'm a convicted felon."

The man took out a note pad and jotted something down. When he finished, he put it back into his breast pocket.

"Your criminal record will be taken care of. I'll see to it personally."

Aric looked confused.

"What do you mean?"

"I mean your record will be expunged. It will go away, be erased. It'll be like it never existed."

Aric moved his forearms back off the table and leaned his back against the padded vinyl booth seat.

"What does it pay?"

"You'll have a salary of $130,000 dollars per year, plus bonuses and of course an expense account."

Aric narrowed his eyes.

"Will I have to expunge anyone?"

The other man laughed out loud.

"You'll have to practice the skills the Army taught you, plus some others that we'll teach you along the way."

"So I may have to kill someone after all?"

"You'll have to stop asking questions. Just do as you're told immediately like you did in the military. You'll have to be precise and careful. You will never be able to reveal anything to anyone outside of the organization. These are the rules, and breaking the rules means instant termination."

Aric saw the serious look in the man's face. His eyes looked cool-blue and deadly, but, at the same time, his personality seemed well adjusted and functional, not like a cold-blooded killer at all. Nonetheless, Aric sensed that this man was not to be trifled with, and that, indeed, he would eventually be instructed to *expunge* someone in the performance of his duties. Would it be any different than when he had been in the Army? He had killed before, several times in fact, but he had always known why he was killing.

Aric looked away, out the big window and into the parking lot. He was flat broke, with no prospect of a job, no friends and no family. His rent was past due and they were going to repossess his car. Something inside him made him pause, but he quickly pushed the tenderness down. He needed this. It was a good thing.

"So what do you say, Aric? Can I tell the boss that you're the newest member of the team?"

Aric hesitated one last time. Then he forced a smile onto his lips and stuck his hand out to seal the deal.

"Okay. It's a deal."

The other man smiled as if he'd known all along.

"All right, then. I'll be in touch with you by week's end. If you need to contact me before then, call me at this number."

Aric took the business card and looked at it.

It read: *Mike Simmons – Floral Designer.*

Aric nodded his head, but didn't ask any more questions. No matter what the details were, this was an offer he couldn't refuse. It was his salvation.

• • •

The next morning, Aric Baxter stood naked in front of the bathroom mirror, staring deeply into his own green eyes. By most women's standards, he was considered to be unusually attractive, but his low self esteem had always protected him from potential arrogance. There were a lot of things hidden inside him, things he'd never seen, things he didn't even know he was capable of doing, and, last night, he'd made a deal with the devil so to speak. He didn't know how he knew; he just knew. The seriousness of what he'd done had hit him the moment he woke up this morning.

Aric listened to the radio announcer for a moment. He was blaring on about the impeachment hearings again. Aric had no use or interest in political things. They bored him. He reached over beside the mirror and turned the radio off. He didn't care who the current President was, so long as he left Aric Baxter alone.

Aric looked back into the mirror at his handsome, ruddy face. On the one hand, he was no choir boy. He'd done a lot of things to a lot of people, but, on the other hand, he'd never been owned before either, and that's what this felt like. He was beholden to a man he'd never met. A lot of his life had been like that, shrouded in mystery and veiled in shadow. He didn't even know his real name; didn't know his real parents; didn't even know his birthday. Sure, the state had given him all those things, simply because he couldn't get on without them, but the simple truth of the matter was this: Aric Baxter was an orphan. As a baby, he'd been left on the proverbial doorstep of society. Abandoned. Unwanted. Unloved.

Aric turned away from the mirror and pushed the thought out of his mind. He was a loner; always had been and always would be, and no one and no thing could change that. He had never owed another man and he wasn't about to start now. As soon as he had breakfast, he would contact Mike Simmons *Floral Designer* and call the whole deal off. Aric smiled. Yes, that's what he would do. He felt better already. It felt good to be independent again – unbeholden.

Suddenly, there was a surprise knock on the door. He was expecting no one, and his mind went to full alert. Aric pulled on his boxers and then a t-shirt down over his head and around his muscled, young torso. On his way to the door, he grabbed his 9 millimeter Glock off the night stand. He looked through the peephole to make sure it wasn't the landlord. Somehow he still had to find the rent money. It was a package delivery man, so he opened the door slowly.

"Good morning, sir. Sorry to wake you. I need you to sign here please."

Aric looked down at the package. It was about the size of a briefcase, but wrapped in heavy, brown paper. The man handed him a paper, and Aric signed it without reading. The courier walked away, leaving Aric alone at the door, holding the package. It was heavier than he thought it would be.

Quickly, he stepped back inside and closed the door quietly so as not to arouse the landlord. He pushed the dirty dishes off to one side, making room on the table for the package. Then he set it down and just looked at it. He wasn't expecting a package. He had no friends, no family, no one to send him anything.

Aric ran his fingers slowly over the surface of the paper, and then he smelled something and bent down closer to determine what it was. It was definitely wafting up from inside the package. He placed his thumb underneath the fold and carefully tore the paper open, and soon, he was looking at the most beautiful, black briefcase he'd ever seen. The smell was leather, and he loved the scent of leather.

Just then, the phone rang in the other room, and he hurried over to answer it. He hoped it wasn't the landlord.

"Hello."

"Good morning, Mr. Baxter."

Aric recognized the voice of the platinum-haired man right away.

"Did you get the package?"

"Yes. But I haven't opened it yet."

"The combination is five, four, seven, two. Memorize it. It is also your employee number and you'll need it throughout your years of employment with us."

Aric struggled to get the courage. He paused a moment, then rushed forward.

"Listen, I wanted to talk to you about something. Something important."

There was no hesitation in the other man's voice.

"I'm sorry Aric, but I can't speak right now. Open the brief case. I'll be in touch soon."

Aric heard the click and then a dial tone as the line went dead. He placed the old phone back into its cradle. He was getting a bad feeling about this.

Then he looked over his shoulder at the leather briefcase on the dining room table. It seemed so out of place in his dirty, unkempt, studio apartment. The briefcase literally shone with brilliance. He walked over to it, partially mesmerized, wanting to smell the leather again. He felt like a small-mouthed bass chasing after a shiny, artificial lure. For the first time, he wondered what was inside it, but he couldn't even remember the numbers, since he hadn't paid close enough attention during the phone call.

Carefully, he replayed the conversation in his mind until he recalled the numbers five, four, seven, and two. It was a skill he'd always had. Aric's memory was almost flawless. He dialed in the first number, then the second, then the third, but he hesitated on the fourth. He felt like he was teetering on the brink of something very big, something that would change his life forever. Something inside told him not to open this Pandora's box, that a price would be paid for it, and that some inner control would be lost. But he wanted to know what was inside. Why all the mystery? What is inside this silly, little box? It was too heavy to be empty. The nagging questions refused to go away.

Aric struggled against his curiosity, but then his weakness became strong and he dialed in the fourth number. The tumblers clicked free. He put each of his hands on either side of the case and held them there. The curiosity was eating away at his resolve now, like some virus that was slowly and methodically taking control of every cell and pixel of his body. His will power crumbled and fell. He had to know.

When he opened the case, he couldn't believe his eyes. He'd never seen so much money in his whole life. There was an aching in his chest, and he realized that he had stopped breathing. He sucked in some air and held his breath again. There was so much money that he could smell it. Leather and cash; the room was full of it now. His eyes traveled over the money of various denominations. It was crisp and clean and new. He reached down and touched it, picked up one of the many packets and fanned the bills with his fingers like one would a deck of cards. There was also a cell phone, passport and three credit cards all bearing his name. He picked one up and held it up to the light. It looked real. It felt real. There was a neat stack of business cards as well. He read the fancy, black words, *Aric Baxter – Business Consultant.*

But he didn't want to be owned! He was a lone wolf! He was independent! He went into the other room and came back with the business card he'd been given last night: *Mike Simmons – Floral Designer*. Somehow, he didn't quite believe that. And then the stronger, more independent part of him welled up inside. He would not be owned! He started to enter in the number on the cell phone, but was interrupted by a knock on the door. It was a loud, angry pounding.

"Hey! I know you're in there! I just saw the delivery guy!"

It was the landlord. Aric lowered the phone slightly, trying to think of what to do.

"I want that rent! And I want it today!"

Aric paused. He looked down at the money, then over at the door. It shook on its hinges as the landlord pounded away.

"Open up this door right now or I call the police to have you thrown out!"

Aric's heart sank. The cell phone slowly slipped from his fingers and landed onto the open briefcase.

"Open the door! Now!"

Suddenly, the realization of his situation came crashing back down upon him. He had no choice. He picked up a stack of money and walked over to the door. Two minutes later, the landlord left happily, and Aric was amazed at how easily the conflict had been resolved. All it took was a small stack of green paper.

The rent was paid, but the heaviness in his heart remained. He walked back into the bathroom and looked at his green eyes in the mirror. There were tiny flecks of brown on the outer edges that he'd never noticed before. He looked closer, but the dark flecks remained. Aric's brow furrowed with tension. He felt different.

9

"Repent! Turn from your wicked ways! Repent, for the kingdom of God is nigh!"

Joshua Moses faithfully marched up and down the busy afternoon sidewalk, preaching repentance to everyone passing by, whether they wanted to listen or not. Many of them shrunk away from him, while others looked on with sadness, and a few, even with quiet and secret longing.

Following closely behind on the sidewalk, young Officer Charles Macy watched every move Joshua made. He had been assigned to watch this crazy homeless man over an hour ago. The Sergeant had said to stick to him like glue and to report in every 15 minutes. Charles had done that, but there was never anything new to report. The man just walked up and down preaching the same words over and over again. Up until a few years ago, Charles had gone to church every Sunday since he was born, but he'd never seen anything like this before.

"Repent in sackcloth and ashes! Return to God. Humble yourselves and pray while you still can. Behold the time of judgment is nigh. Come to God quickly - before He comes to you!"

It was a hot, early June day, but the old man, dressed in a long, heavy, burlap robe, seemed not to feel it. His feet wore only leather-thonged sandals, and his arms were bare from the elbows down. Joshua had been preaching the same message for the last 2 hours, moving up and down the better part of town with no results, but oddly enough he wasn't discouraged. He felt close to Sara when he was obeying God, and he had even developed a friendship with God during the last 40 days.

After the angel had touched his forehead, Joshua had been unconscious for several hours, but when he had awoken, there were several things different that he had noticed right away. Joshua's body had been transformed somehow. He no longer needed to sleep or eat or drink. More importantly to his tired, old body, he no longer felt pain or fatigue. Also, his awareness of spiritual things had changed as well. Joshua not only had a new name and a new body, but he also saw the world with new eyes, spiritual eyes.

Joshua stopped in the middle of the sidewalk and turned around. He looked directly into Officer Macy's eyes and Charles' heart froze inside his chest. Joshua walked up to the policeman and spoke softly to him so that no one passing by could hear.

"The god of your fathers is a lie. You have lived an upright life, but the one true God now wants more. No longer can you live in comfort and complacency. The time has come when God will spew all lukewarmness from his mouth. He would rather have you hot or cold. Come with me and follow the Lord Thy God, who is mighty and pure, whose love flows from everlasting to everlasting."

Officer Macy backed up a step and placed his right hand on his 9 millimeter Glock semi-automatic pistol. Joshua laughed out loud, and then his face became a dead calm in an instant. Both the suddenness and the extremity of the change frightened Charles so much that he couldn't move. He tried to brush it away, but he couldn't. The young officer had just joined the force a few months ago, and they had failed to prepare him for this at the academy. He tried to reason with himself, but that didn't work either. This man had nothing, and Charles was heavily armed, but his instincts told him that this strange, old man was dangerous.

Sensing a confrontation, some of the passers-by had stopped and were now starting to form a small crowd around them, but were careful not get too close. Charles grew more nervous by the second, but Joshua took advantage of the situation to convey his message.

"You are all as an unclean thing. Like lepers, your souls have become infected and rotted, and the stench of your sinful and idolatrous hearts has reached the Lord's throne in heaven. Repent now and be saved. Repent now before it is too late, for the time is short and judgment draweth nigh. Draw close to God and he will draw close to you."

Officer Macy backed up another step and used his left hand to key the microphone on his shoulder. After a short conversation with his Sergeant, the old man preaching all the while, he received his instructions. Officer Macy was to arrest the old man for creating a public disturbance and bring him in for questioning. His Sergeant would send backup. He removed the handcuffs from his utility belt and took a step forward.

"I'm sorry sir, but you're creating a public disturbance, and I'm afraid I'm going to have to place you under arrest for violating Section 7(3)c of the municipal code. You'll have to come to the department with me."

His voice was shaky and his legs turned to rubber. Officer Macy had all he could do just to remain standing, much less make the arrest. Joshua moved closer and extended his arms out to Charles.

"There is wisdom in your fear. If God came today, your soul would be burned up like chaff on the threshing floor. But there is still time for you Charles. God has seen the curiosity in your soul, your thirst, your longing. Repent!"

The blood drained from the young man's face and Joshua smiled softly.

"How ... how, did you know my name?"

Joshua's smile broadened.

"You're wearing a name tag, Officer Macy. Right there over your pocket."

Charles' face flushed with embarrassment. Joshua again extended his arms outward.

"Do quickly what you have come to do."

With the last of his courage, Charles reached out and locked the handcuffs around the old man's wrists, but then, to his amazement, they fell helplessly to the cement sidewalk with a metallic clatter. Charles looked down at them, lying there, still locked shut. Then his gaze moved up to Joshua's face.

"Who are you?"

Joshua smiled again.

"My name is Joshua Moses Talbert, but to God, I am Faithful."

The old man turned and left Charles standing beside his dead handcuffs. The burlap of his robe seemed to blow easily in the wind, but he felt no breeze.

"Repent! Come to Jesus! The hour draws nigh!"

He moved off down the sidewalk. Fifteen minutes later, Officer Macy was still on the sidewalk, not saying anything, just staring out at the crowd. Three City Police cars were now parked nearby. They had pushed back the crowd and were waiting for further orders. There was the sound of sirens coming closer, and the growing herd of onlookers shuffled on down with him, anxious to see what would happen next.

Suddenly, five State Police Cruisers pulled up and screeched to a halt, followed by a TV news van. Seven State Troopers piled out and pointed shotguns at Joshua Talbert and yelled for him to get down on the cement. But Joshua didn't move. He simply smiled knowingly and kept on preaching.

• • •

President Vermeulen had uncharacteristically sent away his aides so that he could watch the newscast in private. Daniel watched the big-screen TV with intensity. He knew in his heart that God was working through this strange man in burlap, so he had cancelled all his afternoon appointments so he could watch it in real-time. God was on the move. He could feel it.

Daniel turned up the volume and listened to the newscast.

"There's a SWAT team here now, Jamal, and I can see them positioned on the roof of a hardware store across the street. The police aren't telling us much, but it appears as if the State Police have wrested control from Wooster City authorities. A hostage negotiator has been brought in, which, in itself seems a bit strange, since the man is out in the open and has no visible weapons or hostages."

The TV camera moved off the female newscaster, and onto Joshua who was standing on the sidewalk yelling at the top of his lungs. Officer Charles Macy sat beside him with legs crossed, just looking out at all the show of police power as if he had suddenly become autistic.

"Repent! The Lord God almighty has seen your sin, your abominations from heaven, and he is coming to harvest all who love him."

A State Police Lieutenant stood behind a cruiser yelling back with a bullhorn. City Police Sergeant Alvin Malkowitz stood helplessly off to one side. He wanted to intervene, but the Chief was on a fishing trip, and wouldn't be back until tomorrow. But when he caught the person who called in the State Police, the Chief would have their hide for sure! He detested the State Police and their methods, and he knew the Chief did too. They always seemed to look for the most extreme response and then magnified it a hundred fold. The preacher was a dead man. He knew that, but there was nothing he could do to stop it. He just had to watch. Alvin remembered his boyhood, and wondered how this could happen in America.

"Get facedown on the ground and spread out your hands with your palms up. Get down now! Get down!"

The camera moved back to the newscaster.

"Wait now. There's another man coming forward as well. He's a plain clothes officer, probably the negotiator. He seems to be unarmed. We'll zoom in and see if we can make out what they say."

The negotiator walked slowly and carefully up to Joshua, who, when he saw him, stopped yelling and smiled politely.

"Why hello there. How are you today?"

The negotiator held out his arms with his palms facing upwards.

"I have no weapons. I just want to talk to you. Do you mind if we talk for a while?"

Joshua took a step forward and thrust his hand out.

"Sure, name's Joshua Moses Talbert. I'm God's prophet, sent to declare God's love and his coming judgment upon the world."

The negotiator's eyes narrowed. Then he carefully moved his hand forward and grasped Joshua's big, strong hand in his own.

"I see. Well, my names Jonathon Aaron Jones, and I'm the state's hostage negotiator sent here to keep you from getting yourself killed."

"Really? But I don't have any hostages, and you can't kill me unless God wants me dead, so I'm not really all that concerned about it. But I thank you for your good intentions. However, if you'll excuse me, I must be about the Lord's work."

"Wait! Please. Just talk to me a minute. Are you telling me that Officer Macy here is not your hostage?"

Joshua cocked his head to one side and grinned.

"Are you serious? Officer Macy there has a 9 millimeter Glock strapped to his side, and he can leave any time he pleases. I have no desire to stop him. But, he is also free to follow me in the Lord's work, should he choose to do so."

"So why is he just sitting there? Why does he look so catatonic?"

Joshua looked out at the other policemen hiding behind their cars and smiled playfully.

"He's not catatonic. He's in the spirit. He's worshipping God and he has shut the rest of us out. He'll come out of it soon enough, when God is done with him."

Jonathon Jones looked down briefly at the sidewalk and then back up again.

"Mr. Talbert. Do you realize how crazy all that sounds? What you're describing can't possibly happen. It's impossible. So why don't you just come along with me and we can go to a secure facility where you and I can talk some more? We can get you the help you need, Mr. Talbert."

Joshua nodded his head in sudden realization.

"Oh-h, I see. Call me Joshua, please. You think I'm crazy because you don't understand the spirit. I get it now."

He folded his arms up across his massive old chest and laughed.

"What's so funny?"

Joshua stopped laughing and moved one hand up to his chin as if thinking. Then he responded.

"Look into my eyes, Jonathon Aaron Jones, and tell me. Are these the eyes of a lunatic? Do you really believe I mean to hurt people? Do you believe I'm a danger to myself and to society?"

Jonathon looked deeply into Joshua's eyes before answering. When he did, he spoke with slowness and precision.

"You look sane to me. And that confuses me a bit, because what you're doing is going to get you killed. And that's not something a sane man wants to do. Do you understand what I mean?"

Joshua nodded.

"Of course. I'm not daft! No one wants to die for no reason. But you have to understand that I truly believe what I'm telling you and that it's real. If I die today, then it's because God has allowed it. It's part of his plan. I believe that. I have faith in God and all he does. I consider it an honor to die for the cause of Christ."

"And just what cause would that be, Joshua?"

"Why preaching the gospel of repentance and salvation to the world of the lost. That's a pretty good cause."

Jonathon nodded his head in mock understanding.

"I see. Well, I just want you to understand that if you don't give yourself up, then these officers will stop at nothing to take you into custody, dead or alive. Do you understand?"

Joshua nodded.

"And do you understand why they want to arrest you?"

"Of course. I'm violating Section 7(3)c of the municipal code, disturbing the peace. I'm also in violation of the Freedom From Religion Act. I know all that. But I have to obey God rather than men. And right now he's telling me to preach, so that's what I'm going to do."

Jonathon squinted in the sunlight.

"So you're telling me that God talks to you? You can hear his voice?"

Joshua shrugged impatiently.

"I'm telling you that over 2,000 years ago Jesus Christ died on the cross for your sins. After that, he rose from the dead, and now he wants a relationship with you today. I'm telling you that this country has collectively fallen from God's grace, and the time to repent and return to him is now! Do YOU understand?"

Jonathon nodded.

"I understand. Go ahead and preach. But it's on your own head now, not mine. I did my best to talk you out of it. I'm going to leave now."

Joshua smiled.

"Good. Don't forget what I told you."

This time Jonathon smiled as well.

"How could I ever forget someone like you? Is there anything you'd like me to tell the Lieutenant in charge before he takes this to the next level?"

"Yes, tell him he's not in charge. He only thinks he is. Tell him Jesus loves him and to repent from his sins and turn to God."

Jonathon shook his head helplessly from side to side and turned and walked away in dismay. This man would be dead in 5 minutes, and there was nothing he could do to stop it.

"Repent and seek the Lord's face! Confess your sins to God and he will forgive you!"

Joshua turned his back on the police and walked away. The Lieutenant with the bullhorn tried one last time to stop him.

"Stop! Get down on the pavement! Stop, or we'll open fire!"

The newscaster then broke in with a commentary, but the camera remained on Joshua.

"He's just walking away now, Jamal. He's ignoring the police as if he's not even afraid of them. I think they're going to shoot him if he doesn't stop! I'm not sure, but I think the police are going to kill an unarmed man just because he's talking about God. He just keeps ..."

Suddenly, a shot rang out, then another, and another. Soon a whole chorus of shots exploded into the air and Joshua turned to meet the hail of bullets.

Back at the oval office, President Vermeulen watched the television in awe and disbelief. He stumbled over to his desk and pressed the button on his intercom system.

"Vicki! Get in here! Get in here now!"

*"The United States government must not under-
take to run the Churches. When an individual, in
the Church or out of it, becomes dangerous to the
public interest he must be checked."*
— Abraham Lincoln —

10

When the bullets came for him, Joshua could see them before they hit. It was as if they were moving in slow motion. He saw 9mm pistol bullets, buckshot pellets, and even high-powered rifle bullets from the snipers. At first, he was tempted to step out of the way, but there were too many of them, so he just relaxed and waited for them to rip his flesh to shreds. He was ready to meet God and Sara, with no regrets.

But the bullets never penetrated; they simply hit his body in every conceivable place, skirted around the skin and continued on out into space. The bullets continued coming for a full 20 seconds until every last policeman had exhausted his ammo supply.

When it was over, Joshua looked down at his body, checking for wounds. He saw none and smiled. Almost casually, he walked over to the State Police Lieutenant who was hiding behind a cruiser as his men reloaded. The Lieutenant stood up and started to back away slowly when Joshua got close. He came to a halt with his back firmly against the car.

Joshua reached down and took the bullhorn from his limp hand.

"May I borrow this, please?"

The Lieutenant's eyes were glazed over in terror and he nodded his head helplessly.

"Why are you trying to kill me, Lieutenant? Was it something I said? Preaching the love of God? Is that a felony, or a misdemeanor?"

The Police Lieutenant struggled to regain his composure, but he stuttered when he spoke.

"I, I, I'm sorry sir, but you're under arrest."

Joshua smiled again, this time looking deep into the man's soul.

"I think not. It appears that this matter is outside your jurisdiction."

The police were reloaded now, but this time they didn't fire. They waited for orders, but their boss remained mute. Joshua heard a scream and turned around.

"He's dead! Charles is dead!"

Officer Charles Macy's body lay broken and contorted on the sidewalk. Sergeant Malkowitz knelt over his fellow officer, a pool of blood growing on the cement beside him. The Sergeant looked up with tears in his eyes and yelled at the Lieutenant.

"You idiots! You killed him! His wife just had their first baby. You just killed the baby's father! This man was my friend! Why did you kill him?"

The Lieutenant didn't answer. He looked down at the sidewalk, then back up again. His fellow troopers looked over at him for leadership, but he had none to offer. One by one, the troopers placed their pistols back into their holsters.

The news reporter was the first to come forward, speaking as she walked, with her camera operator close in tow.

"Oh my God! I don't believe it! The State Police appear to have missed the prophet and shot a Wooster City Police Officer."

She moved closer, following Joshua back to Officer Macy.

"The prophet is kneeling down beside him now. The other police are just standing there. Now, one officer is calling for an ambulance."

She looked on in disbelief as Joshua reached down and touched the dead man's chest. Joshua sensed the absence of the man's spirit, and a single tear rolled down his cheek. He let the bullhorn drop to the cement as he bowed over the man's body and began to pray.

"Please Jesus. Please heal his body and send back his spirit, as a sign to the world that you are the all-powerful and loving God. Please heal this man for your glory and to help bring about the repentance of the lost."

Joshua stood back up, and reached down his left hand and pulled Charles Macy back up to his feet. His blood remained on the sidewalk, but the bullet holes in his body were gone. Charles Macy looked around him at all the commotion, appearing to be noticing it for the first time.

"Follow the Lord, Charles. He loves you beyond measure. Never will He leave you. And never will He forsake you."

And at that moment, Officer Charles Macy knelt down and gave praise to Jesus Christ. The news reporter and the cameraman were right behind him now.

"Darrell, are you getting all this?"

Joshua retrieved the fallen bullhorn, and placed it back up to his mouth before moving off down the sidewalk. He talked softly now as he walked, but the words could be heard around the world.

"Repent and be saved! Confess your sins to the Lord Jesus Christ and he will be faithful and just to forgive you your sins. Jesus loves you. Come all you who are weary, and Jesus will give you rest!"

• • •

Wooster City Chief of Police Randy Spooner had been watching the whole thing seated at the booth of the Old Towne Country Bar and Grille just off Highway 79. He let his hamburger and fries grow cold and congeal on his plate beneath him, as his eyes remained transfixed to the 25-inch TV screen above the bar. They kept replaying the video of his young officer being killed over and over again and Randy flinched every time the shots rang out. And then he had watched as the old man had appeared to raise him from the dead.

There was a crowd forming around the television now, and Randy had to stand in order to see the screen clearly. He had spent the last two days at fishing camp with his buddies and had come into town for supplies and a bite to eat.

At the moment, there was a myriad of conflicting emotions running through him that he just couldn't seem to sort out. He was furious with the State Police for invading his little town; he was sad for his slain officer; but then happy because he was apparently no longer dead. Randy looked down at his cell phone again - still no service. He listened intently now to the news broadcast, in an attempt to glean more information, but all they did was replay the same tape over and over again.

"The City Police Officer is back up on his feet now, Jamal. He appears to be unhurt, despite the bullet holes in his uniform and the blood on the sidewalk. It's amazing! I've never seen anything like this before! I know that man was dead! We have it on video! He was shot and killed by the State Police right in front of us!"

Randy pushed the plate away from him, stood to his feet and threw a 10-dollar bill down onto the table and walked out of the grill.

Once inside his car, he drove as fast as the twisting country roads would safely take him. He turned his radio on and listened to the newscast, but it caused him even more anxiety without the video footage. Finally, when he reached highway 79, his cell service returned and he placed the first of many phone calls. It took him three hours to get back to his office.

11

Senator Dexter sat alone on his bed as the high-priced prostitute finished putting on her clothes and left through the servant's entrance. He liked being 53 years old with the ability to have any woman money could buy. Sometimes, he even had the special pleasure of possessing a woman that money could not buy. He liked that even better, though the process was a bit more complicated and barbaric. But, nothing was impossible for him. He could have it all. He was the boss.

But it hadn't always been so. Long ago, in the distant past, he could barely recall a time when someone resembling himself had been a better man. It had been a time when he still had decisions to make, alternatives that would set him down roads that led to power and glory, or, conversely, to peace and joy. But those days were long gone, and now he was simply following the path of cause and effect that he had chosen long ago, reaping the selfish, material benefits of his ill-conceived decisions. Successful as he was, the honorable Devin Dexter was a tortured soul.

But those thoughts of earlier times were buried deep and he was only cognizant of them at the most rudimentary level. Now, because of all the many sins he had chosen in his life, he was left with only the fruit of his transgressions as a shallow consolation. So, he lay there now, savoring the impeachment proceedings that were getting into full swing, because that's all he had left. President Vermeulen, that self-righteous, God-fearing, obstacle to his rise would soon be ruined and run out of the White House in disgrace. He despised President Vermeulen, not out of envy or simple hatred, but just because he had managed to keep himself intact in a career that robbed so many others of their sanity and their souls. More than anything else in life, he wanted to destroy Dan Vermeulen.

He thought about the impeachment, and relished that the scandal would ensure that his party regained control of the White House in the next election. And, of course, he would be their nominee. After the destruction of so many blue state cities in the bombings, his party was left with a greatly reduced base, and they had been struggling to recover ever since. They had gained ground, but still hadn't yet fully recovered. Devin knew that something extreme was needed or they would never overcome the damage caused by the Muslim extremists who had murdered 15 million of their constituents.

To many in his party, Devin was already the front runner despite the fact that he hadn't yet declared his official candidacy. But Devin would never be satisfied with simply humiliating Dan Vermeulen and running him out of office. No, that would never be enough. He wanted blood. He wanted his pound of flesh. And he would get it, one way or another.

As long as anyone could remember, Devin had always had a bit of a mean streak, and, like whisky, it had strengthened with age. While it was true that he had killed several people personally, he had been responsible for the deaths of many, many, more. But Devin had discovered early on that it was always so much more satisfying to slowly humiliate his victim first.

When he was a child of about 10 years old, his mother had caught him teasing the cat, and had spanked him. The cat had paid for his sins the next day, buried to its neck, and then run over with a lawn mower. It had been a terrible accident. He smiled as he remembered it, but, no matter how hard he tried, he couldn't recall what had happened to the little boy to push him to such extremes. He rarely thought of his childhood, because he could remember so little of it. In reality, it had been nothing worth remembering. Some things caused so much pain that they cried out to be forgotten.

And now, Dan Vermeulen, Mr. President, was buried up to his neck, and Devin was coming toward him with a John Deere of epic proportions. He could hardly wait for the splatter. After all, nothing runs like a Deere!

However, there was one unforeseen item that bothered him: this *so called* prophet in Wooster, Ohio. He could ruin everything. Devin had seen spiritual revival break out before, and the results were always the same. Yes, it was best to nip this one in the bud right out of the gate.

Last night he'd been watching a horror movie where occultists were putting hexes on people, sacrificing them to Satan, and cutting themselves. That was partly Hollywood, but Devin knew that it was also mostly real, that people had been worshipping demons like Molech and Baal for centuries, and would likely continue for centuries more. But Hollywood had only scratched the surface, because Devin had discovered that the real power, the greatest power, had nothing to do with hexes or spells or even human sacrifice, despite the fact that those things appealed to him; the real source of power lay in the act of total dedication and commitment of the human heart to someone greater than humanity. Christianity had known this truth for almost 2,000 years, and the Jews for even longer. But Devin was the antithesis to all of that, the flip side of love and honor. Because Devin had discovered the vast power of hatred and treachery, and that he was the real master, indeed, had dedicated his life's work to serving himself.

He rolled over and picked up his phone off the night stand and punched in a number. There would be no hexes tonight – no spells, no magic, just old-fashioned, brute force. It brought a smile to his face.

The phone rang four times before anyone answered, and Devin grew impatient enough to swear aloud.

Finally, a sleepy voice came on the other end of the line.

"Hello."

"Yes, Mike, it's me."

There was a pause.

"Yes, sir."

Devin liked that. The man knew his place. He knew the rules and who was the master.

"I have a job for you. Two jobs, in fact. We need to meet. Right away. At the normal place in 45 minutes!"

Devin hung up the phone without waiting for a reply, confident that Mike was already out of bed, putting on his pants and halfway there. Yes, the man knew his place. Devin liked that, and he paid a fortune to ensure that it continued.

*"The legitimate powers of government extend to such
acts only as are injurious to others. But it does me no injury
for my neighbor to say there are twenty gods or no god. It
neither picks my pocket, nor breaks my leg."*

— *Thomas Jefferson* —

12

"Yes, I understand what it means. Either we'll be hailed as patriots and heroes, or we'll be tried for treason."

General Taylor held the satellite phone close to his ear and spoke softly so as not to be heard by others in the park. Even though the call was scrambled, he was careful not to mention any names.

"It won't work without your help. You have to be on board or I can't execute. No one person will know of the other's involvement. You will have plausible deniability. Only I will know of your participation, and you know that you can trust me. I've proven myself over and over again to you. Twenty years has to mean something."

There was a hesitation on the other end and General Taylor furled his brow.

"Listen. You owe me. You know that. Now I'm collecting. I need your help to make this work. All I need is information and your talents for a few weeks. There is little risk to you."

The old general listened to the silence and then smiled in satisfaction as the response came through.

"Thank you. And your country thanks you as well. I knew I could count on you. I'll be in touch through the normal channels. Please let me know beforehand if you find anything unusual."

The General pushed the button and ended the call. He placed the phone back in his jacket pocket and let out a sigh of relief. Just a few more calls and his operation would be fully manned. On paper, everything worked fine. But anything could go wrong, and usually did. This was risky business. This time, he must execute the plan with flawless precision, because if he got caught … He didn't even want to think about it.

He took out his phone and called Vicki Valence again. It was time to report in, but he would tell her only what she needed to know. The phone rang and finally picked up.

"Yes. Do you recognize my voice?"

General Taylor looked down as he spoke.

"Excellent. We are almost ready to begin execution. I will call you again at zero hour. There will be very little time, so please be ready."

He paused before speaking again.

"Are you sure you want to go through with this? There can be no backing out once we begin."

He nodded his head involuntarily and looked over at the old man on the bench feeding the pigeons.

"Okay then. As you wish. Get ready for a fast ride. Good bye to you."

Vicki Valence closed her cell phone and placed it back in her purse. She wrung her ice-cold hands nervously before checking her make-up one last time. Then she left the restroom and walked down the hall to the oval office for her meeting. She wanted so much to tell Dan, but she knew better. He would never agree to what the General was doing. Besides, this way she was protecting him in more than one way. If she was caught, then nothing could be traced back to him.

She walked into the office and pasted on a smile.

"Good afternoon Mr. President. You wanted to see me?"

13

Aric didn't have expensive tastes, and he had always led a simple lifestyle, saving as much as possible, pinching pennies where he could, but the fact remained, that he'd never had much opportunity for extravagance until now. So, for the first few days, Aric had done nothing but sit and look at the money, counting it, over and over again, but never spending it. Finally, on the third day, he ran out of food, and was forced to spend twenty dollars on groceries. That left only 129,380 dollars of the original 130,000.

He still felt uneasy about the money and his new job, but there appeared to be nothing he could do about it now, so he simply convinced himself that this situation couldn't be as bad as he'd first imagined.

Then a funny thing happened to Aric. The longer he looked at the money, the more he wanted to spend it. And finally, he did spend it - a lot of it. So much so, that by the time Mike Simmons called him to arrange another meeting, over half the money was already gone. It had happened so quickly, that Aric had hardly seen it leaving his hands. But he had acquired a lot of stuff: new clothes, cameras, a car, computer equipment, even a big screen TV. He'd always wanted one of those.

So when Aric pulled up to the fancy restaurant in his new sports car, the platinum-haired man simply smiled knowingly. He'd seen this happen before, and it was always the same, always like clockwork. In fact, he would have been disappointed to learn that Aric had any of the money left at all. To the contrary, he was counting on it.

"Nice car, Aric."

Aric smiled sheepishly, and sat down at the table across from him. The waiter tried to pull his chair out for him, but Aric resisted the help.

"I got it. Thanks anyway."

Aric was dressed in a tailored blue suit, one of five that had been delivered to him, and he was a little surprised to see that it was almost identical to the one his new boss was wearing, assuming that's what he was, his boss. His mind wandered for a moment as he tried to figure out how they'd gotten his exact measurements. The suits had just turned up on his doorstep, along with some other things he hadn't requested. He could feel himself changing, no, more than changing, being changed, and already he was beginning to not recognize himself. The waiter quickly took their order and scurried away.

"I've got a job for you, Aric. But I need it done right away."

Aric nodded his head but said nothing. He hadn't expected it to start so quickly. Mike waited for him to ask questions, but when Aric didn't, he waded forward with his instructions.

"You are to go to this room, in this hotel."

He slid a piece of paper across the table to him. Aric picked it up and read it to himself – room 302. Then he handed it back to him.

"Don't you want to keep that?"

Aric confidently shook his head.

"I won't forget. Don't worry."

Mike nodded and smiled slightly.

"Yes, we'd heard that was one of your special ... qualities."

Aric wondered if he was going to have to kill someone now. He hoped not, since he wasn't carrying his pistol. He made a mental note never to be without it again. Mike interrupted his musing.

"Over the next few days, you're going to undergo a series of practical tests, designed to ascertain your proficiency levels in a variety of skills we deem necessary for the organization. If you are lacking expertise in any of these skills, then you'll be given additional training in the most expedient manner."

Aric narrowed his green eyes a bit.

"Expedient? What does that mean?"

Mike found himself wanting to reach over and slap Aric across the face, then lecture him about the importance of adequate vocabulary, but, instead, he resisted the urge and ignored his question.

"This is the only time we'll forewarn you. In this particular test, surprise is not a necessary component. But all other tests will come without notice."

The waiter came and served a bottle of wine. Mike took the small glass, held it up to the light with a scrutinizing eye, he tasted a small sip, then nodded to the waiter, who then poured them each a glass.

Aric took a sip of his wine. He hated wine. In fact, he hated alcohol of any kind. It all tasted like cough syrup to him. In high school, then later in the army, everyone had kept telling him it was an acquired taste, but Aric had resisted that notion. He had never been much of a follower, and he had no need for acquired tastes; he already had enough tastes and hungers to last a lifetime. Besides, his foster parents had both been alcoholics, and watching their excess had left a bad taste in his mouth. But he sipped the wine now as he had seen on television. In fact, throughout the entire meal, he simply mimicked Mike and those around him. Just in case this was a test, he wanted to fit in as best he could.

The meal was served, course by course, and just as dessert was served, a slender, attractive woman in a tight, black skirt walked up and hesitated at their table. She looked down at Aric and smiled. Aric smiled politely back. The skirt came halfway up her shapely thighs, and Aric struggled to keep his gaze fixed on her face. She turned and walked away, confident that her exit was being watched. Aric forced himself to tear his eyes away from her. Mike was watching him, and he smiled knowingly.

"Go to her."

Aric cocked his head to one side.

"Excuse me?"

Mike nodded his head.

"Don't question orders. Room 302. I said go to her. I won't say it again."

Aric hesitated, then nodded his head in return and moved his seat back.

"Are there any other more specific orders sir?"

Mike shook his head and took a small sip of his wine. Good, he was starting to learn. There might be hope for him after all.

"No! I would have told you if there was. Just do what comes natural to you. And remember – we are watching – always watching."

Aric's chair made a light scraping sound as he stood up and strode out of the dining room towards the elevators. Mike watched after him with a gleam in his eye, knowing exactly what his boss saw in this particular man, knowing full well what made him so special and why the most powerful Senator in America was willing to risk everything for this seemingly washed-up and mundane little man. Mike put the thought out of his mind. He didn't get paid to think, only to act. Thinking could get him dead. The rules were simple – obey and be rich - disobey and die.

Like so many others in his line of work, Mike had been trained in the United States Special Forces, then had been recruited into the CIA. Now, for the past 6 years, he'd been working for the Senator. In his opinion, Senator Devin Dexter was a lunatic, but he didn't care about that so long as the money kept rolling in. There wasn't a whole lot that Mike Simmons wouldn't do for money, and the things he couldn't do, he just hired out to someone else. As he watched Aric walk after the beautiful girl, he wondered if he'd ever been that young and dumb. Offhand, he couldn't recall being like that, but, then again, so much had changed over the years. He had changed, and things he'd thought he would never consider doing were old hat to him now. Killing was easy, so long as the person deserved to die, and that moral judgment became easier to make as the contract price went up. When it all came down to it, Mike figured just about anyone deserved to die, assuming the price was right. He re-called his strict Baptist upbringing, after all, we've all sinned and fallen short of the glory of God.

Mike picked up his cell phone and reported in to his crazy boss. Just a few more years and he would be happy to retire from this business and sit by the ocean, sipping drinks with tiny umbrellas, and letting his money do the work for him.

• • •

Aric paused outside room 302, standing there mutely, his hand hovering indecisively a few inches from the door. Mike had said that they were watching him, always. He glanced down the hall, but saw no one. What did that mean? And why would they even want to watch him? Who were *they*? Aric took a deep breath and let it out in an agonized sigh. What had he gotten himself into? But the door opened unexpectedly, and his questions were put on hold. Her voice was soft and sultry.

"It sure took you long enough to get up here."

The woman in the black dress reached out her arm and hooked her slender fingers behind Aric's neck and pulled him in. Aric was surprised at how easily he was coaxed into the room. He stared dumbly ahead, not knowing what to say or what to expect. In the end, he remembered Mike's words "Just do what comes natural to you" and he gave the woman control and just responded as most men would.

She didn't say anything as she moved him with surety and confidence on over to the large bed. Aric's back touched the mattress, and the woman straddled him at the waist, hiking her skirt all the way up as she came down gently on top of him.

"You'll learn to like me, Aric. I promise you."

Her voice was gentle and seductive, like the soft feel of cotton flannel on skin too long untouched. Her fingers softly caressed his face, and Aric soaked it all in like a half-starved child, anxious for any touch or feel from another human hand. He had always avoided women in the past. He was a lone wolf, and there was no room for intimacy in his life.

Aric looked up into the woman's face. She looked to be about his age, no wrinkles, perfect skin, her green eyes smiling at him mysteriously. Somehow, she looked strangely familiar. Aric started to speak, but she placed her hand over his mouth and shushed him gently.

"Don't talk, at least not right now. Just let me guide you."

Her hands moved down to his throat and then to his chest. She massaged him gently, then effortlessly removed his tie, his jacket, and then his shirt.

"By the way, I don't believe we've been properly introduced, and I'm not the kind of girl to sleep with strangers. My name is Calley."

The woman bent down, exerting pressure on Aric's waist as she did, and he groaned involuntarily. She touched her soft lips against the skin of his throat and then moved down until she reached his chest. She lingered there a moment and then continued on down.

Aric closed his eyes, relaxed his guard, and let the wolf inside him howl.

• • •

Afterwards, Aric lay on the bed alone, with only the satin sheets covering his nakedness. Calley was in the shower, and he listened as the water cascaded over her beautiful, glorious body. There had been just a few women in his life. In fact, Aric could count them all on one hand. When he'd been younger, he'd tried briefly to fill the lonely void inside him with a woman's touch, but there were always strings attached. Women always wanted a relationship, and when they didn't get it; things turned ugly, even with the most beautiful and congenial of women. It didn't matter though. He was a lone wolf. He took another sip of champagne. Perhaps he could acquire one more taste though.

Aric shrugged that thought off, and put the glass of champagne down on the night stand. He still couldn't help but wonder why all this was happening. Aric wasn't a religious man, but he knew enough to realize that these people weren't doing all this just to be nice to him. They wanted something in return, but for the life of him he couldn't imagine what he might have to offer to people like these. And then there was the matter of this girl, Calley, and her eyes. She was beautiful and talented, but there was something about her mysterious, green eyes that left him feeling both enchanted and discomfited. He didn't know what it was, so he lay there, basking in the afterglow of the girl and the champagne. It was odd that he'd never liked champagne before.

• • •

Inside the shower, Calley scrubbed at her skin in a futile attempt to remove the dirt and filth. But it would never come off; it simply ran too deep; it ran straight into her heart. She had slept with many men in her young life, but never had she felt so corrupted as she did at this moment. There were certain moral and social taboos that one should never cross, and Calley knew that. But, one by one, she had crossed them all. First, she had slept with her father. True, the first time it had been against her knowledge, but after he'd made her pregnant; it no longer seemed to matter so much. It was just more sewage under the bridge.

She struggled to keep from weeping out loud, grateful for the sound of water that washed away her tears. And now, she had ... done something even worse. Her tears grew hot and rolled off her face and down the drain. A part of her wanted to die, while another part of her wanted to kill. She scrubbed harder on her white skin, but there was no soap strong enough. She just wanted to go home to her baby.

14

He knew that, technically, it was against the law to be with her like this, but she was so beautiful, and young, and in love with him, that Devin Dexter couldn't stop himself. The twenty-six year old lawyer held the beautiful, 15-year old girl in his arms and kissed her softly. Their love was mutual, but forbidden, at least for a few more years. He had always liked them younger, but he wasn't sure why. Perhaps it was their undomesticated spirit, or their untainted hope for the future, or their innocence. Yes, it was their innocence, young girls were so trusting, and that trait drew him without mercy, like gravity, he couldn't resist its pull.

His lips moved over her own now, touching, caressing, inviting her eager response, and he was not disappointed. She pulled his weight down upon her in the back seat of his car and unfastened his pants and then her own. Within seconds they were joined together in an unholy way. She looked deeply into his eyes as her fingernails dug into his skin and they both moaned lightly."

Senator Dexter awoke to the sound of his own moans and sat up straight in his bed. Even before he looked, he knew what had happened.

He could feel the wetness on himself and pulled back the silk sheets in disgust. The dream was still fresh in his mind. It always seemed so real. Her hands were so soft, and her lips so moist and warm, that it took control of his body in uncontrollable ways, especially while he slept and had no power to override it.

He had known her over 25 years ago, and she was, without a doubt, the undisputed love of his life. But Esperanza was gone now, and for decades had been, just a shimmer in time, just a fading dream that came to life in moments of stressful living, an evanescent curse from his past that had latched on to his coat-tails and followed him into the future, refusing to die.

Senator Devin Dexter had grown to hate and despise anything or anyone he could not control, so the 25-year-old memory of his young lover, coming at him without his permission, was the most despicable thing to him on earth. He pushed her memory out of his mind, but she would not return to her rightful place in his past. She had always been uncontrollable, untamed, and resistant to comply with his demands. To a point, he liked that, so long as he got what he wanted in the end. In retrospect, Calley's mother had never denied him that, and to this day, he became aroused upon meeting a woman with a Hispanic accent. He had always loved to listen to her speak in her native tongue, regardless of the fact that he couldn't understand a word of what she was saying, or perhaps, because of it.

Reaching down with his right hand, he placed his fingers on the pulse of his wrist. It was racing wildly and out of rhythm.

After cleaning up the mess, Devin reached over to the top drawer of the night stand and pulled out two bottles of pills. He took one to calm his pulse and then two more to help him sleep without dreams. With pills, he could regulate his heart, his sleep, his eating, his sex life, even his bowels, but nothing his doctor prescribed could help him forget. There was no medical technology available that could strip away the memory of the only woman he'd loved, and the woman he had …

Devin didn't finish the thought. The unpleasant recollection would just nullify the medication and keep him awake. That was all in the past. It was ancient history, a shadow of ill-begotten choices, a choice that continued to haunt him through his youth, into middle-age and on into the present. In a fleeting moment of honest despair, he admitted that his ill-fated passion would never leave him, never give him rest. Her memory was the blessed curse of his life and the bane of his existence.

Devin pulled the blanket back up over his shoulder and closed his eyes, waiting for the medicine to take control. Sometimes it did, sometimes it didn't. Tonight he hoped for the best and was not disappointed.

• • •

Calley had met the honorable Senator Devin Dexter quite by accident, or so she had thought at the time. Little had she known that he had planned it out from the start, had sought her out, and then arranged the meeting and their ensuing relationship. Everything with Devin seemed to be planned and orchestrated down to the last detail.

It had been over three years ago while she still worked for the high-class escort service. She had never intended to become a call girl, indeed, had never set out to attain it. Girls just don't grow up playing prostitute, saying, 'I want to be a whore when I grow up!' It just doesn't happen, and Calley had been normal in that respect.

But Calley had also been an orphan, moving from one foster home to the next, staying only long enough to be molested, before she was pulled out and then moved on to the next dirty old man with an apathetic wife. In cruel fashion, Calley had learned about the dark side of humanity at a very young age, and by the time she was 14, there was nothing she hadn't done with a man, at least, nothing she cared to talk about.

Back then, Calley hadn't realized how beautiful and desirable she was to men. She was slender, about 5 feet 5 inches tall, slender and petite with long, shiny black hair. Calley was the kind of woman who turned heads no matter what room she walked into. Men loved her, while women despised her. Although ignorant of her beauty at first, over time, she came to know it all too well, and to loathe her beauty more than anything God had given her, assuming there was a God. Sometimes she wondered about that too.

Devin Dexter had been so nice at first, showering her with expensive gifts, asking only that she be discreet and that she please him in a million ways imaginable. And his imagination had proved unbounded. Calley shuddered when she recalled some of the things she'd done with him - all for money – she was a whore, a despicable whore, at least on the outside. But on the inside, she still felt like a child, a little lost child, needing to be loved.

Calley moved closer in bed to her tiny, 1-year-old daughter. She prayed that God would make her Clarissa unattractive, at least average. Average would be good. Average would spare her daughter the pain that Calley had endured in payment for her stunning beauty.

It was an unusual human trait, but Calley didn't blame Devin, God, or anyone else for her predicament. She had done stupid things and was now reaping the consequences of her own actions. She might be a whore, but she was no stupid whore. She understood the world of cause and effect. Her predicament had been the product of her own doing. She'd had it all coming, or so she thought. Now, after all these years of pain, she was beginning to wonder. "Did she really deserve all that had happened to her?" She wondered quietly.

But on the flip side, she still remembered her first foster family. She'd stayed with the Murphys for 4 years until she was 6, and they had shown her nothing but love. That's how Calley knew how to love her own daughter. She owed that to them, but she would never forgive them for leaving her. That one act by them had set off a chain of events that had ruined her life. Her next foster father had been a full-blown pedophile. She shuddered now under the covers and moved as close as she could to her daughter. Calley put her hand on her daughter's chest and felt the gentle rising and falling of her breathing. She would do anything to protect her daughter – anything. She would even sleep with Aric. And tomorrow, she was supposed to do it again, and again, and again. And she would. Calley would do anything to protect her little girl. That was the one constant in her life. No matter what else happened, Calley would do anything, perform any act, endure any humiliation, even sacrifice her own life in order to protect the only person she valued.

Yesterday, Calley had wanted to tell Aric the truth, but she hadn't dared. Devin was capable of doing anything, and she had her daughter's safety to think about.

At first, thinking about Aric made the normal, healthy part of her feel warm and happy, but then she remembered what she'd done with him and the warmth was replaced with dirt and frozen cold. No, she could never tell him the truth. Devin would kill her for it, and then Clarissa would be unprotected and the heinous cycle would be repeated: a little orphan girl, all alone in the world, good for nothing but the sadistic satisfaction of a few selfish men.

But Devin was more than selfish. He was crazy – she knew that – but it was not a normal crazy; he was Stephen King crazy, the kind of crazy that people write books about. Worse yet, he was smart to boot. But fortunately for her, the apple hadn't fallen too far from the tree, because Calley was smart too. She would wait. All she had to do was keep herself and Clarissa alive until he made a mistake. Then, she would free them both. But she had to be smart. She had to be patient. She had to wait, but in the meantime ... Her body felt cold beside the warmth of her daughter. She recalled a Bible verse from her childhood: one that had been quoted to her over and over again as she was being abused. "Children obey your parents in the Lord, for this is right." Calley wondered what kind of a sick God would order a child to obey to her own detriment and harm.

Yes, Devin was a sick man, but he was still her father, her father and the father of her child. She hated him. She wanted to kill him ... but, in the meantime ... she would obey. She had no other choice.

"Who does not see that the same authority which can estab-
lish Christianity, in exclusion of all other religions, may es-
tablish with the same ease any particular sect of Christians,
in exclusion of all other sects?"

— *James Madison* —

15

George Stollard had been a United States Secret Service Agent for most of his adult life, and he was 43 years old today. At 6 feet 2 inches tall, George had always been muscular and solidly built, but he was at that frustrating time in his life where he was past his physical prime, but still at the apex of his career. Most of his peers, and superiors, would admit that there wasn't a whole lot about guarding the President that he didn't know. He had been assigned to the White House detail for three administrations now, and he loved it. They had even tried to promote him numerous times, but he had threatened to quit if they took him away from his one and only love: protecting the President of the United States. George was the epitome of the phrase, 'married to my job', and that probably explained his 2-year marriage ending in divorce. But that had been 20 years ago, and he hardly thought about it anymore. She'd been a good woman. He'd just been too busy for her, and he harbored no hard feelings and no regrets. Last he'd heard, she was married and living happily in Georgia with a husband and three kids.

Agent Stollard hadn't been surprised when he was sent off to set up the advance party to Wooster, Ohio to make the way safe for the President to follow. George was the best, and they knew it.

George ran his palm from front to back across his graying, blonde hair as he watched the television screen closely while the 24-hour news network showed the video clip over and over again of the alleged prophet being shot at by the police. He made a mental note to speak directly with the Police Chief there. He would commandeer some of his men as a courtesy, but none of them would get close to the President, except perhaps the Chief himself.

He was amazed as he watched the video tape. How had they missed him so many times? And it really did appear as if the young officer had been killed and then raised from the dead. But George didn't believe that. He didn't believe in anything except his job. Without that, he was nothing.

The other men in his detail were grabbing a bite to eat at the local diner, but George would eat later. He wanted to see this prophet fella for himself, plus get the lay of the land.

He rounded the corner and walked up to the small, city park which was now surrounded by police cars and cordoned off with yellow police tape. George quickly slid underneath the tape and walked forward. A young officer quickly came over to him with a frown on his face.

"Excuse me, sir! You can't come in here!"

But George already had his badge out and flashed it at him quickly.

"Agent George Stollard, U.S. Secret Service. Point me to the officer in charge, please."

The young man looked at the badge in awe.

"Wow! I've never seen one of those before. Is that real?"

George stifled a laugh. He remembered being that young – almost.

"Yes, officer, it's real."

He held it up higher and let him get a good long look at it.

"Who's in charge here, please."

The officer, with stars in his eyes answered as best he could.

"Well, no one right now. It's lunch time. The Chief is supposed to be back in an hour though."

George didn't hesitate.

"Call him now, and get him down here right away. I wish to speak to him."

The young officer looked surprised.

"Ah, well, I don't think I can do that, sir. The Chief doesn't like being disturbed during his lunch. It's meat loaf day at the diner."

He balked a moment more.

"I think he'd get mad at me."

George looked over at the prophet, who was now sitting on the grass, with his back leaning up against an Oak tree. Off to one side was a man in a police uniform and a small group of seven others, just sitting there, listening to the prophet talk.

"Is that the guy there?"

The man nodded.

"Yup. That's him. Strange old bird. Never seen anything like him."

George looked closely.

"Who's that policeman with him?"

The man perked up and smiled.

"That's Charlie!"

"So what's he doing out there?"

"Oh, just talking I think. He's the one they shot."

George moved his gaze over to the young police officer and cocked his head to one side.

"He doesn't look hurt to me. You guys really shot him?"

"No way! Not us! It was the state boys that done it. They're gone now though. The Chief booted their butts outta town just as soon as he got back from his fishing trip. I don't think I ever saw him so mad before."

George looked back out at the small group sitting on the grass. He'd seen all the news broadcasts of the man being shot and then raised from the dead, but he hadn't really believed it.

"He doesn't look shot to me."

Just then a white SUV with City Police markings pulled up and screeched to a halt beside the police barricade. A middle-aged man, graying at the temples, opened the door and hopped out nimbly, like he was the 17-year old star quarterback of the local high school football team. He saw George and walked over immediately.

"You Agent Stollard?"

George nodded his head and pulled out his badge. He held it up a moment. The Chief looked down briefly, but was not as impressed as his young officer had been.

"Let's not mince words Mr. Stollard. I'm not overly fond of Federal interference. I keep a nice, quiet, little town here, and I've never needed any help from the Feds before. I think we can handle this one religious fanatic."

George smiled faintly. He liked this guy already. He held out his right hand; it stood poised there, waiting. The Chief looked down at it; then he looked full into George's eyes. He saw something there he trusted and reached out, grasping the hand firmly and pumping it up and down.

"You misunderstand my presence, Chief. You don't need us. We need you."

The Chief's lips turned up slightly at the corners, but he pushed them back down for the moment. In his 20 years of law enforcement, he had learned not to trust strangers too quickly.

"Now how could I possibly help the United States Secret Service, Mr.

Stollard?"

George hesitated a moment before stepping a few yards off to one side. The Chief looked perplexed, but followed him curiously. The young officer tried to follow, but the Chief waved him back. He turned back around to face George.

"All right, Agent Stollard. What's so important that you can't speak in front of my men?"

George looked over and smiled with his large, blue eyes. They had long been his greatest physical attribute. He looked the Chief up and down as if measuring his worth before coming to a decision.

"Chief, the President is coming. And we need your help in making things secure."

All the blood drained from the Chief's face, and was quickly replaced with a million questions.

"When will he be here?"

"Tomorrow afternoon."

"That's not much time."

George nodded.

"Yes, I know. That's why I'm here."

The Chief reached up and stroked his chin thoughtfully, but George quickly interrupted him.

"Chief, can we go somewhere private? We have a lot to talk about."

The Chief nodded. They both got into his SUV and drove away.

Joshua Moses Talbert looked up from his teaching long enough to watch the two men drive off. His eyes glistened and smiled, but he quickly went back to his new disciples.

16

Devin Dexter sat on the bed, propped up with pillows, watching the videotape of Aric and Calley. He looked on, smiling with pride as he watched his daughter perform unspeakable acts on another man. He reached over to the lamp stand and picked up the pharmaceutical bottle, uncapped it, and took out three capsules. He popped them into his mouth like candy and then washed them down with a cup of water by the bed. Senator Dexter had been blessed with an insatiable sexual appetite, but, in later years, had become cursed with all the erectile abilities of a wet sea sponge. But these new pills were a form of super Viagra cocktail and they left him ultra ready, functional and standing stiffly at attention for hours. The doctor had warned him about the possible side effects, nocturnal emissions, increased heart rate, high blood pressure, and inability to focus due to alterations to the central nervous system, but Devin didn't care. Sex was about the only physical pleasure left in life, and he wasn't about to give it up yet.

The Senator hadn't always been this broken inside, but decades ago, he had made life-altering decisions, choices, which when made, created irreversible consequences that answered only to the laws of cause and effect, and those choices, had caused a tiny crack to grow and widen within his soul until finally he had passed the point of no return.

Sometimes it was difficult for him to maintain a decent hold on what was considered good by society and what was considered evil. Always, in the public eye, he was forced to maintain a manual awareness of those ever-elusive societal expectations. What was appropriate, and what was not? It was a nuisance that his high ambitions forced him to endure. Someday, he just wanted to let himself go, without having to worry about what other people knew or thought.

There was a knock on the door, and he yelled impatiently.

"Enter!"

Mike Simmons walked in only a few paces and stopped, pretending not to notice the large, flat-panel video screen up on the wall, playing pornography of the worst kind. That was one of Mike's most important job requirements: selective attentiveness. He knew what to see, and what not to see. He knew when to listen, and when to play dumb. And, most importantly, he knew what to remember and what to forget. Sometimes Mike wondered, is there anything I won't do for money? So far, there wasn't.

"She's here, sir."

Devin smiled and nodded his head politely.

"Good. Show her in, please."

Mike turned and walked out. Devin waited on the bed, and a few moments later, Calley walked into the room. She was wearing that pretty flowered dress he liked so well, the short, silky one that fluttered up with the slightest breeze. It made her look younger. He liked that. He hated to see his children growing up so quickly, and he wanted to hold on to them forever. In his own mind, all fathers were like him. Family was everything.

"You sent for me, father."

She pretended not to hear or see the movie screen. She knew the rules too, and she would play by them as long as she had to. Devin nodded.

"Yes, please sit down Calley."

He patted the bed beside him and Calley obeyed without a sound.

"So what do you think of Aric?"

Calley steeled her insides, walling off her emotions. She just had to get through this. All she had to do was endure.

"He's a nice enough boy. We haven't really talked much though."

Devin laughed out loud and glanced over at the screen.

"Yes, I can see that. He has quite an appetite for you. I knew the two of you would be close. I wanted it. I want you to keep seeing him, getting to know him in deeper, stronger ways. Not just the physical. Do you understand?"

Calley nodded wordlessly. Devin thought to himself 'So long as she kept quiet, it was easy to mistake her for her mother from so many years ago.' He put the thought out of his mind.

"But don't tell him about us yet. He's not ready for it. I'll tell him myself when the time is right. I have plans for him, very big plans."

Devin looked over at the screen where Calley's image was intertwined with Aric's. The timbre of his voice lowered and seemed to reach out hungrily. The pills were starting to work already.

"So how is my granddaughter doing? Is she growing up strong and beautiful?"

Calley winced. Inside her mind, she stabbed his body with a million sharp knives, but on the outside, she smiled.

"Yes father. She's everything you could ever want. You will be very proud of her."

The Senator smiled again.

"I'm proud of you too, Calley. Very proud."

The muscles in Calley's loins tightened. She knew all about her father's pride and what he would do with it. She forced herself to relax.

"Thank you father. I live to make you proud."

Devin reached out his wrinkled hand and placed it on the young, perfect skin of her shoulder. He gently caressed her and then reached over with his other hand and pulled her onto his lap.

"Then make me proud again, Calley. Make me proud."

Calley winced inside, and then turned off a secret switch inside her brain and smiled. Her eyes glazed over into vacuous orbs and looked out past him. In a few hours she would only remember what had happened, but nothing of the details.

There would be no pictures in her mind. None, save the peaceful picture of Clarissa, sleeping soundlessly, safe in her bed at home, away from all these troubles and cares.

Calley closed her eyes and obeyed.

17

Aric sat on the bed in his old, rundown apartment, wondering why he shouldn't just run out and rent a nice duplex in a better part of town. Perhaps he would do that later today. He had the money. He could afford it.

For the past week, he had been seeing Calley everyday, for several hours at a stretch, always enjoying her company and her talents immensely. But there was still something strange about her, something out of place that nagged at his brain, holding him back, keeping him from giving himself completely over to her charms. He didn't know what it was, so for now, he just continued to enjoy her company. Was it even possible to fall in love with a prostitute? The two of them never mentioned it, but Aric knew she must be getting paid to sleep with him. He wasn't vain enough to think that she was doing it for free. Besides, in his experience, no one did anything for nothing. There was always a catch. There was always a price to pay.

Aric stared blankly at the television. He liked the 24-hour news channel and the Weather Channel the best. Seldom did he ever actually listen to the words, but he just wanted some noise to distract him from the thoughts and questions inside his mind. Thinking too hard was not good for a man in his position. He should just be grateful for his many blessings.

"The President's aid, Vicki Valence, released a carefully worded statement today, regarding the President's feelings on the *Bulletproof Preacher* as he is becoming known in the Omaha Beltway. In the statement, Ms Valence says, and I quote, 'The President wishes this brave man all the best and will continue to pray for his well being daily.' End quote."

Aric looked up at the picture of the Bulletproof Preacher they were now flashing across the screen. The visage of his old face was set hard and stern, with skin wrinkled so deep that shadows seemed to fall down inside each facial crevice, and the man's eyes, they seemed to penetrate anything he looked at, delving down, reaching, uncovering, laying waste to any secret left untold. Aric turned away. The man gave him the creeps. Thank goodness he would never have to meet him.

The newscaster went on to talk about the continuing impeachment proceedings and Aric picked up the remote and switched to the weather channel. He hated politics.

The disassembled Glock Model 19 lay in pieces on his lap. He closed his eyes and practiced putting it back together again. He had spent the last two days on a combat range outside the city, polishing his point-shooting skills. He loved guns; they were a fun tool. Mike had been keeping him busy with training, and Aric liked that; it was almost as if he was back in the military, without all the saluting and spit-and-polish bull that he hated so much. Last week he'd attended a school on knife fighting, learning to do things that he'd never dreamed were possible with a blade. Next week he was scheduled to attend a private lesson on information extraction. That one scared him a little.

His thoughts came back to Calley. Did he love her? The questioned nagged at his brain inexorably, giving him no peace, twisting his brain into acrobatic, cerebral contortions. Women were like that. They always messed him up. It was best to be alone. He opened his eyes and looked down at the pistol. But did he love her? Something inside said yes, while another said no.

The cell phone on the lamp stand beside him began to ring. It had to be either Mike or Calley; they were the only ones with his number. He secretly prayed it was the latter.

"Hello."

Every muscle in his body came to attention simultaneously. It was not Calley.

"Yes, sir. Of course."

Aric sat rigidly on his bed, nodding as if Mike were standing beside him.

"I understand. I'll do that, sir. Right away."

He nodded again at the empty wall beside him.

"I'll be there by tomorrow night, sir."

Aric looked down at the pistol in his lap, staring at the dull, black polymer and metal, wondering ...

"Yes, sir. Have a nice day, sir."

The phone clicked off, and Aric set it back down on the lamp stand. So now it was starting. It was time to earn his keep. A combination of excitement and dread filled his heart, but he was starting to get used to all the ambivalence, so he just shrugged it off. He was committed. He had no choice.

But he couldn't help but wonder – why Wooster – why Ohio? What could be so important there? A sudden knock at the door pulled him away from his thoughts.

It was Calley, and he walked to the door and let her in. She glided in like an ethereal princess, never seeming to touch the floor as she moved. She was magic to him, making him feel alive for the first time in his life.

He looked at her, and she returned his gaze. He seemed to melt in her presence, like so much wax held over a flame.

"I love that dress. Thanks for wearing it."

It was the pretty flowered silk one that came halfway up her thighs.

"Thank you. A lot of people seem to like it."

Calley moved to him and kissed him hard on the lips. She felt his hands move down her waist and lift her up. Aric carried her effortlessly over to the bed, and they laid down together, in carnal heat and passion, satisfying the moment, putting out the fire of their natural passions in an unnatural way.

Aric put the nagging doubt behind him and clung to her flesh, wanting so much for this to be real. Did he love her? More importantly, did she love him? But for now – it didn't matter.

Calley held him close. Even though she knew it was wrong, Aric felt less wrong to her than any man she'd ever been with. The wound inside her festered and boiled as she gave herself over to the sickness, one more time.

• • •

"Romper, bomper, stomper, boo. Tell me, tell me, tell me do. Magic mirror, tell me today. Did all my friends have fun at play?"

Aric looked at the slender, black-haired lady on the television screen. She was looking through a round, hand-held mirror, talking to it as if it were a real person. Aric was channel surfing again, alone in his motel room in Wooster, Ohio.

Tomorrow, he would kill a man.

"Oh, I see Tommy, and Susan. And look, there's Phillip, and Cathy, Marissa and Chris."

Aric remembered the 'Romper Room Show' from when he was in

elementary school. He still watched it now at age 26, on occasion, just to see if the woman called out his name. Of course, they were all reruns, and she never called his name. He'd read on the internet, that the original magic mirror had been stolen in a Los Angeles parking lot during a mugging. Aric had stopped believing in magic years ago.

"And I see Joshua, and Aric."

Aric stiffened in the bed and looked hard at the screen.

"That's right, Aric. I can see you. I'm watching you. I can see everything you do."

Aric sat up in bed.

"Don't kill Joshua tomorrow. Just be a good little *Do Bee* and fly on back home before it's too late!"

The tan-skinned woman on the screen smiled at him. Aric raised the remote control and pointed it straight at the television.

"Now don't you dare turn me off, young man!"

Aric pushed the button, but nothing happened.

She smiled again.

"You see, Aric. You want to be a good boy don't you? Just be a good little *Do Bee* and make your mother proud of you."

The remote control dropped from his hand and landed on the quilt without bouncing. How was this happening? Aric's voice rang out hollow and empty in the dark motel room.

"Who are you?"

The woman said nothing. She just stared back at him, smiling all the while.

"Are you my mother?"

There was no answer. Aric lost his temper and yelled at the top of his voice.

"Are you my mother? Tell me you're my mother! I want my mother! Tell me you're my mother!"

There was a sudden pounding on the motel door, and it woke Aric from his dream with a start.

Aric sat up in bed, drenched in sweat, suddenly feeling chilled. He called out weakly.

"I'll be right there!"

But the angry pounding continued. Aric got up, retrieved his pistol from beneath his pillow, and moved toward the door. He left the chain intact and opened the door a crack.

"Yes, what's wrong?"

The bleary-eyed truck driver stood there in white boxer shorts, his middle-aged paunch jutting out and sagging down with gravity. The tired man looked at him in the faint light of the neon sign above the motel.

"I'll tell ya what's wrong son, I gotta get up in two hours and drive straight on through to Texas with a truckload of kidney beans! And I sure can't do it without any sleep! I don't know what kind of kinky stuff ya got going on in there, but will ya please stop screaming for yer Momma and let me get some sleep!"

Aric nodded sleepily.

"Yeah. Sorry."

The man stormed back to his room next door and slammed the door shut behind him. Aric closed and locked the door. He stood there for a moment, resting his sweating forehead against the cold steel door.

Then he walked slowly into the bathroom to relieve himself before going back to bed. He was supposed to kill a man tomorrow – a man named Joshua Moses Talbert - the man they called the *Bulletproof Preacher*. Because of that, Mike had told him to use a knife just to make sure. What kind of craziness was that?

Aric shook himself off and then rinsed his hands at the sink. He splashed some cold water on his face, and then looked into the mirror in front of him. The words in the dream came back to him, as if they were real, as if they were being spoken by God himself.

"Magic mirror, tell me today. Did all my friends have fun at play?"

Aric shook his head to no one in particular. He looked down at the gold Rolex on his wrist and the 45-dollar boxer shorts he was wearing. He wasn't having fun - not anymore. This wasn't play. This was real.

Aric crawled back into bed, stared up at the ceiling, and waited impatiently for the sun to rise.

18

"I just need to talk to him, that's all. I need to make sure he's no threat to the President."

Chief of Police Spooner listened to Agent Stollard talk and then nodded his head. It made sense. The man was bulletproof and a lunatic. If he was in charge, he wouldn't let the man near the President of the United States with a 10-foot pole.

"Do what you have to, Agent Stollard, but I'm telling you, don't expect much cooperation from him. The guy's totally whacked out. He says some pretty crazy things."

George glanced over at the Bulletproof Preacher and then quickly back to Chief Spooner.

"Do you really think he's crazy?"

Randy Spooner hesitated a moment and then looked down at the ground, nervously digging the toe of his boot into the pavement.

"I don't know. Crazy like a fox maybe. Why else would he be doing all these things? I certainly wouldn't accuse him of normalcy."

George smiled. He'd had seen some pretty weird things happen in the past twenty years, but this one took the cake.

"Normal, Chief? Is there such a thing anymore since the bombings?"

The Chief shrugged his shoulders and looked away. He couldn't deny it, normal had definitely changed since the war on terror. George turned back to Joshua, who was sitting at the base of a tree in the park. A half hour ago the old prophet had sent his followers away to be alone.

"I'm going over there to talk to him now. You coming with me?"

Chief Spooner laughed out loud.

"No thanks Agent Stollard. I've already had the pleasure. The guy is spooky. Makes me feel real uncomfortable, if you know what I mean."

George nodded his head, but he really had no idea what the Chief was talking about. He was just one old man. What harm could he do?

"I'll be right back, Chief."

George walked over to Joshua and stopped about 6 feet away. He just stood there, not saying anything, watching the old man, and sizing him up. Joshua looked over and met Agent Stollard's gaze head on, but he didn't say anything. George Stollard reached into his jacket pocket and pulled out his Identification and badge.

"Agent Stollard, United States Secret Service. I need to ask you a few questions, Mr. Talbert."

Joshua nodded his head, but remained silent. He looked away.

"Do you hold allegiance to the United States of America, Mr. Talbert?"

Joshua said nothing, so George continued.

"Have you, or anyone you've known, ever been a member of a group subversive to the United States government?"

Joshua turned back and smiled. George saw the intelligence and sanity. At that moment, he formed an immediate and lasting opinion.

"Come closer, Mr. Stollard."

George shifted his weight nervously to one foot.

"Why?"

Joshua grinned openly, showing the coffee stains on his front teeth.

"Why are you afraid, Mr. Stollard? I've raised my hand against no one, not even your comrades who tried to kill me."

George took a step closer.

"They're not my comrades. Did they really shoot you?"

Joshua nodded.

"Yes, many times."

"But how do you explain that?"

Joshua leaned his back up against the Maple tree and let the bark slide across his robe until his butt touched the ground.

"Sit down please."

George looked over 30 yards to where Chief Spooner was standing. He saw the Chief smiling and shaking his head. With a heavy sigh, George moved down to the grass on the park floor, sitting opposite the old prophet. Then he waited for the old man to speak.

"It's a miracle. God protected me from the bullets. That's all. Maybe I shouldn't even call it a miracle. The supernatural is commonplace to God. All in a day's work for him I suppose."

George shook his head and plucked up a single green blade of grass.

"I don't believe in miracles, Mr. Talbert."

Joshua smiled again.

"So what do you believe in, if not in God?"

George didn't hesitate with an answer. He simply pulled open his jacket to reveal the semi-automatic pistol in its holster.

"I believe in a six-inch bullet grouping at 50 yards. I believe in brute force. I believe in the law of the jungle – tooth, fang and claw – and that bad people will always try to kill good people."

George smiled at his own witty response, satisfied at his quick thinking. But Joshua Moses Talbert shot right back at him without so much as blinking and eye.

"You're right, Mr. Stollard, and the evil you speak of is highly placed."

His words trailed off into the air, then he looked George fiercely in the eyes and moved his head and shoulders forward. When he spoke, it was with a low, guttural hissing that seemed unnatural to George, so much so that it caused a chill to run down the length of his spine.

"They are going to kill the President, Mr. Stollard."

George stopped breathing.

"Why do you say this?"

Joshua didn't answer. George raised his voice.

"Who are *they*?"

Joshua looked back down at the grass beside him and frowned.

"Your task, Mr. Stollard, is to protect the President and to restore him to power. This country has raised a stench in the nostrils of heaven, and the President is the only man who can lead this nation back to God before it's too late. God is giving America one last chance."

George threw the blade of grass down onto the ground beside him.

"Answer my question! Who are *they*? Tell me what you know!"

But Joshua closed his eyes and leaned his head up against the solid trunk of the Maple tree, as if he didn't hear a word that was said.

"You'd better tell me what's going on, NOW!"

George's face turned beet red. He wasn't used to being ignored as if his badge and authority meant nothing. In a sudden uncontrolled burst of frustration, he reached over and tried to grab onto Joshua's robe.

"What the ... !"

But George never finished his sentence. He was shocked as the cloth of the robe slipped through his fingers as if they were coated with hot grease. He tried again, but the harder he squeezed, the faster his fingers slipped off Joshua's robe. Finally, he pulled his hands back and examined them close to his face. They were dry and clean.

"Who are you?"

Joshua answered without opening his eyes.

"I am Joshua Moses Talbert, but to God ... I am Faithful."

• • •

Joshua could sense the man sneaking through the darkness toward him, but he remained still, making no move to prepare for the rush. Instead, he would just wait and see what God had in store. Besides, there was no hurry, and he would rest soon enough anyway.

Aric was dressed in a black sweat suit and wore a dark ski mask over his face. The TV crews had all gone to sleep for the night, and it had been easy to get past the local police guard who was snoozing at his post beside an empty box of Dunkin' Donuts. The poor man was probably deep inside the mother of all sugar comas by now. Aric nervously fondled the ebony handle of the tactical killing knife with the fingers of his right hand. It had been several years since he'd actually killed a man, and he wondered if he could still do it. He shook the doubt and apprehension away. He had to do it. He was committed! It was a do or die situation.

The old man was sleeping with his head slumped down onto his chest. He was a big man, so Aric decided to approach from behind the Maple tree and slit his throat quickly before he had a chance to wake up and resist. He didn't want to look into the old man's eyes. He always hated that. The eyes of a dying man, somehow, always seemed to appear different, especially in the moonlight.

Aric was 6 feet away now. It was the jumping-off point, now or never. He crouched down and coiled his legs to spring. It would all be over in a matter of seconds.

And then, slowly, the old man's head lifted off his chest and turned around to stare directly into Aric's masked face. Aric hunkered down behind the bush, trying to dissolve himself into the soil, but it didn't work.

"Have you come to kill me, Aric?"

Aric's heart shot up into his throat and for the first time in his life he was too afraid to move. He didn't answer. He couldn't.

"What's wrong, son? Cat got your tongue?"

Joshua stood up slowly, brushed the dirt and small pieces of bark off the back of his robe and then walked over to Aric, who was still hiding behind the bush.

Aric finally began to master his fear. He looked into the old man's eyes and saw him smiling back at him. Those turquoise-colored eyes made him shiver.

"Isn't this ironic? You're out here doing the will of your father, and I'm here doing the will of mine."

Joshua smiled before speaking softly.

"Have you given any thought to what you're about to do, how it will change you, how it will lead you down a path that doesn't return?"

Finally, Aric found his voice.

"How did you know my name?"

Joshua laughed out loud and sat down beside Aric and the bush.

"I'll take that as a no."

Joshua stared off into the darkness for a moment, then he clasped his gnarled, old hands together and placed them in his lap.

"Ya know, Aric, we all start out life the same way, full of hope, potential, full of dreams. But ... somehow, things go wrong. For you, it was the death of your mother and the evil of your father. Some would say that you never had a prayer."

Aric's eyes narrowed and his visage hardened.

"I have no mother and father."

Then Aric hesitated and his eyes softened and his head rose up.

"Did you know them?"

The old man shook his head.

"Only what's been told to me by someone in the position to know. By most standards, your mother was good, while your father was evil."

Aric's thoughts went back to the motel room, to the Romper Room dream. He had no memories of his mother or his father, and that lacking was the greatest void in his life, steering him, directing him, misguiding him every step of the way. He had always felt powerless to do right, even though his desire had usually been for good.

"Did you know that the President is coming to see me tomorrow, Aric? The President of the United States of America. Wow! I've always wanted to meet the President."

And then his old eyes wandered off into the darkness and then moved up to stare at the moon.

"You're not a murderer, Aric. I'm sorry, but it's just not in you. At least not yet."

Aric watched him, his fingers all the while moving back and forth on the ebony knife handle.

"But ... somehow, seeing the President just doesn't seem to thrill me like I thought it would. I have nothing but bad news for him, Aric. And I fear he's not going to like me when I'm done."

He looked down from the moon and deep into Aric's green and brown speckled eyes.

"Have you ever had to tell people bad news? Sometimes I hate being the messenger of God."

There was a look of pity in Joshua's eyes now, and Aric couldn't hold the man's gaze. He looked down at the ground instead.

"Take off your mask, Aric. I'd like to see your face before I pronounce on you."

Aric looked back up.

"Pronounce on me? What are you talking about?"

Joshua smiled, and when he did, a hundred wrinkles turned upward with the ends of his mouth.

"That's okay, son. I'll get it for you."

Aric reached up to stop the old man's hand, but as soon as he touched him, he felt paralyzed. Joshua squeezed Aric's hand lightly, while reaching over with his other and pulling off the ski mask. Aric's bare face reflected the moonlight and suddenly he felt very naked and exposed.

"Well, now aren't you a handsome young fella?"

Aric let the knife slip from his hands and fall to the ground.

"I'm so sorry, Aric. I really am. You have been given a tough lot in life. It's not your fault. Well, not all of it. But you need to know that God has never left your side. He was always there for you, always talking to you, always trying to guide you in the right direction. It's just, well, it's just that sometimes you don't listen so good."

Joshua laughed again before going on. He remembered his Sara and her pretty smile. It had taken him years to listen to her.

"God never gives up on us, and he sends people to give us a way out of whatever kind of trouble we've gotten ourselves into."

The old man shifted his weight to his left side and held the ski mask up to the moonlight.

"Take you for example. Satan is a usurper of all things left unattended, and he has snatched you up and thinks for certain that you belong to him forever, but I know better. God still hasn't given up on you, Aric. It's still not too late. You believe that you came to me, but I really came to you. God sent me to you, Aric."

Joshua tossed the ski mask off to one side. It landed on the ground 3 feet away, hardly making a sound.

"Are you ready, Aric?"

Aric shook his head.

"Ready for what?"

Joshua lowered his head and smiled.

"Well, okay, I'll just get on with it then. If it's any consolation, I wasn't ready either. I'm not sure anyone ever is."

Aric was starting to feel rational and sane again until the old man reached over and placed the palm of his right hand on Aric's forehead. His hand was so big that it covered most of the young man's face. Immediately, Aric felt something like hot wax running across his head. Like a slow, rolling wave, it moved down until it covered all his body. And when Joshua spoke, Aric felt the earth vibrate beneath him.

"God has chosen you, Aric. He has set you apart, consecrated you for his own holy purpose. And here are the terms of your consecration unto the Lord: you are forbidden to lie with a woman, neither shall a blade touch your skin, you shall do your best to honor all the words of the Lord as best you know them. You shall honor the terms of this consecration until your task is done."

Joshua moved his hand away but the warmth lingered. Despite the circumstance, it was a very pleasant feeling.

"Of course the rest is up to you, Aric. You can uphold the consecration, or you can break it. But you need to know that this is your last chance to expunge the deal you've made with the devil's imp."

Aric looked up sharply.

"Did you just say *expunge*?"

Joshua ignored the question and continued on.

"And I have one final word of prophecy for you."

The old man raised his open hand out in front of him and held it between Aric and himself.

"And you shall be sacrificed by the enemies of the Lord. You will be cast down and you will be trampled under the feet of men, and your father shall imprison you and you shall remain in chains. After that time, if you have remained true, and if the forces of good prevail, then you will be raised up and set in a place of honor by your true father."

Aric just stared over at Joshua in total disbelief and shock. The plan had been so simple. He was just supposed to slit this old man's throat and walk away. Aric didn't know what to do next.

"By my father? I have no father. I'm an orphan."

Joshua smiled sympathetically.

"There are no orphans, Aric. You have a father. You just have to seek him out."

Aric mulled this over in his mind for a moment. It all sounded cryptic to him, like a huge riddle that he didn't have the patience to solve. Then he remembered the real world.

"I'm supposed to kill you. If I don't, they'll probably kill me."

Joshua shook his head slightly from side to side.

"Well, I'm no theologian, but I'm pretty sure that killing me would violate the terms of your consecration. Besides, you can't kill me. Not yet. But my time is drawing closer, and I welcome it."

Joshua's eyes looked off into the distance as if contemplating something in the distance.

"Don't worry about it, they won't kill you, at least not right away. But it's your choice. It always has been."

Joshua reached over and picked up the knife that had slipped from Aric's hand. He turned it over and over again, examining it. He tested the sharpness on his finger and a drop of blood beaded up and ran down the length of his finger. He wiped the blood off on his robe and offered the knife to Aric.

"Go ahead, Aric. It's up to you."

Aric hesitated, then reached out to take the knife. The ebony grip felt reassuring again in the palm of his right hand. He looked over into the old man's eyes in pleading fashion.

"Tell me what I should do."

"I can't do that, Aric. Not even God can do what you ask. Your life is up to you. That has always been God's way. Only men of power and greed want to control other people, but God just wants you to be happy."

At that moment, Joshua paused and smiled, wondering how he knew all this. And then it hit him: Sara had been unknowingly teaching him, preparing him for this mission for all the long decades of their marriage. He wondered if she was looking down on him now, wondered if she was happy with him, wondered if he would soon be with her. A big part of him wanted Aric to slit his throat and send him back home to be with Sara.

Aric moved his left hand and closed the folding knife. Joshua bowed his head as if all the years of his life were pressing down on him at once. Aric felt suddenly exhausted and let out a huge sigh.

"I need time to think."

He put the knife back into his pocket.

"What can you tell me to get me out of this mess?"

Joshua smiled. At last the boy was starting to ask the right questions. Joshua crossed his legs and looked into his eyes.

"To those who have ears to hear, let them listen to the words of God's prophet."

Joshua moved closer and spoke in hushed tones.

• • •

Off in the distance, a man in a grey suit, took the night vision binoculars away from his eyes and picked up his satellite phone. After a brief conversation, he opened up his jacket and placed the phone back in his pocket. Things would happen quickly now.

19

Back inside his motel room, Aric stood in front of the bathroom mirror, wondering what to do next. By morning they would know he had failed, and that didn't leave him much time.

He picked up his cell phone and punched in Calley's number. It rang and rang and rang, but no one picked up. Aric threw the phone down onto the bathroom counter in frustration. It was after 1AM, so her phone was probably turned off. He wanted to go to her, but with a sinking feeling in the pit of his stomach, he realized that he had fallen in love with a stranger. He didn't even know where she lived. He didn't know her last name. He didn't know much of anything. All he had ... was a cell phone number.

Aric looked back up into the mirror and gazed deeply into his own green orbs. He saw the brown flecks, how they were growing, spreading, taking over everything, and he shuddered. All of a sudden, his life had become crazy, and he had no one to blame but himself.

He didn't believe in the supernatural. At least he never had before, but, still ... The old man, the Bulletproof Preacher, how else could he be explained? Aric remembered the hot wax again flowing down his head and into his torso. It was like he could feel it happening all over again, and it had a calming effect on him that made him more sure and gave him confidence. Perhaps more importantly, all of a sudden the wrongness of what he was doing began screaming out to him, yelling into his soul so loud that it hurt. Killing people for money? Where did that come from? And all because he was behind in his rent?

But the supernatural thing; that was too much; that was just way too much for him to grasp right now. But still ... it had happened. There was no denying what he had experienced. What was it the old man had told him? 'You don't have to believe, just act like you believe'. Aric searched desperately for other options, but he found none. He felt painted into a corner, and they were going to kill him!

Tears welled up in Aric's eyes. He just wanted Calley to hold him, to stroke his face, to ease his fears, but at the same time, the idea seemed ludicrous to him. How do you fall in love with someone you don't even know? He forced himself to think about it for a moment, and he had to admit that if someone else were to tell him this story he would laugh at them and tell them to run! He thought hard. They owned Calley too, just as they owned him. She had all but told him so at their last encounter, discreetly whispering into his ear 'They have my baby girl.' He turned inward and searched for the lone wolf and found it huddled in a corner, cowering like a whipped puppy. And, at that moment, Aric realized the truth. He was a loser. His life was a waste of breath and blood. It would have been better if he'd never been born. He was alone. He was an orphan, and that fact alone was sufficient to explain the depths of his desperation.

Aric let himself fall to the floor and sobbed onto the ceramic tile like a child. The Romper Room words came back to him hauntingly: 'Magic mirror, tell me today. Did all my friends have fun at play?' There was no magic mirror. The magic was dead, but the mirror remained, and it showed him now for what he really was: a failure, a screwed-up, miserable failure – an orphan. A childhood chant came back to him now like a malevolent mantra from days gone by. 'Nobody loves me, everybody hates me, I think I'll go eat worms and die!'

At that moment in time, Aric would gladly eat worms just to get himself out of this mess, but it wasn't going to be that easy. Think! Think! Think! Tears dropped down onto the ceramic floor tile. What had the old man said? 'There is no such thing as an orphan, Aric. We all have a father. You just have to seek him out.' He had a feeling the old man knew more than he was saying, but that thought was no consolation to him now.

Aric moved to his knees and propped his elbows on top of the toilet seat. He hesitated for a moment, took a deep breath, and then he clasped his hands together and tried something new. He prayed.

"Okay God. They're going to kill me now, so I need you. Please help me. I don't believe you'll do it, but I'm willing to try if you are. Besides, the old man said you would help. Okay. Thanks. Bye."

Aric cried until his eyes were dry, and then he walked out of the bathroom and stopped dead in his tracks. A wave a fear and adrenaline rushed over him as he looked at the man sitting in the dark corner. In the man's right hand, he was holding a Beretta 9 millimeter pistol, and it was pointed directly at Aric's chest.

"Don't move or I empty the magazine."

Aric didn't move or speak. He hadn't expected God to answer his prayer so soon. He knew he was a dead man, but how had they found him so quickly? And then he remembered the words of Mike Simmons – *Floral Designer*, 'And remember – we are watching – always watching.'

The man's voice spoke softly, but the Beretta pistol accentuated his words, giving him authority.

"Sit down on the edge of the bed please."

The man's voice was polite but firm. Aric's shoulders slumped down as he complied.

"Lieutenant Baxter. I've been watching you for a while. When you made a deal with the devil, did you think he would never come to collect his due?"

Aric looked over at the man in the shadowed corner and braced himself for the bullets, all the while praying "Please God, I'll do whatever you want. Just don't let me die."

• • •

Calley heard the phone ring again, but she didn't answer it. She knew who it was, and she was forbidden now to see him. Aric had been trying all night long to reach her, but she dared not answer. Her father's orders had been explicit. 'Do not talk to him. Do not see him!' And she could tell by the tension in his voice that he was very mad. Something had happened – something, unforeseen. The honorable Senator always planned things out, and things always went according to his plans. But ... this time, something was different, and Calley saw it as a ray of hope.

She knew her phone was being monitored, but she wanted desperately to speak with Aric, to tell him the truth, to enlist his help. If only ... if only she could think of a way. Calley looked down at her sleeping baby and smiled sadly. She wanted to take the risk, but what about Clarissa? What would happen to her little girl if she was caught? She shook her head and turned her face toward the wall. It was too risky, too dangerous for her baby. She couldn't do it.

Calley went back to the living room and sat on the couch, waiting for the Senator to come. He rarely visited her here, always insisting that things transpire according to his terms and conditions. Most of the time, she saw him at his home, where everything was under his direct control.

But something was definitely different for him to come here with such short notice. What was it? What was wrong? Where was Aric? What had he done to aggravate the honorable Senator? Calley had to know.

Calley turned on the television just to have the noise, and the voice of the President came to her like a soothing ointment.

"And to all Americans, I urge you to stay the course. I urge you to keep the faith. I implore you not as your President, but as a common citizen like yourself – do not be afraid. Never give up! Never give in to despair! You and I have been through many things together, horrible things, terrible things, frightening things, but one thing remains true and clear. We have survived. We are still here. America goes on and on and on. Not because we're better, or stronger, or more right, but just because we never give up. We are not held captive to our fears. The darkness and the unknown, they scare us, but they do not control us. No matter what happens, we must hold true to our faith in God. He is our father, our heavenly father, the creator of all things. In him, we move, and hope and have our being. God is our refuge and strength, an ever present help in time of trouble."

The President looked deep into the camera, as if he could see into Calley's very own soul, as if he was speaking just to her and not the millions of others tuned in.

"I know you're afraid to do the right thing. I know that. But I need your help now like never before. I need America to overcome her fears with a deep and abiding courage. I need each single American: every factory worker, farmer, mother, father, I need each of you to search your heart and find what is good and right and true, and then you must do what your heart tells you.

Follow your heart, with bravery and unflinching loyalty to truth. And above all, you must hope. Always hope. Never give up. Be brave. Do the right thing."

And then the President walked off the podium and the news person took over, commenting on the impeachment proceedings. Things were not going well for him. They played a video clip of Senator Dexter.

"Because the President shows no signs of remorse or change of heart, the Senate will continue, indeed accelerate, its investigations and proceedings. President Vermeulen will be called in for questioning as soon as a mutual time can be arranged."

The reporter raised his voice above the others chiming in with questions and was rewarded for his volume.

"Senator Dexter, there has been speculation that you plan to announce your bid for the Presidency soon. Is there any truth to that? And are you concerned that this impeachment may appear to be partisan and that it may benefit you politically?"

Senator Dexter frowned, but lost no time in rebutting the accusation.

"First of all, my bid for the Presidency is just a beltway rumor and I'll neither confirm nor deny its validity. Second, my career ambitions and my personal feelings have no bearing whatsoever on my duty to move forward with these hearings. All due haste must be taken, in order to resolve the crisis and move on to America's healing. The sooner we get this over, the better for the country. That is my only motivation."

Slightly perturbed and showing it, the Senator waved off other questions and moved away from the podium.

Calley turned the TV off and looked down at her hands resting nervously on her lap, and, for the first time she realized, her father was vulnerable. The President's words echoed in her mind again, giving her courage and boldness.

"Follow your heart, with bravery and unflinching loyalty to truth. And above all, you must hope. Always hope. Never give up. Be brave. Do the right thing."

Calley whispered a prayer and made her decision. She would act. She would do the right thing. She got up and walked to the bedroom, where she waited for the Senator to arrive. He would never see it coming. She would make sure of that.

• • •

General Taylor had sat quietly listening to Aric's story for over 15 minutes, carefully examining every word and comparing it with other things that he knew to be true. He watched the young man's body language, looking deeply into his eyes, all the while, keeping the pistol pointed at the center of Aric's chest.

When Aric was finished, he exhaled, and it was as if all the air in the world had just escaped from the Earth's atmosphere, leaving the planet in a total vacuum. General Taylor could see that the man cowering before him was terrified and broken. But now, what tact should he take? He thought about it for a moment. This was an opportunity, but if he didn't do it right ... He chose not to complete the thought; it was too scary to even ponder.

"You don't recognize me, do you Aric?"

Aric looked over at the dimly lit corner. General Taylor reached out with his left hand and turned on the lamp beside him. Aric's eyes immediately squinted in recognition. He had seen this man before, but he couldn't quite place him, and something felt different. General Taylor smiled and nodded.

"Yes, I see faint recognition in your eyes, but I'll let you chew on it for a while. But first, tell me Aric, are you ready to put all this nonsense behind you and finally do the right thing?"

The old general threw out the bone of hope and Aric was quick to fetch it up.

"Yes sir! Yes sir! I am sir! I want to do the right thing. It's just ..."

General Taylor leaned forward with anticipation, knowing that the boy's next sentence would redeem his soul or seal his fate.

"It's just, that I've been doing the wrong thing for so long that I'm not sure what the right thing is anymore."

General Taylor nodded with satisfaction. That was the correct response, and he knew it to be true before it was even uttered. The General lowered the gun slightly and Aric started to breathe again. Perhaps he wasn't going to die after all, at least not by this man's hand.

"You have special ops training; is that correct?"

Aric nodded. The General had read his file, so he already knew more about Aric than he let on.

"Listen, Lieutenant, your country needs you. If you serve with honor and distinction, then all your sins will be expunged. I will see to it."

Aric's ears perked up at the word *expunged*. There it was again. It seemed to be the recurring theme of his life.

"However, should you fail America, this President, or cause dishonor in any way, shape, or form, I will personally put a bullet in your skull."

General Taylor paused, waiting for an answer, but Aric said nothing.

"Can I count on you, Lieutenant?"

Aric looked down at the nine millimeter Beretta and vigorously and obediently nodded his head. As he nodded, the general smiled for the first time that night.

"All right then. Based on what you've told me and on what I already know, I have a plan that just might work. But we'll have to work quickly and without mistakes."

General Taylor laid his pistol on his lap, and Aric's shoulders dropped down as his muscles finally relaxed.

"Okay, here's what you're going to do."

20

"So if she's such a ball and chain, Dave, then why do you even put up with the old hag? Just get rid of her."

Senator Dexter and Vice President Thatcher were sitting across from one another, separated only by a glass-topped coffee table. The Vice President, normally surrounded by the Secret Service, had dismissed them and they were in the other room out of earshot, which appeared to embolden the senior Senator. The Vice President couldn't believe what he was hearing, and he couldn't help but wonder what the Senator meant by that. And when did they all of a sudden get on a first-name basis? The audacity of Devin Dexter was amazingly overt and bold, causing the Vice President to shift uncomfortably in his chair, already regretting that he had acquiesced to this meeting.

"You're joking right?"

Devin Dexter smiled just like a man who had drowned a puppy and enjoyed it, and it sent a chill down the Vice President's spine.

"I don't joke, Dave. I see what I want, and then I go after it. That's how I've gotten where I am, and that's why I'll be President someday."

Senator Dexter spoke in a matter-of-fact tone, as if it had already happened and he was just waiting to move into the White House. Dave

Thatcher let the crack about the White House pass by without challenge. He just wanted to get through this and on to his next meeting.

"I love my wife, Senator, and I didn't say she was a ball and chain. I was simply trying to be sensitive to her needs, and I don't consider that a constraint to me of any kind."

Devin Dexter was disgusted by the man's lack of fortitude, letting a woman hold him political hostage like that. There was no excuse for it, and a real man would take the woman into the bedroom and remind her of her place. But Devin suddenly realized that this must be one of those things that is inappropriate for him to say, so he would back off for now. He tried to gracefully withdraw by feigning sympathy.

"Yes, I see what you mean. It's a real pickle. Better keep her happy then or she'll ruin you politically. I guess that's why I never married. I like a simple life, free of those types of complications."

The Vice President tried to look deep into Devin's eyes but couldn't hold his gaze. He shuddered and looked back down at his hands folded over his crossed legs.

"Please get to the point, Senator Dexter. I have a full schedule this morning."

Devin Dexter wanted to reach across the table and throttle the man's neck, but he knew that he could never get away with it, at least not yet, not here in the Vice Presidential residence at the Naval Observatory, so he held his temper in check.

"I wanted to talk to you about the impeachment proceedings."

Dave Thatcher looked up surprised.

"Senator Dexter, with all due respect, you and I are on opposite sides of the aisle, so what makes you think I would want to talk to you about that?"

Devin wasted no time getting to the point. His gaze hardened and his voice took on an ominous, businesslike tone.

"I want you to testify to the Senate against your boss."

The Vice President uncrossed his legs and his heart rate shot up another 20 beats per minute. He struggled to master his emotions.

"And why in the world would I want to do that? Dan Vermeulen is my friend!"

Devin Dexter laughed out loud.

"Oh come on Dave, let's be blunt here. You stand poised to become the next President of the United States. Now don't sit there and tell me that deep down inside you're not praying that the President is removed from office by the Senate. I know better than that. You're a politician, and you've been wanting to be President your whole life. And let's face it, you're not getting any younger."

Devin watched the Vice President's nonverbal signals as he waited for a response. Dave Thatcher, a seasoned, lifelong politician, for the first time in his life, had no idea what to say. He just wasn't used to such directness. On the one hand, yes, he wanted to be President more than anything, but not if he had to dirty his hands to get it. He thought as fast as he could and came to an abrupt decision, born more out of gut instinct and fear more than brainpower. He quickly stood up and moved toward the door.

"I'm afraid our time is up Senator Dexter. I have another appointment that I just can't miss."

Devin's blood began to boil and seethe with rage, but he didn't dare show it. The Vice President was weak, too weak to grasp his own success, even as it hung there ripe, ready to be plucked by his own hand. And Devin Dexter hated weakness more than anything. He slowly stood up and spoke through clenched teeth.

"I was hoping you'd do the right thing by the country on this, Dave. It would help us to avoid so many other ... unpleasantries."

Vice President Thatcher, having regained a bit of his pride and his composure, opened the big mahogany door and motioned with his left hand for Dexter to leave.

"Did you just threaten me Senator Dexter?"

Upon hearing the word *threaten*, the two Secret Service Agents standing outside the doorway turned and frowned. One placed his hand on the grip of his pistol, while the other looked to the Vice President for direction. Devin accurately read the no-win situation and tried to make light of the comment. He laughed heartily.

"Just a little political humor, Mr. Vice President, that's all. No need to take things so seriously."

Vice President Thatcher, pretending not to hear, issued curt instructions.

"Agent Simonson, will you please make sure the Senator makes it to his car please."

With that, the heavy, mahogany door swung shut. Dave Thatcher walked back to his desk and picked up the phone. His hands were still shaking slightly. Something had to be done about that man. He was dangerous.

21

James Thurgood was a former Marine Corps marksman, but now he worked for himself. He had been a good shooter in the Marines, but now he was world class, capable of consistently bringing down man-sized targets at beyond 1,000 yards. He had always wanted to be known as the undisputed best, but his present career path paid him good money to be the best and to keep a low profile, so he reluctantly complied.

He was resting in the prone position atop a wooden platform that he had built specifically for this purpose. It was portable, but stable, and he could strip it down and pack it up in just a matter of seconds. The shade from the big oak tree above him provided concealment and was a welcome relief from the sun. He was thankful for the lack of wind today. Wind was just one more variable that could throw off his shot.

He nuzzled his brow up to the eyepiece of the Leupold scope and looked down into the park. The old man was just sitting there under the tree – waiting. James put the crosshairs on the center of the man's head and held it steady, took a shallow breath and held it. His finger eased back on the trigger, slowly and straight to the rear. There was a loud 'click' as the firing pin came forward and struck the empty chamber.

There was always an incredible adrenaline rush before a kill, and he constantly struggled to control his heart rate and breathing. Dry firing always helped him calm his nerves on a job. James had killed before, many times in fact, always at a distance, but it always seemed so personal to him. And he liked it that way. Most people have an aversion to taking the life of one of their own species, but James wasn't shackled with that burden. Killing was just part of life. He was a predator, a very well paid predator. In fact, they were paying him so much that this would undoubtedly be his last job. If his hand was steady and his aim was true, he could eliminate both the primary and secondary targets and he'd be set for a long life of luxury.

He imagined himself somewhere warm, by the ocean, with a tropical breeze caressing his face. And there would be women, beautiful women, always pleasing him, always thinking of just him. That's the way he wanted it. That's the way it was supposed to be.

James forced himself back to the focus at hand. None of that would happen though if he missed the shot. There was a commotion down near the park. People were scurrying to get into position, and then the President's motorcade pulled up and rolled to a stop. He pulled the charging handle back on his high-powered rifle and chambered a round.

The sniper took a deep cleansing breath and tried to relax. Then he placed his eye back up to the scope and settled in for the kill. Just 5 more minutes until retirement. He smiled softly and placed his finger on the trigger.

• • •

George Stollard had tried his best to persuade President Vermeulen not to meet with Joshua Talbert, but he could not be deterred. George had even gone so far as to tell him that he could not guarantee his protection if he insisted on going through with this. In the end, George had become adamant to the point just shy of insolence, but he had walked away disappointed.

Then he had gone back to Joshua with a detail of four men and attempted to take him into custody, but Joshua would not go. When they had tried to force him, their fingers miraculously slipped off his cloak just like before. In the end, George had politely asked the Bulletproof Preacher to meet with the President in private, in a controlled area, where he could better protect him. But Joshua had refused, offering no explanation.

Now, George was nervous as a frog in a blender as the presidential limousine pulled up to the park. He had tripled the usual number of agents, and used every other law enforcement agency in the area to help seal off the outer perimeter. Only a few reporters and TV cameras were within sight, and they had been searched and inspected to invasive levels. No one would get within 500 yards of the President unless George said so.

Joshua Talbert looked on at all the commotion but seemed unaffected by it. He watched casually as the limousine stopped and the President got out and walked over. A horde of Secret Service Agents huddled around him for protection, and a pang of sympathy suddenly welled up inside the old prophet.

George Stollard was in the lead with the President and his protectors close behind. He glanced across the road at the building tops. They were all covered. He even had an agent in the tree over Joshua's head. George had given him the call sign *Zacchaeus*. Given the situation, it seemed appropriate.

Joshua turned and made eye contact with Agent Stollard who was frowning. Joshua smiled and nodded his recognition. He understood the conflict, but was amused by it nonetheless.

• • •

James Thurgood placed his finger lightly on the trigger. He had sanded the skin of his forefinger above the first knuckle and made it very sensitive to the touch, almost to the point of pain. Now, he felt the trigger against his smooth skin, waiting, waiting, waiting.

• • •

The President stopped in front of Joshua and extended his right hand forward. There was an ear-to-ear grin on his face that seemed anything but presidential. Joshua reached out his right hand and grasped Dan's hand firmly in his own. George Stollard was coiled like a spring, ready to pounce should Joshua make a wrong move.

"Thank you so much Mr. Talbert for meeting with me on such short notice. I appreciate it."

Joshua smiled warmly and replied.

"Well, I was in the neighborhood, just hanging around the park. It's no problem."

The President laughed out loud so hard that his head leaned back revealing his throat. Agent Stollard became even more uneasy. The President's laughing faded, giving way to a more serious look. Finally he spoke.

"Mr. Talbert ..."

Joshua cut him off.

"Please, call me Joshua."

The President hesitated and nodded. He wasn't used to being interrupted.

"Sure. No problem Joshua."

• • •

James rested the crosshairs gently on the back of the President's head, waiting, hoping that he would shift slightly to the left and give him two kills for the price of one bullet.

• • •

Off in the distance, George could hear the excited voices of the news reporters as they explained what was happening before them. The President continued.

"Joshua, I just wanted to meet you and perhaps talk to you for a while. I've got some things weighing pretty heavy on my mind right now and I thought you might be able to help me out."

Joshua silently nodded his understanding.

"I know you're a man of God, Joshua, and I need some help right now. I need to know what God wants me to do next."

The old man took a step backward until his back touched the large Maple tree. He slid slowly downward, allowing the heavy bark to scratch his back as he went.

"Please, Mr. President. Sit down. My old bones grow tired of standing."

George Stollard opened his mouth to intervene, but he was silenced with a wave of the President's hand. Dan Vermeulen crouched down to the ground, giving no thought to the expensive suit pants on the bare, black dirt of the park floor.

• • •

The sniper cursed out loud when his targets sat on the ground. They were too low and all he could see was the back of a Secret Service Agent. He moved his eye back up to the scope and waited patiently for them to stand back up.

• • •

Joshua sighed and looked up at the sky. He saw the Special Agent on the limb above him and tried to ignore the submachine gun he held in his hands.

"Mr. President, God has not changed. He is always the same. And he wants now from you, what he has always wanted from all of his people."

The President nodded his head.

"And what is that, Joshua? I need to know, so can you be a little more specific?"

Joshua pretended not to hear him.

"And if the sheep are without a shepherd, who shall lead them?"

The President looked confused, but Joshua looked into his blue eyes and smiled before continuing.

"You know what God wants, Dan, what he has always wanted. He wants you to obey his word, speak his word, lead his people into a boldness and a faith that can only be done by example."

The President grew exasperated.

"But I thought I was already doing that! I'll probably lose my presidency for what I've said so far. What more does God want from me?"

The old prophet's face grew stern and cloudy.

"God wants you to come with me into the wilderness, where he will speak to you directly, where you will grow in wisdom and in stature, where you will become equal to the task he has set before you."

Dan Vermeulen cocked his head to one side in confusion. Then he moved doggedly to his feet like a tired man after a 3-day forced march.

• • •

James smiled as his primary target moved back into his crosshairs. He settled in for the shot.

• • •

"You think God wants me to go into the wilderness with you? Where is that? For how long? Who will run the country? I'm the President! I can't just up and leave!"

Joshua moved lightly to his feet, giving the impression that his 70 years of age were no encumberment at all. He reached out his right hand and held it there.

"Mr. President, if you are willing, please take my hand."

• • •

The smile returned to James' face. Someone up there loved him. He lined up the crosshairs on both heads.

• • •

George Stollard shifted uneasily from his right foot to his left and back again. He braced himself to move forward. The President extended his hand but stopped halfway. George uncharacteristically interrupted the tension in a commanding voice.

"Mr. President, I believe it's time for us to be heading back now."

George hated all the President's aids. Normally they would be tasked with handling these situations, but the President had left them all behind, kicking and screaming back at the airport. The President was without counsel, and he seemed to hesitate, but then his face relaxed and he let the air escape from his chest all in one, big sigh.

• • •

His finger pulled slowly to the rear until it rested on the trigger. The pressure increased slightly, ever so slightly, and the crosshairs were perfectly aligned. He took a deep breath and let it out halfway. James mastered the final adrenaline rush and pulled the trigger slowly to the rear.

• • •

Joshua saw the acquiescent look and smiled. When he spoke, his voice boomed out like thunder.

"And, lo, there was a great earthquake."

There was a few seconds of silence and then the ground began to tremble beneath them. Several Secret Service Agents fell to the ground, but George caught his balance and coiled himself to spring onto the President.

But Dan Vermeulen had already reached out his hand and clasped it firmly into Joshua's meaty palm. Joshua's voice spoke again, this time softly, barely audible in a thunderous whisper.

"And the sun became black as sackcloth of hair!"

No sooner had he spoken the words when George Stollard sailed through the air, diving to save his charge. But in the half second it took him to cover the distance, the sun turned black and the world was left in shadow. When James' deadly projectile reached the space the President occupied, it met nothing but air.

There were screams and yells around him, and George Stollard scrambled around on the ground, trying to find the President. One of his men rushed forward into the blindness and landed on top of him. George pushed him away and yelled into his microphone.

"All units, harden up! The President is missing! I say again. The President is missing!"

*"Leave the matter of religion to the family altar,
the church, and the private school, supported entirely
by private contributions. Keep the church and state
forever separate."*

— Ulysses S. Grant —

22

The slender figure of Vicki Valence paced back and forth inside the conference room on board Air Force One. There were several others in the room, all watching the live newscast from the park, but she was the only one pacing, the only one who appeared to be nervous.

She had been in Dan's office when Secret Service Agent Stollard had tried to persuade the President to cancel this appointment with Joshua Talbert. Vicki had been amazed when she had heard Joshua's simple but curt warning: 'They are going to kill the President, Mr. Stollard.'

Vicki's blood turned cold. The man she loved was going to die. She didn't know how she knew. She just knew it. Perhaps it was just a woman's intuition for the man she loved, but it didn't matter. All that concerned her was that Dan was in danger and she couldn't protect him. Joshua's other words haunted her as she stopped in front of the TV. 'Your task, Mr. Stollard, is to protect the President and to restore him to power. This country has raised a stench in the nostrils of heaven, and the President is the only man who can lead this nation back to God.'

Vicki wrung her fingers nervously over each other. What could the prophet possibly have meant by the term *restore* him to power? The question vexed her as she tuned in to what the newscaster was saying.

"I don't believe this! The President of the United States just sat down in the dirt beside this old man and they are talking to one another."

The image of the President sitting on the dirt horrified Vicki. How could they possibly spin this? This was so unpresidential!

A man's voice off the screen chimed in.

"Susan, can you make out what they're saying?"

"No, Scott, they're too far away. All we can do is zoom in with our lenses and let you watch this unusual event as it transpires. The President is getting up now Scott. He looks a little upset. The old man is getting up too and they're talking again."

Vicki looked on curiously. She wanted to know what was happening.

"What's this? It looks like the old man is offering his hand to the President. But the President's not taking it. There could be a story behind this, Scott. No, wait, the Bulletproof Preacher is yelling out loud enough for us to hear him.

"And, lo, there was a great earthquake."

Scott, the newscaster from off camera sounded perplexed.

"Did he just say something about an earthquake?"

"Yes, Scott, I think he did. I don't know what it means though. Wait! The President is reaching out his hand now. Yes, Scott, they are shaking hands and this meeting appears to be over before it's started. This has got to be a first for me. This President has always been well known for brevity, but this is ... "

Suddenly the camera picture began to shake up and down and there was a loud roar like thunder coming up out of the ground.

"Oh my god! What's happening?"

Vicki looked on helplessly from inside the safety of Air Force One as Secret Service Agents were falling to the ground. But Dan Vermeulen and Joshua Talbert remained steady and upright. And then, suddenly, the lights went out, and when they came back on, the man she loved ... was gone!

• • •

Vice President Thatcher watched intently on the TV as his boss reached out and grasped the old prophet's hand, then the ground shook, the darkness came and the President was gone. The dismayed Vice President pushed the button on the remote and replayed the scene over and over again.

After watching the newscast no less than five times, he plopped himself down on the couch in his office and tried to breathe slowly to calm himself. Almost aloud he said, 'How did he do that?' He'd suspected all along that Dan Vermeulen had planned something big, but this; this was incredible, supernatural, bigger than anything he could have imagined. Dan couldn't have orchestrated this. Could he?

The door to his office flew open and his Chief of Staff rushed in.

"Dave, we've got to get to the White House. The entire cabinet is waiting. It's happening, Dave. There is going to be a transfer of power!"

Vice President Thatcher looked up and noticed the unrepressed glee on his Chief's face and frowned.

"Linda, I'm not going anywhere until you wipe that grin off your face. The President of the United States is missing, perhaps even dead! Show some respect! This man is my friend!"

The woman stopped and her smile faded away slowly.

"I'm sorry Dave. I just thought you would be excited about it. You've been working toward this moment your whole life."

The disgruntled VP thought to himself for a moment. Yes, that was true. He couldn't argue against that point. He had always felt destined for greatness, for power and prestige, and now it was finally here! But inside him, there was a desperate struggle waging between the strongest part of him and the weakest. The best part of Dave Thatcher wanted to mourn for his friend and lose himself in the search to find him, but, the worst part, the selfish part, the part of his soul that wanted what was best for himself no matter what the cost to others; that part of him was secretly hoping that Dan Vermeulen's body turned up floating facedown in a reservoir.

Yes, he and Dan were friends, but ... A part of him wanted Dan to be safe, while another part, a deeper, darker part, the part that seldom saw the light of day, that part wanted the President out of the picture, no matter what the cost.

Dave Thatcher put on his overcoat and walked resolutely to the door, thinking all the while, 'I am a disgraceful man for feeling these things.'

Despite the conflict, the longer the Vice President thought about the transfer of power, the more giddy he became, but he was careful not to betray his innermost feelings. It was a truth that he fought against and refused to allow the light of day.

• • •

Senator Devin Dexter sat in his office, looking on in a state of naked shock and awe. He watched as Joshua and the President shook hands. He watched the camera picture shake. He watched as every ounce of light was blotted out and the camera blackened over. Then a mere few seconds later the light returned and his nemesis was gone.

The Senator stroked his chin and his dark, green eyes squinted beneath his tensely furled brow. This was unexpected, and it was not part of his plan. He thought for a moment more, but came up with no reasonable explanation as to why his enemy would orchestrate this move. It was politically illogical and counter-productive.

But, first things first. He would figure it out later. He picked up the phone and called his Floral Designer.

"Yes, Mr. Simmons. Are you watching the news?"

"Yes, I am sir."

Devin swiveled around in his office chair forcing his voice to lower.

"Don't say anything. Just listen. I am very displeased with the performance of your assistant. This failure cannot be tolerated. I'd like you to conduct an exit interview and then terminate his employment, effective immediately!"

He paused for effect.

"Do you understand exactly what I want Mr. Simmons?"

Mike Simmons understood all too well. He had terminated employment many times at the Senator's insistence.

"Yes, sir. I'll see to it right away, sir."

Devin thought for a moment before continuing.

"And then I want you to immediately issue a new contract to someone more competent. Double the fee and take half for yourself! Make sure it gets done at the earliest possible date!"

The middle-aged Floral Designer did the math quickly in his head.

"Yes sir! I'll get it done right away, sir!"

Mike closed up his cell phone and breathed out a huge sigh of tension. This job was getting complicated. But still, ten million dollars just for arranging a hit? He could retire. Thoughts of his own tropical island with servants and bare-breasted island girls danced through his mind. He quickly made another phone call, doubled-checked to ensure his pistol was where it should be, then rushed off to perform the exit interview. It would only take a few minutes.

Then the thought occurred to Mike, 'Maybe he would just do the hit himself and keep all the money?' Then he shook his head. No, it was best not to get greedy in the home stretch. He knew of other people who were better qualified for the job than himself. This was an outsource job.

23

Aric looked at the TV screen overhead. He had been in the little café for close to an hour now, just waiting, thinking, and watching the news. It all seemed too surreal. Just a few hours ago he had been poised to kill the man on the screen, but he had failed, and now his life was changed forever, caught up in another man's plot. He was beginning to feel like a pawn on a very elaborate and confusing chess board. Ironically, Aric didn't even know how to play chess.

"It has been over 12 hours since the disappearance of the President, but there are still no leads as to his whereabouts."

Aric looked down at his coffee, stirred it a bit and then looked back up at the beautiful, female announcer. Despite all that had transpired, and all the mess his life was in, he still caught himself wondering about the mundane things of life. For example, why were all the women in the news business so beautiful? He couldn't remember the last time he'd seen a fat, ugly female reporter. They were replaying the tape of the earthquake and the momentary blackout again, so Aric watched it quietly for the hundredth time.

"And there you can see the President grasping the preacher's hand, and then, 'poof' he's gone, as if by magic!"

Aric smiled wearily. Even a gorgeous blonde like the one on the screen still sounded ridiculous saying *poof* on national television. And then his thoughts wandered back to Calley. He was worried about her, and he wanted desperately to see her, but not for the physical gratification, as great as it was, the libido had been scared out of him by all that had transpired over the past few days. It was probably best, since doing that would violate the terms of his consecration.

Aric suddenly smiled and placed his face in his hands and rubbed his stubbled cheeks like a man who desperately wanted to go to sleep and never wake up. *Consecration*! He didn't even know what the word meant, and he was supposed to follow its terms? He thought about the prayer he'd said to God, and wondered if he would stay true to his promise. He didn't know for sure if God had answered his prayer, but … something different was happening. Besides, he was still alive, and that was something he hadn't expected.

"You okay, buddy?"

Aric looked up and saw the man behind the counter looking at him with brown, searching eyes. He wore a dirty, white apron and a Ted Nugent 'Whackmaster' baseball cap to cover up the bald spot on top of his head. Aric regained his composure and pointed up at the TV screen with his left hand.

"So what do you make of this guy?"

The older man looked up at the screen and then quickly back down to Aric.

"Which one? The President or the preacher guy?"

Aric took a quick sip of his coffee.

"The preacher guy."

The aproned man bent down and leaned on top of the bar with both his palms.

"I think he's the hand of God."

Aric looked up surprised.

"Really? Why's that?"

The man laughed out loud.

"Are you kiddin' me? This guy dodges bullets on national television, he rose a guy up from the dead, and now he's abducted the President of the United States right in the face of the Secret Service. This guy's the real thing man. This guy's got power!"

The man stood there and waited for Aric to respond, but Aric said nothing. The man became impatient and pointed up at the screen with his thumb.

"So what do you think?"

"About the preacher guy?"

"No! I mean the broadcast babe!"

The man lifted his hands off the counter impatiently.

"Of course I mean the preacher guy! That's who we've been talking about ain't it?"

Aric nodded and held up his coffee cup.

"Can I get some more please?"

"Not until you tell me what you think of the preacher guy."

"Excuse me?"

"You heard me."

Aric was in no mood for games and he wanted to respond with a verbal wise crack of his own, but he didn't. Instead, he forced himself to remain calm. For a moment, he was quiet while he organized his thoughts, and the man behind the counter waited patiently since they were the only two people in the café.

"Well, I guess it's like looking at your reflection in a pool. You can see yourself, and you know what you're seeing, but it doesn't seem quite real; it doesn't look right. Then the wind picks up and ripples the water and it looks even less like it did before."

The man behind the counter shook his head back and forth.

"Listen son. You've been thinking too much and drinking too little. Just tell me in plain English! Is he a man of God or isn't he."

"Do I get the coffee if I tell you?"

"Yeah sure. And it'll be on the house too."

Aric smiled gingerly, as if a smile too big would be painful.

"Yes. I think he is. I think everything they say about him is true. But I don't think he dodges the bullets. I think they just go right through him without hurting anything. And I think he magically transported the President somewhere. I don't know why."

Aric held out his coffee cup again.

"So do I get my free coffee now?"

The old man laughed out loud.

"Sure thing kid."

He walked over to the pot and brought it back. Then, while he was pouring Aric's coffee he continued talking.

"So is the old guy a good guy or a bad guy?"

The question prompted Aric to think back to the night before when he had met Joshua Talbert in the park to kill him. He still remembered the paradox of the old man's eyes. They seemed to be simultaneously fierce and gentle, old but new, and patient but firm. They were strong eyes and he hadn't been able to resist them.

"I think he's a good guy. You?"

The waiter set the coffee pot back down on the counter and thought for a moment.

"Yeah. I think so. He's a good ole boy."

Aric took a sip of his coffee. Then, for the first time, he noticed the blue, oval name patch sewn on the man's shirt right above his breast pocket.

"Say, Bill, you don't happen to know what the word *consecrated* means do you?"

"Yeah, sure. I know what it means."

Aric looked up surprised.

"You do?"

Bill stood up straight and folded his arms across his chest in an authoritative manner.

"Yeah, wise guy. I know what it means. Do I look stupid or something?"

"No, no, of course not. It's just that I don't know what it means, so I figured you wouldn't either."

Aric took another sip of his coffee.

"So what does it mean?"

Bill unfolded his arms.

"You wanna know about consecration?"

Aric nodded.

"Yeah. What's it mean?"

Bill picked up the coffee pot and walked back over to set it on the warmer. He picked up a damp rag and began wiping down the counter.

"Consecrate means to set something apart for a special purpose."

"Really? What kind of purpose?"

The old man stopped wiping with the rag.

"How the heck should I know? What do I look like, a theologian or something?"

Bill reached down below the counter and picked up a large black book and slammed it down on the top of the bar.

"Here! Look it up in the concordance. It's all over in there. Consecrate, consecration, consecrated, all those words are in the Bible all over the place."

The Bible stared up at Aric. It just lay there, waiting. Aric looked back down at it, but hesitated. He'd never read the Bible before. He'd never felt the need, but ... now, things were different. All of a sudden the words of God seemed more relevant than they had before.

"Yeah, there's a lot more people reading the Bible today than there was yesterday. I started reading it after the rag heads bombed all those cities. I figure it might help somehow."

Aric reached down and touched the shiny, black leather, feeling the tiny bumps all across the face of the cow hide.

"So, did it help?"

Bill shrugged his shoulders before replying in a matter of fact tone.

"It didn't hurt."

Aric opened the Bible and found the concordance in the back. He looked up the word *consecrate* and saw a whole list of verses to look up. He picked one, but didn't know where to find it. Bill showed him how, and Aric quickly moved from one verse to another, reading one verse and then moving on to the next.

Fifteen minutes later Aric was still reading and Bill had moved on to another customer who had just come in. Aric then found a dictionary in the back and looked up the word *consecration*. It said 'A sacred dedication to God for a special purpose.'

Aric thought about it for a second. A prophet, a Bulletproof Preacher, and a man with special, magical powers had dedicated him to God for a special purpose. A shiver ran down his spine and goose bumps popped up all over his arms. He was dedicated to God for a special purpose?

Aric took a sip of his coffee, but it was almost cold. He couldn't help but wonder, in light of all that had happened, 'What was his special purpose?'

He lowered his head and continued reading, totally unable to stop.

24

Timm Sawyer was 73 years old, and he had been a pastor his entire adult life. This email thing was new to him, so he stumbled across the keys slowly, trying to figure out how to send a hotmail message using the directions written down for him by his 8-year old grandson. These were humbling times.

Timm had no idea why God wanted him to do this; it seemed a bit bizarre. But the old man wasn't one to question God, so he just typed out the message as best he could using his two forefingers. In the subject area, he typed the words *Freedom March*.

God had spoken to him last week about it, but Timm had resisted at first. It wasn't the Old Testament audible voice thing or the burning bush of Moses; it was just a soft feeling that he must do something, that God wanted it, and then a gentle prodding to make a stand for God and freedom, because the two really were synonymous. Besides, only lunatics heard audible voices and Timm wouldn't admit it even if he had heard voices for fear that they would lock him up.

And then the gentle prodding to action changed shape into something more tangible and specific. *March to Omaha* was all he heard. The incessant sentence took on mantra-like status inside his brain, sometimes waking him at night, but never giving him rest. When he finally told Ruth, his wife, all she said was "He's God – you're not. I'll pack your bags." And that was his confirmation, because he had never been away from her overnight in all their 51 years of marriage. Ruth had never stood for it. Her reasoning was like this "If I wanted to sleep alone, then I wouldn't have married you!" And that was that. She packed his suitcase.

So yesterday he'd put an ad in the paper. It simply said: "If you love God and freedom, march to Omaha on July 19th. Make a stand!" It had seemed silly at first, but that was the message he was prompted to write. So now, he typed that same ad into the body of the email and, after he'd figured out which buttons to push, he let the power of hotmail do the rest.

It was crazy and he knew it, but the old pastor was more sure of this one thing than anything else he'd ever done. It wasn't his job to ask why, just to do the task that God had laid before him. After all, it wasn't that much to ask of an old man. Omaha was only 500 miles away.

After sending the message, Timm Sawyer got up and walked out of the library. The rest was up to God.

• • •

George Stollard squirmed uncomfortably in the high-backed leather chair inside the White House Situation Room, while, across from him, sat the Director of the FBI, the Director of the Secret Service, Vicki Valence, and Vice President Dave Thatcher, who was now officially the acting President of the United States.

The Vice President was about to speak when the door opened and his Chief of Staff, Linda Vaughn, walked in like the queen entering her court. Vicki looked up and tried her best to suppress her displeasure. Vicki had never liked that woman. She was too pushy and thirsty for power, and now that she had it, Vicki felt very uncomfortable.

Linda walked to her seat beside the Vice President.

"Sorry I'm late, Mr. President. I was dealing with the Press Secretary."

Vicki squirmed in her chair, but remained silent. Dave Thatcher wasn't the President yet, and the fact that he hadn't corrected his cocky Chief of Staff spoke volumes to Vicki. The real President, the one the people had elected, wasn't dead, he was just missing. She had cried all last night over him, but something inside her said that Dan Vermeulen was alive and well. When Linda Vaughn looked over and saw Vicki Valence, she frowned.

"What is she doing here?"

Vice President Thatcher looked at his Chief of Staff and then over at Vicki. He raised his palms up in a neutral gesture.

"Vicki was more than just a Senior Advisor to the President. She was also a close, personal friend. She requested to sit in, and I saw no reason to disallow it."

Linda grunted in a masculine tone. She disapproved, but would say nothing for now. The Vice President turned back to Agent Stollard and stared at him for a moment.

"So, Agent Stollard, you would prefer us to believe that President Vermeulen just vanished into thin air, leaving absolutely no clues as to his whereabouts?"

George sat rigidly in his chair, obviously uncomfortable with the situation. He wanted to launch into a verbal tirade of self defense, but he restrained himself. His entire life had been built on restraint of one type or another.

"I'm just telling you what happened, Mr. Vice President, I'll leave you to draw your own conclusions. All I know is ..."

Linda Vaughn was quick to interrupt him.

"I've read your report, Agent Stollard."

She picked up the file folder in front of her and tossed it onto the table haphazardly, causing the contents to spill out onto the oak top.

"In my opinion, it isn't worth the paper it's written on."

George clenched his jaw and felt his teeth grinding together involuntarily.

"Well, Ms. Vaughn, it was very expensive paper. The United States Secret Service uses nothing but the best."

Linda Vaughn's face clouded over, while Vicki smiled quietly to herself. She liked George Stollard already. The Vice President took over the conversation from there, and his Chief of Staff was suddenly uncharacteristically silent.

"Well, let's just put that aside for now and figure out what we're going to do, assuming there is anything we can do."

He looked over at the FBI Director.

"John, will you bring us up to speed on the investigation? What have you found so far?"

John Palance had been in the FBI for 27 years, and had headed just about every department the Agency had to offer before rising swiftly to the directorship. Dan Vermeulen had seen his talent and appointed him as quickly as he could.

"Well, Mr. Vice President, we have all the resources of the FBI working on this, plus we're getting excellent cooperation and support from the CIA, the NSA, and the Secret Service."

Linda Vaughn suddenly broke in before he could finish. John Palance hated to be interrupted, but he tried to maintain his patience.

"Why are you bringing in the CIA? They have no jurisdiction here in the U.S. Is that even legal?"

She let her last syllable crescendo upwards in pitch in a sarcastic slur. The FBI Director maintained his composure and answered in an emotionless tone.

"Actually, Ms. Vaughn, there is a strong case for bringing in the CIA since the kidnapping or murder or potential torture of a sitting President has far-reaching national security ramifications. This has never happened before in the history of our country, so we don't know exactly how much danger our country is in right now, but I can imagine scenarios that could potentially shake the very foundations of the nation. Besides that, it is entirely possible that President Vermeulen is no longer on U.S. soil, and that would mandate the use of the CIA, since they are better equipped to operate outside the United States. Therefore, I believe we should use every resource at our disposal to find out what has happened to President Vermeulen and bring him back to safety, including the CIA."

He hesitated for a moment, letting his words sink in.

"Don't you agree, Ms. Vaughn?"

Her eyes narrowed a bit, and she almost smiled openly. This man was baiting her, even casting aspersions on her character. Good enough. She could handle it, for now that is. But later on, when her boss was the un-disputed leader of the free world, she would exact her revenge. She curtly nodded her head.

"Of course, Mr. Palance. I would never suggest otherwise. I'm just playing devil's advocate to ensure all angles are analyzed sufficiently."

The Vice President, uneasy with the present exchange, prodded the FBI Director to continue with his report.

"Well, we've done everything humanly possible to find the President, but we're just not getting anywhere. It appears to be just as Agent Stollard suggests."

The Director stopped talking, but the Vice President prompted him for more.

"Meaning … ?"

"Meaning, Mr. Vice President, that it appears as if President Vermeulen has vanished into thin air, on national television, leaving no clues or physical evidence."

Vice President Thatcher was noticeably growing impatient.

"So what exactly have you done so far Mr. Palance and what more do you plan to do?"

"So far we have a positive ID on the suspect, Joshua Moses Talbert, who is originally from a little town in southwestern Michigan. He is 70 years old, a widower as of last year, and he's been farming his whole life. He has no special skills, no training, and before two months ago, he'd never left the state of Michigan. We have an international manhunt going on the size and scope which the world has never seen. Right now we're in the process of interviewing every single man, woman, and child from Mr. Talbert's hometown. But quite frankly, Mr. Vice President, I don't expect to find a whole lot."

Vice President Thatcher could hardly believe his ears.

"You mean to tell me that an old man, a farmer, with no special skills, was able to abduct the President of the United States, in broad daylight, under triple Secret Service protection, without leaving a clue as to his whereabouts?"

"In a nutshell, sir, that is correct."

The Vice President shook his head from side to side as if dumbfounded. He looked over at the FBI Director, set his jaw resolutely, and practically screamed out the next words so loud that Vicki jumped in her chair.

"That doesn't make me feel very safe, Mr. Palance!"

He glanced over at the Director of the Secret Service, as if to say 'And that goes double for you!'

"Mr. Palance, you renew your efforts. You find out for me where the President has gone and you get him back. And don't give me any supernatural stories about alien abductions or acts of God! You just find me the President, and you find him now!"

A single bead of sweat popped up on the brow of Director Palance, but he didn't wipe it away. Right now all he could think of was 'Politicians! Can't live with them, can't ...' He thought better and let the words die an early death. Besides, he was in the FBI, not the CIA, so he would follow the rules. He simply nodded to the man in power.

"Yes, Mr. Vice President. We'll get it done."

• • •

After Vicki Valence left the meeting in the situation room, she hung back and waited for George Stollard to exit with his boss. She pulled up beside him and fell in line with his stride.

"Thank you for your service, Agent Stollard. I know that you did all you could. It wasn't your fault."

George Stollard sucked in a deep breath and held it in his lungs. He'd been over and over the events and couldn't come up with anything he could have done differently, knowing what he knew at the time.

"Thank you Ms. Valence. I appreciate what you're saying."

She stopped walking and George followed suit.

"Well, George, I'm not just saying it. I really mean it. Don't be so hard on yourself. You protected Dan for a lot of years, and as I recall, you tried to talk him out of this silly notion of meeting with this crazy preacher man."

George smiled softly.

"Yes, I did, but you know the President. Once he gets it in his head to do something."

Vicki nodded in agreement.

"Yes, well, Dan can be a stubborn man."

She reached her hand out, and George hesitated a moment before meeting her halfway. Finally, he reached out his right hand and grasped her soft palm firmly in his own. When he pulled it away, he kept the tiny paper note concealed in the palm of his hand.

Vicki saw the confused look on his face, but she simply smiled and nodded reassuringly.

"Have a nice day, Agent Stollard. I'm sure I'll be seeing you around."

George Stollard quickly placed his right hand into his pocket and let the note fall to the bottom. His boss broke the silence.

"What in the world was that all about George?"

He shook his head, still watching her slender figure as it moved down the corridor.

"I don't know sir. I really don't know."

The Secret Service Director furled his brow before answering.

"Well, don't act dumb, George, because I saw her give you her phone number."

George turned toward his boss with a look of concern all over his face, but his boss simply smiled in response.

"I don't care George. What you do on your personal time is your business. Just keep it out of the White House."

He looked George squarely in the eyes.

"Understand?"

George nodded.

"Yes sir. Absolutely sir."

His boss turned and started to walk away. Then he stopped and casually whispered over his shoulder.

"Besides, she's awful cute, and you've had a really bad week. Get some rest George. You have 3 weeks vacation saved up and I'm ordering you to take it now. I think this is a good time for it."

George stood dumbfounded at both Vicki Valence and his boss. He hurried back to his office to read the note in private, wondering what she might possibly want with him.

• • •

George sat in the booth of the pizza place with his back to the corner, facing the main entrance. Over the years it had become difficult for him to relax, even when he was off duty, so he quickly scanned the restaurant, taking note of all the exits and all the people who were in the building. Deep inside, to the core of his being, George Stollard was a warrior, and some things never changed.

He saw an old man over in the corner with long, silver hair and a whisker-stubbled face staring at him. George made eye contact with him and gave a slight nod with his head. The man lowered his eyes. There was only one alpha male in this room, and it was George Stollard.

A woman walked in with her teenage daughter to get their take-out order. George watched closely out of the corner of his eyes. He noticed that the girl was a snotty, spoiled brat, treating her mother with disrespect. George had been married once and only for two years. He had never been a father, and sometimes he regretted that, wondering what it would be like to worry about someone you loved. Other people seemed to really like it. His brother had 6 kids, and for him the sun rose and set on his family. George suspected that it was supposed to be that way; that America was built on family values, and that when it ceased to be so, America would cease as well. But George wasn't like his brother. He was a protector, a sentinel, guarding the gates of democracy and freedom by watching over the symbol of freedom, the President of the United States.

George let out a huge breath and forced his head up a little higher. His sole purpose in life was to guard one man; that's all he had been tasked to do. But he had failed. The President had been swept away by an old man wearing a gunny sack, and he had been utterly powerless to stop him. Two days ago George hadn't believed in magic, flying saucers, or God, but today, well, today was an entirely different story, because the President had disappeared into thin air, in front of his very own eyes without so much as a whisper of evidence. So today, George believed in everything: Bigfoot, Martians, ESP, and the Loch Ness Monster. And he certainly believed in Joshua Moses Talbert and the power of the God he served.

His mind wandered back to the old man in burlap, and he found himself analyzing his words to him again.

"Your task, Mr. Stollard, is to protect the President and to restore him to power. This country has raised a stench in the nostrils of heaven, and the President is the only man who can lead this nation back to God."

The weaker part of George, the primitive, egotistical part, wanted to rip the old man's head off, but George doubted that was possible. He would never get around Joshua's magic. For heavens sake the old man was bulletproof, and George still remembered how he had tried to grab his cloak and the burlap had slipped through his fingers like hot grease. Life wasn't fair! The realization screamed out at him now, giving him the mother of all headaches. As if his job hadn't been hard enough already, with a thousand screaming terrorists and whackos trying to kill his boss. Now, he had to deal with unstoppable, unrestrainable, bulletproof people! George thought to himself 'If there is a God, then he must be up there laughing himself silly at George's predicament.'

"Hello George."

He looked up and Vicki Valence stood before him in blue jeans and a white t-shirt with her black purse slung over her left shoulder. George cursed his lack of vigilance. He was getting old and impotent, and now even women were sneaking up on him in broad daylight. George moved hastily to his feet.

"Hello Ms Valence."

He waited for her to be seated, and then he sat down as well. For a moment, there was a clumsy silence, but it was broken by a teenage boy who walked up with a pad and paper in his hand.

"Can I get you guys anything?"

George looked over at Vicki.

"Are you hungry?"

Vicki smiled slightly.

"Famished."

"How do you like your pizza?"

"Hot and in front of me."

George smiled for the first time in weeks.

"I guess we'll have a medium, deep dish, meat-lovers pizza."

He glanced over to Vicki for her approval and she nodded. The boy wrote it all down before looking back down.

"Anything to drink?"

"Mountain Dew for me. Vicki?"

George looked over and caught her studying him. Her eyes were large and brown and very penetrating.

"Water is all. Thank you."

The waiter left and the silence returned. Finally, George broke the deadlock.

"Why am I here, Ms Valence?"

"Please, call me Vicki."

"Okay, why am I here, Vicki?"

She looked down at the Formica table top, placed her hands on top of it and began to fidget as she spoke.

"You're here because I need your help. I need your help finding Dan."

"The President?"

Vicki nodded.

"Yes, I'm in love with him. Did you know that?"

George laughed out loud for a moment but quickly brought the emotion under control.

"Of course I know that, Vicki. Everyone in the White House does."

She looked surprised.

"Everyone?"

"Well, everyone but the President."

Vicki picked up her napkin and started to tear off small bits from the corner and pile them up in front of her.

"Yes, for the leader of the free world, he's not all that bright."

Suddenly George felt a little sympathy for the woman in front of him. She was obviously in agony.

"I don't know what I can do that the FBI isn't already taking care of. It was my job to protect him, but it's theirs to get him back."

A flash of anger swept over Vicki's face like a sudden storm.

"Yes, but you didn't protect him did you! You failed, and now he's gone!"

As quickly as the storm popped up, it suddenly lost force and died off to nothing. George sat there unresponsive, appearing to be unaffected by her emotional outburst.

"I'm sorry, George. That was out of line. I shouldn't have said that. I shouldn't have even thought it. Please forgive me. I'm a bit emotional right now."

The teenage boy returned with their drinks and quickly moved away again.

"That's okay. I've been beating myself up with it ever since it happened. You're not thinking anything that I haven't already thought myself. I know I failed."

George took a sip of cold Mountain Dew. There was a dryness in his mouth that just wouldn't diminish. Vicki looked over at him with pleading eyes.

"But wouldn't you like to get another chance George? Wouldn't you like to help make it right?"

George set his red, plastic glass down on the table. Condensation was already forming on the outside making it wet to the touch.

"Of course I would. I'd give anything to erase the mistake and get the President back. But there's nothing we can do. The FBI has the resources and the where with all to handle these things and they'll be the ones to get him back. The FBI is the best hope right now. All we can do is sit back and watch it on the news."

George looked up and saw Vicki Valence smiling, and it confused him.

"What? Why are you smiling like that?"

She took a sip of her water and then set it back down on the table resolutely.

"George, what if I told you there was something we can do that the FBI can't, and that it's the only way to help the President. Would you want to be involved?"

George rotated his plastic glass around and around with his fingers as he pondered the proposition. She seemed awful sure of herself, and George had been watching her from a distance for many years now. This woman was no dummy. In fact, in all his years at the White House, she was one of the smartest advisors he'd ever seen. Finally he nodded.

"Yeah. Sure. I could be persuaded to get involved."

Vicki smiled. Then she looked out across the dining room and nodded. A man that George somehow hadn't yet noticed, stood up slowly and walked over to their booth. Vicki slid over to the wall and the man sat down beside her. George went on full alert and folded his arms across his chest in order to bring his hand closer to his pistol. Vicki Valence, still smiling, lowered her voice to a hushed tone.

"George, I'd like you to meet General Thomas Taylor."

George was already studying the man's face. He had warrior eyes. The general reached his big hand out across the table.

"It's good to meet you, George. I've heard a lot about you."

George recognized General Taylor's name and reputation. The man across from him was a living military and covert operations legend. He had seen him at the White House several times. He looked at Vicki and then back over at the general. Finally, he extended his right hand out over the table and grasped the general's hand firmly in his own. After a half-hour discussion, George Stollard nodded his head, and the deal was on.

25

When Calley answered the door, she saw the imposing, emotionless bulk of her father's employee, Mike Simmons. Standing behind him were two more men, both dressed in suits and wearing sunglasses. Her immediate thoughts were: they look so ridiculous, dressed like they're in a gangster movie and wearing shades at night. Mike's words were clear and brief.

"The Senator is waiting for you in the limousine. Bring Clarissa and enough clothes for a week."

Without a word, Calley turned and walked to her bedroom. It would be pointless to argue, and against her best interest and the interest of her daughter. She knew from experience that they would take her by force if she resisted, so Calley quickly packed her bag, and then another one for Clarissa. She dropped the bags at Mike's feet and then went in and gently wrapped her sleeping daughter in a blanket, being careful not to wake her.

Out in the limo, she reluctantly handed the sleeping form of her daughter to Senator Devin Dexter. He looked down at her peacefully sleeping and smiled.

"You've given me such a beautiful grand daughter. She looks just like you."

On the outside, Calley smiled, while inside, she tore her father to shreds with her bare hands, all the while thinking 'She's not yours, she's mine, and you can never have her!' But once again, Calley was the perfect picture of restraint. She knew it was time to be meek and supportive or her daughter would pay the price.

"Thank you father. She has my face and your intelligence. She's a lucky little girl."

Senator Dexter made eye contact with her and she could tell that he was probing her for any signs of insincerity. She met his gaze and smiled as lovingly as she could.

"Thanks for letting us come over and visit father. Clarissa just loves to play at your house."

Convinced that all was well, Dexter nodded his head and handed the baby back to her after the door closed and the limo started to move.

"And what about you, Calley? You like it there too, don't you?"

"Of course father! Of course I like it! I covet any chance I can get to be with you. You're so busy all the time that we don't get to see you enough. It's just all the more special at your house. It's more like family."

He didn't say anything, and Calley could tell that something was bothering him. It was obvious that his plans weren't going as anticipated, and that's why he had come for her. The Senator always needed release when he was under stress. The rest of the drive was silent and 15 minutes later they pulled into the entrance of his estate. Calley knew what was expected of her, so she quickly took Clarissa into her room and laid her in the crib.

Next, she took off her clothes and bathed as thoroughly as possible in scented soaps and oils. The lingerie she picked out was his favorite, not too kinky, but sufficiently sexy and alluring. Once she was physically prepared, she walked over and looked down into the crib. In a quiet, motherly whisper she talked to her baby.

"I'm doing this for you sweetheart; it's for you, so that someday you won't have to. I love you so much."

Then she took her cell phone out of her purse and dialed Aric's number. The recording picked up, but she didn't leave a message. If he was smart enough, he would find her. She left the cell phone turned on and hid it behind the curtain on the window ledge.

Last of all, Calley steeled her will, walled off the portions of her mind that she saved for future use in another life, and began the long walk down the hall to her father's room. The door was unlocked as she knew it would be, so she opened it and stepped inside. Devin Dexter had the blankets up to his waist and a hungry smile on his face. Calley knew exactly what to say.

"Daddy, I can't get to sleep. Can I lay down with you for a while?"

The honorable Senator reached over with his left hand and pulled down the blankets for her. Calley walked over and slowly glided into his bed. But this time, his touches almost made her sick. She wouldn't last much longer and she knew it.

26

"This isn't the wilderness! What am I doing here?"

Joshua interlocked his fingers behind his head and ignored the President of the United States. He was starting to get on his nerves.

"You said you were going to take me to the wilderness so that God would speak to me and tell me what to do next."

The old prophet breathed a heavy sigh and leaned back, closing his eyes to the beating of the hot sun above them. The two of them had been here for three days already, just sitting here, looking out at all the rubble of the city. It wasn't what the President had expected, and he was becoming more and more vocal about it. Joshua wondered to himself if Sara had considered him to be this whiny for all those years they were together. He pondered the question for a moment, realizing that Sara had been patient with him. He breathed a heavy sigh and thought to himself. 'Yes, Sara, I'll be patient with him, though I'd like to strangle him right about now.' But Joshua didn't say that. Instead, he forced a gentle smile onto his lips before speaking.

"No, Mr. President. I believe my exact words were: God wants you to come with me into the wilderness, where he will speak to you directly, where you will grow in wisdom and in stature, where you will become equal to the task he has set before you."

Dan Vermeulen cocked his head off to one side impatiently.

"Isn't that what I just said? So where's God? Where's my wisdom? We've been sitting here for three days now!"

Joshua smiled softly and looked out at the desolation of the city that was once called Detroit. The bomb that had been detonated here had been a small one, only 15 kilotons, but still, the damage had been severe. There wasn't another living soul for miles, and the city would be uninhabitable for many more lifetimes, along with much of Toronto across the river in Canada.

"Be patient, my friend. God will come to you in all due time."

Dan Vermeulen looked out at all the concrete desolation of the city and suddenly hung his head in discouragement. He knew he was being a pain, but it was just too difficult for him to be here. Being in the nuclear-devastated city reminded him too much of his own family and how they had died. Why would God want him here, amidst all the death and destruction, the rotting corpses, the twisted and tangled steel girders, and the concrete rubble that piled onto itself haphazardly like a careless child's building blocks. The President of the United States formed saliva in his mouth and spit angrily off to one side on the radioactive pavement, watching it sizzle in the heat of the summer sun.

"I just wish God would kill me and be done with it!"

Joshua looked up and over at him, as if he'd suddenly noticed he was there for the first time.

"What did you just say?"

Dan Vermeulen stared off into the rubble and a lone tear welled up in his eye.

"You heard me. I haven't wanted to live for years, not since my wife and kids died."

Joshua smiled with compassion. Perhaps they had found some common ground after all. He found himself nodding involuntarily in agreement.

"I know what you mean. I look forward to death more than anything I can think of."

Dan tore his gaze away from all the rubble and locked his eyes on Joshua in surprise.

"You want to die too? Why? You're God's prophet. You have every reason to live."

A sudden breeze kicked up and blew a lock of Joshua's greasy, gray hair back away from his face.

"My reason for living was Sara, and she's dead after a lifetime of love and devotion to the likes of me."

Joshua looked down at the blackened pavement.

"She was my reason for living. But she's gone now, and I won't see her again until I die."

Joshua looked back up and locked his eyes on Dan.

"I welcome death, whether it's quick or whether it's racked with pain. Either way is fine with me. This temporary purpose that God has given me was an answer to prayer. It helps me make it through the day, but it's not like being with people who love you. It's not the same, and never will be. It's just another distraction from loneliness. It gives me something worthwhile to do while I wait to die."

Dan stood up and walked over to sit down beside the sagging old man.

"But you're a prophet of God. He chose you above all others to spread his words of love and coming judgment. You should be honored. Bullets bounce right off you. You've got power. That's got to mean something."

Joshua dug his sandal into the pavement, twisting his toe back and forth as if trying to burrow down into it.

"Yes, it means that I have to keep on living, that God isn't through with me yet."

Joshua's eyes suddenly narrowed and suddenly seemed more dangerous.

"I waited for those bullets to hit me, to tear through my flesh and into my body, but they just hit my skin, skirted around me and passed on by, leaving me alive and lacking, leaving me alone and without the woman I love. She was all I ever wanted."

Dan didn't know what to say. He felt the same way. So he just started talking.

"You have any kids Joshua?"

The old man shook his head slowly back and forth.

"Nah. We both wanted them, but Sara wasn't able. She cried sometimes because of that. I think she wanted kids more than anything else. That's why she helped with the Sunday School so much, just to be around the children."

And then, for the first time in three days, Dan Vermeulen thought about the well being of someone other than himself.

"I had two kids. They were great. Sandra was 7, and Michael was 3."

Joshua watched as Dan closed his eyes and talked.

"I can still see them so clearly when I close my eyes and think about them. Sandra was a chatterbox. She hardly ever shut up. And she said some of the funniest things. I remember one time she asked me why Mommy's breasts were bigger than mine."

Dan laughed out loud as he spoke.

"Here I was the President of the United States, the leader of the free world, and I didn't know what to say. I was tempted to call in the Surgeon General for a conference, but, in the end, I told her to ask her mother."

Joshua nodded his head in encouragement, before he spoke.

"Yes, kids will do that to you. Do you remember that old Art Linkletter show where he said, *Kids say the darndest things?"*

Dan looked over at him a little confused.

"Art Linkletter?" Who's that?"

The response made Joshua feel older than usual. He ignored the question and asked one of his own.

"So what's it like, having kids I mean?"

Dan looked over at the old man, seeing him in a different light. They were no longer Dan Vermeulen, President of the United States, and Joshua Moses Talbert, Prophet of the Most High God. They were just two guys sitting on radioactive rocks and talking about life.

"It was great Josh. It was the best thing I've ever felt. The most important job in the world is raising your kids. And when you do it with a woman like Jeanette, well, then it's something extra special."

And then they talked about women, well into the afternoon and until the sun perched itself down on the western horizon. Just for a day, they forgot about the troubles of America, the job to be done, and, when they had exhausted all conversation, they quietly watched the evening sky, turn to yellow, then red, then slowly become dark as the stars appeared above them.

And in the following days, the President and Joshua became friends, and somewhere in the process, Dan Vermeulen felt himself growing in wisdom and in stature, becoming equal to the task that God had set before him. Little by little, all that was inside him was poured out onto the pavement as an offering to God. Then, he was gradually filled up with something better, something that God could use.

27

They were all seated in George Stollard's living room, the three people who most wanted to save the President. George had bought the house in the Omaha suburbs shortly after moving to the new White House with the President's security detail. It was a rustic house, decorated with dead animals and guns, having the faint odor of mildew and wood smoke. George was hardly ever there, but it gave him privacy and a place to store stuff and build equity for use in retirement, assuming he ever did quit working.

"You got all this information from Aric? Are you sure about all this, George?"

Vicki Valence had a shocked look on her face and an edge of disbelief in her voice.

"Positive. No doubt about it."

George laid Aric's cell phone back down on the glass top of the coffee table and opened a manila folder in front of him.

"Aric reports directly to this man. His name is Mike Simmons, but you can bet he's no Floral Designer."

He handed the business card to the General, who turned it over in his hand with his fingers.

"Did you get a good set of prints off it?"

George nodded.

"A friend of mine is running them right now. We should have the results soon. I'm guessing this guy is former Special Ops, and, if that's the case, we should know everything about him up until the time he separated from government service. The way Aric explains him, he's a pretty scary guy."

Vicki took the card from the general.

"Why is it we want to find this guy again?"

The general patiently and methodically answered the question.

"He's the best lead we have right now. The President was last seen with Joshua Talbert, and this Mike Simmons character ordered Aric to kill the preacher the day before he was set to meet the President."

George interjected.

"And that was just one day before someone else tried to assassinate the President as well."

Vicki nodded.

"I see. So if we find Mike Simmons, then he'll lead us to his boss, and his boss is someone who wants Dan dead."

General Taylor picked up where she left off.

"It's more than that Ms Valence. Simmons' boss wanted the President and the preacher dead. They recruited Aric, who, by the way, wouldn't have been my first choice for something like this. These guys are well trained, well organized, and well funded. They could have gotten the best assassin in the business, but instead, they chose Aric. There's a connection somewhere that we're not seeing. There is definitely something special about Aric, something that we won't discover until we find Simmons' boss."

George Stollard took back the card and replaced it inside the envelope before taking up where the general left off.

"This guy Simmons is the first domino. If we can find him, then maybe, with a little luck and a lot of work, maybe everything else will fall into place and make more sense. So that's job one: find Simmons."

Vicki nodded her head in understanding.

"Okay, so how are we going to do it?"

George looked over at the General and smiled. He slowly got up and walked over to his living room window. His lifted his left hand and patiently tapped the glass with all four fingers. When he turned back around, there was a thoughtful, but determined gaze in his eyes.

"Ms Valence, the general and I have got lots of toys, lots of toys that most people don't even know about."

Vicki folded her arms across her chest impatiently.

"Really? So are you going to tell me about them or just bask in your superior knowledge?"

George laughed out loud and even the general smiled a little.

"You bet, Ms Valence. We'll tell you as soon as you need to know. We've got toys that we haven't even taken out of the box yet. And I just can't wait to play with them!"

Vicki looked over in disbelief. The President of the United States was missing, the man she loved could be in danger, and all these guys could talk about was toys! She looked down and shook her head.

"Well, these toys better be good, because I don't see how we're going to find this guy."

George Stollard looked back out the window at the Spruce tree on his lawn. He was confident. They would find him, and when they did ... hell and all his horsemen wouldn't be able to stop George from killing the man. Come hell or high water, he would get his pound of flesh!

28

Devin Dexter cursed out loud at the television broadcast in the back seat of his limousine.

"How can his approval rating go up when no one even knows where he is? He's not even acting as the President right now!"

The Senator listened intently to the news broadcast talking about the missing President Vermeulen, the stalled impeachment proceedings, and the latest turn in the country's spiritual mood.

"In addition to the President's rising approval rating, latest polls show that momentum for impeachment has all but died away since the President's disappearance. For an in depth look at that, we go now to Investigative Reporter, Alan Townsend from inside the Omaha Beltway. Alan, what details can you tell us?"

There was a moment of silence until the picture switched over to a man in his thirties who was standing in front of the fountain at the War on Terror Monument.

"Well Susan, this unforeseen turn of events has the opponents of President Vermeulen in a tizzy and scrambling to regroup. Just a few short days ago, the majority of the Congress, both House and Senate, were overwhelmingly crying out for President Vermeulen's head on a platter, but now that he's missing, it seems almost political suicide to come up against him. Latest polls show that a resounding 69 percent of Americans are now against the impeachment proceedings. Couple that with a presidential approval rating of 64 percent, which is up from an all-time low of 32 percent just a few days ago, and we've got ourselves the making of a real showdown between Congress and the White House."

Susan McAllister's voice broke in with a question.

"I'm wondering, Alan, where does all this newfound support come from, and what is the impetus?"

Alan Townsend waited a moment to respond before launching into his reply.

"Well that's the puzzling thing, Susan. According to all our polls, the President is gaining support not just from one group, but from across the board. This is a widespread turnaround, and it doesn't seem to be sympathy related. When asked for their reasoning, most people cite the President's last few speeches as moving them back to the center of the mainstream. Many even claim that the President has given them a new interest in God and spiritual things."

Losing all composure, Devin Dexter lashed out with his right fist and punched the TV screen as hard as he could. The small set exploded, cutting his hand, and shooting glass into his face. The limo driver slowed down and looked into his rear-view mirror. He was aghast to see the Senator's bloody hands clamped over his face. The driver made a quick left turn and headed for the nearest hospital. Through the blood seeping into his hands, Senator Dexter was swearing like a drunken sailor.

He pulled his hands away from his face and looked through the blood in his eyes to the shattered television screen.

"Damn those cowards! Let them play this way, but I won't be stopped. I have power they don't even know about, and I'm not afraid to use it. If I have to, I'll tear this country apart!"

The limousine pulled into the emergency room parking lot and the driver ran in to get assistance. Devin waited inside, impatiently bleeding all over the black, Corinthian leather upholstery. When they came out to get him, he refused the wheelchair and pulled away in anger.

"I can do it myself! Just get away from me! Don't touch me!"

Senator Dexter stormed inside and didn't see the man take his picture with a cell phone. Within the hour, the picture was sold to Fox News and was all over the TV, radio, and the internet.

• • •

Pastor Timm Sawyer sat in the uncomfortable wooden chair inside the tiny library of his hometown. This was the only computer in the library, so he had to make an appointment to use it. Now, he struggled to remember how to log in to his hotmail account. He took out the scrap of paper with his username and password and slowly typed them into the appropriate fields.

It took a while for the program to load up, but when it did, the old man was shocked to find that his mail box was full. There were well over a thousand messages in his inbox. The first email was a disappointment, asking him if he was satisfied with his sexual life and promising huge discounts on male enhancements. Timm wondered what a male enhancement was, but quickly deleted the message according to his grandson's written instructions. The next email was more interesting.

"Dear Mr. Sawyer,

My family and I will be joining you on your march to Omaha as you walk past Chesterton. God bless you and thank you for taking this initiative.

170

God Bless.
Amy and Phil Masters."

The next one read:

"Dear Mr. Sawyer,
My husband and I think you are a total lunatic. But that's okay, because so are we. We wouldn't miss this for the world, and we haven't been this excited since the sixties!
Power to the people!
Lou and Evelyn Collins
Meadowbrooks Retirement Village
P.S. Will there be special food available for those of us who are lactose intolerant? We are also allergic to peanuts.

Timm chuckled and sent out a quick reply:

Dear Mr. & Mrs. Collins,
I will bring you soy milk and cast out any peanuts in Jesus' name! See you in Omaha!
Godspeed!
Pastor Timm Sawyer

Timm spent the next 3 hours reading and answering emails until his fingers were pained with arthritis. He was about to stop and rest when he came across a message that was different from the others.

Dear Pastor Sawyer,
My name is Agatha Buhler, and I'm a Producer for Fox News. Your march to Omaha is all over the internet, and we would like to interview you

on the air. Unfortunately, we have been unable to reach you by telephone. Please call my office as soon as possible at (731)299-8762.

Best regards,
Agatha Buhler
Producer, Fox News
Omaha, NE

Timm hurriedly copied down the number on a piece of scrap paper. His hands were shaking so bad he could hardly write. He quickly scanned through the rest of his email and found similar offers from CNN, MSNBC and Headline News. He would have to finish his email later. His hands just hurt too much.

The old man quickly logged off and headed back home, but was shocked to see his front lawn crowded with people waiting on his front porch. In addition, there were three news vans out front on the street. When he walked up to the sidewalk, someone yelled, "There he is! It's the Freedom March Man!"

Timm never made it to the porch, and spent the next 4 hours giving interviews and talking to people who wanted to help organize and manage the march on Omaha. Finally, at 9PM, his wife came out and chased them all away. Ruth served him meat loaf and baked potatoes and then helped him into bed. His bones were tired to the marrow, so he prayed a simple prayer "Thank you God. I'm an old man and I hurt, so please help me." Timm closed his eyes and quickly fell off into deep sleep.

In the morning, it started all over again.

29

The pavement really dug into his knees, leaving holes in the fabric of Dan's five-hundred dollar suit pants, but he gave it no thought. He was busy talking to God. Dan didn't know what day it was, he didn't even know how many days he'd been here in the burned-out city, but neither did he care.

Joshua was sitting on the hood of an old car, leaning his back against the windshield, at least it looked old; but then everything looked old after a 15-kiloton blast. He stared out over at Dan's kneeling form and smiled. He could hear his weeping from 20 yards away and he was pleased with it. The President of the United States was finally a humble man, an emptied out shell and then filled back up with something good. He was now a tool that God could use.

But it had been a slow train coming. Dan Vermeulen had grown used to the pampering of the White House and the sycophantic nurturing that never questioned him and treated him like royalty. The glass of the windshield was shattered, but Joshua's burlap robe was so thick that it didn't bother him.

Last night he had a dream. He saw Sara, waiting for him in a green, open field, surrounded on its edges with towering oak trees, and a small creek running through the middle of it. Sara was sitting on the bank just looking over at him and smiling, all the while the tall flowers and grasses were whipping around her in the breeze. It was good to see her smile, even if it had been only a dream. His time was getting closer. He felt it drawing near, and the realization brought him comfort.

Over on the pavement, Dan got up and brushed the tiny gravel pebbles off his knees. Some of them were stuck in his skin, but he picked them out and threw them to the ground. He had lost 15 pounds without realizing it, but he felt better than he had in years. Some days they fasted, while on others they ate canned food, because that's all there was in the deserted city. Dan suddenly felt hungry, so he walked on over to where Joshua was lying on the hood of the old Ford Crown Victoria. Dan noticed that it had government plates.

"Hey old man! You hungry yet?"

Joshua smiled at Dan's dig. He'd taken to ribbing him for his age the past few days, but Joshua didn't mind. It was all in fun.

"Who you calling old, sonny? When's the last time a bullet bounced off you?"

Dan laughed out loud and put his left foot up onto the bumper of the Crown Vic.

"So we going to eat or what? I'm starving!"

Joshua moved slowly down off the hood and dropped onto the ground.

"Well, come on then. Let's head over to that supermarket again. I think they're having a special on barbecued Spam this week."

Dan shook his head in disgust.

"You've been out here way too long. Is there even such a thing as barbecued Spam?"

The old man grunted and started walking off down the road while Dan followed. The dress shoes he was wearing had given him blisters on top of his blisters, but they were already starting to heal and to form large calluses.

"There must be or else it wouldn't be on sale. Think about it, Dan. We could wash it down with some Hawaiian Punch."

"Fruit Juicy Red?"

Joshua nodded.

"Oh yeah. Nothing but the best for God's chosen prophet."

Dan's footsteps could be heard on the pavement whereas Joshua's sandals were totally silent. He chided Joshua playfully.

"I was thinking more of a nice Merlot. What do you think?"

Joshua shrugged and played along with Dan's culinary game.

"You mean like Ripple or Boone's Farm?"

"Oh man, that is so disgusting! You would ruin a good can of Spam with cheap wine?"

Joshua smiled but didn't answer. Dan had noticed that both of them had grown quieter the last few days. It wasn't that they didn't get along, because they did. In fact, Dan didn't remember liking any man as much as he liked Joshua. He had become both a father figure and a friend to him. The sun was beating down hard, and sweat was dripping off Dan with every step. He looked over at his companion and shook his head.

"Don't you ever get hot in that burlap thing?"

Joshua shook his head.

"No. It breathes pretty good, for a gunny sack that is."

Dan nodded.

"Hey listen, Josh, I think I might want to stop off at that Wal-Mart and pick up some blue jeans and tennis shoes. What do you think?"

Joshua stopped and turned back toward his friend. He peered deep into his eyes. It had been almost a week since Dan had even hinted at leaving Detroit.

"Are you ready?"

Dan nodded.

"I think my heart is ready. I'm just not quite sure yet where God wants me to go."

Joshua turned back and started walking again. Dan hurried to catch up.

"It'll come to you soon. I'm sure of it."

Dan smiled. Something was different inside him now. He had somehow changed. He felt excited, and, most important of all, he wanted to live again. He hadn't felt like this since Jeanette. But now, he had made peace with God, and was anxious to do whatever was asked of him. In his heart, Dan knew he could be happy again, and he longed for a fresh start.

He hurried his pace and passed Joshua on the left. He could almost taste that Spam!

30

Aric hated politics. He always had. But now the world was in-fested with it and there was no escaping the spin and the ma-neuvering. He muted the television and threw the remote down onto the couch beside him. The talking heads were babbling on and on about how the blue states had been weakened in the electoral college by the bombing of the east and west coast cities which were traditionally lib-eral strongholds. Now they were heaps of ash and the balance had tipped back to the conservatives. The south and most of the Midwestern and Plains states, the heartland of America, had been spared, except for some residual fallout. Because of the population shift and the resulting change in the electoral college, most experts were predicting the conservatives would finish regaining the Congress, and might possibly hold on to the white House, depending on the outcome of the impeachment proceed-ings. It was looking better for the President, assuming he was still alive to share in the victory, but Aric didn't really care. He had too many other concerns, like staying alive and trying to save Calley. He wanted to try and call her, but George had taken his cell phone somewhere, and the number was programmed into its memory.

George Stollard had told him to wait here in his house until they were ready to make their move, but he was finding it increasingly difficult to stay put. He looked out the window at a Robin perched on a branch in George's backyard. He had a worm in his mouth, and it reminded Aric that he hadn't yet eaten breakfast. He got off the couch and walked into the kitchen.

Inside the refrigerator he found a quart of milk, but it turned out to be curdled. There was also some spoiled cottage cheese, and moldy bread. He closed the refrigerator door and moved on to the cupboard. Eventually, he ended up walking back to the couch with a can of cold pork and beans and a lukewarm cup of instant coffee. He made a mental note to get some groceries later on.

He unmuted the television and the words of the newscaster immediately caught his attention.

"So are you telling me, Pastor Sawyer, that God came to you personally and told you to organize a political march to the nation's capitol?"

The camera shifted to the meek-looking, old man who seemed to squirm uncomfortably in his chair before answering.

"Well, no. I wouldn't put it exactly like that. People would think I was crazy if I started hearing an audible voice of God. It was more a feeling that God wanted me to do this. And he kept putting the words *March to Omaha* inside my head and I couldn't get them out. I tried, but I just couldn't do it. Lord knows I'm too old to be walking all that way."

The thirty-something brown-haired woman smiled and prompted him with more questions.

"So what exactly do you hope to accomplish by this march, Pastor Sawyer?"

Timm didn't say anything at first, and the camera zoomed in on his face as he turned away from the host and focused his eyes deep into the camera.

"I hope that people will realize that God is the only way to happiness, that we need to put aside our differences and work together to help our fellow man and to rebuild our country."

He hesitated and there was a moment of clumsy silence, but the announcer didn't interrupt.

"I hope that people will discover on this pilgrimage the God-sized hole inside their hearts and seek to fill it with his love and with his grace. Because, ultimately, there are only two questions in this world worth asking: 'Who is my master? And How can I best serve him?' I guess that's what I wish to accomplish. Beyond that, I just want to go home and be with my wife."

The announcer smiled again and looked back into the camera as she spoke.

"Wow! That's a pretty tall order, Pastor Sawyer, and a noble one at that. We at TV 8 wish you all the best in your pilgrimage."

Timm nodded his head.

"Thank you ma am."

"And just one last question, Pastor Sawyer. Are you a Republican or a Democrat? People are just dying to find out."

The old man sagged his shoulders and seemed weighted down by the question. When he spoke, it was softly and barely audible.

"I'm just a man, just a man who loves his neighbor and wants the best for America. And the best for America is God."

The beautiful host turned back to him and nodded with a smile. Then her head moved back to the camera as she wound up the story.

"And there you have it, America. Just one man's dream for bringing the nation closer to God and serving his fellow man. The marches will take place all across the uncontaminated states and move to their climax in Omaha on July 19th."

Timm piped up suddenly as if he'd just forgotten something very important.

"Oh yes ma am, if I can interrupt. There's just one more thing. I was supposed to tell you about our website. We're on the internet you know."

The television host nodded for him to continue.

"Go ahead. What is the address?"

"The address? What address?"

"The URL."

Timm looked confused, like an old man suddenly thrust into a strange, new world with no frame of reference.

"I mean where can we access your website on the computer? www dot something or other?"

Suddenly Timm's eyes lit up.

"Oh yes. I have it right here."

He leaned back in his chair as he dug his right hand down into his pocket and pulled out a scrap of paper.

"My grandson wrote it down for me. He'll be 9 years old next month you know."

She looked at him again, both amused and impatient.

"No, I didn't know that. So what is the address?"

Timm pulled out his reading glasses and squinted down at the paper.

"The address is www.marchforfreedom.com. It's really important that you type in all three of the Ws, because it won't work without all of them. I tried it with two and it just won't work."

Timm smiled, proud of his newfound computer savvy.

"And there you have it folks, go to www.marchforfreedom.com for all the latest info on God's freedom march to Omaha. Back to you Steve."

Back inside the Stollard house, Aric picked up the remote control and turned off the television. He thought about God again and the promise he had made to him, then he looked over on the coffee table at the Gideon Bible lying there. He'd stolen it from the last motel he'd stayed in. In retrospect, he supposed that was a sin, but it hadn't seemed important at the time. Besides, people took the towels and those little soaps, so the Bible didn't seem like that big a deal to him.

Aric set down the can of pork and beans and picked up the Bible. He opened it up and read the first verse he came to.

"Then little children were brought to Jesus for him to place his hands on them and pray for them. But the disciples rebuked those who brought them. Jesus said, 'Let the little children come to me, and do not hinder them, for the kingdom of heaven belongs to such as these.'"

Aric closed the Bible and thought about it. Why could he relate to that? Even at 26 years old, he felt like such a child. He was a grown man, but he still felt like the little orphan boy under the guardianship of the state. The words of Romper Room came back to him once more.

"Romper, bomper, stomper, boo. Tell me, tell me, tell me do. Magic mirror, tell me today. Did all my friends have fun at play?"

And then it occurred to him, if God was his father, as Joshua had told him, then that made him a child, a child of God. The thought gave him comfort, and, just for a moment, he felt more like a child, and less like an orphan.

Aric reached down and picked up the stolen Bible again. He wanted to know more.

31

"What do you mean you're pregnant? That can't be possible!" Young Devin Dexter looked pleadingly into his lover's eyes, hoping for some type of recantment on her part.

"I mean I miss my period! I not bleeding! I going to have a bambino! How other can I say it!"

Devin's mind raced methodically, already going over the options, trying each one on for size to see which was in his own best interest and which was not. He had been secretly seeing Esperanza for almost a year now and had always assumed she was using birth control. It had seemed like a logical assumption at the time, though he was regretting the choice now. He slowed his mind down. Damage control - think damage control.

"I'll pay for an abortion. I'll drive you there and back and we'll get the whole thing taken care of."

As soon as he said the words, he sensed she wouldn't go along with it. Her once-beautiful face contorted in disgust and she screamed at him.

"What! Kill my little bambino!"

Her young, lithe figure, spun around and began to run, but Devin was too fast for her. He quickly reacted and began to give chase, and when he caught her, he grabbed her right arm above the elbow and twisted her around. There was a loud smack as her left hand swung around and met his right cheek. A red patch welled up instantly, and that side of Devin's face began to heat up as blood rushed to the spot. The rest of his face flushed, mingling with the slapped surface, erasing the evidence of the strike. Before he could control his anger, with one quick motion, he raised his right fist and brought it careening down into her chin. When she saw it coming, she tried to back away, but not in time. He heard the cracking of bone and she dropped to the ground against the rock and ceased to move.

"Senator Dexter! Senator Dexter!"

Devin Dexter was stripped mercilessly away from his day dream and looked out across the sea of reporters, all waving their hands frantically like spoiled children who had the right answer and wanted to be called on in class. But these little brats didn't have any answers, all they had were questions, the answers to which Devin had no intention of giving them. Finally, he pointed to a man from MSNBC who usually asked him softball questions.

"Senator Dexter, in light of the President's rising poll numbers, are you still intent on carrying through with the impeachment proceedings?"

Devin made a mental note to never call on that reporter again, then he made an effort to slow his pulse and keep his face from turning red with anger. Usually it was an easy thing to do, but it was becoming more and more difficult lately.

"The government of the United States does not run based solely on poll numbers! If that were true, then we would all be at the mercy of dozens of diametrically opposed special interest groups and nothing would ever get done."

Devin paused, happy with his response so far.

"Instead, we follow a little piece of paper called the United States

Constitution to the letter. That being as it may, President Vermeulen will have his day in court, so to speak, if and when he is found. Just because the President is missing, doesn't mean he is absolved of all his egregious legal trespasses."

The reporter raised his hand again, but Devin looked away from him and called on someone else with a superior wave of his finger.

"Senator Dexter, isn't it true that a bi-partisan group of Senators and Representatives came to you with an honorable plan for diffusing the impeachment proceedings and you turned them away?"

Devin's slightly receding forehead was nearly bursting with overloaded blood vessels.

"There is nothing honorable about circumventing the Constitution just because a handful of individuals find it politically expedient. The House of Representatives has handed down articles of impeachment, and the Senate is bound to act on them. And we will carry out our constitutional duties if and when the President is found."

More arms shot up, but he ignored them all.

"In closing, let me just add, that my own personal meditations go out for Dan Vermeulen, wherever he is. Let us all hope in our own way, that the leader of our nation is rescued from whatever fate has befallen him."

Devin walked away from the platform and off the stage, ignoring all the pleas to answer more questions. The press were all monkeys, useless lower-level primates, and he hated them! He veered off to the right and his security detail followed him.

"I need to use the head!"

The man closest to him moved on forward and walked into the bathroom. Once he'd thoroughly checked it out, Devin was signaled and walked inside by himself. He turned on the faucet and stared into the mirror in front of him. His green eyes looked bloodshot and swollen, so he cupped his hands under the faucet and splashed some cold water into his face and eyes. His lightly bandaged fingers moved to his wrist and did a quick check. He'd already replaced the broken television after losing his temper in his limousine, but the cuts on his fingers would take longer to heal. His pulse was a bit fast and erratic, but nothing to worry about. He hated it when people asked him how he'd hurt his fingers. After all, it was none of their business. And then that stupid picture of him walking into the emergency room all bloody and battered, had shown up on Fox news. Of all the journalists, he hated Fox the most. Fair and balanced? Yeah right!

He pulled out a bottle from his right coat pocket and dumped a few pills into the palm of his hand. He selected four and dumped the rest back inside and screwed the cap back on. The big capsules always went down hard, but the effect was worth it. After a few of these, Devin didn't care what questions people asked him. With the help of his little medicinal friends, stress rolled off him like water off a duck's back.

He looked down at the bottle. Devin could have sworn that he'd just filled it, but already he was running out. Momentarily, he wondered if someone had been stealing his pills. He made a mental note to watch the servants at his estate more closely. It never paid to let down one's guard.

Suddenly, he thought of Aric and Calley. They were his legacy, and it bothered him that things weren't going better between them. Perhaps it was time to bring Aric in. Devin had never been one to openly carry emotional baggage before, but in his later years, he had been more and more inclined to yearn for the closeness of family at a time like this. It wasn't that he felt normal family ties, because he didn't even understand what normal was, he just didn't want to be alone anymore, and he wanted to be worshipped by blood relatives as well as by colleagues and strangers. To him, that seemed like the right relationship, and he would pursue it to the end.

Esperanza came to his mind again. That night, so many years ago, when he'd hit her, had been the last time he'd ever seen her. He had left her lying there facedown on the edge of the field on that country road, thinking that she had died from his own hand. At first, he'd been scared, but then, gradually, when the police didn't visit him and it appeared that he'd gotten away with murder, the fear began to give way to relief, and then to joy. For many years, he'd thought that was the end of the story, and he'd moved on to politics, money, and bigger and better things. After all, even though he'd loved Esperanza as much as his twisted soul could, he reasoned that the two of them had no future together. Besides, he'd been only 26 years old, the son of privilege, born into money and power, whereas she was the 15-year old daughter of an illegal immigrant from Mexico. But Esperanza had been beautiful beyond comprehension, even at the young age of 14 when they'd met in that same field, and he'd become bewitched by her beauty almost immediately. Of course he'd always known it was wrong for a man his age to be with her, that's why they always met secretly, but morality and the laws of the land weren't enough to dissuade him from taking her for his own. He thought about her now, wondering what would have happened if he'd done things differently, but he shook his head and spit into the sink beside him, disgusted at his own flirtation with weakness. He knew in his heart, that if he had the chance, he would take her again. It was his right.

For twenty years Devin had been convinced that the love of his life had died in that open field on that dark night in October, but then, five years ago, something had happened to cause him to doubt what he knew to be true. He started dreaming about her, and then, while on the campaign trail, talking to a group of local businessmen, he'd looked into the crowd, and there, just as clear as he'd seen her in that deserted field so many years ago, he thought he saw her beautiful face staring back at him. She had been there only for a moment, for just a whisper, and then her image was gone. But that tiny wrinkle in time had changed his life forever, given him purpose and an obsession that he'd thrown himself into with a fervor transcending anything he'd ever experienced. After that day, he'd hired a private investigator, telling him that he wished to find a woman from his past. When that PI failed, he hired another, and another, and another. He'd spared no expense, believing that his seemingly unlimited source of money could solve any problem. But the location effort had been hampered from the start by the fact that twenty million Americans had just died in a terrorist attack. Nine cities had been destroyed, along with most of their public records. If Esperanza had been in one of those cities, then she was no doubt already dead. It had indeed been pure luck that Devin had survived that fateful day. He'd been one of only a handful of congressional leaders who'd lived through the attack. In reality, Devin's political career had been waning, but now, the terrorist had given his career the boost it needed by eliminating most of his competition and moving him up the congressional food chain. Ironically, he was forever indebted to them.

In the end, Mike Simmons had not found her; however, he did find her two children, Aric and Calley, his children, two people, blood relatives that he'd never known existed. Government records showed that Esperanza had given them up to the state at birth and then disappeared completely. So, he'd pursued a relationship with first Calley, and then Aric. At first, he'd been surprised by how much Calley looked like her mother, and he'd decided right from their first meeting, that he had to possess her. The only thing Calley had lacked, was her mother's Hispanic accent, but he could live with that.

But Mike Simmons had so far been unable to locate Esperanza, and Devin's lifelong dream of getting her back had not materialized. In all likelihood, she had probably died in the bombings, and now it seemed, that Calley and Aric both were also turning on him, and Devin Dexter just didn't respond well to rejection. If he couldn't turn them, if they refused to love him and become what he wanted, then he would be forced to … exact damage control, more damage control. The honorable Senator Dexter had become an expert at turning liabilities into assets. If they wouldn't bow to his will, then somehow he would make their fates benefit him. He just didn't know how yet.

Feeling suddenly very alone, he turned away from the mirror and walked back out of the restroom into the dog-eat-dog world of the political pack to fight another day. Someday, he would find Esperanza again, and when he did, he would either love her, or kill her without mercy. Or, perhaps, he would do both.

32

General Tommy Taylor walked out of the doctor's office with his shoulders sagging heavily from the weight of his diagnosis. His PSA levels were extremely elevated, and the biopsy had revealed a high-grade tumor. According to the specialist, he had only a few months to live.

The sun was shining down hard today, bouncing off the concrete and coming back up in his tired, old face. It was ironic that he had survived countless excursions behind enemy lines, a dozen or so firefights, been wounded three times, and now he was being snuffed out by tiny, little cells that weren't behaving the way they should. He was an old soldier, and he felt frustrated, somehow cheated of the opportunity to die in battle for his country. The last thing he wanted was to die a humiliating death, lying helpless on a gurney with tubes and wires poked into his body. He had always thought he'd go the way of his ancestors, with the smell of cordite in his nostrils and a smoking gun in his hand. It was the only way for a real man to die, the only honorable way.

But ... he wasn't going to live long enough to let those crazed, megalomaniac doctors get hold of him. They had wanted to admit him right away and begin a battery of tests and then radiate him and poke him full of holes with needles. Besides, he would rather die than wear one of those disgusting blue, backless hospital gowns! No, it was over for him, and he had no regrets.

This would be his last mission, and then ... General Taylor picked up his head and held it high as he strode proudly to his car, climbed in quickly and then drove away. He had to meet with George and execute the next phase in the operation.

The doctors had thought he was foolish for not submitting to them. Screw them all! He would choose his own time and his own way. He drove to the rendezvous faster than he should have, not even bothering to buckle his seat belt. He found the act of defiance both satisfying and liberating. No man is more dangerous than he who has nothing to lose. This turn of events empowered him, and, in his way of thinking, elevated his chances for success. There was nothing more important than the mission. As he drove and turned right he thought to himself, 'The mission – whatever it takes!'

33

There were about a hundred people out at the road, waiting for him to kiss his wife good bye. Pastor Sawyer looked his wife in the eyes and smiled, and Ruth returned his gaze with the deepest respect that she saved for him and him alone, then she reached over and moved a lock of his fine, white hair back in place. They had been through a lot together, experienced a lot of hard times, but she had always stuck by him, encouraging him, supporting him, even when she knew he was screwing up. But this time, in her bones and in her soul, Ruth knew that her husband was doing the right thing, the thing that God both wanted and demanded. Her husband was making a stand, and for that she was very proud of him. She looked back into his eyes and smiled her encouragement and love.

Times had changed. In the moment it took to nod her head, she looked back at their life together, starting out from scratch, going from church to church, living on hot dogs and macaroni and cheese, raising children on a shoe string with nothing but love and a promise for better times. They had survived cold wars, desert wars, gas wars, terrorist wars, and even the nuclear bombing on American soil, but, through it all, she had always known that God and Timm would be with her. But now, her husband was going on a pilgrimage without her, because God was sending him where she could not follow. Ruth wanted to go along, but she knew her health wouldn't allow it. Besides she was needed here to take care of the grand kids. His leaving made her angry, but she apologized inside and tried to hide it from her husband. He didn't need the added burden of an emotional woman right now. Instead, she showed him support and encouragement. It was her job, and she loved him.

"When will you be back?"

The old man looked down and shook his head from side to side.

"I have no idea sweetheart. I'll hurry if I can. You know that."

She reached out and he reached back. They hugged in a warm embrace, forgetting for a moment the people watching from the road.

"Don't you dare get yourself killed old man! You be careful, and get back here as soon as God is done having his way with you."

Timm took half a step back and looked deeply into her eyes where tears now welled up just as they had 60 years ago when they had fallen in love as school kids.

"You haven't changed a bit, my love, and if I had to do it all over again, I would jump at the chance be with you. You are the love of my life, and I have no regrets."

She threw her head forward and buried her face in his flannel shirt and cried. After a minute, she pulled back and nodded her head.

"Okay. I can do it now."

Timm nodded proudly. She was a strong woman, and he loved her more than he loved himself. He reached out his hands and she clasped hers to his. They both gently bowed their heads in prayer. She went first.

"Dear God. Please keep this old man safe. He thinks he's still young, but he's not. Do what you want with him, but please send him back to me safely when you're done. I love you and thank you."

Timm waited a moment to make sure she was finished, then spoke his own prayer.

"Dear Lord, please keep my wife safe while I'm gone. I place her in your hands. Please give her peace and help her not to worry about me. I love her and I love you. Thank you God. Amen."

After one last hug, she reluctantly let go and watched as he walked off the porch and onto the sidewalk. Ruth looked on as he greeted the marchers with smiles and excitement. He had always been good with a crowd. He would get the job done. She knew it in her heart. God had chosen the right man.

The crowd began to move off down the road with Timm in the lead. He thought about looking back, but then he remembered the verse in the Bible, 'And Jesus said unto him, No man, having put his hand to the plow, and looking back, is fit for the kingdom of God.' For a moment he hesitated, and then he thought better of it and turned and waved and blew his wife a kiss, because he already knew that he would never be fit for the kingdom. It was only through the death and resurrection of Jesus that he would enter into heaven.

Back on the porch, shivers went up and down her spine when she saw him wave. All around them the world was falling apart, but at 73 years old, her husband still had time for romance. She was comforted in the fact that the world could never touch their love, because it was rooted in spirit, something beyond this physical world.

Ruth raised her hand to wave before blowing him one final kiss. She watched until her old eyes could see him no more, then she walked back inside to take the cinnamon rolls out of the oven. The grand kids would be anxious to eat them when they got here.

She stopped and looked over her shoulder back through the window and out into the empty street. Yes, God knew what he was doing. He had chosen the right man. She put on her oven mitt and opened the hot door.

34

Vicki got up off the couch and walked out of the room, leaving George, Aric and General Taylor hunched over maps and intelligence reports that were spread out across the coffee table and the floor. This whole thing was getting too complicated for her. She wondered how men handled all the details and the stress. Normally she could handle it too, but not now, not with Dan missing. The stress was just too much for her and she found herself unable to focus on even the smallest of details for more than 5 minutes at a time.

They were in there talking about assets in the CIA, contacts in the pentagon and the FBI, as well as certain people of undisclosed origin who had names like Iron Mike and Trusty. She guessed the latter were prior military types who now worked as contractors in the civilian world.

She opened George's kitchen cupboard and looked around for some coffee creamer. There was no food in this man's house, and it smelled terrible. Vicki looked over at the stack of dirty dishes in the sink and shuddered. George Stollard was a good man, but he lived like a pig. She walked over to the sink, filled it up with soapy water and put the dirty dishes inside it to soak. It was funny how things changed. She shook her head from side to side in disbelief. A short while ago she was a Senior Advisor to the President, meeting with heads of state, with people waiting on her hand and foot. Today, the President was missing and she was looking on helplessly as three men plotted the covert operations that would help protect the man she loved, assuming he was still alive. In an effort to feel useful, she found a clean dish rag and began washing down the Formica counter tops. They were filthy dirty, and she doubted they had been cleaned in months. She found some scouring powder and used it liberally to scrub out the stains. She thought about the situation as she cleaned.

General Taylor was an unusual man, and it seemed to her as if he had friends everywhere. He didn't even work for the government anymore, but he was able to obtain court orders, tap phones, bug apartments, and procure any weapon imaginable. Once this past week he had even managed to have a spy satellite rerouted in order to get detailed pictures of Senator Dexter's estate. A chill suddenly came over Vicki. That man was scary, and if they got caught doing this, they were likely to end up behind bars. Vicki pictured herself in an orange jump suit and caught herself wondering what shoes she would wear to match such a gaudy color.

Dan had been missing for so long now that she had to start wondering, even though she fought against it, is he still alive? She put the thought out of her mind and moved back to wash the dishes. The food was dried on and wouldn't budge. They would have to soak for a while longer.

She bent her head down and leaned on the counter for support. The thought came back to her, hauntingly, always there, always hovering, always crying out to her to be noticed and acknowledged. 'Dan is dead! The President is dead!'

Suddenly, losing control, she raised the dish rag to her eyes and cried softly. She didn't hear George Stollard come up slowly behind her.

"Vicki? Are you okay?"

She jumped and turned around, jerking the rag down to her side and wiping the tears away with her free hand.

"Yes, of course! I'm fine. Just don't sneak up on me like that!"

George nodded and apologized.

"I'm sorry. I didn't mean to startle you. I just came in here looking for another pencil. Mine broke and I can't find the sharpener."

She turned back to the sink and her voice took on a sudden edge.

"It's because you don't clean anything George! You need to put things away when you're done with them, and you need to do the dishes and sweep this floor! The way you live is ...!"

And then she stopped in mid sentence and began weeping softly to herself. George hesitated clumsily before stepping forward. He put his right hand on her shoulder and stepped to the right side of her.

"It's okay, Vicki. I understand. I'm worried about him too."

Her sobbing slowed and she turned around to face him.

"Really? I thought you hardly knew him?"

George smiled sympathetically.

"The secret service knows everything. We just don't tell anyone about it. But we see Dan when no one else does. We see him when he's alone, we hear his prayers, and we watch over him when he's sleeping. The President is never alone, because we're always watching over him, protecting him, keeping him from any harm."

Vicki looked up at him pleadingly.

"Do you know things about him that I don't know?"

George thought for a moment, deciding what he should say and what he should not.

"Did you know that he hasn't been sleeping well lately?"

Vicki nodded her head.

"Yes, I could see how tired he was getting and sometimes he had rings under his eyes even in the morning."

"Did you know why he wasn't sleeping?"

Vicki shook her head.

"The President has nightmares almost every night."

Vicki threw the dish rag into the sink and leaned forward.

"Really?"

George nodded his head up and down.

"Yes. He has two dreams that haunt him every night. In the first, he relives the bombing of Medina, and he watches in horror as the women and children die in the blast."

Vicki moved her hand to her mouth.

"Oh my God!"

Her eyes took on a faraway look as George continued.

"And in the second dream, he is on the White House lawn, and he sees the First Lady and his kids playing, waiting for him to return from the summit meeting. He runs to them, and they run to him, but just before they embrace, the suitcase bomb explodes and he watches as the skin is melted off their bodies. Sometimes he wakes up screaming in the night and I come in to check on him. Sometimes he tells me about it, and I always want to talk to him, but I know it's not proper. I have to stay professional."

Vicki was weeping now with her face buried in her hands. George took half a step forward and she fell forward against him with her head on his shoulder. His hands moved out to avoid touching her, but then, he brought them down slowly and softly onto her back.

"It's okay Vicki. We're going to find him. Don't worry about it. We're going to find him and bring him back safe and sound. It's my job. It's what I do."

Vicki recognized a little bit of herself in George. She moved her head off his shoulder and looked up into his face.

"Do you promise?"

George looked down at her desperate eyes and red cheeks. He nodded his head in assurance.

"I promise. I swear it."

And then he added.

"Or I'll die trying."

• • •

It had been George's idea to use Calley's cell phone number to trace it back to her. He brought in his friend from the FBI and soon they had narrowed the search down to within one city block. They were there now in a communications van that said Richter's Painting Service on the outside, cruising back and forth, waiting for the signal to come in strongest and to get a lock on Calley's exact location.

Aric and George slid open the door and stepped out onto the sidewalk. Aric was wearing a pair of denim cutoffs with a blue T-shirt and George had on a pair of black jeans with a long shirt pulled down over his pistol. George took a quick look around and headed for the alley between the used book store and the coffee shop where the signal was strongest.

Once they reached the brick wall at the end of the alley, George looked around for a door that led into one of the buildings but found none. As long as Calley's cell phone was turned on and functioning properly, it would continue to ping the nearest cell tower and they could trace its signal, and that signal had led them here.

Aric walked over to the big, green dumpster in the back, left corner and began poking around through the trash. George walked to the opposite side and scanned the ground and the window ledge for anything unusual. It had to be here somewhere, or perhaps inside one of these buildings, and, hopefully, when they found Calley's cell phone, they would also find Calley.

Aric glanced over out of the corner of his eye to where George was standing. He liked George Stollard. George was a good man. But, like most men in his profession, he didn't open up much, and that just made it easier for Aric to make his next move. Aric had played along with them for as long as he had to, but he'd never intended to let them take the lead indefinitely. Besides, he didn't need Calley's cell phone anymore to know where she was, and George and General Taylor were taking way too much time. Calley needed help, and she needed it now.

"Hey George! Look at this over here in the dumpster."

George looked up and walked on over.

"What is it? I don't see anything."

Aric pointed to a trash bag deep in the back corner, surrounded by old newspapers.

"I thought I saw a light blinking in those newspapers."

George leaned in closer to get a better look, bracing himself on the edge of the steel dumpster. Behind him, Aric raised the broken broom handle high over his head and brought it crashing down on the back of George's skull.

The Secret Service Agent slumped forward and then crashed to the dirty, cement floor of the alley. Aric bent down and placed his fingers on the man's throat until he found a pulse. It was steady and strong. Quickly, he removed George's pistol, extra ammo, and his wallet before standing back up and whispering a prayer.

"Dear God. Please help me. I don't know if I can do this on my own. I just know that I have to try."

Aric moved to the left wall of the alley and pulled down the rickety, steel ladder of the fire escape above him. Deftly, he pulled himself up and onto the stairs and after a few seconds, disappeared into the red, brick building.

George waited a few more moments to make sure Aric was out of sight, then he moved to his knees and then slowly back onto his feet, all the while, rubbing the bump on the back of his head. Already, a terrible headache was starting to creep in. He looked up to the fire escape where Aric had disappeared and then back down into the dumpster at the green, blinking eye of Calley's cell phone. He thought to himself, 'The things I do for my country.'

He reached down into the dumpster and retrieved the cell phone with two fingers, being careful not to erase any fingerprints or other evidence that may be on it. After placing it in a heavy Ziploc bag, he sealed it up and walked back out of the alley and stopped in front of the van. Before stepping inside, he took one last look around. So far, the general had been right about everything, so he would continue to trust him. But George had a feeling, an instinct, that the old man knew more than he was saying, a lot more.

• • •

Across the road, in a tiny, dimly lit, third floor apartment, Mike Simmons, *Floral Designer*, was making arrangements.

"Units one and two, stay with Aric."

"Roger that. We have him in sight now. He's hailing a cab on Burns street."

Mike nodded in satisfaction to no one in particular. He was the best at what he did, and he'd earned every penny of the millions he'd saved up over the years working for Senator Dexter and others like him. All of them were so arrogant, so drunk with power, that they seldom saw him for what he really was. Arrogance was a weakness, he knew that, and he always exploited it for all it was worth. Mike Simmons was the best Floral Designer in the business, and he always won the game.

"Units three and four, stay with the van. Record any calls coming out and any conversations inside. I want all the intel I can get."

"Roger that. He's making a cell phone call now. We'll route it through to your laptop."

Mike smiled and pulled up his email program. He had seven new messages, but he ignored them all as they were of no consequence. He pressed F5 and refreshed his screen. The powerful computer hesitated and then after a few more keystrokes, the voice of George Stollard came through loud and clear.

"General, it's done. He hit me on the head, just like you said he would. Took my pistol and my wallet as well. I had sixty bucks in there!"

General Taylor smiled at George's discontentment before answering. He liked George, but he still didn't trust him. But then again, General Taylor didn't even trust his own mother, and that trait had kept him alive over the years.

"Don't worry about it George. I'm good for it. Come on back to base and we'll find out where our little bird flies to. Then we'll move in. Don't worry. Everything is going as planned."

Mike Simmons smiled and almost laughed out loud, but quickly quelled his emotions. He thought to himself, 'Well, perhaps not exactly as planned.'

• • •

"You're sure of it? There's no mistake?"

Devin Dexter sat in his recliner in the den. His grand daughter, Clarissa, was playing at his feet, while Calley sat off to one side reading *Women's World* magazine. Devin let out an exasperated sigh, and then thought for a few moments before issuing more instructions to Mike Simmons.

"Well, I guess we have no choice. Bring him in. I want to hear it from his own mouth."

And then he added as an afterthought.

"And make sure no one sees you. I don't want any links to me."

Devin pushed the button on his cell phone and closed it up before setting it on the ivory-legged magazine table beside him. Calley looked up from her reading material and watched discreetly as the Senator reached down and picked up her baby girl. She hated it when he touched her, even more so than when he touched Calley's own body. Aric hadn't called her, and then, her cell phone had come up missing. Calley felt betrayed, used, and let down by him. There was no more hope, and she knew that if she was going to get out of this, she would have to do it herself. She had been here for several days now, and more and more the Senator was speaking openly to her about his treachery. This bothered her. Either he was losing his mind, or he no longer saw her as a long-term threat. She quickly disregarded the latter. Devin Dexter trusted no one, and he saw every person as a threat. And as far as losing his mind, that was a given. He was crazy, but cunning as well. He was too smart to openly discuss his plans for gaining power in front of her. Unless ... unless he had already planned to kill her. That would explain his lack of discretion and his loose lips. If he had already planned her demise, then he would have no need to feel threatened by her. His voice broke the silence.

"Well, Calley, you'll be happy to know that your brother will be joining us soon. That makes you happy, doesn't it?"

He looked over at her, all the while bouncing Clarissa on his knee, and watching Calley's response intently. Calley felt terrible as the reality of what this meant reached down into her soul and stripped her of all hope. But she pushed it down as if repression was second nature, because it was.

"Yes, father. That's wonderful! It'll be so good to see him again! When will he get here?"

Devin's stare turned to ice along with his voice. More and more, his appetite for her had been waning, and she knew this was not good news for her and Clarissa. So long as she pleased him in bed, they would remain safe, but she held on to the President's words in quiet desperation. "And to all Americans, I urge you to stay the course. I urge you to keep the faith ... do not be afraid. Never give up! Never give in to despair!"

But the President was gone, nowhere to be found, and Devin Dexter, even though things were not going exactly as he'd planned, he was still free to do with her as he pleased. He was in control, and she knew that her life was his. The smile on her face threatened to fall off like some cheap novelty moustache with not enough glue, but she held it there with a sheer strength of will and love for her daughter.

"He'll be here soon enough."

And then, he walked over and placed Clarissa in her lap and walked away, speaking menacingly as he left the room.

"Put her in bed, and then come to my room."

After he was gone, Calley's smile dropped to the hardwood floor and lay there, taunting her, daring her to pick it up and try again. But she couldn't. His hunger for her had died, and, in its place, all that was left was hatred and malice. She was doomed. She knew it. In her heart, all hope was gone.

She looked her daughter in the face and held her closely. She would die before letting him have Clarissa, but would she get the chance? Calley got up quickly and rushed off to put the baby in bed. First things first. Leaving her daughter and going to him was becoming more and more difficult, but, also, more and more important if she was going to save both their lives.

She put on something risqué and knocked on his bedroom door. He beckoned her with the word "Come!" and she obeyed without question. Over the next hour, she did her best to satisfy him, but she could tell that her efforts were falling short. She was just going through the motions now, and he could sense it. Her days were numbered. Oh, how she wanted to kill him!

She returned to her room and took a long shower, and then she lay down beside her sleeping baby, wondering, 'is this the last time I'll be with her?' In desperation, she called out to God, but heard no reply. Finally, she fell asleep, into the black abyss, but even her father haunted her there, threatening her, warning her, keeping her from satisfying unconsciousness.

35

The President of the United States was wearing brand new bib overalls, and his feet were shod with white, Nike running shoes. He wore a white T-shirt, and he had a canvas back-to-school knapsack on his back, bulging with cans of Spam and a few extra clothes.

"I guess I'm ready now, Josh."

Joshua looked over at his President and smiled broadly. Just a few months ago he had thought he would never smile again, but now, now things were different. He was filled with hope and pride, and a sense that he had done something good in the world. But he still missed his Sara.

"Yes, Dan. I believe you are."

He leaned heavily on the Ash wood rake handle they'd picked up at the Wal-Mart. The burlap robe, disheveled, gray hair, beard, and the varnished wooden staff all gave him the look of a modern-day prophet. Dan shifted his weight nervously from one foot to the other before he spoke.

"Any last words oh mighty prophet of our Lord?"

Joshua laughed along with Dan. He placed his right hand on Dan's left shoulder and turned to walk.

"Let's just walk a spell and see what pops out of my mouth."

Both men turned and walked toward the outskirts of the once-great, but now burned out shell of a city. It was a desolate wasteland, but for the past several weeks, both of them had lived inside the urban tomb, had survived, even flourished and come out the other side feeling fresh and renewed.

"You realize they're going to impeach me for this, assuming I live long enough that is."

Joshua nodded his old head and sighed.

"Yes, I know. But don't lose faith. God has a way of surprising us. God can do anything, and he usually does."

Dan looked out over the rubble and laughed out loud again, this time much louder than before. Joshua looked over quizzically.

"I was just thinking about Forrest Gump."

"The movie?"

Dan smiled.

"Yep. Life is like a box of chocolates. You never know what you're gonna get."

Joshua's barreled chest heaved up and down and his laughter echoed off the burned-out brick buildings around them.

"Well, I suppose that's one way of putting it. Sara and I watched that movie three times. She loved it."

Then his laughter faded and he grew quiet. Abruptly, he stopped and stood in the dust. Dan followed suit. They turned and looked at each other. Dan had washed up at the culvert and shaved, but Joshua was dirty, dry and wrinkled. They seemed like total opposites as they stood there, but something about them, the most important part, was the same.

Dan looked over at his mentor through new eyes, and he didn't see a wrinkled old man who smelled musty. Instead, he saw a loving man of God who was willing to give it all for what he believed, and he knew, beyond anything mortal, that this was the best-kept secret of Christianity. And someone had to spread the word.

"You keep that sense of humor, Dan. Something tells me you're going to need it in the days to come."

They walked on again and didn't stop until reaching the city limits sign. Dan looked over at Joshua with a look of concern.

"What's going to happen to you now, Josh?"

With his left hand on the staff, the old man leaned forward as a grim look came over his face. For a moment, he didn't answer, wondering how much he should tell him about the future. In the end, he kept silent, just standing there.

"Are you going to be okay, Josh?"

Joshua nodded.

"I'm in God's hands, and that's an enviable place to be. I'll be okay."

"You're welcome in the White House anytime. I could use an advisor like you."

Joshua moved the staff from his left hand to his right.

"I'm just a farmer, and I'm starting to miss the ground."

Dan nodded his head in understanding.

"I have a very nice rose garden. Stop in and see it some time."

A faraway look came over Joshua's eyes, and he looked out across the deserted landscape beyond the city.

"My time is almost up, Dan. My task is almost finished. I may not see you again."

Dan Vermeulen stood dumbly on the pavement, soaking in the realization that he was saying good bye to his new friend on earth. A tear welled up in his eye, and he reached out his right hand. Joshua looked at it, hesitated, then reached out and firmly grasped Dan's hand in his own.

"Godspeed – Mr. President."

Dan lingered a moment, then loosened his grip and felt Joshua's hand fall away. Joshua pulled a large, black Bible out of his robe and held it out to him.

"This belonged to Sara. I'll be seeing her soon, and I no longer need it. This book has been good to me, and I'd like you to have it."

Dan smiled and stepped forward. He embraced the dusty, old man as hard as he could, but he could barely get his arms around the bulk of the big man's chest.

"Thank you."

Dan withdrew and accepted the big book, holding it in his hands reverently, like he would the original stone tablets of Moses. The eyes of the two men met one last time and held steady, and then the President turned and walked away. A few paces out, he stopped and turned back around.

"If you get there before I do, please tell Jeanette and the kids that I love them."

Joshua nodded his head and then watched until Dan was out of sight, then he sat down in the dust and prayed, gathering the courage and strength to do that one final task.

36

Vicki Valence was in George Stollard's kitchen doing the dishes, again, and she was none too happy. It had been almost a month, and they were still no closer to getting back Dan than the day he'd disappeared. Vicki wasn't a feminist, not by a long shot, but in her experience, most men liked to pretend competence, when what they really needed was a woman to show them how to get the job done right.

Her hands were moving unseen below the surface of the dishwater, while an inch of suds and bubbles floated around on top. She was a Senior Advisor to the President of the United States, the real President, and here she was playing housewife and nursemaid to a couple of James Bond wannabes! She could hear George and General Taylor in the next room talking about the latest turn of events. In short, General Taylor had been outsmarted by his opponent. While he and George had allowed Aric to escape, hoping to follow him to Calley and whoever his boss was, that plan had failed. They had been tracking him electronically, when all of a sudden, the signal had disappeared, leaving them no clue as to Aric's whereabouts, and their only link to the kidnapper was gone. She had never heard the General swear or lose his composure before. He always seemed so in control, but now, things were different, and the general was scrambling to rally his forces and come up with an alternate plan. But so far, it didn't look good for the home team.

"Hey Vicki!"

She heard George's voice and her hands stopped moving in the water. She thought to herself, 'Don't say it again, George! Don't you dare!' And then the words she dreaded came out of his male mouth.

"Will you please bring me in another beer?"

That was the last straw! She let out an unstifled scream, brought her soapy hands up to her face and held them there for a moment. George and the general ran into the kitchen to see what was wrong. George had his pistol drawn and aimed up at the ceiling, expecting the worst. She moved her hands away from her face and dried them on the dish towel beside her. George looked around and then slowly lowered his gun.

"You okay, Vicki?"

She cocked back her right arm and threw the dirty dish towel into his face.

"No! I'm not okay! Dan is out there and he could be dying right now, and all you care about is another beer! I'm not your slave, and I don't take orders from you or anyone else. I answer to the President and the President alone! Do you understand me?"

George looked over at General Taylor, his jaw still hanging open dumbly. He put his pistol back in his hip holster and walked over to the refrigerator.

"General, you want one too?"

General Taylor, still in a state of heightened surprise shook his head from side to side. George grabbed a cold can of beer, popped open the top and walked back into the living room, giving Vicki an annoyed stare as he left. The General backed slowly away and followed him.

Vicki heard them talking in hushed tones about her in the other room.

"It must be hormones or something."

"Yeah, maybe we should call a doctor and get her a prescription."

Vicki held her breath and walked out the kitchen door onto the wooden deck attached to the house. She grabbed her cell phone as she walked, making sure to slam the door on her way out. She muttered one word in a muffled voice, but she said it with all the conviction of a linebacker blitzing a quarterback on fourth and long.

"Men!"

She looked out at the birdfeeder and wiped the moisture from her eyes. It was all she could do just to keep from screaming again. Gradually, her composure returned and she opened her cell phone, determined to make something happen. This just wasn't her style, sitting around waiting for men to do the job while she was relegated to KP duty! The phone rang against her ear, and then, finally, after six rings, Eleanor Thatcher picked up on the other end. She'd been trying to contact the Vice President for days now, but his Chief of Staff, Linda Vaughn, had been denying her access all along. She despised that woman.

"Hi Eleanor. How are you today? This is Vicki Valence."

"Yes, Vicki, I recognize your voice. It's been a long time. We should have lunch."

Vicki and the Vice President's wife spoke for 15 minutes and then hung up. Vicki walked off the deck onto the soft grass of the back yard and tried to think of what more she could do. A plan was forming, but she needed help. Vicki Valence had never been very good at waiting. She bit her lower lip as she thought, then George Stollard came out the back door, carrying a beer in each hand. He looked at her and smiled sympathetically. She gave him a nasty grin that silently said, 'Get out of my face you egotistical, male, chauvinist pig!'

"I thought you might like a beer. So here it is. I brought you one."

George took a step toward the deck railing but then hesitated, wondering if it was safe to approach her. Vicki narrowed her eyes and furled her brow, trying her best to look mean and imposing. She could tell that he meant it. And then she thought to herself, 'What the heck, he's just a man. What does he know about women? Probably nothing.'

Vicki smiled slightly. George saw the softening in her and smiled as well. He took a few more steps away from the house and started down the steps of the deck. Just then, a deafening explosion rocked the house behind him, knocking Vicki off her feet. She felt the blast and the heat push against her face as she was slammed down to the grass.

As she looked up at the sky, broken boards, fire, smoke, and debris sailed on by her and into the neighbor's lawn. She thought she saw George's body sail on by as well, but couldn't be sure. And as she lost consciousness, her last thought was 'I'm going to die.'

37

Eleanor Thatcher was a woman of honor. She sat up in bed, with two fluffy pillows propped behind her back. Her husband, the Vice President of the United States and the acting President, sat beside her with a patchwork quilt pulled over him. The quilt had been made from scraps of cloth by her great grandmother during the depression back in the 1930s and it was one of Eleanor's most valued possessions, though it looked out of place in the elegant surroundings of the Vice Presidential residence at the Naval Observatory.

Her husband was reading a Zane Grey novel with his glasses down low on his nose. She wondered how much longer she should wait before taking the bull by the horns and forcing him to spill his guts to her. Her wonderment lasted a scant 5 more seconds, then she reached over with her right hand and stripped away Zane Grey and threw it on the quilt beside him.

"Hey! You lost my place!"

She raised her arms and crossed them over her chest in a determined stance.

"The way you've been moping around the past few days, you're lucky I didn't rip it in half! Count yourself lucky, old man!"

A heavy sigh escaped from the Vice President as he recognized her mood. It was going to be a long night.

"All right, Eleanor, what do you want to talk about?"

Dave had met Eleanor in grade school and they had both grown up in the Kansas wheat fields together. While everyone else in the world practically genuflected when he entered the room, Eleanor remained exempt from all that. As far as she was concerned, he was still a young farm boy who liked to sneak up into the hay loft with her. Dave Thatcher would never admit it publicly, but Eleanor was his conscience, and whenever he got out of line, she was quick to rebuke him. The Vice President tolerated it for three reasons: one, he loved her more than any person alive, and, two, because she'd earned it, and last, and the most painful reason of all, because she was always right. If there was one thing Dave hated, it was when she told him he was screwing up. He disliked coming home from the oval office or from a huge dinner with heads of state, only to have his wife sit him down like a little, lost child and say: "Dave, you're screwing up boy!" However, his experience had taught him that there was one thing far worse than this humiliation, and it was when she said nothing at all and allowed him to embarrass himself in front of the world. He was the acting President of the United States, but she would always be there to remind him of his roots as a Kansas farm boy. She was as dependable as the sun itself and they were a team. His wife may not be the power behind the throne, but she certainly carried her weight and supplied enough voltage to make her presence known.

"Something's bothering you, David, and you haven't told me what it is."

The Vice President turned away and looked over at the wall.

"What are you talking about? Nothing's bothering me!"

Eleanor reached over with her left hand, grabbed his chin and rotated it back until she was looking him in the eyes.

"Don't you hold back on me now, old man! We've been married for 41 years and I know when there's a burr under your saddle. Now spill it! Let's go!"

Dave Thatcher looked into his wife's eyes and tried not to smile. The woman was the same immutable person he'd fallen in love with 50 years ago in grade school, and, even after all these years, he still couldn't get enough of her. She was his partner for life, and he both trusted and respected her more than anyone else. Nonetheless, he was still a man, so he stubbornly resisted.

"I feel fine, Eleanor! There's nothing bothering me!"

The 61-year-old woman looked down her nose at him and frowned. He always resisted at first; it was part of the game, but, in the end, she would play him like a fiddle, and he would enjoy making music with her.

"David! It's a sin to lie, especially to your wife!"

The Vice President's green eyes twinkled, but he refused to smile. Something really was bothering him, and it had been ever since Dan Vermeulen's disappearance. He lowered his eyes to keep her from reading his thoughts, but it was already too late.

"Is it Dan?"

He was silent for a moment, then nodded his head up and down slightly. Eleanor reached over and hugged him as she talked.

"Oh, David, that's not your fault. He disappeared into thin air, and we have no idea where he's at. If you ask me it was an act of God, and in his due time, God will fix it. Until then, there's not a whole lot anyone can do, not even the acting President of the United States."

The 62-year-old Vice President shook his head sadly.

"It's not that, Eleanor. It's something worse than that."

His wife leaned back and looked into his face.

"Something worse? What?"

He took her hand into his and looked down as if in shame.

215

"Eleanor, it's just that I keep getting these feelings inside that I don't like."

Eleanor nodded her head.

"Yes, keep going. I'm listening."

"Well, on the one hand, you know how I've always wanted to be President, but ..."

Even after all these years, Eleanor thought it was funny that men had so much trouble expressing emotions, but, she had learned to just accept it as fact and try to deal with it as best she could.

"But what? Tell me."

Dave folded his arms across his chest and squirmed his legs beneath the quilt.

"I never wanted to become the President this way. It's bittersweet. I miss Dan. I owe a lot to him, and he may be the best friend I've ever had. But still, I find myself, way in the back part of my mind, hoping that we don't find him."

Eleanor nodded.

"Yes, keep going."

Dave's face turned away again, but Eleanor pulled it back again with her left hand. She was surprisingly strong for such a petite woman.

"David, you have to talk about it!"

He reached up and touched her wrinkled hand with his own.

"It's hard for me to show you my faults, Eleanor. I want you to be proud of me."

She smiled and stroked his face with her hand.

"Don't be silly, Dave. I've known your faults since we were kids, and I suspect you've known mine as well. But that doesn't change how much I love you, that doesn't change that I will always stand by you, even if you disregard me and treat me like I was a fool. You're a good man, and you've earned my loyalty and devotion. You know that. Don't you?"

Dave smiled and kissed her on the cheek before pulling back and gazing fondly into her eyes.

"I'm getting pressure from Congress to make my presidency more permanent. Most people don't believe that Dan will ever be found and they don't want the power vacuum. You've always given me good advice. What should I do, Eleanor?"

Eleanor reached over and turned off the lamp on her side of the bed.

"You know I can't tell you what to do, David. You're my Vice President."

Unsatisfied, he pressed her for more.

"Well, your Vice President is calling on you for counsel. What do you think I should do?"

Eleanor smiled inside. She loved it when he asked so nicely. She hesitated a moment for effect.

"Well, first off, my Vice President is a man of impeccable virtue and character, and I'm sure that he will do the right thing in the end, but, if I were to counsel him, it would be to simply remind him that he's a man, and that all men have two sides. I would caution the Vice President to act out of the strongest part of his character. All men have a selfish side, a side that advances their own desires above the good of the people they were elected to serve. But My Vice President is better than that. Even though there's a small part of him that wants to be in charge more than anything else, the stronger part, the part that would lay down his life for the ones he loves, would rather be second in command with honor, than first in command with shame."

When she had finished, Eleanor hugged him again and he hugged her back.

"Eleanor, remind me to give you a raise."

She laughed and picked up his Zane Grey novel.

"Here, better get back to your book before it's too late."

He accepted the book, opened it up and pretended to be reading, but he knew instinctively that she wasn't through with him yet. She started to roll over, but stopped halfway.

"Oh, by the way, Vicki Valence called me today. We had a really good talk. Apparently she's been working with George Stollard and General Taylor trying to find Dan. They've made some headway."

Dave Thatcher put down his book and looked over at her in surprise. "Why didn't she call me?"

"She said she's been trying to contact you for days but Linda Vaughn won't put the call through."

Suddenly, things started to click inside for the Vice President, and a new plan of action began to form in his mind, one based on the strongest part of his character.

"Honey, do you have Vicki's cell phone number?"

Eleanor smiled as she rolled back over.

"Yes dear. It's in my cell phone beside the lamp."

And then, as a well-planned after thought.

"Ya know, David, I never did trust that Linda Vaughn. Kind of makes me wonder why she wouldn't let Vicki talk to you."

With that final seed planted, she rolled over and closed her eyes with a smile on her face. The Vice President looked over at his wife and then down at the cell phone beside him, wondering if it was too late to make some phone calls. Then he concluded, 'Of course it's not too late. I'm the Vice President. I can call any time I want.' He picked up the phone and punched in the number.

Eleanor Thatcher relaxed her breathing as she pretended to be asleep. She was in love with her husband. He was a good man, and he always did the right thing, after a bit of prompting.

38

Vice President Thatcher sat behind Dan Vermeulen's desk inside the oval office. He hadn't touched a thing, preferring to leave things alone as a reminder that he was only keeping the seat warm until Dan's return. His wife had helped him to see that, and he would never forget it again. He knew in his heart, that the best thing he'd ever done was to marry a farm girl from Kansas. Eleanor had always been his greatest asset and the strongest part of his character.

But what should he do now? Two days ago when he'd spoken with Vicki Valence, she'd been in the hospital, and he'd found out about things he'd not been told, things that, in fact, had been kept from him. She had recounted to him how there had been an attempt on George Stollard's life, that his house had been blown apart, that he was in the hospital with serious wounds, and that General Tommy Taylor, an American military legend, was dead.

Vicki had brought him up to speed, telling him that the general and George had been trying to locate Dan Vermeulen and were making some headway, but not enough. Apparently, they were getting closer than they knew, close enough that is to get them all blown up.

The Vice President looked at the picture of Dan Vermeulen and his family, sitting upright on the desk in front of him. This whole affair was bigger than Dave Thatcher knew; it was even bigger than the Oval Office. He knew it instinctively, and he also knew that he was not equal to the task, and he wanted Dan Vermeulen back now more than ever and without reservation. He just had to figure out the best way to go about it. If only he knew where Dan was and whether or not he was alive. That was job one, to get the President back in this chair. Dan Vermeulen was the only man with the courage and conviction to lead this country back into greatness. He still remembered Dan's last televised speech. His words had been stunning, inspiring, and downright profound.

"And to all Americans, I urge you to stay the course. I urge you to keep the faith. I implore you not as your President, but as a common citizen like yourself – do not be afraid. Never give up! Never give in to despair! You and I have been through many things together, horrible things, terrible things, frightening things, but one thing remains true and clear. We have survived. We are still here. America goes on and on and on. Not because we're better, or stronger, or more right, but just because we never give up. We are not held captive to our fears. The darkness and the unknown, they scare us, but they do not control us. No matter what happens, we must hold true to our faith in God. He is our father, our heavenly father, the creator of all things. In him, we move, and hope and have our being. God is our refuge and strength, an ever present help in time of trouble."

Dave Thatcher had grown up in the church, but had never carried on a serious relationship with God. But now, in light of recent happenings, he was rethinking that decision. He'd been raised to believe in God, that he was good, that God loved him, but had never acted on the information. There just hadn't been the need, and to act on it carried a lot of effort that was easier to avoid by putting it off. But how could he put it off anymore? He'd seen the bullets bounce off Joshua Talbert, and he'd seen Officer Macy rise from the dead. He believed in God now more than ever, but belief demanded action. Would he act? Would he find his spine?

Yes, Dan Vermeulen was the man for the time. He was the leader who could take this country out of the wilderness and back into the promised land. His job, David Thatcher, the Vice President, was simply to stay the course, keep things afloat until his return.

With a resolute nod, he typed in an email to the following people: The Director of the FBI, the Director of the CIA, the National Security Advisor, and the Director of the Secret Service.

Meet me in the Situation Room at 8AM tomorrow morning. This meeting supersedes all others.

Signed, David Thatcher - Acting President

Linda Vaughn, his Chief of Staff, was purposefully not invited.

Then he picked up the phone and made arrangements with the Secret Service to visit George Stollard and Vicki Valence in the hospital. It was a meeting that was long overdue.

• • •

Vice President Thatcher waited outside the White House Situation Room a full 5 minutes before walking inside. He knew everyone was there, but he just wanted them to sweat a while longer. He was still dressed in his workout clothes, and had yet to shower after his 45-minute exercise program. This, too, he did by design. He wanted to remind them that, while they felt compelled to wear formal business attire, he, the Acting President, could wear anything he pleased, just because he was the boss and he made the rules.

When he walked in, all eyes moved nervously to him. He ignored their looks and strode confidently over to his high-backed, leather chair.

He wanted them to feel like they'd been called into the office, or wood-shed, whichever was more appropriate. Dave Thatcher settled himself in, looked up, and then with a penetrating gaze, fixed his eyes first on John Palance, 27-year veteran of the FBI and now their Director. John returned his gaze and held it. Dave thought he sensed a bit of unspoken attitude, but he could live with that, for now.

His gaze moved on to Norman Stearns, Director of the Secret Service, who stared back at him like a stone-faced poker player. Dave smiled inside. These Secret Service guys were such stoics, but he admitted that perhaps that was a necessity in their line of work.

And sitting beside Norman Stearns was Harvey Keitel, Director of the Central Intelligence Agency, a man who remained a total enigma to Dave. He was spooky, but good at his job and loyal to Dan Vermeulen; that's all Dave cared about right now. He wanted to surround himself with people who cut through all the crap and got results. The country didn't need anymore politicians, just people to shoulder the load and get the job done.

Across the table from Harvey sat Melissa Cohen, Dan's National Security Advisor. She was close friends with Dan, so he would trust her until she gave him reason not to. He made eye contact with all of them, one by one, and then he picked up the phone and punched in Linda Vaughn's cell phone number.

"Linda, this is Dave. I'm in the situation room. Will you come down here please? Right away."

Then he hung up the phone and turned back to others at the table. He locked eyes with Melissa Cohen.

"Melissa, I'm sorry to hear that your son isn't feeling well today. I assume it's nothing serious?"

His statement was twofold: to let them know he cared, and to let them know that he was keeping track of them. It was Dave's belief that everyone worked better when they felt accountable to some higher power, whether that higher power was him, or God almighty. She stuttered, and he could tell she was taken aback by the question.

"Uh, uh, yes sir. He's doing well. Thank you for asking..." She hesitated before finishing her sentence. "... Mr. President."

Dave made eye contact with her and smiled.

"Thank you Melissa, but from now on please refer to me as Mr. Vice President. Dan Vermeulen is the President, and my loyalties are to him and to him alone."

She returned eye contact, and the nervous look on her face started to fade away.

"Yes, Mr. Vice President. I'll do that, sir."

Just then the door swung open and Linda Vaughn rushed into the room, pulling up short when she saw the heavy hitters inside the room. The fact that she had not been told about this meeting, indeed, had no clue as to its existence, did not bode well for her.

"Good morning Mr. President."

Dave nodded but didn't speak. Linda stood there a moment, waiting for an invitation to sit down, but, to her dismay, none came.

"You called for me Dave?"

The Vice President nodded but still said nothing. Linda pointed to a chair.

"Would you like me to sit down, sir?"

Dave shook his head.

"No, Linda, this won't take that long."

He then looked over at Norman Stearns, Head of the Secret Service.

"Norman, will you show them both in, please?"

Norman Stearns stood up stiffly and walked over to the door. He signaled to the Secret Service Agent outside and then came back in and sat down. The whole while, Linda Vaughn watched and stood, growing more and more nervous by the second. The Vice President spoke.

"First, Linda, I want to thank you for serving me with such devotion and enthusiasm. Your loyalty has not gone unnoticed."

Linda started to relax a bit. She nodded and smiled. This was getting better. Just then the door opened again and Agent George Stollard was wheeled into the room. He had a large bandage on his forehead, and his left arm was in a sling. There were cuts and scratches all over his face. Behind him, pushing the wheel chair, was Vicki Valence, dressed in blue jeans and a plain, white t-shirt. Her face was also cut in a few places, but not as seriously as George's.

Linda Vaughn sucked in her breath when she saw them, but was afraid to ask why they were here. Dave Thatcher nodded to them and smiled weakly as they took their places at the table. Once they were settled in, the Vice President looked back up at Linda Vaughn, still standing there alone.

"Ms Vaughn, it's been brought to my attention, that Vicki made repeated attempts to contact me, but you refused her access. Is that correct?"

Linda squirmed back and forth in her chair, wondering how to get out of this mess. She didn't answer.

"Ms. Vaughn? A yes or no answer will suffice."

She looked over at Melissa Cohen, who promptly turned away from her. Norman Stearns of the Secret Service had his eyes locked onto her like a laser-guided bomb, but she ignored his tense stare.

"Don't keep us waiting, Ms. Vaughn. We have a lot to do this morning."

She waited a second, then simply said, "Yes." Dave nodded and then looked down at a manila folder in front of him. He took out a series of photos. One was a view of George Stollard's home, blown to bits and almost level to the ground. The second was a picture of George Stollard and Vicki Valence being loaded into an ambulance by paramedics. And the third, was the most telling; it was the battered, burned, and bloody corpse of Major General Thomas A. Taylor, lying in the smoking debris, twisted, and half-covered with wreckage. His eyes were closed in permanent sleep.

"Pass these down to Ms. Vaughn please."

They were passed down to her, and when she held them in her hand, the photos shook nervously.

"Vicki came to you and asked for help in the most important business this country has right now and you turned her away."

He hesitated, weighing his words carefully.

"Because of you and your petty politics, Ms. Vaughn, a great American General is dead and no longer of service to his country."

He stood up abruptly, and sent his chair flying back toward the wall.

"Ms. Vaughn, you're fired!"

Then he turned to Norman Stearns.

"Mr. Stearns, please have Ms. Vaughn escorted off White House grounds. Please make sure she doesn't come back, not even for a guided tour."

Norman Stearns smiled in satisfaction and walked over to the door. He opened it, spoke softly to the agent outside, who then walked in and stood before Linda Vaughn. She stood there mute, unable to speak. The Secret Service Agent put his right hand on her left shoulder and firmly guided her to the door. It closed, and Linda Vaughn disappeared.

• • •

Back in the Situation Room, Dave Thatcher looked around the table at the five people remaining and smiled resolutely.

"My father always taught me it's best to get hard business done early in the day."

Then he looked over at Vicki Valence.

"Vicki, it would appear that I'm in need of a new Chief of Staff. I trust you, and you're more than qualified. Besides, it only makes sense, since it will make for a smoother transition when Dan returns to his duties."

His gaze softened, but Vicki was so overwhelmed that she was unable to speak.

"Please, Vicki. I need you. And Dan needs you too, here at the White House, doing what you do best until his return. As my Chief of Staff, you'll be able to do more for him here than out there on the street getting blown up. Don't you agree?"

Vicki glanced over at George Stollard, who was smiling as much as the bandages would allow. She turned back to the Vice President.

"Of course, Mr. Vice President, whatever you say. I'll begin immediately."

Dave Thatcher nodded and smiled.

"Excellent!"

Then he looked over at George.

"And you, George, your vacation is hereby cancelled. We need you here to help with this operation. As soon as you're ready, you'll be the point man, coordinating operations between the FBI, Secret Service, the NSA, and the CIA."

He looked around sternly at everyone at the table again. Some of them looked at each other, but only for a moment.

"Does everyone here understand that George Stollard is in charge of this investigation and the subsequent effort to bring back the President and whoever it was who abducted him?"

He didn't wait for an answer.

"There will be no department loyalties and competition here, just a concerted, cooperative effort to work together and bring back Dan Vermeulen. George reports directly to me and for the next few weeks, you report to George. Give him everything he asks for and anything he needs that he doesn't know enough to ask for."

Then he looked them all in the eye again, one by one, getting the confirmation he wanted.

"Don't worry about a thing. This meeting has been recorded, and I take full responsibility for whatever the outcome. This is my decision, and I stand by it."

He stood up, signifying the end to the meeting.

"Now, if you'll excuse me, I need to take a shower."

He put his hand on George's shoulder as he walked past him.

"Good luck, George."

As he neared the door, he turned around and called back to Vicki.

"Well, Ms. Valence, you're my Chief of Staff and we have work to do. Are you coming or not?"

He smiled as she stood up and followed him to the door. George reached up and winced as he pulled the bandage off his forehead. There was a mass of dried blood near his hairline.

"All right then, let's get started. I'll tell you everything I know, and then you all can reciprocate."

The door closed behind the Vice President, and George Stollard was left in charge.

"The highest glory of the American Revolution was this: it connected, in one indissoluble bond, the principles of civil government with the principles of Christianity."

—John Quincy Adams —

39

Senator Dexter sat in front of his massive, mahogany desk inside his office at the new Dirksen Senate Office Building in Omaha. He had just sent away his Chief of Staff and ordered no disturbance for the next half hour prior to his next meeting. His friends in the Senate were losing their will, and he had to shore up support for the impeachment proceedings. Ever since Dan Vermeulen had turned up missing, the political assault on the President had been put on hold. Privately, Devin had been furious and had lobbied against the delay, but publicly, he'd had no choice but to support it. His closest advisors had reminded him that continuing an attack on a missing President would be perceived as piling on and not in the best interest of his public image. Dan Vermeulen, so long as he was missing, would be awarded, by default, the coveted and useful 'victim' status. Victimhood would never get anyone elected President, but it certainly was enough to keep a sitting President in power, at least under these circumstances. Besides, the President's last few speeches had been powerful and forthright, sending his poll numbers up for the first time in months.

But Devin Dexter didn't buy any of it. To him, it was all a political ploy by Dan Vermeulen to salvage his administration and keep his job, and, Devin had to admit, it was a stroke of genius. Despite the fact that Dan Vermeulen had been missing for weeks, his favorability poll numbers continued to climb, and now, Vice President Thatcher was growing a spine as well. Devin hadn't seen that one coming, but none of that mattered so long as he could get to the President and finish him off before he returned to the safety of the Secret Service.

This morning, after the staff meeting, his Senior Advisor had remained in his office and had asked him point blank. "Why are you so desperate to follow through with impeaching a man who may already be dead?" The question had seemed naïve to Devin, and he had refused to answer his underling, primarily out of arrogance, but also because that was privileged information. His advisors didn't need to know why he ordered them to do certain things, they simply needed to be about their master's bidding without asking questions. Later on he would deal with this particular advisor. The number one rule in Devin's world was 'Always remember your place in the pecking order.' In short, Devin was at the top, and this man was below him, therefore, he had no right to ask questions. It was the natural order of things.

Devin thought about it now; it had been such a naïve question, serving no useful purpose, but he felt compelled to answer it now privately, since he could no longer remember why he was destroying Dan Vermeulen. Insanity was that way. It sometimes began with a single bad decision, then escalated into a series of poor judgments, finally, culminating in deliberate choices of evil that changed a person's character forever, leaving him out of touch with the rest of his race. And that's what made it so easy, because the normal rules of humanity no longer applied to Devin

Dexter, simply because he was now insane. He hadn't seen it coming, but after a while had discovered himself striving for it. In the end, there was a particular point where he'd surrendered his conscious will and given it over to whatever evil force had conspired to possess him. That was the way it always was with insanity and always would be. There was no such thing as 'not guilty by reason of insanity', because all insane people, at some point in their lives, had chosen the path they were on. It was a deliberate choice, and they were accountable by virtue of that choice, despite the fact that they no longer remembered it. The fact that they felt no responsibility was of no consequence, because, in the end, they would answer to their masters.

It was the law of human existence; everyone has to serve someone; everyone has a master, whether they realize it or not. Therefore, after their last breath, after their last pulse of blood faded into eternity, they would return to their master and whatever accountability he had in store for him. Dan Vermeulen, who had chosen sanity, service, and compassion, would return to the God Jehovah, while Devin Dexter, who had chosen to serve only himself, would descend to the consequence of that lifelong decision. He always had a choice, and the one true God would always accept a man who turned from self to serve others, it's just that Devin Dexter had neither intention nor desire of doing so, no desire to serve, and his only yearning was to dominate and to be worshipped. In his conscious mind, he would never lower himself to serve another. The fact that he was a created being, and, therefore, must be subordinate to someone or something, didn't even cross his mind. The world belonged to him by virtue of his willful conquest, and he would rule by his own whim.

But still, his inability to finish off even the memory of his enemy frustrated him to the core of his being, and he wouldn't rest until Dan Vermeulen's legacy was tarnished forever. It was the obsession that drove him forward.

His thoughts wandered now back to other business. Calley, his daughter and lover, had changed. He couldn't quite put his finger on it, but something about her was different, and it made him feel uneasy. Besides, she no longer excited him as she used to. For anyone else, the thought of sleeping with your own daughter would have been a sufficient sickness, but Devin had progressed even beyond that. Like a fix, Devin always needed something more, something stronger, something sick beyond restraint. Then his thoughts settled on Clarissa, his daughter, his grand daughter, and the evil inside him began to fester and bubble out of control. At first, he tried to push it down, but it wouldn't obey him; it just kept growing, and growing, and growing, until, finally, his desire for verboten things swallowed up any sense of family and decency and left him panting for the day when she would become old enough to be used. Or was she already old enough? A smile twisted across his wrinkled, old face as he reminded himself that nothing was beyond him, moral constraints did not apply to him, and his only limitations were the ones he chose to impose upon himself. But why impose any limits at all? It was a good question, and he pondered it alone in the privacy of his office.

And what should he do about his son, his only son, who had betrayed him? Devin allowed himself a moment of personal pain as he pitied himself for the way his children had treated him. Both of them had turned from him, refused his gifts, and rejected his fatherhood. The thought angered him, and burned inside him, growing into a vengeance that gradually took control and silenced anything resembling reason. Yes, his children must be punished; they deserved it. He couldn't recall its origin, but the old adage 'spare the rod and spoil the child' came to mind.

He looked down into his Franklin Planner. After dinner tonight, he was free. Yes, tonight he would take Aric to the wood shed. The smile spread onto his face like a cancer, growing, malignant, deadly, and unstoppable. If not, there was always Clarissa.

40

"He did what!"

George Stollard, dressed in a white shirt and tie, threw his sports jacket down across the chair in front of him. FBI Director John Palance swiveled around in his chair to look directly at George.

"I said Aric just bought fifteen thousand dollars worth of merchandise on your credit cards. He also withdrew five hundred dollars in cash from an ATM machine. We have it on video, would you like to see it?"

George plopped himself down in his chair and laid his arms up on the table. He hadn't been getting much sleep the past few days.

"Yeah, sure."

And then he added.

"How am I going to pay for all that? It'll take me years to bounce back from this!"

John Palance nodded to an assistant who typed a few strokes into the computer. The screen up on the far wall lit up and came to life, showing Aric Baxter standing in front of the ATM machine. He was smiling. George swore out loud.

"That son of a ...!"

But John cut him off.

"Now look at this. Watch his lips."

Aric held the stack of twenty-dollar bills in front of the camera and laughed. His lips moved, but no sound was evident. John Palance, who was usually reserved and professional burst out laughing.

"He just said, 'Thanks George', and then he walked away to spend your money."

George stood up quickly, sending the chair backwards 3 feet.

"I never trusted that kid! He was the most unscrupulous little whelp I've ever seen! When I get my hands on him ..."

"Now George, just calm down. The kids is doing you a favor."

But George burst in before the FBI Director could finish.

"A favor! The little brat is going to bankrupt me! First my house gets blown up and now this!"

John Palance couldn't help but smile, but then he pasted a serious look onto his face before responding.

"Don't you see what he's doing George? He's leaving a trail for us to follow. Anyone who watches CSI knows that we must be tracking all these transactions. He wants us to know what he's doing and where he's been."

George nodded and sat back down slowly.

"Yeah, I know. It just makes me mad. I hope the President has a mind to pay for all this. So where's the little brat at now?"

John Palance shook his head back and forth.

"We don't know where he is. We only know where he's been. He keeps moving faster than we can keep up with him. We keep hoping he'll rent a car, then we could track him real time, but he's not that stupid."

George placed his left hand under his chin and thought.

"So what do you think he's up to?"

John leaned back in his chair and rocked it back and forth a bit. He was in great shape for his age, and his biceps bulged out beneath his dress shirt.

"I think it's just like you said. He's going to try to break into the Senator's estate and rescue that woman of his."

George crossed his right leg over his left knee and frowned.

"From what I've seen of the Senator's complex, there isn't much chance he'll succeed. They'll catch him before he gets 10 feet onto the property. That place is wired to the hilt."

John nodded in agreement.

"Yes. He's destined to failure. No doubt about it."

George threw up his hands in desperation.

"So hey! You're the G man! What are we supposed to do? I think the Senator's involved in the assassination attempt on the President. Can't we just go in there and get him?"

John shook his head sternly.

"No way, George."

"Why not? It's a matter of national security. He may have the President there."

John Palance scoffed.

"I agree, but that's just conjecture. We're just guessing. We need proof before we break down the door of the most powerful member of the United States Senate! Besides, we have to do it legally. We have to follow the Constitution on this. The man has rights!"

George stood up again and pounded his fist down hard on the table before raising his voice.

"I couldn't care less about his civil rights! I care about the President! I have to get him back! It's my job!"

Remaining calm and poised, Director Palance replied in a soft tone.

"Yes, I can see that. However, *my* job is to uphold the law, and I can't commit felonies in order to follow through on a hunch and a bit of circumstantial evidence and possible coincidence. If we don't do this right, the honorable Senator Dexter will have our heads on a platter. He would launch a congressional investigation that would destroy the bureau and cripple the country for years."

George ground his teeth together in frustration. On the one hand, he liked John, and he knew he was doing his best, but, on the other, it just seemed like every time he suggested a course of action, the FBI quoted the law and said it couldn't be done. George composed himself and sat back down slowly. George looked over at John and locked eyes with him. John returned the stare, but then his eyes slowly began to soften.

He thought for a moment, and then reached into his coat pocket that was hanging on the chair next to him and brought out a small electronic device. At first, George thought that it was a recorder, but then he remembered that everything said in this room was recorded anyway. It was standard FBI procedure.

"What is that thing?"

John pressed a button on the box before speaking.

"It's a portable jammer. It will interfere with any electronic device you may have brought with you today on your person."

George looked a bit confused.

"No offense, George. I just can't take any chances. My career is on the line, along with the reputation of the bureau."

He hesitated a moment and then continued.

"If you repeat any of what I'm about to tell you, I'll deny it and call you a liar on national television if I have to. Do you understand?"

George leaned forward in his chair and slowly nodded his head. He wanted to hear what was so important and dangerous to the FBI.

"I'm going to speak candidly to you, George. I've helped you about as much as I can. With the evidence we now have, there's nothing we, the FBI, can take action on."

He paused a moment.

"However ... if, by chance, you were to go to Harvey Keitel over at the

CIA, I know for a fact that he has the assets you need."

George narrowed his eyes before speaking.

"Harvey's a spook. Do you trust him?"

John smiled softly.

"Not only do I not trust him, but the man scares the hell out of me. But ... he's a patriot, and I trust that. Sometimes ... "

John Palance started to say more but thought better of it.

"Let's just say, George, that the FBI's hands are tied by the law and the U.S. Constitution, but Harvey Keitel, this guy's a regular Houdini, and he doesn't feel bound by such trite things as the law and due process."

He looked away from George and then quickly back again.

"Do you catch my drift, George?"

George smiled lightly and nodded his head slowly up and down. John Palance smiled.

"Good! This conversation is over and it never occurred."

He then pushed the button on his electronic device and placed it back into his coat pocket as if it never existed. George thought for a moment and then got up slowly and deliberately from the chair.

"Listen, John, I just remembered something that I have to take care of this morning. But I'll check back with you this afternoon. You've got my cell number if you need me."

John nodded. He liked George. Not only did he have his cell number, but he was also tracking George's whereabouts twenty four seven, at least until this whole thing was over.

George walked out of the room, went down the elevators and left the FBI building. He was entering uncharted waters, and this whole covert ops world made him nervous. But, he would do whatever it took to get back his President and repair the results of his failing. It was a point of honor.

41

There were printouts scattered all across the dirty, shag rug of the cheap motel room floor. The rug was an ugly, yellow color, with black cigarette burns and mud stains scattered intermittently across its width. Aric picked up the satellite photo of the Dexter estate and scanned it with an eye for breaking in. There were armed guards, dogs, surveillance cameras, and a myriad of alarm systems that he would have to deal with. Frankly, he didn't see his odds as very good, but he had to try nonetheless. Calley and her baby were counting on him.

He would go there tonight and watch the place to try and find a weakness. He had already been to several stores, maxing out George's credit cards, buying equipment he would need. Over in the corner, he had a pair of night vision goggles, binoculars, a hunting rifle with scope, a set of camouflage clothes, a rucksack, a razor sharp survival knife, more 9 millimeter rounds and extra, high-capacity magazines.

When Aric looked over at the gear, he felt like he was going off to war, and perhaps he was. If they caught him, he was dead.

Suddenly, a thought occurred to him, 'Will God get mad at me for killing Senator Dexter or will he help me?' Nothing like that had ever been a concern for him before, and thinking about it now made him feel uneasy and conflicted. Life had seemed easier before he'd answered to anyone. Was it okay to kill an evil man who was hurting someone you loved? Aric put the thought to rest for now. It must be. Aric had been reading his Bible lately and had learned that God had killed all kinds of evil people in the past, and had ordered people like King David and Joshua, and Gideon to kill thousands of people, even women and children, so what would it matter to kill just one more?

He put the thought out of his head for now; it was getting in the way of the mission. The mission must come first, always the mission. Aric took another bite of the supreme pizza he'd ordered an hour ago. It was already cold, and it just didn't taste as good as the last one he'd had, but he was starving, so he wolfed it down regardless. He liked the golden brown and greasy pan crust.

So many things had happened to Aric in the past few weeks that he couldn't sort them all out. He had gone from destitution and pending homelessness to a well-paying job and all the satisfaction that Calley could give him. Then he'd met Joshua Moses Talbert and everything had changed again. If he had just killed the old man, then everything would have been fine. But, Aric knew better even as he thought it. Joshua was the wild card in the deck, and the normal rules didn't apply to him. To go up against Joshua and his God was to fight a losing battle. Besides, Aric had made a promise to God himself, and he would make good on it, no matter what it cost him. On the other hand, it was also a losing battle to go up against Mike Simmons and the Senator. No matter what he did, Aric felt like he was going to die tonight, and that remained his strongest case for doing the right thing.

What was it that Joshua had whispered in his ear? "Don't live for something that isn't worth dying for." Calley and her baby: they were worth risking his life for, even worth losing it. It wasn't about sex, because he had already decided that would not happen again with her. Ever since he'd prayed to God that night in the motel, lying on the cold, ceramic tile of the bathroom floor, he had seen the world through different eyes.

He still couldn't put his finger on it, but once the initial pleasure of making love to Calley had subsided, something about the whole affair just began to feel wrong. And it was something more than the mere sin of fornication, he felt that it was deeper and more profound than that, something that he wasn't seeing, as if a very important part of the picture was obscured from his view. Nonetheless, he had made up his mind. No matter what the cost, he would rescue Calley and her daughter, or die trying, preferably the former.

All of a sudden, Aric began to feel a little sleepy, then light-headedness crept over him. He raised his hand to his forehead and was surprised to wipe beads of sweat from his brow. It was hotter in here than he'd thought. Aric moved his right foot beneath his butt and heaved himself to his feet. Surprisingly, he fell backwards onto the bed and stared up at the ceiling, which was now spinning around faster than he could follow it. Something was very wrong.

The door to his motel room opened partway, then Aric heard the chain lock give way and then a creak as it opened slowly the rest of the way. He heard footsteps, and then saw a face suspended over him, hovering in and out of focus. Aric tried to reach behind his back to pull the pistol out of his belt, but hands came down and clamped over him securely, disallowing any movement. A strong-smelling rag came down over his nose and mouth, and Aric's last thoughts were, 'I'll never eat pan pizza again.'

· · ·

When Aric woke up, the left side of his face was resting plushly on the black, Corinthian leather of Devin Dexter's limousine.

He came out of his dream lightly, slowly at first, and then he thought he heard music, but it wasn't rock and roll or country and western like he was used to; they were violins, and, suddenly, Aric wondered 'Am I in heaven?'

Finally, he lifted up his heavy head and slowly came to a sitting position. Directly across from him, smiling victoriously was a man with gray hair, in his fifties whom he had never seen before, though he looked strangely familiar to him. Aric gave the man a brief nod and then moved his hands up to cradle his face. He had a terrible headache.

Beside the man sat Mike Simmons, holding a Glock pistol, which was pointed directly at Aric's chest. Aric spoke to him without even looking in his direction.

"Hey Mike. How's it goin'?"

Mike Simmons didn't answer, but the other man laughed out loud before responding.

"I knew I would like you, Aric. I just knew it!"

Aric looked up and gazed at the man again, taking note of his impeccable suit, his shiny shoes, the perfectly knotted tie, and the faint smell of Old Spice in the air.

"You must be the guy who holds Mike's leash?"

Devin Dexter nodded.

"Well, I wouldn't exactly put it that way. Mike is a free agent, my most loyal employee, but he is free to come and go as he pleases. Mike has never let me down."

Aric glanced over at Mike, then down at the pistol pointing at his own chest.

"I suppose that makes you my boss too?"

Devin nodded again.

"Allow me to introduce myself. I am the honorable Senator Devin Dexter, ranking member of Congress, multi-millionaire many times over, and, of course, your father."

Aric moved his gaze quickly back over to Devin.

"My father?"

Devin nodded, but he saw Aric's eyes narrow a bit in disbelief.

"You don't believe me?"

Aric chuckled as much as he could, considering his predicament. They were undoubtedly going to kill him, so he didn't know why they would play games like this beforehand.

"No I don't. My father is dead. I never knew him."

Devin glanced over at Mike Simmons and gave a slight nod. Immediately, Mike lashed out with his free hand and struck Aric on the face with his big, meaty left fist, nearly knocking him unconscious. He rocked his head backwards, then it fell forward again and Aric cradled his head softly in his hands. The pain was excruciating. Then he heard the Senator's voice again, and this time it had more of an edge to it.

"Don't ever say that again. If you do, then Mike will shoot you in the left knee."

Aric looked over at Mike and saw him smile, confirming that he would indeed follow through with the threat, perhaps, was even eager to do so. Then he turned back to the man claiming to be his father.

"If you're my father, then why have we never met?"

Devin considered the question a moment before turning his head toward Mike and nodding his head again. Once more Mike's fist lashed out and careened into the side of Aric's jaw, knocking his head back and stunning him for several seconds. Mike was amazingly fast for someone as large as he was.

"Don't you know, Aric, that children should be seen and not heard? What has your mother been teaching you all these years."

Aric looked up, wondering if he should answer the question, wondering what would happen if he opened his mouth. In the end, he decided it was best to remain quiet for now. Devin Dexter smiled.

"Good. You learn quickly. I like that. Apparently the apple didn't fall too far from the tree, though, it fell farther than I would have liked."

The Senator moved forward a few inches before speaking again.

"So, Aric, son, what do you think I should do with you now, considering the fact that you let me down, betrayed my loyalties, and disrespected my trust? Hmmm, what do you think I should do?"

Aric didn't answer. He didn't dare. There was no way he would give that big goon another excuse to punch him again. When Aric remained silent, Devin continued.

"Too ashamed to speak I assume. I don't blame you. At least that shows a little bit of remorse and honor."

He leaned back in the plushness of his seat again and lifted up a glass of Scotch that Aric hadn't seen until now. The Senator took a small sip and then savored the flavor a moment.

"There's nothing like a good, 12-year-old Scotch. Don't you agree?"

That question felt safe enough to answer, so Aric spoke curtly.

"I've never been much of a drinker."

Devin smiled.

"Well, that's a shame. You probably don't smoke fine cigars either then?"

Aric shook his head slowly from side to side, but winced at the pain it caused him.

"No, not really. But I've been told they're acquired tastes."

Devin nodded in agreement.

"Yes, that's true. And I see you've acquired a taste for my daughter, Calley, as well."

Aric lifted his head up in surprise and heightened interest.

"Calley?"

Devin laughed out loud.

"That's right."

Then he shook his head slowly from side to side.

"You know I really like you son. It's just too bad you turned on me. I would have given you the keys to my kingdom. We could have ruled together, Aric."

And then he paused and a look of sincere sadness came over his face.

"It's such a shame, such a waste. Because now ... I have to kill all of you, you, your sister Calley, and her daughter."

Upon hearing that, Aric screamed and launched himself over at the Senator, wrapping his hands around his throat. He began to squeeze as hard as he could, but suddenly his grip began to loosen and then his hands fell away completely as Mike continued to bludgeon him with the butt end of his pistol. Finally, Aric slumped backward into the seat and fell into unconsciousness.

The honorable Senator Devin Dexter, always concerned with appearances, regained his composure, then straightened his tie and ran his fingers through his gray hair in an attempt to tidy up his discomfiture. When he was done, he placed his glass into the cup holder. He hadn't spilled a drop.

"Mike, let's go somewhere a little more controlled and private. My son and I would like to get to know each other a little better. We don't have much time together."

Mike opened the black divider and barked out an order to the driver, who quickly took a left turn and sped off into the night.

42

"You're kidding me? He actually said that? The Director of the FBI actually said that I'm a regular Houdini and that I don't feel bound by such trite things as the law and due process?"

George sat across the table from Harvey Keitel, a short, stout man with a receding hairline, wearing jeans and a blue rugby shirt that fit loosely around his torso. They had agreed to meet on neutral turf at the small café on the outskirts of town, just the two of them.

"Yes, that's almost word for word. If you ask him, maybe he'll give you a copy of the recording."

George had been joking with his last remark, but Harvey looked serious when he answered.

"Trust me, George, if that conversation was recorded, then the media was destroyed the moment you left the room. John Palance is no rookie, and he leaves nothing to chance. He would make a formidable adversary."

George raised his eyebrows, surprised by the comment.

"Really? Are you speaking from experience?"

Harvey took a sip of his coffee and then set the cup back down. It was steaming hot.

"Of course not, George. You heard the Vice President. We practice interdepartmental cooperation. The CIA and the FBI are on the same team. We're the perfect picture of love, peace, and harmony."

Harvey smiled.

"You don't believe me?"

George leaned back and placed his right arm up on the back of the booth. George found it amusing that they had both argued over who would face the door with their back to the wall. In the end, they had flipped a coin and George had lost.

"Well, it's not that. It's just that John painted a little different picture of the CIA than you do. To be honest, Harvey, I don't think he trusts you."

Harvey leaned his head back and laughed out loud.

"Of course he doesn't trust me. I'm a spook!"

Suddenly, George felt uneasy and looked carefully around the empty café.

"Should you be advertising that in public, Harvey. Aren't you guys supposed to be secretive about who you are?"

Harvey picked up his coffee cup again.

"Don't be silly, George, I was just on national television last week. Anyone who wants to know who I am, already knows. I have no secrets."

Then he smiled again.

"Well, none I want to talk about."

This time George was the one who smiled. He was finding Harvey Keitel, the nation's top spook to be very humorous and pleasant.

"You're not what I was expecting, Harvey."

"Yes, I know. I deal with that all the time."

Then he got serious.

"But let me tell you something, George. This town is full of people who don't trust one another. It was even worse back in D.C."

Then he swiveled in the booth to his left and pointed out toward the curb across the street.

"Let me give you an example. You see that black panel van, the one from Arco's Heating Service?"

George nodded.

"Now you see the second floor window in the corner of that building behind it?"

George nodded again.

"Even as you and I speak, our every word is being recorded."

Then he reached up with his right hand and waved to the black van.

"Hey guys. How's it going? Go ahead, George, say hello to John Palance and the FBI."

George looked dumbfounded and chose not to wave.

"Why do I get the feeling you're not joking about this? You're serious, aren't you."

Harvey nodded.

"Now watch this. As I count down from three … three, two, one. My people in the second floor will lay down some communications counter-measures that will render the G men in the black van totally useless."

George looked out the window of the café, waiting for something to happen. Suddenly, the driver's side window rolled down and a man in sunglasses shoved his left arm out the window and held up his middle finger in their direction. The van started up and then drove away. Harvey reared back his head and laughed some more. After a few seconds, he settled back down and returned to his coffee. George was still amazed.

"Okay, well, that was educational."

Harvey lifted up his right hand to beckon over the waitress.

"Miss, may I get some more coffee please?"

She came over and filled both their cups. Harvey winked at her but she turned and quickly left.

"You see, George, no one trusts anyone any more."

George didn't respond. He no longer knew what to say. Since Harvey had totally taken control of the conversation, he waited for Harvey to continue and was not disappointed.

"So, George, now that we're alone, tell me, what is it you want from me?"

All of a sudden, Harvey Keitel had gone from loud and boisterous, to quiet and subdued. It was a little spooky that he could change so quickly.

"I'm not sure yet, but I was hoping you could tell me that."

"Just tell me what your situation is, George."

George then explained everything that had transpired over the past few days, then he paused.

"I suppose, Harvey, I was hoping, since the FBI is powerless to arrest or intervene, that I could elicit the assets of the CIA to crash into the Senator's house, and help me rescue the President."

Harvey stroked his stubbled chin thoughtfully before responding.

"Actually, George, the CIA doesn't do a lot of crashing down doors. Most times we get in and get out quickly and no one ever knows we were there. It makes it easier. There's less political fallout that way. You see, George, we like to operate in the dark, and when people turn on the lights, like the FBI, or Congress, we get nervous and start shredding files. Understand?"

George did and nodded.

"So can you help me?"

Harvey didn't answer. Instead, he waved to the waitress again and ordered a slice of blueberry pie.

"Do you want a slice, George?"

"No thank you."

"What a shame. A good slice of pie will liven up your spirits. You shouldn't get so serious all the time, George. You need to lighten up a bit."

The waitress brought the Director of the CIA his blueberry pie, and he tore into it like a man starved. A few minutes later, he was done, and he pushed the plate away from him. Neither man had talked as he ate.

"You know, George, I've made some really good decisions after a slice of homemade blueberry pie. It's my favorite."

George couldn't wait any longer.

"So, does that mean you'll help me or not?"

Harvey picked up the paper napkin, dabbed a blueberry stain from the corner of his mouth before laying it back down on the table.

"It means, George, that I'm going back to my office now. I'll make a few phone calls on the way back, and by time I get there, I'll have all the information I need to decide. Fair enough?"

George narrowed his eyes, not sure what would happen next, but he was in no position to press for more. In the end, he simply nodded.

"I'll have my people send over all the files of everything we've collected so far to give you a head start. But Harvey surprised him again.

"That won't be necessary, George."

George eyed Harvey suspiciously but said nothing.

"Don't trust anyone in this town, George, especially a spook. I already have copies of everything you've collected."

He stood up and threw a twenty-dollar bill on the table.

"Let me give you a tip, George 'Always pay in cash.'"

And then, as he walked away.

"I'll be in touch."

This time, George knew better than to offer his cell phone number.

43

There was a naked light bulb hanging from the ceiling above, but it was turned off, leaving Aric in almost complete darkness. He could smell the dampness all around him, and his jeans were soaked from laying on the concrete floor in his own urine. The soreness in his wrists were beginning to ebb down into his fingers from the heavy, nylon zip tie that bound his hands behind his back, and his ankles were also bound tightly together. Aric had no idea how long he had been here, only that his bowels were crying to burst out, and that his stomach felt stabs of pain from the hunger.

He kept thinking back to his first meeting with Mike Simmons, regretting the day and wishing he could take the ill-fated decision back. It had been a mistake that he may not live much longer to regret. Aric Baxter had the distinct feeling that he was about to be *expunged*. A part of him wanted to blame God, but deep inside himself he recognized this was folly. God hadn't made these choices. God hadn't accepted the money. He had – Aric Baxter – and only Aric Baxter would be held accountable for that act. Aric would pay the price for his sins. It was cause and effect. Finally, after 26 years, he understood.

Looking back, he realized that all his feeble efforts were but folly.

Even the good he tried to do, rescuing Calley and her daughter, would not come to fruition. Aric was horrified to admit that he couldn't point to one, single selfless act in his life. He had lived in self, and now he would die in self. A great and sudden sadness swept over him.

And then he thought of the promises he had made to God. He thought of Joshua Moses Talbert, and the terms of his consecration. "God has chosen you, Aric. He has set you apart, consecrated you for his own holy purpose. And here are the terms of your consecration unto the Lord: you are forbidden to lie with a woman, neither shall a blade touch your skin, you shall do your best to honor all the words of the Lord as best you know them. You shall honor the terms of this consecration until your task is done."

So far he had kept the terms, but, in all honesty, he'd neither had the time nor the opportunity to lay with a woman in the past weeks. The shaving part had been easy, and his beard was getting fairly heavy now, heavier than it had ever been. He had no idea why Joshua, that crazy old man, had told him such silliness, but, still ... he believed in it. Besides, the consecration was all he had left to hold on to now.

Just then, he heard the jolt of iron on iron and the creaking of the heavy, wooden door as it swung open on the rusty, old hinges. A beam of light burst in and blinded him, threatening to overwhelm his senses and render him unconscious. Aric struggled to focus his eyes, then he looked directly into the light and saw the outline of a body, standing there in front of him.

The body stepped forward, his eyes made their final focus, and he gasped in astonishment.

• • •

The man in white raiment stood outlined in front of the door for several seconds and then stepped inside slowly. He walked over and his tall, sturdy figure bent down and looked deeply into Aric's eyes. When he spoke, it was softly, but with a volume and power that ripped into Aric's aching skull.

"You have kept the terms of your consecration. You must continue to do so. There is peril to your own soul."

Aric's eyes finished adjusting to the light and he could see deeply into the other man's eyes, but he turned away, unable to hold his gaze. Something was separating the two of them, something that he didn't yet understand.

"Who are you?"

The being, for Aric was now convinced that he was not a man, sat down on the dirty, cement floor beside him without becoming soiled.

"My name is Caedlin, and I am our master's servant, sent to encourage and strengthen you before the final trial."

Aric lowered his head in disappointment.

"You mean it's going to get worse?"

The bright figure nodded his head slowly.

"Yes. It always gets darker before it gets light. That is the way of such things as these."

"Can't you just let me go and help me rescue Calley and her baby? It seems like God would want that."

The man of bright light looked down sympathetically before reaching down to caress Aric's stubbled face.

"That is also what God wants, but the trials have come to make you strong. The fire prepares you for the life to come. It is a small price to pay for a life of sin and self."

"But I don't want to pay. It hurts too much. I just want to get out of here."

The being in white linen nodded its understanding.

"No one does, but it's an offer you can't afford not to choose. The pain is fleeting and will soon be gone."

Aric tried to smile, but could only manage a hint of it.

"Can you help me?"

Caedlin nodded and immediately a burst of power surged from his fingertips and onto Aric's face, flowing into him and through him, saturating and renewing every molecule of his body. It lasted a full ten seconds, and when it subsided, Aric felt totally refreshed. The pain in his wrists and hands was gone, and he no longer felt the pain in his joints. Suddenly, he felt dry and warm, as if he was sitting on a pillow and covered with a blanket. The emptiness inside his stomach was filled, and he found himself wanting to sing, but he didn't know the words to say. His comforter spoke again.

"As iron sharpens iron, so one man sharpens another."

Aric suddenly looked confused.

"Iron sharpens iron? What are you talking about?"

"I mean that when you have come through the fire, you shall be as shining brass."

Aric thought about it, but still didn't understand the relevance. Right now it didn't matter to him. The pain was gone and he felt renewed. Caedlin stood up.

"I have to go now, but the peace of our Father, who is in heaven, will stay with you. He loves you and will be with you always, even to the end."

And then Caedlin was gone, and Aric was plunged back into darkness. But the light inside him remained.

44

It had been a long day, and George hadn't slept in 20 hours. He could barely stay awake as he drove home, so he stopped off at an all-night latte place for a pick-me-up. As he got out of his car and walked up to the door his mind wandered. The investigation was going slowly, and they still had yet to find the smoking gun that would empower the FBI to raid Senator Dexter's home and arrest him. Even more disappointing, George had heard nothing from Harvey Keitel at the CIA.

Just a few hours ago there had been a rumor break that someone had seen President Vermeulen in Indianapolis, so George had dispatched an agent to check it out. It was the fourth time this week that someone had spotted the President. All three times prior it had turned out to be a bogus lead, and lately, George was feeling more like a reporter for the National Enquirer than a United States Secret Service Agent.

As George walked into the little caffeine station, he looked around carefully for anything suspicious; it was just a security habit, something he did without even thinking. He walked up to the counter. The college kid was sitting there on a stool listening to a walk man and reading a sports magazine. George noticed an unusual tattoo on the young man's shoulder of a camouflaged cross and wondered what it meant. When the kid didn't move to serve him, George cleared his throat impatiently. Finally, the clerk threw down the magazine and removed his headphones.

"You want some latte or something?"

George sighed in disgust. This kid was going nowhere in this business with customer service skills like that. Nonetheless, he forced a smile onto his face.

"Just a regular latte please"

The boy looked at him and smiled for the first time.

"Sure thing. What size?"

George smiled back at him.

"Better make it a small. I need just enough gas to make it home and get in bed."

The boy nodded and stepped over to the machine with a paper cup. George remembered his days in Washington DC. Before the bombings there had been a Starbucks on every corner, but now, you had to look for them. Life had become somewhat diminished since that day, especially if you'd been poor to start with. George thought about his brother's family in Kentucky and sighed. They were dirt poor and didn't even know what a latte was. He still sent them money every month for food. When he got done with this case, he should visit them.

"Any flavoring with that?"

George thought about his growing midsection and his slowing middle-aged metabolism and declined.

"Better not."

The boy finished the latte and handed it to him. The little insulated cup jacket slipped down onto the counter top, so George picked it up and pushed the jacket back into place.

"That's six dollars and eighty-five cents."

George pulled out his wallet and handed the boy his credit card, but was waved off.

"Sorry man, but our computer is down tonight. We're only taking cash until it comes back up."

George hesitated and thought about saying something in protest, but stifled himself. It wasn't the boy's fault; besides, computer networks were much less reliable than they had been. The infrastructure just wasn't what it had been before the bombings. It was no one's fault. George opened his wallet, but could find no cash. He rarely carried much of it. Finally, he found some in his left, front pocket.

"Here's some. Oh wait, this isn't enough."

The boy counted out three dollars and twelve cents in change on the counter top. George looked up at him in disgust. This day just kept getting better.

"Don't worry about it man. I'll cover the rest."

And he put his left hand in his pocket and fished out 3 dollars and some change. George looked him in the face, and it was then that George noticed the softness of the boy's blue eyes. George smiled sincerely and spontaneously for the first time that day.

"Thanks. I appreciate it."

And then George did something unusual. He struck up a conversation with a total stranger for no reason at all.

"So what are you listening to on the earphones?"

The boy looked down at the counter.

"Oh, just listening to a sermon on tape."

George was surprised.

"Really?"

"You seem surprised."

George placed his wallet back into his pocket.

"Well, yeah. I guess I am. Sorry."

The boy shrugged it off.

"That's okay, man. I get that all the time. My parents think I'm a Jesus

Freak. That's what they call me. But I don't care. Well, I do care, but I can handle it okay."

George smiled again. There was something about the boy's openness that was disarming.

"Well, sometimes parents just don't understand the enthusiasm of youth. You going to college near here?"

"Not yet. I'm still trying to raise up the money. But I hope to. I know I won't go no where without an education."

Suddenly, George felt compassion for the boy, and it was uncomfortable for him. George didn't know how to handle it, so he tried to make a clean exit.

"Well, don't work too hard. In the meantime, try to have some fun, okay."

George turned to leave with his latte, but the boy stopped him cold in his tracks.

"I am. Tomorrow I'm going to meet the Bulletproof Preacher."

George turned and adrenaline surged into his system.

"The Bulletproof Preacher? He hasn't been seen since the day the President turned up missing. You must be mistaken."

The boy shook his head back and forth confidently.

"Nope. I'm sure. He just joined the freedom march not fifteen minutes ago. I just heard it on the news. He's going all the way to right here in Omaha. I thought I'd head out tomorrow and see if I could maybe meet him someplace in between, maybe Iowa or somewhere. I just want to spend some time with the guy and see what he has to say."

George didn't answer the boy. He had already pulled out his cell phone and punched in the number to the White House Secret Service detail. When they answered, he told them who he was and asked for confirmation of the rumor. George then hung up and was about to make another call when his phone rang. It was a voice mail from FBI Director

John Palance, saying that he had already dispatched a team from the Indianapolis FBI field office. His agents would have the preacher in custody within a few hours and they would call him as soon as they knew more. George listened to the message again before hanging up his phone.

"Wow! Neat!"

George had forgotten all about the boy standing there behind the counter. He looked up now and saw the boy gaping at him in splendor. He had just listened to the entire conversation.

"Are you a secret agent or FBI guy or something?"

George laughed softly. He really liked this kid, but he just didn't have time for him. Nonetheless, he pulled out his federal ID and flashed it.

"George Stollard, United States Secret Service."

The boy was grinning from ear to ear.

"So does this mean you're going to meet the Bulletproof Preacher too?"

George nodded.

"I suppose it does. He's someone we need to talk to."

The boy leaned forward.

"He saved the President's life you know. Some people say he kidnapped him, but he only took him to protect him from the assassin's bullet."

The smile on George's face faded away.

"Where did you hear that?"

"I read about it in a blog on the internet. They say that the President and the preacher have been holed up somewhere together until it's safe to come out, and now they'll both come back and lead the nation back to God. Do you know the President?"

George winced at the question. It reminded him of his failure, and he didn't want to answer it.

"Yes. I do."

George turned to leave again.

"So what's he like?"

George stopped again, but this time he thought before answering. He was sworn to secrecy, so he had to be careful what he said publicly about his charge. Besides, he liked the President.

"He's a good man. He's real. He's the same man in public as he is in private. But I can't tell you any more than that."

The boy looked confused.

"Why not?"

George took a step forward and made direct eye contact with the young man. He had wanted to use this line his whole life.

"Because if I did, then I'd have to kill you."

At first, the boy looked surprised, then George smiled and the boy's face lit up like a firefly.

"Wow! Cool! Neat!"

George shook his head as he walked toward the door. He opened his cell phone again and began to make a torrent of calls to make sure everything was getting done. Suddenly, his tiredness was gone and he was ready for another day. On his way to the car, he took a sip of his latte. Next time he would get some hazelnut flavoring. Finally, they were making some headway.

45

She sat alone on the bed waiting. Calley looked up into all four corners of the room and saw the small video cameras. They were watching her as always, always watching, always enjoying the perversion she had grown to hate. But this would be her last performance, because the next time she got the chance, Calley would squash Devin Dexter like the bug he was, even it meant the forfeiture of her own life. She had it all planned out. She just needed a little opportunity.

Her daughter, Clarissa, had been taken from her yesterday, and the thought of what might be happening to her drove Calley crazy. A half hour ago she had taken a sedative just to calm down enough to perform one last time. At least she knew that Aric was still alive, and that he had tried to come back for her. She only wished that she had told him the whole truth when she'd had the chance. But now it was too late. They were watching her too closely.

Just then, the door opened and Aric's motionless body was flung onto the carpet and the door immediately closed and locked again. She sprang from the bed and rushed to his side. Kneeling beside him, she cradled his battered face in her hands. They had beaten him severely, but at least he was still alive.

"Aric! Can you hear me!"

There was no response. Calley hurried into the bathroom and came back with a wet cloth and a towel. She worked on his face, cleaning away the dried blood, dabbing at the wounds, and trying to make him presentable for the movie they were supposed to make for the honorable Senator Dexter. When she had finished, she cradled his head on her lap and rocked him gently back and forth like she would her own baby.

The key to survival was usefulness. She had to provide a product that the Senator wanted or else he would simply eliminate her and Aric too, before she had a chance to kill him and free her daughter. After several years of experience, she knew what he wanted, but in order to provide it, she needed Aric to cooperate. She needed him to come to.

After a few more minutes, she laid his head down on the carpet and returned to the bathroom with a cup of water. She took a deep breath and hurled the ice-cold water into his face. Aric sputtered a moment and then his eyes opened. Calley knelt down beside him and helped him move to a sitting position.

"Aric, are you okay!"

Aric sucked in one deep breath after another until he could speak.

"Hi Calley. An angel named Caedlin came to me and healed my wounds, but then Mike came and beat me again. I feel like a truck ran over me."

Calley felt sorry for him. They had beaten him into delirium. She offered him the towel and he accepted it, gingerly dabbing at the wet blood. Every time the soft cotton towel touched his face he wanted to cry out in agony, but his pride wouldn't allow it.

"I'm sorry, Aric. I'm so sorry."

And then Calley leaned forward, covered her mouth with her hand and whispered into his ear.

"We have to make love now, Aric. Please."

Aric stopped drying himself and looked up in disbelief.

"What? You're joking, right?"

"Quiet! Only whispers. And keep your mouth covered so they can't read your lips. The cameras are recording it all!"

It was then that Aric noticed Calley was dressed in black laced lingerie and wore more eye makeup than usual. He was about to speak when she covered his mouth with her hand and whispered into his ear again.

"Aric, please! They're going to kill my daughter unless we do what they want. I need your help."

A confused look came over Aric's face as he sat up with his back leaning against the white, painted wall. Finally, he moved his hand up to his mouth and whispered softly.

"Is it true? Are you really my sister? Is he our real father?"

All the blood drained from Calley's face when she heard him speak. She couldn't answer him aloud, but only nodded her head in shame, once more wishing that she had been the one to tell him. Aric lowered his eyes, not knowing how to respond. On the one hand, he was revulsed at himself for what he'd done to her, for what he'd enjoyed with her, on the other, he loved her and felt compassion for her and her daughter.

"What's your daughter's name?"

Calley seemed confused by the question, but answered nonetheless.

"Her name is Clarissa."

Aric thought a moment and tried to smile, but the gash in the left side of his lip wouldn't let him. He remembered the terms of his consecration and shuddered. But even without the consecration, he couldn't make love to his own sister, not knowingly, not even to save a little girl's life. It was different now.

"I can't do it, Calley. Not anymore."

Her brow furled and her eyes narrowed in fear but then quickly changed to anger.

"Of course you can! Don't be silly!"

Her voice no longer a whisper; the volume rose with each word.

"You've already made love to me seven times and now you all of a sudden can't? What's wrong? Aren't I attractive? I was always your sister, but you still took what you wanted!"

Aric looked into her eyes pleadingly.

"Please, Calley. You're my sister. I didn't know it then. It's different now. Please. Let's find another way. Don't give up hope."

Calley began to scream as loud as she could and flailed her arms up and down, beating his injured face with her fists. Aric raised his arms up to block her punches and finally managed to grab her wrists and bend them down behind her back. When she realized her efforts were useless, Calley went limp in his arms and sobbed uncontrollably on his right shoulder, leaving his shirt wet with her tears. Aric held on to her as she heaved up and down on his shoulder with each mighty sob. Eventually, the sobbing slowed and finally stopped altogether. When it did, Aric picker her up and carried her over to the bed. He laid her down and spread a blanket over her scantily-clad body. She was exhausted, both in body and spirit, perhaps beyond repair.

Aric looked up at the camera in defiance. He was angry for all the pain they had caused her, and he wanted to kill them for it. But right now, he had neither the means nor the energy to exact such a vengeance. He walked to the other side of the bed and collapsed beside his sister, praying in a soft voice so as not to awaken her.

"Dear God. Please forgive me. I've made such a mess of things and I'm sorry. All hope is lost for us both. We deserve it. But the little girl, Clarissa, she deserves better. Please God. I believe in you. You are my real father. Please find it in your heart to spare her life."

Then Aric relaxed his muscles and went to sleep, his last conscious thought being, 'That's odd, I don't feel like shining brass.'

46

An hour later, George's latte was cold and he still hadn't taken a sip. He sat in the FBI conference room with the Director and several other agents, waiting for word from the Indianapolis field office. When Special Agent Neilson finally called in, John Palance put him on speakerphone. George was not surprised by the outcome. The FBI agents had attempted to take Joshua into custody and failed. They had drawn their firearms in an attempt to persuade him, but of course he'd just laughed at them. Special Agent Neilson's voice sounded nervous and unsure. George was relieved they'd had the common sense not to shoot, since Joshua had joined the freedom march and was surrounded by innocent civilians. When the agent was done, George cut in before John Palance could speak.

"Are you with the subject now?"

"Well, yes, I mean no. He's about 30 yards away. I had to move away from the crowd so I could hear enough to make the phone call. I have three agents watching him though. He's not going anywhere."

George wanted to laugh at that statement, but refrained. He knew from experience that a thousand FBI agents could never keep Joshua Moses Talbert from doing anything against his will.

"Okay. Here's what I want you to do. I want you to go back to Joshua, and ask him politely if he will speak with George Stollard. Make sure you say please. Do you understand?"

There was silence on the line.

"Agent Neilson. Do you understand?"

Finally a reply came.

"Yes. Affirmative. Are you sure?"

John Palance interrupted.

"Just do as you're told, Agent Neilson!"

Then he muted the speakerphone.

"George are you sure what you're doing? This isn't exactly normal procedure."

George smiled.

"Trust me, John. Joshua Talbert isn't exactly a normal man. We have to do it this way. We have no other choice."

A few second later the voice of Joshua Talbert came over the speakerphone.

"Hello George. Do you believe in miracles yet?"

George was relieved to hear his voice.

"Are you okay, Joshua?"

The prophet seemed to ignore the request.

"The Lord God almighty has chosen you, George. You are consecrated to his divine and mighty purpose."

George hesitated, and then made a decision. He answered briefly.

"Yes, I know. I accept that. I believe."

John Palance looked over at George skeptically, but said nothing.

"Do you remember what I told you, George?"

"Yes, well, most of it."

Joshua said the words again.

"Your task, Mr. Stollard, is to protect the President and to restore him to power. This country has raised a stench in the nostrils of heaven, and the President is the only man who can lead this nation back to God before it's too late. God is giving America one last chance."

George shifted nervously in his chair. He hated being reminded of his greatest failure, but he understood now why Joshua had used the word 'restore' even prior to the President's disappearance. Joshua had known all along what would happen.

"I remember. That's what I've been trying to do. But how can I protect and restore him if I don't know where he is? Truth is we don't even know if he's dead or alive!"

Joshua's next words thundered into the speakerphone and echoed around the sterile confines of the conference room.

"He's alive, George! He is coming again! And, if he lives long enough, he can save this land!"

George yelled back into the speakerphone.

"Where, Joshua! Where is the President!"

But there was no answer, and George just knew that the old man was smiling on the other end.

"Joshua! Talk to me! Joshua! Where is Dan?"

And then the line went dead and George cursed under his breath.

• • •

Aric was awakened by the slamming of the door as it crashed against the door frame and three men rushed in and over to the bed where he and Calley lay. He tried to sit up quickly, but the soreness in his muscles wouldn't let him. They grabbed him and dragged him out of the room as Calley sat up and screamed.

• • •

By the time Senator Dexter walked into the wet, dank room, Aric had been tied to the chair and has once more been beaten severely about the face and chest. His arms were bent around the back of the chair and his hands tied behind him. His ankles were duct-taped to the legs of the chair. Every time Mike Simmons punched Aric in the face, blood sprayed out onto the cinder block wall and his head flew violently back, threatening to snap his neck.

The other men who had helped were gone now, and wouldn't return so long as the Senator was in the complex, and then, only to dispose of the body and clean up the evidence. Devin looked down at his son, shook his head from side to side and frowned.

"It's such a waste. You could have ruled beside me. It would have been great! You and I, father and son, ruling the world, just one, big happy family."

The Senator motioned to Mike to bring a wooden chair over to him. Devin sat down.

"But no! You had to go and develop a conscience. How inopportune!"

He reached over with his right hand and pushed Aric's head up, trying to make eye contact, but couldn't. Aric's eyes were both swollen shut, leaving only tiny slits for him to see. Devin looked over at Mike.

"Go ahead. Get rid of the swelling over his eyes so I can see him. Cut him! I want him to see my face before he dies. I want him to see his father."

Mike stepped forward, brought a folding knife out of his pocket and easily flipped the razor-sharp blade open with his thumb. It glistened in the dimness of the naked bulb swinging overhead. The Senator leaned back in the wooden chair as Mike moved forward, and placed the blade over Aric's eye, hovering, less than an inch away from his skin.

"Do not touch the face of God's anointed!"

The voice boomed out like thunder, shaking the little concrete room. Mike swung around, dropping the knife, and pulling out his pistol in one quick movement. He looked around the room, but there was no one there but the Senator.

"What the hell are you doing? I said cut him!"

Mike looked confused.

"Did you just say something?"

The Senator grew more and more perturbed.

"Of course I said something! I said cut him, and that's what I expect you to do! You will obey me without question!"

Mike hesitated, looking carefully around the room, then he holstered his pistol and slowly bent down to pick up the knife. He heard the voice again.

"It violates the terms!"

Mike stood up with the knife, convinced that he was going crazy and that the voice wasn't real. Then Aric slowly lifted his head and opened his mouth to speak, but the words came out slowly and with great difficulty, one syllable at a time.

"The ... con – se – cra – tion."

This time the Senator moved closer.

"What did he just say?"

Mike looked over at Devin and shrugged.

"I think he said consecration."

"Why would he say that?"

Mike looked down at Aric and thought he saw the hint of a smile forming on his bloody and swollen lips.

"I don't even know what it means. Is he trying to smile?"

A concerned look came over Devin's face. It wasn't supposed to happen this way. This wasn't in his plan.

"I'm going over to see Calley. I'll be back in half an hour. I want his eyes open by time I come back or all your money is forfeit."

The Senator hesitated, and then locked eyes with the man.

"Do you understand, Mike? I want to see his green eyes."

Mike Simmons nodded slowly. The Senator turned and walked out of the room, slamming the door behind him. Mike had never let him down.

47

George Stollard had gone up on the roof of the new Hoover building to think. Most people didn't get up there for security reasons, but George had been given unprecedented access by the Director, by virtue of the Vice President's unusual orders. He stood there now, waiting, thinking, wondering, what to do next? A big part of him wanted to jump in a helicopter and fly to Indiana, but he knew it would be a fruitless waste of time. Joshua had already told him all that he would ever tell him, and Joshua Moses Talbert wasn't the kind of man who could be interrogated or bullied into talking. He would talk when he was good and ready. Besides, the President was alive! That much he had told him, and that was the most valuable information he needed. George had just gotten off the phone with Vice President Thatcher and given him the good news, who had immediately pressed him for a plan to bring Dan back to the White House. But he had no plan, and David Thatcher had not been impressed or amused.

George went over the details in his mind again, desperately looking for something, some small detail that he had missed, but he came up dry again. So much in his life had changed since he'd met Joshua. His life had been orderly, in place, predictable, and boring. What was that last thought? Boring? George found it hard to believe what he was thinking. He'd always loved his job. He lived for it, but, now, his world was bigger. He had more knowledge about a universe that had been closed to him before, the spiritual side of things, and, he knew, that with great knowledge comes great power, and great responsibility, and then after that, accountability.

He'd told Joshua that he believed, but what exactly had he meant? Did he believe in miracles? Yes. Did he believe in Joshua? Yes, without a doubt. Only a fool would not. But did he believe in God? He thought for a moment. Well, he had to say yes to that as well. It was either believe that Joshua produced the magic on his own, or that there was a power behind the throne, that God was there giving him the power to do these miracles. Joshua claimed that it was God, and George had no reason to disbelieve him. Yes, for the first time in his life, George believed in God. But what now? George had to believe that faith required some action on his part, but he just didn't know what it was. He'd never gone to church, but he paused and considered it now.

His cell phone rang and he picked it up immediately.

"George Stollard here."

There was a moment of silence, and then a cryptic voice on the other end.

"This call is untraceable, so don't even try."

George squinted in the sunlight reflecting off the roof.

"What? Who is this?"

"Never mind that. If you want to get the President back, just listen."

George perked up. He wished he had a way to record the call, but he didn't.

"I'm listening."

"Do you remember the place where you bought the latte last night? The small one, with no flavoring, and the kid with the tattoo?"

George was reminded of Harvey Keitel, and immediately knew it was someone from the CIA. How did they know so much about him?

"Yes, I remember. Just off the highway."

There was a pause.

"Meet me there at noon. Alone. We have many things to discuss and plan and little time in which to do it. The op is a go. But we have to hurry. Do you understand?"

George nodded his head. But the voice quickly came back.

"Don't nod your head, George. This is a telephone. Use words."

George looked up and scanned the buildings around him, but he saw nothing out of place.

"George, do you understand?"

He turned his attention back to the cell phone.

"Yes, noon, the latte place. I'll be there."

And no sooner had he responded when he heard a click and the phone line went dead. George closed his phone and looked up. He slowly scanned the buildings around him and wondered to himself. 'How do they do that?' And then he looked straight up over his head into the sky and smiled for the camera.

Then he rushed off the roof and exited the building without telling anyone where he was going. He didn't want anymore FBI company. It would spoil the deal, and these guys were serious.

48

When Mike was alone with Aric, he looked down at the bloodied figure and shook his head from side to side. Things were getting strange. First, he had watched Joshua Moses Talbert dodge bullets on national television, then, the President of the United States had vanished in plain sight, and now, he was hearing voices he could not explain. Yes, things were getting weird, and worse yet, out of control. Weird and strange he could handle, but someone had to be in control or else he didn't know what to count on, who to side with, or even which person to kill.

Mike moved over to the chair across from Aric and sat down. He still held the knife in his hands, but, for the first time in his life, he was having doubts. 'What is in my own best interest?' He thought about it a moment, but didn't know for sure. All he'd ever wanted in life was to make enough money to buy a peaceful house in the Caribbean and live out his days in luxury and decadence. But no, he had a lunatic for a boss, who, quite frankly, was getting weirder and more sadistic by the minute. True, Mike had been paid well, very well, but, truth be told, Mike was starting to find the limits of his own greed. He already had millions locked away in his offshore accounts. Why put up with this any longer? He didn't need this.

Aric raised his head again and looked over at Mike, sitting in the chair across from him. He had heard the thundering voice and recognized it instantly. Throughout his captivity and the beatings, he'd become convinced that he would soon die. There was no other logical conclusion to draw. But now, Joshua was in the room, and anything could happen.

• • •

Calley lay on the bed where she had been with Aric almost an hour before. Aric had thought her asleep, but, with tears in her eyes, she remembered the prayer that he had spoken on behalf of her daughter, just a small child that he neither loved, nor had ever met. She went through it in her mind again and again.

"Dear God. Please forgive me. I've made such a mess of things and I'm sorry. All hope is lost for us both. We deserve it. But the little girl, Clarissa, she deserves better. Please God. I believe in you. You are my father. Please find it in your heart to spare her life."

And finally, just in the last few minutes, it occurred to Calley that Aric's prayer was interchangeable for both of them. Both of them were guilty; both of them needed God's forgiveness; both had made many mistakes and were sorry. But, most importantly of all, both wanted Clarissa, her little girl, to live, to breathe, to have hope and to grow up in happiness. It was, perhaps, the only selfless act of their lives, and they had it in common. They were brother and sister.

Calley thought about it for a minute. It made sense to her. She remembered her first foster family, how they had loved her, how they had held her and treasured her as their own. Unbeknownst to her, so long ago, the seed had taken root, and now, Aric, was loving her and her daughter, was indeed willing to die for them both. And that act, that virtue, was real, and it was something she wanted to know more about, assuming she ever made it out of here alive.

Aric was probably dead by now, but her daughter was still alive. Calley didn't know how to pray, but she had Aric's words, and Aric's words were now hers as well. With solemn slowness, she threw the blankets back away from her and slid down to the carpeted floor. She moved to her knees and propped up her elbows on the bed. Then Calley bowed her head in her hands and prayed to God in black-laced lingerie, hoping that he was real and that he would honor such a sinful woman as herself. She began slowly.

"Dear God. This is Calley. You know me, but I don't know you. But Aric does, so that's good enough for me. I want to know you too. I just hope it's not too late."

She squirmed on her knees, squishing the gold-colored shag carpet beneath her. She hesitated a moment, but then plunged on ahead, repeating Aric's prayer almost verbatim.

"Please forgive me father. I've made such a mess of things and I'm sorry. All hope is lost for us both. We deserve it. But my daughter, Clarissa, she deserves better. Please God. I believe in you. You are my real father. Please find it in your heart to spare her life."

And with that prayer, a great weight lifted off Calley's shoulders, leaving her weeping uncontrollably on the edge of the bed. She didn't know how else to describe it, but, for the first time in her life, she felt clean. Calley thought to herself. 'I have a father who loves me. I have a daughter who needs me, and I have a brother who would die for me.'

Calley raised her hands up to heaven and cried happily before God, but her joy was not to last. Just then, she heard the tumblers on the door lock click, and it began to swing open.

• • •

Aric strained to keep his head up and struggled to make eye contact with Mike Simmons.

"It's all real, Mike. The voice you heard. I heard it too. It's Joshua Moses Talbert. He's coming, and he's bringing God. Do you really want to be around when he gets here?"

Mike feigned courage and mocked him.

"Don't be a fool! You would say anything right now to save your own skin! You're going to die and you know it!"

Aric smiled, but immediately winced in pain as he did.

"Of course I'm going to die, Mike. All of us are. But what happens then? Do you know? I do. I'm going to heaven. I have a father there who loves me."

Mike rubbed the polymer handle of his folding knife and sat up straight.

"I don't believe you. You're as whacky as Dexter. Right now you'd say anything to save yourself."

"Anything? I would say anything?"

Aric raised his eyebrows as far upward as the pain would let him.

"Cut me, Mike. Cut me!"

Mike leaned back in the chair. He looked confused.

"Cut you? Are you nuts? You want me to cut you?"

Aric nodded and smiled again. He didn't know why, but the pain was starting to subside. Mike Simmons sat there, choking on his own indecision and hating himself for the weakness. He only had a little while longer and then Dexter would be back. One way or the other, he had to commit to something. In this case, even no decision was a choice, a choice that could get him killed.

Finally, he decided and reached across with the knife, touching the blade on Aric's grossly swollen eyelid. He expected blood and fluid to squirt out as he moved it lightly across the skin, but instead, not a mark was made. Aric smiled knowingly.

"What the ..."

Mike couldn't finish the sentence. He was in shock, and Aric took the opportunity to recite the terms of his consecration that Joshua had given to him so long ago and to which he had remained loyal.

"God has chosen you, Aric. He has set you apart, consecrated you for his own holy purpose. And here are the terms of your consecration unto the Lord: you are forbidden to lay with a woman, neither shall a blade touch your skin; you shall do your best to honor all the words of the Lord as best you know them. You shall honor the terms of this consecration until your task is done."

"What the hell is going on here?"

Mike got up anxiously and paced back and forth as he pondered what to do next.

"It's the hand of God, Mike. He's real. He's chosen to protect me. I don't know why, but he has."

Mike stopped pacing long enough to turn on Aric and yell in his direction.

"That's absurd! You're just as bad a sinner as I am! You've killed people! You even slept with your own sister! There's no way God would protect you! No way!"

Aric hesitated a moment as Mike Simmons hovered close by, waiting for Aric's explanation, but he had none.

"I can't explain it, Mike. I don't know enough about it all. Until a few weeks ago, I was like you and I had no use for God."

Mike took a single step forward.

"Then why would God use you? Why? Why would he use you when there are so many other good people to choose from?"

Aric hung his head for a moment before answering, and, when he lifted his head back up, there was a calmness in his voice that hadn't been there before.

"It's not a statement about me, Mike. It's a statement about him. I think God loves me, Mike. I don't deserve it, but I think he does. It's the only way I can explain it."

Mike took another step forward and raised the knife up again. He was running out of time.

"I don't buy it, Aric. And I don't have the time to debate it with you right now."

He stepped forward, right up to Aric, and moved the knife closer to Aric's eyes.

"One way or another, Aric, I'm going to cut you, and you're going to bleed like you've never bled before."

The knife moved across his eyelid once more, but still, it didn't penetrate the skin. A frantic look of fear spread across Mike's face. He moved the knife again, trying desperately to draw blood but it was no use. Aric would not bleed.

"Give it up, Mike. You can't cut me. It's against the terms of my consecration. I have to be willing, and I'm not."

In a burst of rage, Mike screamed and lunged forward with the knife and drove it deep into Aric's chest. He stepped back and a triumphant look moved across his face, tenuous at first, but then more and more certain as he saw the hilt of the knife protruding from Aric's chest.

Aric looked down at the knife in his own chest and smiled as it slowly began to work its way out of his chest as if it were a transplant being rejected by his body.

"I'm sorry, Mike. It's not me. It's the hand of God, and there's nothing either of us can do about it."

Mike Simmons, *Floral Designer*, lost control and all reason. In a fit of fear and trepidation, he staggered backwards.

"No! No way! This isn't happening! I don't believe in this!"

Aric looked down at the knife, lying motionless on the dirty cement floor, then he looked back up at Mike.

"So what do you believe in, Mike? Do you believe in God? You must believe in him by now. Look at all the miracles he's shown you! Isn't it time for you to believe?"

Upon hearing Aric's voice, Mike's fear was replaced with anger and determination.

"I'll show you what I believe in. I believe in things that never let me down. This is what I believe. This is what I trust!"

Mike reached back with his right hand and placed it on the Glock semiautomatic pistol. He gripped it firmly and drew it from the holster. With one smooth motion, he pulled up the gun and aimed it directly at Aric's chest.

"I put faith in my Glock!"

Slowly, he eased his finger back on the trigger. Just then, the door knob rotated counter-clockwise.

• • •

Through tear-stained eyes, Calley turned her head and watched as Senator Devin Dexter walked into the room. His dark blue suit was spotless and perfectly pressed. He looked at her, smiled, and then locked the door from the inside, before calmly striding over to the bed.

Calley wiped the running mascara resolutely from beneath her eyes. She was a warrior, and she would fight one last time, to the death.

"Is my brother alive?"

Devin smiled and nodded slowly. He had taken extra pills this time in honor of the special occasion, and his loins were bursting forth with power and anticipation. This time, there would be no foreplay, just an angry, sexual rage, followed by her unwilling submission, a sweet release, and then peaceful sleep.

"He's alive for now, so long as you cooperate."

Calley turned her body defiantly to face him.

"Where's my daughter?"

Devin smiled the way he did when he knew he was in complete control, and he toyed with her like a cat playing with a mouse.

"Don't you mean *our* daughter?"

A sudden rage filled Calley to the breaking point, but she pushed it down, controlling herself, saving it all for the right time.

"I said, where is my daughter!"

Devin took a small step forward and slowly took off his suit coat. It was the best money could buy. He carefully folded it and placed it on the foot of the bed.

"She's back at the house. She's okay ... for now."

He then began removing his shirt, one button at a time.

"I want to see her."

Devin laughed softly to himself. She would never see her dear Clarissa again, that much was sure, but there was no sense in alarming her about it. It would only taint the experience. And this one, last time, he wanted it to be good, the best he'd ever had.

"Of course you can see her, just as soon as we're done with our little ... talk."

Calley forced a playful smile onto her lips. He was going to kill her, and then he would rape Clarissa, maybe not tomorrow or the next day, maybe not for many days, but, eventually, he would hurt her beyond repair just as he had wounded her. Calley thought to herself 'Over my dead body!'

Senator Dexter had his shirt off now, displaying the sagging chest muscles of an aging man who had lived life too hard and too fast. When Calley looked at him, she wondered how she had ever been afraid of him. Now all she felt was a determined and focused rage, but she channeled it into the business at hand. Suddenly, her voice became thick and sultry.

"Let's not waste time talking, daddy."

Calley took a step closer, and placed her fingers on the Senator's belt buckle, loosening the thin, leather belt, and then the snap, then watching as his trousers fell to the floor. Devin felt the cool air hit his bare legs, and he suddenly felt deliciously vulnerable.

"I was naughty at school today, daddy. I got in trouble on the play-ground again."

Devin grew as solid as granite. He wanted her more than ever, and he could barely contain himself.

"Am I going to have to spank you, Calley?"

Calley moved her face in closer until her lips touched his own, then they slowly traveled down Devin's chest to his waist, where they paused long enough for her hands to softly push the waistband of his boxers down to his ankles.

"Oh daddy! You're so big and strong!"

Calley found herself suddenly eye level with the objects of her pain and bondage, and, unless she did something to change it, they would become the future ruin of her daughter. They had brought her into the world, and they had also brought her daughter into being. It seemed a confusing paradox to her, that something so perverse and unnatural could bring forth the beauty and innocence of her daughter.

Calley moved forward, and Devin Dexter leaned his head back in satisfaction. Calley smiled, then quickly, with one violent thrust forward her jaws clamped down like a powerful vice and then she jerked her head backward as hard as possible, putting all her weight into it. Devin Dexter bellowed like a newly banded calf, and then fell to the carpet, writhing in pain.

Blood ran down Calley's chin as she stood to her feet and looked down on her father's squirming body. Calley wiped the blood from her chin and smiled with satisfaction.

"That was good for me, daddy. How was it for you?"

Just then, the door burst open and men with guns ran in and surrounded her. But Calley didn't care. Her daughter was now safe.

• • •

Mike Simmons pulled the trigger again and again, sending bullet after bullet into Aric's chest. A total of five bullets struck Aric's torso, sending up small geysers of blood, flesh and bone.

Suddenly, the door flew off its hinges and George Stollard rushed in followed closely by several men with MP5 submachine guns. George took aim, and, almost as if by script, Mike Simmons swung his gun around. The room erupted with gunfire and Mike Simmons, *Floral Designer*, fell backwards onto the dirty cement floor, plummeting headlong into an eternity of his own choosing.

George lowered his pistol and walked over to Aric who had slumped forward into the confines of his wooden chair.

"You okay, kid?"

But Aric said nothing. George saw the blood and yelled back over his shoulder.

"Get me an ambulance here, now!"

He rushed forward and gently leaned back Aric's head, and then placed his fingers on his throat. The pulse was weak and fading.

"Aric! We've got help on the way! Just hang in there!"

There was a gurgling sound and George saw Aric's lips moving, desperately trying to form words and force out air.

George moved his ear closer. The single word tried indomitably to come out of Aric's mouth one weak syllable at a time.

"Con ... se ... cra ..."

There was a final wheeze and then nothing, as Aric's heart stopped beating and the final breath of life exited his body.

"Aric! Look at me! Talk to me!"

But Aric's green eyes lost their brightness and dulled over like a window shade being closed at dusk. George dropped his pistol to the cement floor, buried his face into Aric's bloody chest and wept. He had failed.

Unseen to George, Caedlin, the powerful angel of light, reached down his hand and lifted Aric from the chair. Aric's earthly bonds dropped away like useless strands and were carried away by the unseen wind. Aric smiled. The blood was gone from his face and his chest, and his clothes were clean and bright and shiny. Caedlin returned his smile.

"Are you ready, young Aric?"

Aric looked down at his old, lifeless body, still bound to the chair, with George Stollard crying into his bloody chest, then quickly back up to the bright and shining angel who towered magnificently over his head.

"Is it over? Did I do it?"

Caedlin nodded as he spoke.

"Well done, thy good and faithful servant."

Aric beamed with joy, his new, green eyes brilliant in the angel's light. Aric took one last look at George.

"Will he be okay?"

Caedlin didn't answer.

"I need to know he'll be okay! He's my friend!"

Caedlin let out a smile and a sigh.

"Aric, it is with him, as it was with you. It's his choice. It is your father's way."

Aric looked up at him.

"My father?"

The angel nodded.

"Yes, are you ready to meet him? He's been waiting for you."

Aric reached down and touched his friend on the shoulder, just for a moment, and then Caedlin swept him away to meet his father.

49

Pastor Timm Sawyer walked slowly with a hunched back. Already, they had gone over one hundred miles and his body was falling apart. His feet hurt; his back hurt; his legs hurt. He was a mess. Regardless of all that, he smiled as he walked beside Joshua Moses Talbert. They had picked up people all along the way, just as he had planned, but the numbers were staggering. They didn't have an exact count, because every time they passed through another town, they picked up more people, but most news channels were estimating well over one thousand people and climbing. Not everyone stayed long term, some only tarried a few miles, but all of them sang along when God was praised. It was like a long, mobile worship service, and Timm couldn't remember when he'd had more fun. He only wished his wife could be here with him. Joshua looked down at him as they walked.

"What's troubling you, my friend?"

Timm laughed out loud.

"Don't you ever tire of knowing what people are thinking?"

Joshua shared his smile.

"I'm not omniscient. I can just see the look on your face. What are you thinking about?"

The first ten miles or so, Timm had been intimidated by Joshua's presence, but then they had started talking, like two old men with a lifetime in common. Now, they felt like old friends.

"I was thinking about Ruth, just wondering what she was doing right now."

Joshua piped in quickly.

"Would you like me to tell you?"

Surprised, Timm looked over and his steps slowed.

"You can do that too?"

The old prophet laughed.

"No. I was just messing with you."

Timm shook his head from side to side.

"You certainly don't act like a prophet."

"And just how should a prophet act?"

Timm ran his left hand through his white hair and then wiped the sweat off onto his pants.

"I don't know. I guess I was expecting a lot of thee's and thou's, you know. King James Version talk. And it's been thirty miles and you still haven't parted any large bodies of water."

Joshua put his hand on Timm's shoulder.

"Doesn't it make more sense to just use the bridges?"

"Well, yeah. I guess. It would be more fun though if you could whip up a miracle or two."

Joshua smiled, showing his yellowed teeth through his grey beard.

"Well, I'm sorry, Timm. I'm just a man though. God does the magic, not me, and he pretty much does it on his own whim. God's like that you know. He's got a mind all his own."

Timm saw he was lagging and picked up his pace again.

"Yeah, I know. God's always been that way. He never listens to me. He just keeps on doing whatever he wants. At least he's predictable."

People in back of the crowd began to sing again and it started to filter its way up to the front.

"Oh, I don't know, Timm. He's not all that predictable. I never expected to be bulletproof."

Timm laughed.

"You got me on that one, Joshua. I suppose I never expected I'd be leading a thousand people to the promised land at age 73 either."

They were silent for a minute, just listening to the singing, and then Joshua spoke again.

"All I ever wanted to do was farm. All I ever wanted was to live out my life in peace with Sara at my side. Funny how things change."

Timm looked over sympathetically. He understood his friend's pain. He would be devastated if Ruth were to die. He relied on her for so many things.

"Yeah, well, I'm sorry about that, Joshua. When Ruth and I die, I hope we both go together."

Joshua smiled softly.

"You will, Timm, you will. But not for a while yet."

Timm looked over, searching the prophet's turquoise-green eyes, wondering if he was serious. He concluded that he was.

"So what about you, Joshua? When are you going to die?"

"Well, no man knows the time, but, I suspect, soon. Very soon. I'm almost done here, and, I'm eager. I miss her."

Timm nodded his head. He understood, and there was no need for more words. As they walked, the singing got louder, so Timm joined in. His voice wasn't good, but it blended in okay.

"Then sings my soul, my savior, God, to thee. How great thou art. How great thou art."

Timm liked the old hymns best. He could tolerate the newer ones, but they just didn't move him like the old words. He looked over at Joshua and paused for a moment.

"How come you never sing with us, Joshua?"

A smile came to the large, barrel-chested prophet before he answered.

"Because I don't know the words."

Timm's jaw dropped open. He was dumbfounded.

"What? You're kidding me! This has got to be one of the most famous hymns of all time! How can you not know the words?"

Joshua's face tightened and a few of his wrinkles went away for a time.

"Because I never went to church."

Timm accepted the answer in silence.

"Sara wanted me to, but, I was just never interested. She always read the Bible to me though, so I know that pretty good. She would sing sometimes too, but mostly while I was out in the field working, so I seldom heard it."

Joshua's eyes grew moist.

"She's the person that God should have chosen for all this, Timm. She was worthy. I'm just an old farmer who can barely turn a straight furrow anymore."

Joshua grew silent again, but Timm eventually added some words of encouragement.

"Oh, I don't know. I think you're doing okay – for a beginner."

Joshua looked over at him and laughed softly. Then Timm finished.

"I suppose God pretty much chooses who he wants, and he has a long history of choosing the ones that you and I wouldn't. In God's eyes, the most qualified is usually the one who is willing, breathing, and pumping blood."

Both of them laughed together and joined back in the singing. Joshua's deep, throaty voice started out soft, but then grew to a crescendo as he learned the lyrics. Soon, he was bellowing out as loud as he could. All the while, the television cameras recorded it all and broadcasted it around the country. With each passing minute, their numbers increased.

50

George Stollard looked through the one-way glass into the FBI interrogation room at Calley, who was still dressed in black lingerie, huddling in the cool air of the room. He turned his head and spoke brusquely to the agent nearest him.

"Why hasn't she been given any clothes?"

The agent looked a bit flustered.

"I'm sorry, Agent Stollard. It's just not a priority with us here at bureau. We were waiting for you to get here first, since we knew you'd want to question her."

George shook his head in disgust. She'd been through enough already. She shouldn't be treated this way.

"How long has she been in there like that?"

The FBI agent looked down at his watch.

"About three hours now, sir."

George turned and wanted to lash out at the younger agent, but he held his tongue in check. He knew he was emotional right now, and he didn't like the out-of-control feeling. Aric had died, because he'd been a mere five seconds too late. George walked over to the door and entered. Calley looked up at him, stopping George in her tracks. She was amazingly beautiful from close up. He walked up to her and stopped.

"Please forgive me, Miss Ramirez."

Calley looked up at him with questioning eyes.

"Miss Ramirez?"

George took off his jacket and draped it over her shoulders. She grabbed onto it and pulled it down over her, covering as much of herself as possible.

"Yes, that's your real name. Didn't you know that?"

George moved to the side and sat down in the chair next to her. Calley shook her head.

"No. I don't even know who my mother was. I think she died at my birth."

"Actually, Miss Ramirez, that's not true. But I'll tell you all about that a little later."

Calley reached up with her left hand and tried to wipe the tears and mascara from her face. George pulled out his handkerchief, dabbed it in the water glass in front of him and handed it to her. She smiled slightly, and George returned the look.

"Thank you, sir."

"Please call me George. I'm not with the FBI, but I'm heading up this investigation by order of Vice President Thatcher. I'm with the Secret Service. We would like your cooperation by telling us all you know about Senator Dexter. In return, you and your daughter will be given safe haven and new lives, should you choose them."

Calley nodded her head and began to wipe some of the blood and mascara from her face.

"Can I see my daughter now?"

George thought for a moment. Standard procedure advised against it, but George needed her cooperation if he was going to successfully put away the Senator. Besides, this woman had been through enough already.

George looked up and motioned to the mirror.

"Bring in the little girl, please."

A minute later, a female agent walked in carrying Clarissa. Calley jumped up and ran to her, cradling the one-year-old baby in her arms, crying openly and hugging her daughter. The baby looked up at her mother and smiled, moving her hand up to Calley's face and playing with her lips as if they were toys. Calley bit down lightly on Clarissa's tiny fingers, all the while making little baby noises. Clarissa laughed out loud, cooing with delight at seeing her mother again.

George looked on, pleased with himself. At least he had saved the mother and her daughter. He pulled a pen and paper out of his shirt pocket and laid it on the table.

"Miss Ramirez, if you could just write down your sizes, I'll run out and buy you some decent clothes. They may not be fashionable though, but you'll be comfortable."

Calley looked up from her daughter and smiled at George. She liked this man. He was a gentleman. He was different than the others. She bent down over the table and quickly wrote down her sizes as best she could while holding Clarissa.

"Thank you George. I appreciate it. Do you think I could clean up a bit first though?"

George nodded his compliance.

"Sure thing, ma am."

Then he turned to the female agent and gave directions.

"Agent Turner, please take Miss Ramirez to a shower so she can get cleaned up. I'll send the clothes over to you as quickly as I can."

Agent Turner nodded and put her hand on Calley's shoulder and started to lead her to the door. Calley stopped and turned back.

"George?"

"Yes ma am."

Calley's eyes lowered as she spoke.

"Is Aric okay?"

George didn't want to answer her. He was still filled with shame at his failure as well as sadness at his loss. He liked Aric. He took a step forward and placed his hand lightly on her back.

"I'm sorry, Calley. We didn't get there in time."

Calley leaned her head forward and cried into George's shoulder, while Clarissa laughed out loud and grabbed onto George's shirt. The emotions bombarded George, making him feel clumsy and out of place, but he stood there stoically, allowing her to cry. After a minute of tears Calley stopped weeping and looked up into George's face defiantly.

"As soon as you get back with those clothes, I'll tell you everything. I'll tell you enough to put the honorable Senator Devin Dexter in prison for the rest of his life!"

Then Calley turned and walked away with her daughter. George looked after her and smiled softly. She was a strong woman, and he liked her attitude.

51

After the President left Joshua in Detroit, he walked south until reaching Ohio. He saw a few people along the way, and was surprised at the extent of their poverty. All along he had known of the living conditions of those close to the contaminated zones, but he'd never seen it firsthand. Before, it had always been confined to the sterility of a newspaper or his daily briefing. But now, out here, in the real America, everything took on such a different face. It had been so long since Dan had been a normal person that he'd forgotten about the daily struggles most people have to persevere. To him, people had just become numbers, or votes, or problems to deal with in the course of his job as President.

But now, he saw the people through different eyes, new eyes, and it moved him and he cried at the outskirts of a deserted little town near the border of Michigan and Ohio. They were living in squalor, eating food not fit for pigs; their hair was dirty and matted, and they stunk from lack of running water with which to bathe.

One particular little girl had affected him the most. She had been sitting on a street corner, clutching a dirty rag doll to her breast, clinging to it as if it were the only hope in a desolate world of pain and suffering. Dan had stopped beside her, his new clothes now covered in dust and sweat.

He had tried to smile, but couldn't.

"Hello little girl."

She looked up at him sadly and responded in a timid voice.

"Hello."

"What are you doing?"

She clutched the doll tighter.

"Waiting."

Dan's interest had piqued.

"Waiting for what?"

She shook her head from side to side.

"I don't know."

Dan had stopped right there and sat down on the pavement beside her. He reached over to her.

"May I hold you? Just for a minute?"

The little girl hesitated, and then walked over to him. She couldn't have been more than 7 years old. Without a word, she'd plopped down in his lap, dropped the doll, and wrapped her arms tightly around his neck. That had been 3 days ago and she was still with him. It was tough going, because he had to carry her most of the way, but it was worth it to him. She was too precious to leave behind. Besides, her parents had died, and she would soon follow them if left on her own.

Finally, Dan had reached a town big enough and far enough away from the contaminated zone to have electricity and running water. It was a borderland, and the people were suspicious of him, but still treated him with courtesy. He didn't dare tell them who he was, and, since he had no driver's license with him he couldn't prove his identity even if he'd wanted to.

No one recognized him until an old white-haired lady who lived alone and felt sorry for the little girl agreed to put them both up for the night. Dan had just shaved his beard and taken his first bath in over a month before sitting down at the table for dinner. It was good to feel clean again. As soon as he sat down, the woman looked at him suspiciously. Dan made eye contact with her and smiled.

"Do you recognize me now?"

The old woman nodded humbly.

"Yes, I think I do. You look just like the President of the United States. I've seen you on television many times. You look shorter in person though."

Dan laughed out loud, and the little girl smiled when she saw him happy. Her name was Missy, and that's the day she began to talk to him openly and with substance. And once she started, there was no shutting her up.

The old woman had told Dan that there was a telephone in the next town south, and then she'd given him a good night's sleep in a clean bed and sent him off with enough food for a day. Dan had thanked her and promised to return and repay her kindness. All she'd said was "Just get back to Omaha and put the country back together again." The next morning, they both walked to the next town. Dan was recognized there as well and given access to anything he wanted. He used the phone, but no one answered so he had to leave a message.

When he left, a small boy walked up dragging a big, red wagon. He gave the handle to Dan.

"Thank you Mr. President. Always remember that Jesus loves you."

Dan bent down and hugged the little boy. Then he gently lifted Missy into the wagon and walked out of town. It was a hot, summer day, but the wagon made it easier.

52

Joseph Clemons moved his wheelchair a little closer to the work bench so he could reach things. After he'd gotten over the shock of accepting a contract for ten million dollars, the enormity of his task began to set in, and he started asking himself, 'how am I going to kill him?' First of all, the President was still missing, so, unless he turned up again, he wouldn't be able to kill him to collect on his money. But the platinum-haired man had assured him that the President would resurface, and that when he did, the job was to be done immediately, before Secret Service Protection could be reconvened. After that, it would be nearly impossible to fulfill the contract.

So Joseph had been preparing diligently, getting everything in place so that he could move with lightning speed once the President was spotted. The last assassin had used a high-powered rifle and had failed, so Joseph decided to go with an explosive device, triggered remotely to ensure he got away. Due to his disability, Joseph wasn't like most hired killers, but rather than see it as a liability, Joseph preferred to accentuate the positive. Quite frankly, no one ever suspected him capable of killing a head of state, and that worked to his advantage. Many an unsuspecting victim had made his job easier by underestimating him or by feeling sorry for him. Sympathy and political correctness were both tools that Joseph Clemons used every chance he got.

Joseph had learned all about explosives in the military when he'd worked for 10 years in the Army as an Explosive Ordinance Disposal (EOD) Specialist before losing his legs in a blast. He still remembered the recruiter talking to him about camaraderie, espirit de corps, teamwork, and pride, but, in reality, Joseph just wanted to learn how to blow things up. In the end, he had learned all he'd wanted to and more. After leaving the Army, he had hooked up with a former buddy who had been working for the CIA as a contractor. He recruited Joseph to do a few odd jobs, which just happened to include killing several people of unsavory character, and he had enjoyed it immensely. Since then, he'd been working free lance, and making excellent money. The fact that people died was of no consequence to him, provided he was the one who lived and earned the money. The way he figured, someone had to die and someone had to live; it's best to be on the right side of that deal. So, oddly enough, Joseph Clemons made a living at killing, and he was very good at his job.

For this particular contract, he would use high-grade military C4, a lot of it, and a remote electronic detonator. He looked at the cell phone on the table in front of him and sighed, and then he picked up the screw driver and began to disassemble it. He'd done this so many times that he could do it with his eyes closed, but, for ten million bucks, he'd keep his eyes open just to make sure.

The television was playing next to him. He picked up the remote and switched from CNN to Fox news. Joseph tried to monitor all the news stations as much as possible just to make sure he got to the President before the Secret Service. He even had a private pilot on standby just to ensure he got there in time to set up. This was the chance of a lifetime, and he wasn't about to screw it up. If he made good on this, he could retire and live a life of luxury anywhere he pleased, assuming it was outside the United States.

Fox news was showing a live report from Solon, Iowa, where thousands had joined the Freedom March to Omaha. The people were singing songs and raising their hands in the air as they walked. Joseph thought it was stupid. Why walk when you could ride? He was suddenly reminded of his favorite Cat Stevens song:

"And if I ever lose my legs

I won't moan and I won't beg

oh if I ever lose my legs

I won't have to walk no more"

Just then, the female announcer interrupted the report with breaking news.

"We now have unconfirmed reports that the President of the United States, President Daniel Vermeulen, has been seen in the town of Randolph, Illinois, which is just south of Bloomington off I74. We repeat, there are now unconfirmed reports that President Vermeulen has been spotted in the town of Randolph, Illinois. We go to you now live to Randolph, with a special report from Amy Dekline at our Fox News affiliate TV 7 news."

The picture cut away from the studio feed on out to the live report in Randolph. The announcer was a slender, twenty-something brunette wearing a dark blue pant suit. When she spoke, she could barely contain herself.

"Thank you Kara. I'm here with a Mrs. Barbara Ramsey who tells Fox News that she has seen the missing President not more than two hours ago. Not only that, she claims to have video footage of the event."

Amy then turned to her left and the picture panned out to include a large, dark-haired woman wearing a very big smile.

"Ms. Ramsey, please tell us now in your own words exactly what you saw."

She moved the microphone over and Barbara Ramsey grabbed it out of her hand.

"Well first off, Amy, I said it's Mrs. Ramsey, not Ms. Ramsey. I'm a married woman you know."

She looked over at the announcer, who had to lean over to speak into the microphone.

"That's nice Mrs. Ramsey. Will you please tell us what you saw?"

"You bet I will. Well, you see I was coming out of the Wal-Mart right over there and up walks this guy in bib overalls with the cutest little girl you ever did see. He was pulling her in a wagon if you can believe that. Now that's not something that you see everyday. He smiled at me just like he was on the campaign trail, only it looked like a real smile. And then he just walked right in. So I ran out to my car to get my camera, and when he came back out a few minutes later, I videotaped him and I have it right here. Only I want ten thousand dollars before I show it to you."

Amy Dekline then reached over and pried the microphone from Mrs. Ramsey's hands, who seemed reluctant to give it up. Once she had the microphone back, the camera zoomed in on her.

"Thank you Mrs. Ramsey. We appreciate that eyewitness account as well as your generous offer. Back to you now Kara."

The screen split now, showing both announcers.

"Thank you Amy. Does anyone there appear to know where the President was going and what he was doing there?"

"No Kara, at least not yet. We're still in the process of interviewing employees and we expect to have more in a few minutes, along with some security footage that Wal-Mart has generously allowed us to use."

"Can we roll that footage now, Amy?"

"I think so, Kara. Jon, do we have that ready yet? No? I'm sorry, Kara, but it will take a few more minutes to get that for you."

Joseph set down his screwdriver and put his hand on his chin thoughtfully. Then he rolled to the living room where his cell phone was lying on the coffee table and dialed the number of his private pilot to make arrangements. It wouldn't be long now but he would have to hurry.

53

At a gas station, somewhere near Des Moines, Timm Sawyer first noticed that Joshua was gone. It wasn't unusual for the old prophet to take off at night and go off to sleep alone, but he'd always returned at dawn, ready to make the day's trek with the others. That had been yesterday, and Timm was surprised at how much he now missed his traveling companion. Sure, there were other people, thousands of them, but none of them made him feel safe or encouraged him the way Joshua did. It was odd, but while Joshua was beside him, he didn't seem to feel so tired, so sore, and so hot and dirty. The absence of his new friend made him miss his wife all the more. According to the road sign they'd just passed, they were still 130 miles away from Omaha, but Pastor Timm Sawyer was already anxious to return home. Sure, he put on a happy face for the crowd, but right now he wanted nothing more than to sit down in his recliner and watch sitcoms while his wife knitted. His old body was tired and sore to the breaking point.

It seemed odd to him, he knew that he was making history, that he was living right through it, and that times like these would probably never happen again, nonetheless, Timm wanted to go home. He was just too tired, and the pain was becoming more than his Ibuprofen could bear.

And then the singing stopped and a strange hush came over the crowd. A man from a quarter mile back, listening to a portable radio suddenly yelled out, 'They're saying the President is alive! They've found the President!'

Upon hearing the news, a surge something like adrenaline coursed through Timm's veins and gave him the boost he needed to continue on. He liked President Vermeulen, and had been encouraged by his speeches right before the disappearance. He wondered now, as he trudged on toward the nation's capitol. What would Dan Vermeulen do? Would he hold true? The answer scared him to the core of his being. He couldn't help but think 'This could be very good, or it could be very, very bad!'

• • •

President Vermeulen and the blonde-haired little girl, Missy, sat at the booth in the Flying J truckstop near Davenport, Iowa just off I80. A truck driver named Zeke Bettendorf had given them a ride from Randolph to here, but now he had to drop off his load and head on back home. Dan had thanked him and graciously accepted the hundred dollar loan he offered. That would be enough to get them back to the White House. Dan had never hitch hiked before, indeed, had never even ridden in an 18-wheeler, but he was finding it to be a good time, and he was in no hurry to make it back to politics. Besides that, something more important was happening: he was finally discovering what America was all about, who the real, everyday Americans were and how they lived, what they thought, and how they felt about a good many things. The little girl was loving it too.

Zeke had helped him out in a lot of ways. Using his CB radio, and at Dan's request, he had spread disinformation as to Dan's whereabouts.

After hearing the news reports about the giant manhunt that the FBI and Secret Service were conducting, Dan had elected to come back in to Omaha on his own terms and under his own power. He had gotten rid of the bib overalls and was now wearing plain blue jeans, a t-shirt, a camouflaged baseball hat, and a pair of sunglasses that he'd bought cheap at the local Goodwill Store. Missy was dressed in similar fashion and they'd given the red wagon to Zeke, who also had a little girl. Now, so long as they remained inconspicuous and low key, they could pretty much travel as they pleased without being rescued by the police.

"Can I have one of your French fries, Mr. President?"

Dan, who was lost in thought, looked down at Missy and smiled.

"Of course you can, honey. But why are you all of a sudden calling me Mr. President?"

The little blonde girl looked up at him with her pretty, blue eyes and smiled as she answered.

"Cuz that's what you are. That's what Zeke said."

Dan looked up at the television above their booth. They were showing a recent interview with Pastor Timm Sawyer again, who had just left Des Moines on his way to Omaha.

"Yes, I know honey. But I don't want anyone to know that right now."

"How come?"

Dan looked back down at her, envying her innocence.

"Because there are some people back at my house that I want to surprise. Besides, people treat me differently when they know who I am. I want people to talk to me like they would anyone else, like you and I do."

"Oh."

She took a fry off Dan's plate and dabbed it into some ketchup. Dan's eyes misted over and he struggled to fight back the tears. He didn't notice her looking at him again.

"Why do you cry so much?"

Dan wiped dry his eyes and tried to smile.

"I'm sorry, Missy. It's just that you remind me of someone that I once loved."

"Was she a little girl?"

Dan nodded.

"Yes, she was a beautiful little girl just like you. She was my daughter. I had a son and a wife too."

Missy set the half-eaten French fry down on the plate before looking up.

"What happened to them?"

Dan shifted uncomfortably in his chair before answering.

"They all died honey."

The little girl moved closer to him on the booth seat.

"That's what happened to my mommy. She got real sick. It was a real bad cold. She went to sleep and went to heaven. I'm sposed to meet her there later on. I don't remember my daddy."

Dan looked down at her and placed his hand on top of her blonde head.

"Well, honey, I'm meeting my family in heaven too."

Suddenly, the little girl's blue eyes lit up.

"Hey. I got an idea! Let's go to heaven together!"

Dan smiled and gave her a big hug.

"Good idea sweetheart. But until then, you can come and live with me."

She looked at him with eyes open wide.

"You mean in the big, white house?"

Dan nodded and she smiled.

"I would like that."

Just then, a large, burly man walked up to their booth and stopped. He wore a Miller Light baseball cap with a blue flannel shirt and dirty jeans with holes at the knees. He didn't say anything at first, he just stared, first at Dan and then at Missy.

"I'm hauling a load of canned goods to Omaha and Zeke says you both could use a lift. Am I right?"

Dan stood up and slid out of the booth.

"Name's Dan, and this here is Missy. We could use a ride and we'd be much obliged."

The older man nodded and reached out to shake Dan's hand.

"My name's Tyler, from Wisconsin, and I know who you are, sir."

And then as an afterthought he added.

"I didn't vote for you, but I'll sure as hell give you a ride!"

Dan smiled and picked up Missy before following. On the way out, he stopped and dropped a twenty-dollar bill with the cashier. She gave it back to him.

"It's already been paid for sir. Have a safe trip. And God bless."

Dan hesitated and then took off his sunglasses so he could make eye contact with her. The middle-aged woman smiled at him and nodded her recognition. Dan and Missy walked out to the parking lot, rushing to catch up with Tyler who was already stepping up into his rig.

. . .

"With all due respect, Mr. President, I think it's a bunch of horse manure!"

"Really?"

Dan looked over at the brazen truck driver. Tyler was a very blunt man, and Dan found his candor to be refreshing.

"So what do you think about the government in general?"

"I think they suck! The whole bunch of them!"

Then he looked over at Dan for just a second.

"Well, present company excepted of course. You seem like a good enough egg to me. And that kind of confuses me."

"How so?"

"Well, I already told you I didn't vote for you so that's no surprise, but I just don't understand how you could do it."

Dan looked confused.

"I don't understand either. Do what? What are you talking about?"

Zeke's face grew stern and he gripped his hands tighter on the wheel as if he was trying to strangle the life out of it.

"You sold out, Dan. You sold all of us down the river! I mean don't get me wrong. It was great the way you protected us from those crazy terrorists, but once we re-elected you, you lost yer nerve."

At first Dan was angry. He wanted to lash out and try to explain to Tyler how much pressure was on him, all the lobbyists, his enemies across the aisle, not to mention the threats from overseas, but, in the end, he realized that all his excuses were nothing but hot air. Instead, he thought about it for a moment and actually listened to what his new friend was telling him. Tyler was speaking the truth. He wasn't eloquent, but it was the truth. In his first term as President, he had felt more in touch with the people, more accountable to them, like he was their servant, but then, after being re-elected, he'd found it easier to compromise, to give in, to go along with people he normally wouldn't even ask over for dinner. No, Tyler was right, and he couldn't blame him for thinking this way. He turned in the big captain's chair and looked at Missy lying on the bunk behind him. Thank God she wasn't awake to hear Tyler's rough talk. Then he looked back over to the burly truck driver.

"Yeah. I know you're right."

Tyler let up on the accelerator a little bit in surprise.

"Really?"

Dan nodded.

"Yes. You're right. Every word you said is true, and I won't make excuses for myself."

Tyler took off his Miller Light cap and wiped his brow, then placed it back onto his balding head.

"Okay. So what are you going to do about it, Mr. President?"

Dan thought about it a moment. He looked out the window at the cornfields, already over head high in mid July, and when he spoke it was with a newfound determination that Tyler didn't recognize, but that he respected instinctively.

"Do other truckers feel the way you do?"

"Well, yeah, most of us. You gotta understand that most truck drivers just wanna haul their loads and go home for a few days with their families. We don't like politics, and the government just seems to get in our way when we're trying to do our jobs. The government is like salt. You put a little on your food and it tastes better, but, put on too much, and it tastes terrible!"

Dan laughed out loud for the first time since they'd left the Flying J. He thought for a moment, and then an incredible idea came to him.

"Say, Tyler, do you mind if I use your CB radio?"

Tyler looked down at the microphone and then back over at Dan.

"Well, no, I guess not. Have at it, Mr. President."

Dan picked up the microphone and thought a moment without keying the transmitter. There were so many things that he wanted to say. He whispered a prayer and suddenly wondered what Joshua was up to. Dan looked down into his lap and fingered the worn, black leather of the Bible that Joshua had given him. Lately, he'd been reading it a lot. He missed the old prophet and wondered if he would ever see him again on this earth. Then he keyed the mike and started blabbing away, pouring out his heart and soul to the heart of America.

Dumbfounded but happy, Tyler just sat back and smiled, roaring down the highway at 10 miles over the limit, daring Smokey to pull him over.

• • •

When Joshua left Timm in Des Moines, he did so with a heavy heart. He would miss the companionship of the old pastor. They both seemed to have a lot in common. Joshua was still in Iowa, just east of Omaha, standing in the corn, which reached up over his head, towering toward the sky. The wind blew and tickled the broad, green leaves against his burlap robe, and the rustling sound of it had a calming effect on him. He sat down now in the dirt and the corn leaves rose up around him, blocking out the landscape, leaving nothing but a sea of green. He placed his head in his hands and wept out loud.

"Dear God. Please. I don't want to do it! I don't know if I can do it. It seems so hard to me. It's more than you should ask."

He looked up past the green leaves toward the blue sky and raised his open palms toward the heavens.

"Haven't I done enough already?"

But he knew the answer before asking it.

"Sara, talk to him, please. You know him better than I do. I want to see you again, but not this way. There must be something better."

But there was no answer except the steady rustling of corn and the smell of green leaves and black dirt. Joshua dropped his hands down into the ground and scooped up big handfuls of soil. He poured the dirt over his head and watched as it dropped down past his eyes and onto the burlap robe. He missed plowing the dirt. He missed his tiny field back in Michigan. If he'd stayed there, his beans would be almost in blossom

308

by now. All he'd ever wanted in life was to love his woman and plow a straight furrow. He didn't want to do great things. He didn't want to lead. He just wanted to go home.

Suddenly, his shoulders became heavy, and he lay down on his back and stared up through the forest of green and out into the blue sky. He felt a bug crawling in his hair, but made no move to stop it. Eventually, he closed his eyes and he went to sleep, waiting for the day.

54

Vicki Valence sat in her apartment staring at the dark television screen. She was exhausted. Vice President Thatcher had been relying on her heavily, primarily because she knew more about being President than he did. But now, after three days away from home, she was back for a short break and a few hours sleep.

She was starting to hate Dan Vermeulen. All this time he'd been alive and didn't call her. He just kept letting her worry about him. Didn't he care enough about her even to call? Inside she cursed her own weakness.

Everything else was falling into place: Calley was under protective custody with her daughter, and Senator Dexter had been charged by the Justice Department with a list of crimes so long that they were almost impossible to enumerate. No doubt he would go to prison for the rest of his life. George Stollard was still trying to track down Dan, and he'd promised to notify her as soon as they knew his whereabouts. She was worried sick, and she hated worrying about any man!

She thought about Aric, who had died in the rescue. She hardly knew the boy except for their brief time together at George's house. He had seemed like such a quiet, tortured soul. She only hoped that he had found some respite from his pain and wondered where he was, if he was with God, and if he was happy now.

Her ears perked up. There was that beeping noise again. It was coming from somewhere in the room. She walked over to the wall and turned off the air conditioner so she could hear better. That beeping noise was driving her crazy. She heard it again; just two, short, high-pitched beeps. And then it occurred to her. It was her cell phone. The batteries must be low. She walked over closer to the couch and listened again.

Her cell phone had been missing for days now, and though she'd torn the place apart looking for it, she hadn't been able to find it. The beeps came again and she moved over closer to the couch. She got down on her knees and looked underneath it, but found nothing except a dirty pair of socks.

"You little bugger! Where are you?"

Two more beeps. She must be close. She walked around the couch, even tipped it over. Then she heard the beeps again and ripped off the black, leather-covered cushions. And there it was, her tiny, little cell phone, still blinking green, but almost out of electricity.

She picked it up and took it over to the charger and plugged it in. Then, with the help of the added electricity, it rang, notifying her she had messages. She scanned through her messages and her heart almost stopped when she heard Dan's voice.

"Hi Vicki. This is Dan. You know, I'm the guy you call, Mr. President, when you're angry. I just wanted to let you know that I'm okay and that you shouldn't worry about me. I'll be coming back soon, but I still have things I need to do out here in the heartland. I know you'll understand. Please prepare a briefing for me of everything that has taken place while I was gone. And please don't tell anyone else about this call, at least not yet. We'll just leave it between you and me."

There was a brief pause before he continued.

"Well, I guess that's about it, except to say ... I miss you Vicki. I'll catch up with you as soon as I can."

And then the message ended. With a smile on her face and tears in her eyes, Vicki replayed it again, and again, and again, for a total of seven times before she saved it to memory. He missed her, and he had called her, only her. Dan Vermeulen was a wonderful man, and she loved him with all her heart.

55

Joseph Clemons rolled on down the sidewalk, dragging his t-shirt cart behind him. He had already sold twenty-three shirts this morning, most of them blue and gold with the words 'Freedom March for Jesus' emblazoned on the front and back. Despite the fact that he was about to make ten million dollars by killing the President of the United States, he gained perverse satisfaction from the idea of making one hundred percent profit on every shirt he sold. It wasn't his fault. This was America, and he was a dedicated capitalist. He would charge whatever the market would bear.

"T-shirts, get your T-shirts, one hundred percent, pre-shrunk cotton. Get your T-shirts now, guaranteed not to fade or your money back."

Joseph realized that most people bought the shirts from him because they felt sorry for him. He wasn't stupid. They thought he was crippled. He could see the pity in their eyes, but if they only knew the truth. Right now, just a few feet behind him in his cart, beneath all his shirts and safe inside a secret compartment, was a shaped charge containing twenty-five pounds of high-grade military explosives. It was more than enough to do the job. In fact, he would probably kill a hundred or so bystanders, but, he didn't care. It all paid the same. Once you've murdered one person, the rest is cake. It didn't matter to him. It was just business.

The earbud connected to his radio told him that the procession was moving closer. Oddly enough, the news was reporting how unusual it was for the President not to have his full security detail with him. Apparently there just hadn't been enough time to arrange it. Normally, this plan of Joseph's would be out of the question, since the Secret Service would have planned the route, then lined it with law enforcement and bomb-sniffing dogs. On top of that, they could change the route without notice, thereby foiling his plans altogether. Oh well, no skin off his back. The President would pay for his overconfidence and lack of vigilance, and, in the process, Joseph would become ten million dollars richer.

Joseph continued down the sidewalk until he came to the base of the concrete wall off to his right. It was only 4 feet tall and ten inches thick, at the base, and it sloped upward and away from him until it connected to the overpass further down the road. The concrete was definitely solid enough to give the explosion something to push against, thereby extending the power and range of the blast. He rolled to a stop on the sidewalk beside the four-foot high cement wall, and then he reached behind him to unhook the cart from his wheelchair. He would need to move out fast when the time came. The leather gloves he wore made his hands sweaty in the hot summer sun, but he needed them to protect his hands and also to deny forensics a good set of prints, although he doubted there would be much left for forensics to examine. He smiled to himself. Oh yes, he was good, real good, and he was already counting the money, unaware of the fact that the man who'd hired him was rotting in the morgue, and that his employer was already destitute behind bars.

Joseph turned his head and looked across the road. There was a man watching him, so he pretended to look away, all the while getting a good peek out of the corner of his vision. It was probably nothing, but he would keep an eye on him just the same. Vigilance and paranoia were second nature to a man in his business. He noted that the man was big and burly, and he wore faded blue jeans with a short-sleeved rugby sheet, and a black baseball cap pulled down low over his eyes. The man turned away and Joseph relaxed his guard for the moment.

It wouldn't be long now. It wouldn't be long at all.

• • •

Despite using spy satellites, advanced facial recognition systems, many thousands of law enforcement personnel across the country, billions of dollars worth of top secret equipment, the NSA, the CIA, the Secret Service, and the FBI, George Stollard still had no idea where Dan Vermeulen was … until … he saw him join the Freedom March on Fox News.

"Hey, can't you make this piece of junk fly any faster than this?"

The pilot glanced back at him and smiled. The multi-million-dollar aircraft they were in was a fully upgraded Black Hawk with special modifications available only to Special Operations Groups. Except for Marine One, it was the fastest and most expensive Black Hawk ever produced.

"What's the matter, George, isn't over 300 kilometers per hour fast enough for you? Keep your pants on. We should be there in 10 minutes."

George settled in and finally buckled his seat belt. He'd already notified the Omaha police of Dan's whereabouts and asked them to provide security until he arrived on site. He looked over to his right at the other choppers in his formation. He saw four Apache gunships, plus two other Black Hawk copters, carrying the twenty Secret Service Agents that would set up makeshift security for the President. Just to make sure, overhead, four F-15 Eagles flew Combat Air Patrol.

His twenty men carried the usual myriad of light arms: MP5 submachine guns, high-powered sniper rifles, semiautomatic pistols, and grenade launchers. Heavier equipment like Stinger anti-aircraft missiles and heavy machine guns would be arriving in SUVs with more agents and heavy body armor about ten minutes after him, assuming the traffic could be cleared in time. With the Freedom March bringing in over two million people from all across the country, the city was packed to overflowing, and George Stollard was as nervous as he'd ever been.

The pilot turned and yelled to George.

"Hey, George, look to port!"

George turned and looked down at the city streets below. Traffic was jammed with hundreds of 18-wheeled trucks, all moving slowly in the direction of the War on Terror Memorial.

"I've never seen so many semi trucks in one place before."

George shook his head in disgust, as his active paranoia worked overtime, imagining a nuclear bomb in every single semitrailer. This was going to make his job a lot tougher.

"How much longer, Larry?"

"Relax, George. We'll make it. About seven more minutes till we set down on the roof."

George felt his cell phone vibrate inside his shirt pocket and answered it, happy to have something to do. It was John Palance from the FBI, notifying him that the Hostage Rescue Team was on standby and at his disposal should he need them. George thanked him and quickly hung up. Then he got another call from the National Park Service. They had tripled security around the monument and were beginning to screen the crowd, looking for anything suspicious. George was beginning to feel a little better when his phone rang yet again. It was his boss, back at the White House. The Omaha Police Department was now with the President and had tried to take him into protective custody, per his direction, but the President had refused to go with them. In response, they had surrounded him with officers and were escorting him to the monument where he would give his speech.

George smiled and hung up. Nothing Dan Vermeulen ever did would again surprise him. He'd protected three administrations over his career, but none had been tougher than Dan Vermeulen. Keeping up with this guy was like trying to catch a greased pig. At least the police were there now and he had some measure of protection. Then, as if remembering something very important, he opened his cell phone and punched in another number.

"Yeah, Dave, make sure the Omaha police have their bomb sniffers on the scene. I want them to clear a path all the way to the monument. Got it?"

George closed his cell phone again and leaned back.

"How much longer, Larry?"

Larry turned back and shook his head in disgust.

"Good gracious, George! You're worse than my kids! We'll be there in 4 minutes."

George nodded his satisfaction and settled back into his seat. They were going to make it. He smiled. This was the job he was born to do.

• • •

The old man in the black baseball cap had been watching Joseph Clemons for over half an hour now, and he moved in closer, winding his way through the growing crowd, trying desperately to get into position before the President got any closer. This was the man; something in his spirit told him so. This was the crucial moment; this was the final task that God had for him. After that, he could go home to his Sara.

Joshua moved past a woman with a baby stroller. He looked down at the baby boy and smiled, but then quickly moved on with an urgent sense of purpose. Suddenly, the man was there, right in front of him, and, before he knew it, their eyes locked. People moved all around them, crowding past him, but, despite the noise and the crowd, Joshua sensed the danger inside the man, the malice, and the greed.

Joshua took one more step forward, and the man's eyes took on a look of fear. His right hand moved into his shirt instinctively and rested lightly on the grip of his Beretta, 9 millimeter pistol. Joshua reached into his pocket and pulled out a twenty-dollar bill and extended it toward the man.

"Can I get one of those red ones that says 'Jesus is Lord' on it?"

Joseph let his right hand fall off the pistol grip and he reached out to take Joshua's money.

"What size?"

Joshua forced a smile onto his lips.

"Oh, just give me the biggest one you've got."

Joseph swiveled his wheelchair around and sorted briefly through a stack of shirts. Finally, he pulled out a red one and tossed it up to the big man standing before him.

"Size triple extra large. Go ahead. Try it on."

Joshua didn't look at the shirt, but directly into Joseph's eyes.

"That won't be necessary. I trust you."

Joseph instinctively wheeled his chair back a few inches. This man unnerved him. From his vantage point, Joshua could see the President getting closer. He was surrounded now by police officers, but the crowd pressed in against him so close he could barely move.

• • •

Pastor Timm Sawyer had been shocked to see the President of the United States walk up to him about a mile back carrying a small girl in his right arm. He hadn't even been able to talk when Dan had first introduced himself, and now, the crowd was so noisy that not even the loudest yell could rise above it.

"Hi. Are you Pastor Sawyer?"

All Timm had been able to do was nod dumbly.

"Well it's good to meet you. My name is Dan Vermeulen and I'm the President of the United States of America. I'm proud of you, Timm, and I'm here to offer my support."

Still, Timm could say nothing.

"Do you mind if I walk with you to the monument?"

Timm tried to talk, but it simply came out as a mumble. He tried to recover and just nodded his head briefly. The President extended his left hand and Timm hesitated and then shook it nervously.

"Relax, Timm. I'm just a man like you. He's God. I'm not."

And then he had placed his left hand on Timm's shoulder and got him walking again.

"Let's get going, Timm. We have work to do."

So they had moved on and Timm stayed as close to the President as he could, considering all the people who were trying to get close to him. Now, another TV camera crew pressed in and Timm was brushed off to the side. He moved forward again and finally caught up again. They were nearing an overpass, and the concrete walls of it started to rise up, low at first, and then gradually higher. They went underneath and came out the other side.

• • •

The three UH-60 Black Hawk helicopters landed atop and on both sides of the overpass and George's feet hit the pavement running. He could see the President down below, just coming off from beneath the highway bridge. He wasn't more than a fifty feet below him. After the other choppers were unloaded, George directed the snipers to take up position and to scan the crowd. Several other agents pulled out binoculars and searched through the sea of people below them, looking for anyone suspicious.

George started to move down the road to get to the dirt embankment and the road below. He glanced up and someone caught his eye. It was a large man in a short-sleeved rugby shirt and blue jeans. He was wearing a black baseball cap. Fear gripped his heart as adrenaline surged through his body. George lifted his mike to his mouth with his right hand and pointed toward Joshua with his left.

"Eagle Eye do you see the man in the black baseball cap?"

The voice came back almost immediately.

"You mean the one beside the t-shirt vendor?"

"That's affirmative, Eagle Eye. I want you to put him in your sights and stand by. If he makes a hostile move, you are authorized to fire."

"Roger that. I'm on him now."

• • •

Joseph Clemons saw the choppers land on the overpass and then watched nervously as they deployed on the bridge. As soon as they began to move down the embankment, he glanced from side to side and began to wheel himself through the crowd to get behind the concrete wall. He yelled and cursed, and finally people made room for him.

Joshua watched him go and smiled in spite of his fear. The President was almost in front of him.

"Dear God. Please help me."

He was ready.

• • •

Dan Vermeulen came out from under the overpass and back into the bright sunlight. The brief shade had been refreshing. He turned to Missy.

"Sweetheart, do you mind walking for a bit. My arm's getting pretty tired."

Missy smiled and slid down to the pavement. Then she placed her little hand in his. Dan smiled back down at her and moved forward once more. He was anxious to get this over with and get back to the White House for a hot shower, some good food, and clean sheets. It had been over a month since he'd slept in his own bed. Then, suddenly, a thought occurred to him: he hadn't had a nightmare since leaving the White House. He smiled to himself. Imagine that. He felt better than he had in years.

• • •

The man in the wheelchair hunkered down behind the concrete wall and placed his hand in a pouch that was strapped to the frame of his wheelchair. Joseph pulled out the cell phone and placed it innocently in his right hand. He punched in a few numbers and the device was armed.

• • •

George and his men were almost there now. Dan Vermeulen looked over his left shoulder and smiled when he saw the Secret Service Agent reach the bottom of the embankment and the road. Dan laughed and waved when he saw George sprint toward him, holding his federal ID up in his left hand as he came.

• • •

Joshua stood in front of the t-shirt cart, sensing that he was missing something. He saw the man in the wheelchair looking out past him at the President from behind the concrete. Then, something inside Joshua told him to reach down and push away the T-shirts in the cart. He did so quickly, and then frantically pulled up the loose board that served as a fake bottom to the cart. He saw the C4 and the wires that connected them all together and shuddered. He looked over his shoulder. The President was right in front of him now, along with hundreds of people.

• • •

Eagle Eye rested the crosshairs on Joshua's head and paused. Was he cleared to shoot? Did he represent a threat? He saw the big man tear away the shirts and then rip up the cart bottom. When he saw Joshua place his hands inside the cart, he took a deep breath, and his trigger finger slowly moved to the rear.

• • •

Joseph Clemons felt giddy with his right forefinger hovering power-fully over the last button. He saw the President halt on the pavement right in front of him, and he grinned from ear to ear as he thought about all the money that would be transferred to his bank account. Joseph ducked down below the wall and pressed the button. The signal went out.

• • •

Joshua looked over at Joseph Clemons and then back at Dan Vermeulen who had just noticed his presence. Dan smiled at Joshua and took one step forward with the little girl in tow. A look of terror moved on to Joshua's face and he yelled out as loud as he could. His voice boomed out like thunder and the crowd silenced around him as everything began to move in slow motion. While Eagle Eye's bullet careened toward his head, and Joseph's electronic command moved at the speed of light, Joshua Moses Talbert threw himself onto the cart with arms open wide, summoning the last of the power on loan to him.

• • •

The deafening blast threw Dan and the small child down to the pavement, along with George Stollard and a hundred other people. A bright, searing light rose up and enveloped everyone within a block. And then, the light and the blast subsided.

• • •

George got up and crossed the final few yards to the President who lay motionless on the pavement. He knelt down beside him and lifted his head in desperation.

"Mr. President! Are you okay!"

There was no reply.

"Mr. President! It's George Stollard! Answer me!"

Dan Vermeulen opened his eyes and then glanced down at the little girl in his arms. She was okay.

"George, will you please get off me. This doesn't look good."

A smile took over George's face as he stood up and reached his hand down to his President.

"Absolutely, Mr. President. Whatever you say sir."

Dan got up and gave Missy a hug of reassurance. It was then he noticed Joshua's burlap robe lying on the pavement about twenty feet away, intact and undamaged. George Stollard was the first to reach it, followed by Dan Vermeulen. They both knelt down beside the piece of burlap. A steady puff of smoke rose up from it, and Dan moved his face over the smoke, letting it rise up passed him on toward heaven. It smelled sweet. George reached down in disbelief and pushed on the burlap, but all he felt was the rough texture of the cloth and the warm pavement beneath it.

A tear dropped down and hit George in the hand. He looked over and saw the President with tears in his eyes and a smile on his face.

"He went home. He's with God and with his Sara."

Then Dan reached down and picked up the burlap robe and clutched it to his chest.

"I envy him."

George Stollard, now regaining his composure and his professionalism, stood up and raised his mike to his lips and shouted instructions clearly.

"Harden up! Harden up! Get down here! Secure the area!"

The President was suddenly surrounded by men with machine guns, and, as George lifted Dan up from Joshua's body, a helicopter which had been hovering overhead quickly landed and took the President and the little girl away.

Down below, Joseph Clemons dropped the cell phone and gaped on in amazement at what he'd just seen. Quickly, he put his gloved hands to the wheels of his chair and began moving away after the stampeding crowd.

But Timm Sawyer didn't run. Instead, he slowly rose to his feet, walked over and stood beside the spot where Joshua's robe had been on the pavement. His hands began to shake and his voice wavered as he spoke.

"Receive him now, oh God our father."

Timm looked down and saw the black, leather Bible lying at his feet where President Vermeulen had dropped it as he was deluged with Secret Service Agents and rushed away. He bent down and slowly picked it up. The old, vellum pages had fallen open to Second Kings chapter 2. He read it to himself now.

> "And it came to pass, as they still went on, and talked, that, behold, there appeared a chariot of fire, and horses of fire, which parted them both asunder; and Elijah went up by a whirlwind into heaven."

Timm reached up to his shirt, clutching a handful of cloth in his hand and pulled down, tearing the fabric a few inches, and then the Secret Service pushed him back onto the curb as the area was secured by law enforcement.

56

Chief of Staff to the Acting President, Vicki Valence, sat at her desk in the White House, typing away on her laptop computer. Dan would be coming back tomorrow, and she would see him for the first time in over a month. She wondered what he would be like, if he had changed, what he felt about her, if anything.

Vicki didn't like working late, but quite frankly, she had nothing to go home to, not even a cat. So, she had stayed late, putting the finishing touches on the brief that Dan had requested she write, detailing everything that had happened while he was gone. It had been a tall order, and anything but brief.

She held her hand up in front of her and watched it shake in the dim light of her computer screen. She was a nervous wreck and she needed rest. For the past month, she had dedicated her life to the return of one man, one man she loved, but who, for all she knew, had no feelings for her. She recalled her first real conversation with George Stollard a few weeks ago when she had first elicited his help in the pizza place.

"You're here because I need your help. I need your help finding Dan."

"The President?"

Vicki nodded.

"Yes, I'm in love with him. Did you know that?"

George laughed out loud for a moment but quickly brought the emotion under control.

"Of course I know that, Vicki. Everyone in the White House does."

She looked surprised.

"Everyone?"

"Well, everyone but the President."

And, in Vicki's mind, that was pretty much the crux of the problem. She was in love with a man who had no clue. He was the leader of the free world and the most popular president in history, and she had been loving him for years without his knowledge. Yes, Vicki Valence was head over heels in love with the man, and she wanted to beat the tar out of him.

"Men!"

Vicki hated the way Dan made her feel weak and helpless. She didn't want to just wait around. She wanted to run up to him and throw herself into his arms, declaring her secret love for him. So why didn't she? Vicki had always been an overachiever, aggressive, a woman who saw what she wanted and then went for it. She certainly hadn't made it to the White House by being timid. So why was it so different with Dan?

And then, in an instant, the answer came to her. Dan was not a 'thing' to be attained, not a task to be completed, or a short- or long-range goal to be met. He was a man, a person, and, more importantly, her friend. That was it. That was the source of her fear. She couldn't all out go for it, because if she failed, then ... she would lose her best friend in life. If she declared her love for him, then she risked losing it all. She sat there and imagined the clumsy silence between them, the way both of them would feel out of place in meetings, and the way they would each avoid each other's gaze. It was no way to run a White House.

Vicki breathed a heavy sigh, closed her laptop and lay her head down on top of it. It was the ultimate catch 22. Living in silence was hurting her, but living without him would be more than she could bear. She whispered a prayer to her newfound God.

"Okay Jesus. Here I am again. Alone. I don't want to be lonely anymore. I love Dan. Can you please hook the two of us up please?"

Her head lifted up suddenly off the laptop and she laughed out loud at the insanity of her prayer, treating God as if he was a computer dating service or some such ludicrous thing. She needed sleep. And then, her laughter faded, and her face relaxed back into a frown. A lone tear formed in the corner of her left eye, hung there stubbornly for a moment, and then let loose, running down her cheek and onto her computer. And then a new prayer formed on her lips.

"Dear Jesus. Whatever you want is fine with me. But, if I have to live alone, then please help me, because I can't make it on my own."

Suddenly, as if in response, her cell phone began to vibrate on her desk. She looked at it, then up at the heavens before picking it up and opening it.

"Hello?"

It was the Vice President's wife, Eleanor Thatcher. She and Vicki had become better friends the past few weeks. Vicki admired her wisdom and the way she opened up and shared her life with her.

"Well, no, of course not. You call anytime! You know I love to talk to you."

Vicki reached up and wiped her left cheek.

"No, I haven't been crying."

She hesitated.

"Well, maybe a little bit."

And then she listened, while the wise, old woman spoke to her in a soothing, compassionate voice, lifting her up, encouraging her and making her feel loved and special. By the time Vicki hung up 45 minutes later, she no longer felt tired. Instead, she quickly finished the President's brief and then hastily left the White House, anxious to reach the pet store before it closed.

57

The last time Devin had been in a prison, it had been on an inspection tour as the Honorable Senator Devin Dexter from the great 'show me' state of Missouri. This time, after a surprisingly speedy trial, he entered inside the walls under a less noble cause, and was given a new name: Federal Prisoner Number 8345278.

Devin hobbled along as best as he could with his hands and feet shackled, but whenever he slowed down, the heavyset guard behind him placed his wooden baton in the middle of Devin's back and pushed him forward. Devin was convinced that the sadistic guard was another mean-spirited Republican. The Judge had given him life in prison, but, with any luck and a lenient parole board, he could still be out by his 87th birthday. That was only a scant 35 years away.

Shortly after his conviction, Devin had taken to talking out loud to himself, all the while remaining upbeat and undeterred.

"Yes, I can do 35 years in here. I'm the honorable Senator Devin Dexter. Someday, when I get out of here, I'll become the oldest President ever to be elected."

The bald, egg-shaped guard behind him shook his head and laughed out loud.

"Yeah, sure. You've got my vote. Now keep moving along, Mr. President."

Devin glanced over his shoulder, but the guard pushed his head back to the front.

"Eyes front little man!"

Devin mumbled under his breath.

"Stinking Republicans!"

They reached Devin's new cell and the guard yelled for him to halt. There was the sound of electricity and then the door opened. Devin stepped inside and then turned to face the door just as it was closing. Devin thrust his hands out through the bars and the guard unlocked his shackles, gathered them up and then walked away.

"Have a nice night, Mr. President! If you need anything, us Secret Service Agents will be waiting for you outside the cell block. Just ring the bell and we'll send in the butler."

Devin growled after him, but this time held his tongue. The Senator turned around slowly and then saw his cell mate, staring at him with a smile on his face. Derek Potter had been institutionalized for most of his adult life, only getting out long enough to break the law and come back inside. Presently, he was doing a 13-year stint for raping an 8-year-old girl and her mother, among other things.

"Good morning Senator. Or should I say Mr. President?"

Devin backed up against the bars, bracing himself for whatever might come next. Derek Potter was well over 6 feet tall and weighed in at 250 pounds. Since he pumped a lot of iron at the prison gym, most of his body was muscle; it certainly wasn't brains. A look of fear and hatred crossed Devin's face. How had his life ever come to this? He was supposed to be in control. After all, he was the most powerful Senator in American history. Devin made a mental note to himself, as soon as he got back into office; he was going to clean up the corrections system. The conditions inside this prison were deplorable! Yes, he would make it part of his campaign platform. Devin snarled at the giant man before him in the roughest, most imposing voice he could muster.

"Stay back you pervert! I can make one phone call and have you snuffed out by nightfall!"

His new cell mate stood there in his boxer shorts, and Devin could plainly see the height of the big man's arousal. Derek put his right hand to his lips and blew Devin a kiss. Then he took a step forward, smiling maniacally as he came.

"C'mere sweet thing! I've been saving something up for you. You can probably guess what it is. I think you're going to like it."

Devin pressed himself up tighter against the bars, determined not to turn his back on his new cell mate.

• • •

Back at the control desk, the two guards listened to the screams and nodded their amusement. The fat one who had taken Devin to his cell turned his head away from his deep-dish, meat-lovers pizza toward his fellow employee.

"He called me a stinking Republican! Can you believe that?"

The other guard smiled and leaned back in his chair.

"That's okay. Derek's an Independent. He likes just about anybody, so long as they give him what he wants."

Both guards laughed and shoved more pizza in their mouths.

"He told me he was going to be the President!"

Gradually, Devin's screams faded away and the cell block went quiet again.

58

The President of the United States lay alone in his bed, wide awake, staring up at the ceiling, wondering ... what had happened to his life. So much had occurred in so little time, that he couldn't eat it all in one bite. It was more than he could process. He thought about it now, trying to take it all in.

Devin Dexter, his arch Nemesis, the man who wanted him dead, and, had apparently tried to have him killed on more than one occasion, had failed and was now in prison. Dan's favorability rating was up another five points today. It would appear that the whole country loved him, but Dan knew those things were fleeting. Surveys and polls were like that. You could be the hero today and the goat tomorrow. But he also knew what was most important. What really mattered to him at the end of the day, when all the advisors and servants went home, after he left the White House and was sitting alone in his rocker, contemplating all he'd done, he wanted an old age of no regrets. He wanted to be able to look back on his life and plainly see that he'd done the work of God, family, and country.

'Sitting alone in his rocker' – he thought it sad that he'd worded it that way. He didn't want to be alone, but he had been for several years now. Jeanette and the kids were gone, and they weren't coming back. Up until recently, Dan had been convinced that he would not survive the events of the past month, but he'd been wrong. Not only had he survived, but, through the grace of God, he had flourished beyond his wildest imagination.

Realizing that he wasn't going to sleep anytime soon, Dan got out of bed and walked down the hall to the next room. The Secret Service Agent nodded and spoke a courtesy to him.

"Good evening, Mr. President."

Dan just nodded and walked on by. He paused outside Missy's new bedroom, and then quietly opened the door and slipped inside. He saw her there, sleeping quietly, holding the teddy bear that Vicki had bought for her. The two had hit it off right from the start. It was odd, but Dan had never noticed Vicki's love for children. He thought to himself, there was a lot about Vicki he hadn't noticed until the past few days, like the way she bit her lower lip under stress, the way she played with her right ear lobe, and how beautiful she was. And then, the familiar guilt returned to him, telling him that his life was over, that he had no right to happiness. His family was dead, therefore he was dead. He watched as Missy's chest rose and fell with the gentle rhythm of her breathing, and thought to himself 'she needs me.' I can't die yet. And the feeling of being needed and wanted by a single person was overwhelming; it felt better than the presidency. He had already decided that he would adopt young Missy, indeed, had already started the legal process. She would be his daughter, and he would have a family again.

Dan raised his right hand to his chin and brushed his lower lip thoughtfully with his forefinger. Nonetheless, it felt like something was missing, something that he would never be able to supply on his own. And then he remembered Vicki today during their staff meeting, how she had looked at him, those large, brown eyes, how she had nervously twirled a lock of her chestnut brown hair, even the way she smelled when she brushed up close. And he knew, suddenly, that she was the one person that he couldn't afford to leave here at the White House when his term of office ended. Unexpectedly, he spoke out loud.

"I'm sorry, Jeanette."

His words disturbed Missy's quiet slumber, and her eyes opened as she looked up at him sleepily.

"Hello, Mr. President."

Dan smiled and walked over closer to the bedside.

"Hello my little pumpkin."

She squinted her eyes and smiled.

"I like pumpkin pie."

Dan sat down on the bed beside her.

"I know you do, sweetheart. I'll have Ramone bake one for you tomorrow. Would you like that?"

Dan knew in his heart that he was going to spoil her rotten, but she deserved it. She'd been through enough pain already.

"Okay. I would like that. Is it morning yet?"

Dan reached down and brushed a lock of her pretty, blonde hair away from her eyes.

"No honey. Not yet. Go back to sleep."

She hugged her teddy bear, whom she had named Zeke, and rolled back over onto her side. Dan pulled the blanket up over her and left the room as silently as he had entered.

With resolution in his mind, he fell back asleep.

59

George Stollard was painfully forcing himself to finish up his vacation. He had already spent a week with his brother's family in Kentucky, but had found it hard to unwind with so many kids running around screaming all the time. Oddly enough, his brother seemed to love it, to thrive on it, as if the chaos of it all gave his life meaning and purpose. That part of life was a mystery to George, and he wondered about it now, wondered what it would be like to wake up in the morning with a kid sitting on his chest, babbling incoherently and drooling. So much of his life had been orderly and regimented, that he'd never experienced spontaneity. In fact, because of the nature of his job, he had come to view spontaneity as a serious security risk. Everything had to be planned out or he just wasn't happy.

But the last month of his life ... George thought about it now; it had been different. Nothing had gone as he'd planned, but, still ... everything had turned out right. And then he looked down at the gravestones in front of him. Well, not everything. Aric and the general were dead.

He stepped up to the first headstone and read the inscription.

"Major General Thomas T. Taylor

For love of country, he gave it all."

And then below the dates he read, "Live hard! Die with a pistol in your hand and a purpose in your chest."

George couldn't help but wonder if General Taylor was perhaps the last of a unique breed of warriors. In his heart, he hoped not. People like the general would always be needed to do the things that others couldn't stomach. Life was like that.

He whispered a prayer and then moved left, over to the fresh grave of Second Lieutenant Aric M. Baxter. The dirt in front of him was barren and empty. George stepped forward and placed the flowers in his hand on top of the headstone and then he knelt down and spoke out loud.

"I'm sorry Aric. I feel like I failed you. I was a few seconds too late and you died. I feel like it was my fault, that you should be alive right now. But ..."

George was interrupted by the woman's voice directly behind him.

"It wasn't your fault, George. You did your best."

He quickly turned around, and his hand instinctively moved to the grip of his pistol. Calley raised her dark eyebrows slightly.

"Are you going to shoot me, George, here in beautiful Omaha National Cemetery?"

George turned his head and then lowered his hand when he saw her standing there with the baby stroller out in front of her. Clarissa was snuggled up and fast asleep. His gaze moved up to Calley, now. The first time he'd seen her she'd been wearing black lingerie with blood on her face. He barely recognized the beautiful woman standing before him now.

"Miss Ramirez. It's good to see you again."

George stood up and walked over to her, offering his hand to her. She reached out and accepted it, taking his tough, callused hand into her own. George noticed how smooth and soft her skin felt and let his touch linger for a moment longer than was appropriate.

"I just came by to see my brother. I come here every morning. We're finally getting to know each other."

George nodded.

"Yes. I'm sorry for your pain, Miss Ramirez."

Calley was wearing a yellow print sundress, with a wide-brimmed hat that shaded her eyes from the rising sun.

"That's a very nice dress. You look good in it."

Calley took half a step forward and smiled. She had gotten to know George better during the week following Aric's death. They had spoken on the phone several times as George kept her informed of the investigation and the charges against Senator Dexter. He had also spoken with the President on Aric's behalf and had the blots on his military record expunged. After that, it had only seemed fitting that Aric and the general be buried side by side.

"Thank you. Not just for the compliment, but for a good many things. For helping with Aric, for being his friend, for helping me find my mother."

George smiled and broke in.

"And don't forget, I saved your life too."

Calley laughed softly, trying not to wake up her daughter.

"Yes, George, and thanks for saving my life as well. I appreciate that most of all."

And then she looked down at Clarissa and frowned.

"If it wasn't for you, my baby probably would have ..."

She bowed her head down to cover her eyes and George stepped forward, placing his right hand on her arm.

"It's okay. It's what I do. It's who I am. It was my pleasure, really."

Calley looked back up and wiped her eyes clean. A bit of mascara was left below her eye, so George reached over to wipe it away. He allowed his touch to linger for just a moment, and then one moment more. Their eyes met, and he quickly pulled his hand away. George shifted his gaze over to the tree to his left.

"So, Miss Ramirez, can I buy you an early lunch?"

Calley looked at him and stayed silent for a moment, basking in his chivalry. She had never met a man who respected her, and here was George Stollard, strong, handsome, capable, and knowing all the bad things about her past, and he still treated her like a lady.

"I would love to George. Do you mind pushing the stroller?"

George looked over at the baby carriage and recalled his thoughts of just a few minutes before. 'Spontaneity is a serious security risk. Everything had to be planned out or he just wasn't happy.' He hadn't planned on meeting a beautiful woman here. He hadn't planned on asking her out to lunch. He hadn't even planned on coming to the cemetery today. It just kind of happened on its own. Perhaps he should give spontaneity a try.

George walked over and put both hands on the stroller and began to push it slowly down the sidewalk.

"You look good with a baby, George!"

She reached up and placed her left hand on George's bare arm. He felt the tingling all the way to his spine.

"Really? I've never seen myself as the family type, but who knows. Weirder things have happened I suppose."

Calley tilted her head back and laughed softly.

"So tell me something about yourself, George, something I don't already know."

George didn't know what to say.

"Like what kind of thing? What do you want to know?"

Calley thought for a moment as they strolled on down the sidewalk.

"Well, let me see. Do you go to church at all?"

George was caught off guard by the question.

"It's odd you should bring that up, Miss Ramirez, because I just went to church last week with my brother's family in Kentucky. I enjoyed it, though I've never really considered myself a religious man per se. But the past month has gotten me to thinking about a lot of things."

Calley nodded.

"Me too. I went to church last Sunday as well. The sermon was boring, but I just liked being there. It made me feel closer to God somehow."

George smiled.

"Yeah, that's how I felt."

"You know, George, I've been living my life for other people for so long that I hardly even know who I am."

George Stollard stopped walking and his tone suddenly became very serious.

"Why that's absurd. You're Calley Ramirez. Your mother was Esperanza from Mexico. You're a strong and beautiful woman, and you have a daughter named Clarissa."

And then he looked her full in her green eyes.

"And you, Calley Ramirez, are a wonderful person."

George began walking again, and suddenly, Calley felt a few inches taller and the sun seemed to shine brighter.

"So George, what do you say we go to church on Sunday together this week?"

George laughed.

"Oh, I don't know Miss Ramirez, church is such a personal thing, and we've only just met."

She squeezed his arm harder and moved in closer. George smelled her perfume and melted at her side.

"I suppose I could go to church with you, just this one time though."

The three of them moved on down the sidewalk, out of the cemetery, and into the rest of their lives.

60

Vicki put her hand on the doorknob and paused outside the oval office. She looked up at George Stollard who was standing at his post, having just returned from vacation. George had been smiling all morning and Vicki wondered what had him so happy. These Secret Service guys were usually so serious all the time.

"What's up with you George?"

George looked down and nodded.

"Oh, nothing much. Same old grind here at the big oval."

Vicki gave him a confused smile.

"The big oval?"

She shook her head from side to side.

"George you have been acting strange ever since you got off vacation. Are you okay?"

He renewed his smile.

"Of course. Never been better. I had a great time. I went to church twice."

She wanted to ask him about it, but didn't have time. Dan had summoned her here for an urgent meeting.

"We'll have to talk about that later."

Then she moved a little closer and lowered her voice.

"George do you have any idea why Dan called me in here so rushed?"

George shrugged and his smile went away.

"I have no idea. Besides, I can't tell you."

Vicki cocked her head to one side.

"You can't tell me? Why?"

George's smile returned again.

"Because then I'd have to kill you."

Vicki's hand dropped down off the door handle.

"George that was funny the first time you said it, but it's starting to get old."

Vicki turned away from George and looked over at Susan Stutker, the President's Personal Assistant.

"Hi Susan. Is he ready to see me?"

Susan gave her the same knowing smile as George.

"Yes, you can go right in, Vicki. He's waiting for you."

Then she leaned forward in her chair.

"In fact, he's been pacing the floor all morning. He's as nervous as I've ever seen him!"

Vicki's eyes grew thoughtful as she gazed off into the distance, wondering what this new piece of information meant.

"Thanks Susan. I owe you one."

And then she turned back toward George and smiled slyly as she opened the door.

"I owe you too, George."

And then she whispered.

"I'll get you for this."

George looked over at Susan and laughed out loud. Susan shook her head.

"George, what in the world has gotten into you lately? You know you shouldn't do that to her. That girl's in enough pain as it is."

And then as an afterthought, she added.

"You men are so vexing! It's a miracle us women put up with you."

George stopped laughing, looked straight ahead, and smiled dutifully.

"She'll find out soon enough. She'll be okay. Vicki's tough."

• • •

When Vicki walked into the oval office, the President was pacing back and forth on the carpet, looking thoughtfully down at a sheet of paper he was holding. He was so engrossed in what he was reading that he didn't hear her come in. Vicki cleared her throat before speaking.

"Good morning, Mr. President."

Dan looked up.

"Oh. Hi Vicki."

Dan looked at her in a different way than she was used to and it made Vicki squirm inside.

"You called for me, Mr. President?"

Dan nodded and then walked over to her. Susan was right. She had never seen him this nervous before. When he came up to her, he reached out and unexpectedly shook her hand. Vicki was perplexed.

"Dan, why are you shaking my hand?"

Dan let her hand drop down and then he turned his back on her. He moved his right hand up to his forehead as if deep in thought.

"I don't know Vicki. It's just a greeting, just a way of breaking the ice. That's all. I'm a little bit nervous right now."

Vicki took a step forward.

"Okay. Can you tell me why?"

Dan turned back around, not realizing that she had stepped forward and almost bumped into her. He seemed totally discombobulated and began to stutter.

"I, uh, Vicki. Well, I. Oh, my this is terrible!"

He walked over to his massive oak desk and threw the paper down on top of the desk pad. Vicki gazed at him curiously as she walked over toward him. Something was wrong and she couldn't help but wonder what it was. Was she about to be fired? She thought about it, but couldn't think of anything she'd done to merit such a move.

When she reached him, Dan had turned his back on her and his right hand had moved up to pinch the bridge of his nose. Vicki touched his back and she felt his whole body tighten. Whatever it was, it must be terrible.

"Dan, listen to me. Whatever it is, we can work it out. We've been through worse and we'll solve whatever problem this is and then we'll move on with your agenda of putting the country back together again. You can do it, Dan. I know you can! You've come so far already!"

She gently rubbed the flat of her hand on the middle of his back in an effort to soothe him, but it only made it worse. Finally, he turned around and threw his hands down in frustration.

"Vicki, I have to talk to you about something!"

Vicki nodded.

"Okay. Shall I sit down?"

"Yes, that's a good idea. Maybe I will too."

Vicki walked over to the chair to the left of his desk, but Dan beat her there and held it as she lowered herself onto the cushion. He had never done that before. Maybe he was firing her. Dan sat down in a similar chair across from her and bent himself down, placing his elbows on his knees. When he looked up at her, she could see the agony in his eyes. A sudden fear came over her. 'Maybe he has cancer or something?'

"Vicki, I strongly believe that we need to make some changes around here. And it can't wait another day. We have to do it right now."

Vicki nodded her head. Okay, so he didn't have cancer. That was good.

"It's about you, Vicki."

Her heart rate flashed upward, and her hands went ice cold. This was it. He was going to fire her. But why?

"Okay, so it's about me. Is it a bad thing?"

Dan turned his head toward the painting of George Washington on the wall to his right, unable to look her in the eyes.

"Well, maybe. I guess it just depends on your own view of it I suppose."

"My view of it?"

Dan threw up his hands and jumped to his feet in frustration.

"Oh, Vicki! Why are you making this so difficult for me?"

Dan walked back over to his desk and picked up the sheet of paper on the desk pad.

"Mr. President, how can I be making it hard for you when I don't even know what we're talking about?"

Dan ignored the question and walked back over with the paper in his hand.

"Just listen to me, Vicki. This scares me to death and I don't know how else to do this, but I have to get it done before I go crazy!"

He lifted the paper up to his eyes, cleared his throat and began to read.

"Dear Vicki."

Vicki's heart sank. It was a 'Dear Vicki' letter. She hadn't gotten one of those since high school.

"Twenty years ago, I met the most wonderful woman in the world. Her name was Jeanette. We fell in love and I married her. We had two kids and we raised a family together. Jeanette was my partner in life, she was my right arm, and I did nothing without talking to her first. She loved me, she gave me wise counsel when I was confused and lifted me up when I was discouraged. If not for Jeanette, I wouldn't be here today in the White House. I owe everything to her."

Dan paused. Tears had welled up in his eyes and he had to wipe them away to keep his sight from going all blurry. Vicki leaned back in her chair and swallowed hard. She didn't know what to say. How could she have ever hoped to compete with a woman like Jeanette Vermeulen?

"And then, on that fateful day when everything changed, Jeanette and my children went away from me. I was left alone, without encouragement, without love, and with a void in my heart that I thought would never again be filled. I missed them so much, that every day I woke up with just one hope in mind: I wanted to die."

Now Vicki's eyes were filling with tears. She still loved him more than ever, and didn't want to be reminded of his pain. It hurt her too much and she just couldn't bear it.

"But then, after years of sorrow and grief, I woke up one morning and I began to realize that the void inside me could again be filled, that I could be happy, and I gradually wanted to live again."

Dan lowered the sheet of paper and looked up at Vicki. She met his gaze, wondering where he was going.

"Vicki, I realize now, that all those things I said about Jeanette are equally true for you. After she left, you were there for me. You helped me through the war, through my grief, and through the rebuilding effort."

Dan hesitated before going on. He looked over at Vicki to gauge her feelings, but her head was down and covered with her hands.

"Vicki, I don't know how you feel about me, but I know how I feel about you. You're the best friend I've ever had and I don't want to live without you after I leave the White House."

Dan moved to his feet and turned sideways, staring at the wall.

"I was hoping, that, maybe, we could get to know each other in a different way, a deeper way. You know, just to see what might happen."

Vicki's hands moved down from her face and then she stood up and wiped the tears from her eyes.

"Mr. President, a part of me wants to ..."

She shook her head in exasperation and then continued.

"Dan, how could you possibly not know how I feel about you? Have you even been here for the past six years?"

She walked up and placed both her hands on the sides of his face and squeezed until his lips puckered out.

"Hello! Is there anybody in there?"

She dropped her hands down and turned her back to him. Dan shook his head from side to side in total confusion.

"Vicki, I guess I don't understand. I still don't know how you feel about me. Are you going to ..."

But Dan didn't have a chance to finish before Vicki walked resolutely over to the heavy, oak door and opened it up. George Stollard was there with his ear pressed close against the wood.

"Hello, George. Why don't you just come on in so you can hear us better?"

George nervously straightened his tie and then took a small step forward.

"Is everything okay in here, Mr. President?"

Dan didn't answer at first. He just threw up his hands.

"I have no idea, George. I'm at a loss on this one. But you better get ready just in case she beats me up."

Vicki gave Dan an impatient stare, and then she crossed her arms over her chest defiantly.

"George, tell the President how I feel about him."

Agent Stollard looked over at the President for direction.

"Please, George. Someone needs to tell me. If you know, let's spit it out. I need to know too."

George turned back toward Vicki and looked her full in the eyes.

"Mr. President, Vicki Valance has been head-over-heels in love with you for several years now."

Dan looked over at Vicki and then back to George.

"Are you sure, George?"

But Vicki interrupted him.

"Hey Susan! Can you hear us from there?"

There was a moment of silence. Then Susan shouted back to her.

"Yes, Vicki. I can hear you just fine. I've been listening on the intercom the whole time."

Vicki took two bold steps up to Dan Vermeulen and moved her face to within six inches of his own. In a lowered voice she said, "Okay, Susan. Please tell your boss who loves him."

Susan's voice came back with no hesitation.

"You do, Vicki. You love the President of the United States more than anyone I know."

Vicki smiled and moved another inch closer. When she spoke, it was in a barely audible whisper.

"Now tell me, Mr. President, you are the leader of the free world, the most popular leader this country has ever known, so how is it even remotely possible that everyone knows I love you except, you?"

Dan tried to back up a pace, but Vicki followed him.

"Answer the question, Mr. President."

Dan looked over at George who immediately nodded his head.

"Better tell her, Mr. President. She holds all the cards, and you don't stand a chance."

Dan let out a sigh the size of Texas and then lowered his head in embarrassment. Finally, he shook his head and spoke.

"I'm sorry, Vicki. I know you think I'm smarter than this, and I probably am smart when it comes to budgets and war strategies and politics, but when it comes to relationships, I'm just as dumb as the next guy. Take away my suit, the Secret Service, the power tie and the oval office, and I'm just a man."

Dan moved forward just a little.

"I'm just a man, Vicki, but I love you. Will you forgive me?"

Vicki's face relaxed and a smile slowly spread across her lips. Susan stepped into the doorway, smiling from ear to ear.

"It's about time, Dan."

George Stollard backed up and then left the room, closing the door behind him.

"Come on, Susan. I think these two need to talk."

The door closed and Vicki Valence moved closer. Her lips met Dan's and they kissed softly. The kiss grew into a loving passion and finally, Dan's arms wrapped around her and they embraced as the picture of George Washington looked on from the other side of the Delaware.

"I'm sorry it took so long, Vicki. I really do love you."

She sighed in his arms.

"That's okay, Mr. President. After all, you are just a man."

61

Pastor Timm Sawyer and his wife Ruth sat snuggled up on the couch together, watching the Fox News Special Report on the Freedom Day Celebration in Omaha, Nebraska. The announcer stood with a microphone in front of the War on Terror Memorial, looking out past the tens of thousands of people who had lined the park to listen to President Vermeulen's speech. Timm looked at his wife before speaking.

"Honey, I think the air conditioner is on too high. Does it seem cold in here to you?"

Ruth Sawyer picked up a quilt that was lying on the couch to her left and spread it over his lap.

"Here, just cover up with this. You know I like the cold, Timm."

Yes, Timm did know that, but it still bothered him that they lived in an icebox during the month of August. Timm sighed and unfolded the quilt. Ruth moved closer to him and covered up as well.

"Now see, honey. Isn't this nice and cozy?"

Timm looked over at his wife and smiled. There were other things he would have said in his younger days, but, instead, he just nodded his head in agreement. It wasn't important. Besides, if being cold made her happy, he'd just bundle up warmer and make her the happiest woman on earth.

"It's coming on now. There's your friend, the President."

Ruth grabbed the remote away from him and turned the volume up higher. Timm found it humorous that Ruth commonly referred to President Vermeulen as his friend. In reality, they hardly knew each other. In fact, they had walked only a mile or so together during the Freedom March, and Timm had been so nervous that he'd been unable to speak. But then a few weeks ago, the Sawyers had gotten a phone call from the President himself, inviting both of them to dine with him at the White House. Ruth had bought a new dress, and they were looking forward to going next week.

The President walked up to the podium and the crowd yelled its praise. Dan Vermeulen waited a moment, smiling all the while. Finally, he raised his hands to quiet them and the noise died down.

"Thank you all for coming here today. I appreciate it."

Dan arranged the papers in front of him and cleared his throat before speaking.

"My fellow Americans, we come here today to the National War on Terror memorial to honor all those who have fallen in order to keep us free. Since the War on Terror began over a decade ago, many brave men and women have died in defense of our great country. I would like to start with a moment of silence with which to honor and thank them for the supreme sacrifice they made so that you and I could remain free."

Five hundred miles away, in the frigid confines of their living room, Ruth and Timm bowed their heads and prayed silently for the families of those who had given their lives to protect them.

Back at the National Monument, Vicki Valence put her arm around little Missy and bowed as well. She sat on stage behind the President and to his right. The President looked up and smiled grimly.

"Let us never forget them."

Dan glanced over to his right as if drawing strength from Vicki and she smiled at him in support.

"Good people of America, over the past six years as your President, I have grown to love and admire all of you. While it's true that I don't know each of you individually, I have been honored and blessed to get to know quite a few of you. And the more of you I get to know, the more proud I am to serve you. Let me just talk to you now about a few of those people."

Dan turned the page of his speech and then looked again into the camera.

"All of you know that last month over two million Americans marched with me to this very monument in the name of freedom. During my time before and on that march, I met a good, many people who enhanced my life and taught me many important things. I met truck drivers who gave me rides. Thank you Zeke Bettendorf from Randolph, Illinois, and thanks to a man named Tyler from Wisconsin who helped me to see some things. I appreciate your help. Some of these people are nameless to me, but still, they reached out and touched me in the most profound way, and I'm a better man for having known them. Thank you little, white-haired old lady from Ohio who gave me a hot meal and a warm, soft bed to sleep in. I am forever indebted for your kindness. A special thank you to the little boy who gave my Missy a little red wagon. It was a great help. And thank you to the cashier at the Flying J truckstop in Davenport, Iowa. All of you, together, made a big difference in my life.

While I was on my sojourn across the heartland of America, I visited the contaminated cities as well as the small communities surrounding them. During that time, I walked from town to town, not as your President, surrounded by Secret Service, riding in a limousine, but as one of you. I traveled on foot, and I didn't have a penny to my name. But all of you took me in, gave me food, gave me a bed to sleep in, and you helped me find my way back to the White House. During that journey, I saw poverty, and sickness, and grief. I saw children living in squalor. I met a little girl named Missy. When I first saw Missy, she was sitting on a street corner all alone. She was holding a dirty rag doll and wearing old, torn, and dirty clothes. She was little more than a rag doll herself. I sat down on the sidewalk beside six-year-old Missy and I asked her what she was doing. She said 'I'm waiting.' I asked what she was waiting for, and she told me that she didn't know. Missy was homeless and living in the streets. She was an orphan, but I knew that she would die without help, so I took her with me, and I am now proud to call her my daughter."

Dan turned around.

"Missy, will you stand up for us please?"

The little girl with long, curly blonde hair and bright blue eyes grabbed on to Vicki's hand and stood up shyly in front of the thousands of spectators. As she did so, a roar went up from the crowd. She blushed and then quickly sat back down. Dan turned back around, all the while, smiling proudly.

"Missy is important, because she is the future of our great country. Someday, Missy will grow into a woman, and it's people like her who will carry on the next generation of America. For better or for worse, America's future is being decided today. There are many orphans now in the areas surrounding the contaminated zones, and they are waiting, waiting for all of us to come to their rescue. They need us now like never before, and I would urge all of you to consider doing what I have done. A task force is being set up to expedite the adoption of those children left orphaned by the attack on our country's great cities. I urge you now, to take those children in, raise them as your own, show them love, and help them make America great, not just for today, but for the future as well."

Cheers went up through the crowd, and Dan waited for it to die down again before speaking.

"And now, I want to speak candidly to you about government. I want to caution you by saying that government can be a friend to the people, or it can be the people's worst nightmare. I am part of the government, but I want to caution you to regard all of us with a healthy suspicion. Watch what we do and hold us accountable. We need your vigilance. We are your servants, and you have loaned us your power to govern. But the government is made up of people, and people are flawed, therefore the government is flawed as well. Some of us mean well, while others of us are just selfish and greedy. Learn to recognize the selfish ones, and when you see them, work and campaign and vote to take away their power, lest they corrupt and enslave you."

Another cheer went up from the crowd and Dan looked back over his shoulder again. He saw Missy and Vicki and was encouraged. He held up his hand and the crowd silenced.

"For those of you who are waiting for the government to ride in on its white steed and save you, wait no longer, because we're not coming. As Americans, you should never wait to do the right thing. Government can help you, but it is better if you help yourselves. Too much government just complicates and slows things down. After all, that's what the government does best; it takes something simple and it complicates it. It's about the only thing we're really good at."

Laughter went up from the crowd, and Dan laughed along with them.

"I urge you now, people, do not make the mistake of outsourcing your prosperity and your happiness. Do not hire the government to heal your sick and feed your poor, because we'll just complicate it and the sick will still be sick and the poor will remain poor."

Dan hesitated before going on to the next point. He took a deep breath and moved on.

"And now let's talk about religion."

The crowd suddenly became quiet.

"There's been a lot of talk about the separation of Church and State going on. It's been a major topic for centuries. In fact, that's why our ancestors came to America. They were looking for religious freedom from a repressive government."

A serious look came over Dan's face.

"Good people of America, the freedom of religion as espoused in the first amendment was never meant by our founders to protect the government against religion. It was set up to protect religion from the government. The first amendment protects the rights of every American, whether Jew, Muslim, Hindu, and Christian. And to those of you who are afraid that a Christian will trample your rights or force on you beliefs not your own, let me reassure you with the words of President Thomas Jefferson who said 'Religion is a matter which lies solely between man and his God, that he owes account to none other for his faith or his worship, that the legislative powers of government reach actions only, and not opinions, I contemplate with sovereign reverence that act of the whole American people which declared that their legislature should "make no law respecting an establishment of religion, or prohibiting the free exercise thereof," thus building a wall of separation between Church and State.'

Dan paused for a moment as if gathering his thoughts.

"Recently, there were a few people who tried to have me removed from office because I sometimes talk about God. I was in direct defiance with the Freedom From Religion Act, a bill which I foolishly signed into law. People, that law went too far. It infringed on the freedom of speech and the freedom of religion. And I apologize now for my mistake. My administration is now working with key members of Congress to see the Freedom From Religion Act repealed."

A huge roar went up from the crowd and Dan was forced to halt his speech. After almost a minute, he raised his hand and quieted them down.

"America was once the most powerful nation on earth, but power has never been the sole measure of greatness. The greatness of a country is determined by the greatness of its people, and the past few months I have learned that Americans are still the greatest people on earth."

More applause erupted, this time louder than anything previously. Dan tried to quiet them, but it took several moments to calm them down. When the applause finally subsided, Dan went on.

"I want each of you to look to your left and then to your right. I want you to see the person next to you, look in his eyes, look at her face, and study each person carefully. And I want you to realize that the secret to all of America's ills lies in the person beside you, or, more directly, the person inside yourself. If your neighbor is lacking, give to him generously. If one of you needs encouragement, offer it freely. And if a stranger needs a friend, then show him kindness. Some things are best done by government, but most things, the everyday, the mundane, the tedious, the grassroots jobs of life, are best done by yourself and the person beside you. If you're waiting for the government to save you, then wait no longer, because the government is you.

'We the people of the United States, in order to form a more perfect union, establish justice, insure domestic tranquility, provide for the common defense, promote the general welfare, and secure the blessings of liberty to ourselves and our posterity, do ordain and establish this Constitution for the United States of America.'

Dan raised his voice higher.

"We the people, we the farmers, we the factory workers, we the moms, we the dads, we the students, we the shopkeepers, we the people who live, and breathe, and bleed and die in this great country! It's we the people who make this country great, and it's we the people who have to keep it great. Not the government, but the people. We the people!"

Dan took a moment to let it sink in before continuing.

"Now, I stand here before you as your President, but it will not always be so. In just over a year, I will leave the greatness of this office. I will hand back the power you've loaned to me, and I will diminish. I will return to the obscurity of everyday life. I will become like you. I will once again become we the people of the United States. And I have to tell you my friends that I yearn for that day.

However, before that day happens, there is work to do. There are miles to go before we sleep, so please, join with me now and for the next sixteen months and follow me as together, we lead this country back to greatness and prosperity."

Applause broke out again, and this time it did not subside for over a minute. The President stood there, humbly waiting. Finally, the applause subsided.

"And now, I speak to you again of freedom. I encourage you to defend those rights which were earned and protected by blood. Our founding fathers recognized the truth of freedom, they realized liberty's power, but they also knew that it was a fragile force that must be continually protected and nurtured. And for that reason and cause, they pledged their lives, their fortunes, and their sacred honor. But with great freedom comes great responsibility, and our founding fathers were willing to die to preserve the natural laws of God and Nature. Indeed many of them made the supreme sacrifice for each and every one of us, and their blood cries out to us now from the ground they fought to free! Their blood cries out to every American who takes his freedom for granted and to every American who sits idly by, waiting for the government to save them. Their blood cries out to us in outrage! 'Did I die in vain? I gave my life, my fortune, my sacred honor so that you and your family could be free!'"

The applause lifted up again, this time even louder, and the thousands of people moved forward, pressing against the ropes that separated the stage from the grass below. George Stollard grew nervous as he looked down on the crowd and yelled into his microphone.

"Keep the crowd back! Make sure they don't make it to the stage!"

Dan Vermeulen looked out happily on the crowd. He was proud to be the President once more. He turned back to Vicki and saw her smiling. Then Missy pulled her hand away from Vicki's and ran up to her father. She jumped into his arms and Dan beckoned for Vicki to come forward as well. She walked up and stood beside him as the crowd thundered its appreciation. Dan held Missy in his left arm and held Vicki's hand on his right side. Finally, after several minutes, the crowd grew quiet again. Dan leaned in closer to the microphone.

"And now, I leave you with one final thought. It is we the people who make this country great, but it is God the Father who gives greatness to his people."

With that, Dan waved and yelled out as loud as he could.

"God bless America!"

The crowd opened up louder than ever as Dan and his family turned and walked off the stage. The Fox news announcer started his commentary as Ruth and Timm Sawyer turned to each other and smiled.

Ruth pointed the remote control at the television and turned it off. There was a strange and sudden silence that overtook the room as the two of them sat mutely in front of the empty, dark screen.

Finally, Ruth Sawyer pulled back a few inches and looked up and into her husband's eyes.

"I'm so proud of you, Timm."

Timm looked down at her and a confused look came over his face.

"Proud of me? Why? What did I do?"

Ruth squeezed in closer to him on the couch.

"You were there, Timm. You did your part. God called you and you answered his voice."

Timm shrugged.

"I suppose so. But it was a small part. It wasn't so big compared to the sacrifices that others made."

Ruth reached over and pulled the quilt back up over Timm's chest. It had worked its way down over the duration of the speech.

"Well, maybe so. But do you know what I think, Timm. I think that there are no small parts. I believe that each person's task is built on the work of the people before him. And when one person shirks his calling, then the people who follow him can't do what they were intended to do. God called you to organize a march, so you wrote an email."

She laughed a moment.

"And then, little Benjamin taught you how to use a computer to send it out."

Timm laughed along with her and then built upon her thought.

"And then you prayed with me, and one by one, and then by the hundreds, and the thousands, the people all came together and did the one, small part they were called upon to do."

Ruth smiled and hugged him closer. Timm hugged her back. After a few seconds of silence, he said.

"Honey, I think you're right. It takes all of us working together, each of us doing our own, little parts. And I think, that perhaps, the only parts that seem large to us, are the tasks that go undone."

For another fifteen minutes, Timm and Ruth sat together on the couch, sharing their body heat, helping each other feel warm, and loved, and safe.

Skip Coryell is the author of six books and lives with his wife and children in the midwestern United States.

For more information about Skip Coryell and his life and writing, go to www.skipcoryell.com.

Other Books by Skip Coryell

Bond of Unseen Blood
We Hold These Truths
Blood in the Streets
Laughter and Tears
RKBA: Defending the Right to Keep and Bear Arms

Available anywhere books are sold.

Signed copies are available only at
www.whitefeatherpress.com

Read this exciting excerpt from Skip Coryell's political thriller *We Hold These Truths*

FBI Agent Richard Resnik stood on the empty, snow-covered runway, watching the little plane fly out of sight. The winds and the blowing snow had suddenly dissipated, just long enough to allow the tiny plane to get airborne, then, as if on cue, they returned with near gale force.

Lance walked up behind him and stopped.

"What is he going to do?"

Richard shook his head in frustration.

"He has a nuclear bomb and an airplane. What do you think he's going to do?"

Lance nodded in agreement at the unspoken fear.

"He'll kill as many people as he can, as soon as he can. That's his nature. His fatwa. This is jihad."

Richard turned to look him in the eye.

"That's right. Chicago is the second largest city in the country, and all he has to do is fly straight down the coast a few hundred miles."

Lance took a step forward, shaded his eyes from the wind and looked out after the disappearing speck.

"Isn't there any way we can stop him? There must be something we can do."

Richard thought for a moment, then shook his head back and forth in despair.

"Unless I can get another plane, or unless the phones come back on, then we're totally helpless. We can't stop him, and half a million people are about to die."

Lance nodded his head. It didn't look good. He kicked the snow with his boot and worked it back and forth, forming a little trench in the snow.

"I guess it's just Spunky now – Spunky and God. That's our only hope."

They were so focused on the end of the runway and the disappearing plane, that they hadn't heard Josh and Hank walk up behind them.

"I sure hope he's sober."

Lance turned and looked at Hank.

"He flies better when he's drunk. He's the only guy who can beat me at chess, drunk or sober. Besides, Spunky's not the kind of man to go down without a fight. He'll think of something, even if he has to die."

Josh McCullen nodded his head in agreement.

"That's right. Spunky's the best. He's a redneck – an American redneck."

Richard gave him a sarcastic look before he spoke.

"Well that's reassuring. The entire fate of civilization may rest squarely on the shoulders of an American, alcoholic redneck, who may or may not be sober. That's just great!"